The Void Beyond
The Cluster Saga
Book Two

Carlos R. Tkacz

For Steph, who believes in me even when I don't believe in myself.

Prologue

We look back now at this time in human history as one of the most trying in our collective memory. It is a story of violence, of trial, and of despair. But even more than that, it is a story of sacrifice, of perseverance, and of duty. It is a story that now defines us, that changed us forever.

-*Excerpt from* The End Times: a Brief History of the End of Humanity *by Ibn Dars-Elat*

They watched as the light from the engines burned brighter and brighter, piercing the starry cosmos and crowding out the light from other stars around. The acceleration bursts were different in their energy signatures and color. New engines. They raced to make new calculations, to update their models on the technologies of the Watchers. Accurate predictions were essential for survival, should their position in space ever be discovered. Should they ever have to run again.

They trained their instruments back towards the outer rim of the galaxy, back towards the little clusters where they had seen the enormous outputs of energy. Things were silent once again, but it was too late. In ten years, the Watchers would arrive, and whatever civilization lived in that sector of space would face the ultimate death: extinction. Whatever battle or experiment had caught the attention of the Watchers must have been quite the sight. They argued over potential causes, and they argued over what to do.

Some, the older ones who could still remember, argued they do nothing. Let the universe take its course. For generations they had found themselves safe, hidden in plain sight as they were. Why risk annihilation for aliens they had no connection to, no trade or shared information with? The younger ones, those who had not been alive at the Great Leaving, argued the opposite. No matter the threat, whomever was out there deserved to be warned. Rtskl led this view.

"How can we do nothing?" she cried in council, floating in the center of the congress hall and casting her eyes about with fire in her vision and passion in her eyes. "Have we forgotten the fate we suffered at the hands of the Watchers, those monsters? Do we not remember what befell our people?"

"That is precisely why we can do nothing," answered the leader of the opposing view, an ancient named Kwllt. "You were not there, young one. You did not see the devastation. You did not watch your society butchered and burned without remorse, without chance of retaliation, without any recourse." Her voice showed her age, cracked like the ancient plains of a dry planet and resonated with time and hollow depth. "We could do nothing. We could only watch as they destroyed us."

Rtskl listened, along with the others in council, in silence and with reverence. She had heard these stories all her life, from the time she was a small one in the communal pod, but they had not lost their power. Fear threatened to overwhelm her, threatened to weaken her resolve, but she waited until Kwllt fell silent, and then she spoke again: "I do not pretend to know the horrors you and yours endured, ancient one. And I mean no disrespect. You saved our people and gave me life. But you saw what was happening. You were there, and this gave you time. This gave you time to prepare, to plan, and ultimately, to escape and live. Do not these creatures out there in the cosmos deserve the same chance? Do they not deserve a chance to defend themselves or to run? If we do not warn them, then what happens when the Watchers find the next target, or the next? Do we simply watch as the universe falls prey to their pogrom? Do we live alone and afraid as all life, all brothers and sisters in the void, suffer the fate we so narrowly escaped?"

There was silence in the hall, the water still as those in attendance did not move. All minds were turned towards the map projected in the murky waters of the screen-cloud where the star map clearly showed the path the Watchers were taking towards the unknown civilization that had just made itself bright in the empty darkness of space. Ten years. The Watchers would arrive, and destroy this alien culture, in ten years. And unless they did something, those poor souls would never know until it was too late.

1

War, regardless of the intentions, never leads to peace. There are always power vacuums left for the ambitious and cruel to fill, hatred bred of violence left to simmer and grow. Rather than peace, war leaves fertile ground in which it may replicate itself.

> *- Excerpt from* Cause and Effect: an Analysis of the Traitor's War, *by Spokayn Erthre*

From low orbit, the firefights on the surface appeared to blossom into orange and red clouds of expanding gas and light. The viewscreen crackled with static from the magnetic and electrical forces shearing at each other on the surface of the planet. Sensor readings came pouring in, electronic whistles and jumbled radio messages and a scattering of voices and footsteps. Casualty reports, troop movements, armament shipments, shuttle landings... and in the center of it all, Leader Eazkaii sat with his hands steepled in front of him like the calm center of a storm. He allowed the information to flow through him, absorbing not so much the details but the overall trends. In his mind, the battle was beginning to take shape, and the shape was not one favorable to the Black Sun.

He was impressed. They had expected the planet Rot to be an easy conquest, something of a sporting vacation while the fleet moved towards larger, more desirable targets. He had underestimated the inhabitants of the planet. Unlike most of the Coalition planets, which had fallen into barely contained chaos after the Inner Cluster's victory and the shutdown of the skip drive network, Rot had managed to keep civil society going. Eazkaii smiled. A challenge is always welcome.

"Sir," an officer to his right, Eazkaii could not remember his name, said tentatively. Eazkaii looked at him, not answering, until the man continued. "We have lost Surface Units Three, Six, Seven, and Nine. The other units are beginning to approach the capital city where the last of the holdouts have barricaded themselves."

Eazkaii barked orders, watching the changing perspectives cycle through the view screen in front of him and listening to the mad shuffling of feet and voices around him as his orders were passed down the lines to their respective recipients. Now the screen showed the feed from a surface soldier's helmet cam. It was chaos on the ground, and the feed was jumpy and unclear. Eazkaii could make out sprinting soldiers and dead bodies, could hear the thumping explosions and crackling of energy weapons. There was a flash of white and the feed went dead. The screen cycled, this time to a camera mounted on a surface vehicle speeding through a city street lined with blown out buildings and littered with corpses. The vehicle was taking fire from all sides; bursts of energy flashed from behind bus stops, from dark windows, from under overturned aircars. Eazkaii could hear the yells of the men operating the vehicle as it careened through a portion of street set ablaze with spilled fuel, could hear the sounds of energy bursts striking the armored sides and the screams of the men as they burned inside. Again, the feed went black, cycling to a drone view from above the same scene in time to see the vehicle smash into the capital building and explode, the hundreds of pounds of explosives in the vehicle's cargo coming alight in a massive inferno of fire and light. Troops fighting in the wake of the vehicle's suicide run rushed towards the new opening in the building, firing into the light and smoke. Eazkaii was pleased. The men in the vehicle had followed his orders without question, willing to die for the cause. What better way to die could there be?

But then something unexpected happened, sending a jolt of pleasure down Eazkaii's spine. The entire capital building exploded in a blinding light, taking out the drone above with it. The viewscreen cycled to a low orbit satellite; the explosion was visible from space, entire city blocks vaporized. At the same moment, reports began flooding in of a new wave of enemy combatants pushing back against the Black Sun surface units. Then the feed went dead. The viewscreen cycled dead feed after dead feed.

"Arn!" Eazkaii called his first officer to his side. "What happened?"

"Sir," Arn appeared at his side on the bridge, furiously scanning through the information flooding his tab. "It appears the inhabitants of Rot have more resources than we thought and have been holding back. They just took out 6 of our satellites simultaneously. Reports are coming in of new enemy combatants entering the battle at every front. Our people are being pushed back."

Eazkaii did not respond right away, staring instead at the static on the screen before him. At the press of a button on his console, the screen switched to the default outer view. The curvature of the planet Rot filled the viewscreen. A beautiful planet, a paradise of oceans and mountains and forests, it appeared as a light blue-green marble swirled with white and orange from this distance.

One of the first to be settled in the Slow Migration so many generations ago, this was truly a planet worth fighting for. Worth defending. And the resources on it – labor especially – would have gone a long way in sustaining the Black Sun's continued conquest. Eazkaii sighed. Such a waste.

"Prepare the weapon," he said gently. "Sterilize the planet."

There was silence on the bridge.

"Sir," Arn said with admirably little hesitation. "We still have over a hundred thousand troops on the surface."

"Then they die in service of the Black Sun," Eazkaii said with conviction. "What better way to enter the oblivion which awaits us all after life?" Eazkaii paused, daring anyone to contradict him, to deny the glory of the Black Sun. "Do it."

Again the mad shuffle of feet around him, this time with a new sense of urgency. The weapon. All in the ranks of the Black Sun knew the rumors of its existence, but this would be the first time the weapon would be used in battle. Eazkaii could sense the fear in the men around him. They feared not for themselves but for what this act made them, for the threshold they were about to cross. Eazkaii took an inner look at himself, gauging his emotions, looking for any sign of trepidation or fear. He felt nothing. And why should he? There was only the cause. All decisions could only be judged in light of the end goal. Nothing else, not morality nor life nor fear, mattered.

"Sir," Arn appeared at his side again. "We are ready."

"Fire."

For a few moments, there was nothing. Then the

bridge crew had to look away for the flash of white light exploding from the surface, filling the viewscreen. When they could look back, a shockwave of light could be seen spreading rapidly across the planet's surface from the explosion point, wiping through the beautiful blues and whites and oranges and leaving an ashen gray behind. The wave engulfed all that was visible on the hanging sphere and turned over the horizon. The entire planet looked as though it had gone blind. The entire thing – the death of the planet Rot – had lasted only a minute or so.

Eazkaii was already thinking about the next target.

2

The movement of peoples is, through a historical lens, one of the most common occurrences in the human story. And, through the same lens, we see that, whenever the natural flow of humans from one place to another, be it because of war, famine, injustice, etc., is stopped, whenever borders are emphasized and controlled, this flow is not controlled. Only more people die.

-*Excerpt* from Lines in the Sand: the History of Migration and Enforcement *by Als-de Garcia*

The ship now coming into view on her screen looked as though it had been through hell. And it likely had, considering the stories filtering out of old Coalition space. Khalihl ordered her ship around in front of the incoming ships, six tattered and barely together cruisers full of refugees from the growing destruction sweeping through what was left of the Coalition. She hailed their lead ship, the *Kindred.*

"This is Q'biin Khalihl, Captain of the *Gibran* and Admiral of the Inner Cluster fleet," she said to the man who appeared on the viewscreen. "I bid you welcome to the Inner Cluster."

"Thank you," the man, obviously short on sleep and

nutrition, said. "I am Gerald Hunth of the ship the *Kindred* and from the moon-colony Mond. I come with 352 refugees seeking asylum."

"I acknowledge your request," Khalihl could hear the tension in Hunth's voice, could see the fatigue in his worry-worn eyes. There was much to discuss with the gentleman, many procedures to go through in order to process these people, but some part of her was not ready for that. These were the first to arrive from the growing conflicts in what had been Coalition space; they had survived whatever destruction had befallen their system, had made the arduous and long journey to the Inner Cluster, likely underprepared for it. They deserved some rest. "There are many things for us to discuss to process your request, but this can wait. Allow my ships to escort you and yours to a moon nearby. There, we can offer your people whatever help they need. We will get to the procedures when you have recovered some."

"Thank you again," the man said, relief and joy plain on his face and in the tears beginning to stream down his cheeks. "Thank you so much."

It only took a few hours for them to reach the nearby moon Khalihl had promised, and as she watched the battered and beaten people file out of their ships and into the waiting arms of the medical staff there to treat them, she marveled at their bravery and strength. These people had been forced to leave everything, an entire world they had built for themselves and for their culture, behind. It would take time for them to recover from the pain and the trauma. This she could plainly see in their sunken eyes and their shuffling gaits. But she also sensed a new hope from them. They had made it, had survived the ravages of the power struggle from which they fled! And then there were the children. Khalihl was filled with hope and joy to see them being exactly what they were, children, and doing exactly what children do, play. Their peals of laughter and the sounds of their feet running on the cargo hold floors lightened her heart and, she could see, the hearts of everyone around.

After the sick and injured had been attended to, after everyone had been fed and clothed, civil servants began the processing. Khalihl wandered from booth to booth, listening to the stories being told and thinking about the events that had perpetuated this crisis. Many of the stories were painfully similar. After Meiind had shut down the equipment allowing for the harvest of human Sources, the already processed and distributed supply of batteries quickly began to dwindle. With this also degraded the Coalition's government and soon there was no central power to speak of. Small wars broke out on planets over the remaining batteries and skip drives. Some of these turned into power struggles spanning systems, and eventually, while many began the process of adapting their societies to the new, lonely realities of life cut off from the rest of humanity, the Black Sun emerged. Khalihl stopped and sat down at one booth where a woman with a child was telling her story.

"There was no warning," the woman said, fatigue obvious in her voice and posture. "They destroyed the colony on Redras, one of our moons, within an hour of appearing in orbit. Seven million souls gone in an instant. Then they began making their demands."

"What is it they wanted?" Khalihl asked after glancing at the worker taking notes and making sure it was alright for her to ask questions.

"They wanted any Source batteries and skip drives we had left," the woman responded, turning now to Khalihl. "They also demanded we renounce any religion practiced on our planet, a regular tribute of resources, and fifty percent of males below the age of 14." This was exactly as Khalihl had heard from every refugee fleeing the Black Sun.

"How did your people respond?"

"They tried to negotiate for less difficult terms. We are not sure what happened when our president went to the ship in orbit, but soon after, an invasion had begun. They came down and began destroying cities and capturing and killing people. My husband…" the woman broke down into tears and buried her face in her hands. Khalihl reached a hand out and gripped the woman's shoulder for a moment before getting up and moving on.

She had heard hundreds of stories now, and each of them were similar. A preliminary, unwarranted, and devastating attack followed by the same list of demands. If those were not fulfilled immediately, then utter destruction ensued. The Black Sun was not interested taking their time nor in reducing causalities. They only wanted resources and power. Their leader only wanted domination.

She found herself at one end of the cargo hold, looking out at the hundreds of people milling about booths and sick beds, volunteers from the Inner Cluster and refugees alike. Seeing them all here, hearing their stories and seeing the anguish written on their faces, she could not help but wonder at the choice she and Meiind had made. Using the Source for energy was murder, that much was clear. But, in destroying the technology, in condemning planets to isolation and suffering, had they allowed something worse to come forth? Were they, in a way, responsible for the billions of lives already lost and the billions still in jeopardy? Were they responsible for the Black Sun and its leader, Eazkaii?

Khalihl turned to leave the cargo hold, her mind

awash with confusion and fear and anger. The halls of the moon base were humming with activity. As she walked towards the command center, absently saluting the soldiers and civilians stopping at attention as she passed, her mind drifted to the person often in her thoughts when she found herself unsure of things: Aasben Raasch. The late CoFleet Admiral who had given his life in treason against the Coalition and to save New Mecca, the man who had led the conspirator trio made up of herself, the Admiral, and Meiind. How many times in the aftermath of what was now being called by Cluster historians and the populace alike the Hero's Battle – the remnants of the Coalition called it the Traitor's Battle – had she wished Raasch was here to guide them again? How many times had she regretted not having more time to learn from the man, to perhaps be with him? In the Inner Cluster, he had become a hero of mythic status, and the Elder Council had added a bust of him to their meeting place, a constant reminder of the man who had saved them despite political and ideological differences. He had been a man dedicated to truth and morality. What would he think of what was happening in the remains of his culture? What would he do?

Khalihl did not have an answer to these questions, and she knew, ultimately, she would have to make her own decisions based on her own thoughts and feelings. She arrived at the control center of the base and sat before a console, inputting a few commands. A stream of information filtered onto the screen in front of her: refugee stats, news of the wars being fought, the latest movements of the Black Sun. Again, everything led back to this one enemy. No matter what happened, she knew, they would become the most important issue to be dealt with.

Indeed, what to do about them was the principle discussion happening in the Elder Council now. Some argued for a preemptive attack; the Black Sun would only grow in strength the longer they waited and become more difficult to handle, these advisors said. And, they thought, the leader of the Black Sun, Eazkaii, an obvious and dangerous megalomaniac, would not settle with simply overtaking old Co space. He would want the Inner Cluster as well. Khalihl agreed with them in this, but she was unsure of their conclusions. Again, Raasch's voice rang in her head. Did he not turn against his superiors because of their decision to attack the Inner Cluster without provocation? While it is true the Black Sun was a serious threat, they had not yet threatened her people in any way. And history was clear on the ways in which interventionist policies often led to long, dragged-out conflicts. It was for this reason, as well as for the faint voice of Raasch in her mind, she had sided with the advisors advocating military preparedness while also providing what relief they could for the people suffering in these power struggles. Waiting was difficult, but it appeared to be the most logical course of action. And yet the stories she had just heard, so like the hundreds of others recorded throughout Inner Cluster space as refugees poured in all over, pulled at her sense of outrage. She felt dragged in different directions; her personal anger wanted recourse but her upbringing prioritized peace and life, arguing to wait and to try to do the most good and the least harm. *So often,* she thought, *it seems the same premises lead equally to different conclusions and courses of action. What does this mean about the premises themselves?*

"Sir?" a voice behind her, that of the base's highest ranking officer.

"Yes?" Khalihl turned to face a woman standing a few paces away, at attention, with a face full of stress and worry.

"A message has arrived for you," the woman said. "From the Elders."

Khalihl could not help a bitter thought: *What now?*

"Prepare my ship, please," Khlahl said, standing with a growing sense of dread and fatigue.

3

*After the collapse of the Coalition, when the skip
network went down, planets were left largely on
their own. Some, planets that relied on trade for
necessary resources, suffered greatly. Others
preferred this and rejoiced in their liberation from
the Coalition and its rules. All manner of social
structures and governments evolved, springing
forth after hundreds of years under single rule,
leading to what has been called the "Social
Explosion."*

-Excerpt from Broken Chains: Social
Evolution in the Post-Coalition Era *by
Nigel Dentree*

The morning light touched his face and colored the
insides of his eyelids pink. He opened them to watch the
sun slowly rise over the horizon, barely a sliver at first,
then some more, and now shafts of light sliced over the
planet's edge in incredibly defined rays of energy. The
landscape began to lighten, moving from the muted colors
of the dark to the gold-washed vibrancy of the sunrise.
Meiind took in what his eyes saw: the miles and miles of
the vines called the Bodhi tree, the namesake of the planet.
The vines were in full bloom this time of the year, and
their vibrant, green leaves soaked in the now warm
sunlight. The sky was changing as well, shifting from the
deep black of night to a pastel purple and red with the

early sunrise and now the pale blue standard of this atmosphere. With more light came more information. Meiind could make out the mirror reflections of lakes dotted throughout the view before him, these fed by underground rivers coursing throughout the planet's crust. To the south, he could see a small farming village carved out of the Bodhi vines, massive circles of crops surrounding a small cluster of buildings. Roads spread from the village in three directions. Thin tendrils of smoke floated up from some of the structures until they reached high enough to be set aflame in color by the rays of the rising sun. Meiind watched from where he sat cross-legged in front of his Bodhi-vine hut, taking in the view as he had so many times before and seeing something new again as he had every morning since he had gone into seclusion. He sat and watched until the sun had cleared the horizon.

With the full force of the sun on display, the air warmed perceptibly and the vine forest came alive with movement and sound. Birds took flight and called out. Small fishing vessels appeared on the lakes. Farmers with their produce carts began to populate the roads. The bells of the village temple tolled into the morning air. Meiind took a few last breaths, deep and slow, and stood to make his breakfast. His joints creaked and his muscles strained from sitting so long in the early cold, but his mind felt refreshed and rested. He savored this freshness of mind and the clarity of attention that came with it. As he went about his morning routine, preparing his tea and porridge, he could sense the distinctiveness of each movement, of each item in his hand, of each smell, and when he sat to eat, of every taste. It gave him immense satisfaction to become so engrossed in the most mundane of details. This sense of attention always, in the mornings, focused itself on his past.

While he ate his morning meal, he usually played the Inner Cluster news broadcasts, trying to keep apprised of events in the universe from which he felt more and more distanced with every passing year on Bodhi. At first, he had been almost manic for information, and he knew now this came from a sense of guilt for the aftermath of his decision to end skipping technology. He had watched and listened as the Coalition fell apart into warring factions, as millions, no billions, were caught up and killed in the fighting. That had been before he had come to Bodhi to try and recover – how many years ago? eight? ten? – when he was still on the prison planet trying to help the poor souls who had been… farmed there. His life before the Traitor's Battle, when he was a mediator for the Coalition, and his life immediately after was full of holes and shadow in his memories. From where he now sat, eating his plain breakfast on the planet Bodhi, in the peaceful society of the Buddhi, those events seemed more than a lifetime away. The memories felt as though he had stolen them, as though they belonged to someone else entirely. He knew the source of this feeling, knew his mind was defending itself from the doubt and pain he felt whenever he allowed himself to reenter those frames of mind, those memories. But, every morning, during and after breakfast, while he sat in his vine hut in silence, he forced himself to think back, to evaluate his actions, to try and better understand his past so he may be rid of it. Today, after he set aside his empty bowl and cup and sat again at the front of his hut to overlook the forest, a new memory came to mind and with it thoughts of someone he had not spoken to since, had not met in his thoughts in many years. *Khalihl*, he thought, *why have I pushed you so far away?*

●●●●

Khalihl had arrived at the prison planet, which they

had begun calling Australia as a kind of historical joke, soon after her battle with the Coalition and the death, the sacrifice, of Admiral Raasch. Meiind watched her ship's fiery reentry, watched the *Gibran* glide silently down to the landing field. They embraced as two survivors on the tail end of a terrible ordeal, as two friends who had never expected to see each other again. Meiind could not help but think: *I am glad you and Raasch both did not die. This is not something I can do alone.*

He told her everything – well, almost everything. He left out the true nature of the president's death, attributing to him instead a kind of villainous tirade, as in the holos, that gave up all the information Meiind had learned through his touch. He explained the president's history and the true nature of the energy that had powered human society and expansion for over 300 years, the true cost of fast interstellar travel. The truth of the Source as it had been used to power human expansion through this corner of the galaxy. The truth of the lie they had all been told, a lie fabricated and developed by the president throughout his centuries long control of humanity. The Source used for skipping came from one, and only one, place: humans. Every skip drive battery represented dead – murdered – humans. Humans farmed specifically for that purpose. The look of shock and disgust that grew on her face as he told his story would stay with Meiind for many years after.

He was relieved, when, after he had exhausted his experiences, she came to the same conclusion: the technology allowing for this must be dismantled. No matter the benefit, no matter how important the Source and skipping had been to human development, it could not be allowed to continue. It was simply too horrifying.

"We must destroy the entire compound," Meiind concluded, "we must destroy every trace of the technology so it cannot be reproduced."

"Think of the consequences for such a sudden loss," Khalihl argued, "think of the planets left isolated. There are planets where the population only survives through skipping, inhospitable mining colonies where food has to be brought in from afar. If you destroy the technology immediately, suddenly, people on planets that are not sustainable will suffer immensely."

"There are already loaded batteries, thousands of them here and more out in the Coalition and the Cluster. These will serve to soften the blow."

"They will not be enough. I agree the compound needs to be destroyed, the technology dismantled, but we should do it slowly, systematically. And we need not throw away the knowledge of the technology. Perhaps one day it will become useful again in a less horrifying way."

"Think about what you are saying Khalihl," Meiind responded, emphatic. "Think of the history of our species. Think about what would happen if this technology ended up in the wrong hands."

Khalihl knew Meiind was right, knew there could only be one course of action. Her mind balked at the implications, at the thought of the difficulties the Coalition would face without skipping. The Inner Cluster would adapt; they were sparing with their use of skip drives anyway. But the Coalition only existed because of the ability to instantaneously travel through the stars. It would be a death blow to the social structures that held the some 300 planets of Co space together, and who knew what terrible things would come forth in the aftermath? History had dire things to say about sudden power vacuums coupled with resource scarcity. But history also had dire things to say about humanity's ability to wean itself from unethical and destructive practices. How long had slavery been in practice? And, after that, wage slavery? How close had humanity come to destruction before they finally let go of fossil fuels? Humanity had evolved, somewhat, but through cooperation and planning. In the years to follow, Khalihl knew, without the centralized Coalition to control things, there would be strife and struggle that would bring out the worst in humanity, as war had always done. This technology could not be allowed to exist in such an environment.

"You are right, of course," she answered after a moment or two, "but I still struggle with the idea. Either way, the potential for suffering is so great. I wish Raasch were here to help you in this. However, it is your decision; you represent the Coalition in this. Do what you think is right."

She walked away, after a brief touch of the hand to Meiind's shoulder, to be with her thoughts and to leave him to his. He watched her, a sense of profound fear building within him. The responsibility was too great, and he also wished Raasch were here to help him. He wished anyone would help. That is why he had called Khalihl, and as he watched her back as she stood a ways away from him, overlooking the slums surrounding the complex, he resented her for her refusal to be involved. Her refusal to even truly engage with the issue and help him find his own way.

●●●●

The memory was vivid, as many had been since he had begun a regular meditation practice. He distinctly remembered the anger, the fear, the worry he would make the wrong decision. The desperate need for someone else to bear the load with him. He remembered the image of Khalihl's back turned towards him, such a human gesture of isolation and removal. In the end, he had done what he thought was right, what Khalihl knew was right, even if she could not accept it, and what he thought Raasch would have done. He destroyed the compound and buried everything, all the technology necessary for Source extraction, deep in the underground cargo holds, sealing off access and leaving drones to guard against intruders. Still, he wondered then and now if this was enough.

His dishes washed and the sun well above the horizon now, Meiind exited his hut to stand in the warming light. There was more activity in the village and on the roads now, and for a moment he simply watched, lost in thought and in the past. *Why do these memories come back now?* he thought. *Why after all these years?* Indeed, he had not thought of that last meeting with Khalihl in years now, had not wondered at his decision in more. There had been little time for such soul searching in the time since the end of the Traitor's Battle and the dissolution of the Coalition. *There must be a reason these feelings flow back to me now. Something is happening.*

His mornings were usually dedicated to his studies: history, philosophy, religion, literature. But with his mind so occupied, he felt he would be unable to focus, he would have to revisit any material he tried to work with today again anyways. He chose, instead, to take a walk through the pathways cut into the Bodhi forests, tunnels through the vines, and allow his mind to wander where it would. He did not want these thoughts disrupting his focus for long. *Better to give them the space and time they demand.*

Space and time, he thought as he set out onto the path leading from his hut to one of the major thoroughfares. *Spacetime.* This was essentially what he had been thinking about for the last decade since the end of the Coalition, wondering at the human understanding of it as opposed to the human experience of it. For the physical universe, everything existed within the planes of that existence, within spacetime and its confinements. The discovery of the Source and its application in skipping had proven something humans had theoretically known for centuries, namely that there were other planes, other dimensions, inaccessible to human experience but still capable of exerting force on it. These other dimensions had existed in human thought like black holes did before the discovery of their actuality, as mathematical necessities to fill holes in universal theories of physics. And yet, when their reality became clear, especially with the advent of skipping, in which ships and people could be moved through spacetime without relation to its constraints via some other dimensionality, this knowledge only led to more confusion. Attempts to explore whatever dimension a skipping piece of physical matter entered into failed; it seemed instruments developed in spacetime could not measure things outside of it. It was as if the tools did not speak the right language.

This, of course, had led to a number of theories trying to explain what happened during a skip, some useful and others full blown crazy. Meiind had read through old books claiming that skipping gave humans access to the divine realm. Others claimed the skipping ship went to hell for a moment. Still more said it was a kind of death, the returning ship and its passengers were not the same people but replicas with the same memories. One popular theory in the 22nd century even claimed skipping was proof the universe was a massive computer simulation, a reemergence of pop culture science fiction from the 20th and 21st centuries. For all the interest in the topic, however, science failed to explain the phenomenon satisfactorily, and humanity, except for a few dedicated scientists, moved on. After all, with skipping, there was much to explore in the galaxy.

Meiind snapped from his thoughts at the sound of a temple bell tolling nearby. He found himself now in the village near his hut, the one he could see when he looked out over the valley. People milled around, some walking to and from errands and some sitting at tables outside of food stalls and talking. There was a sense of slowness he had never seen elsewhere, a sense of deliberate and precise action to the people he saw as he walked through the small cluster of buildings. In the years Meiind had spent on Bodhi with these people, he had often wondered at the pace of life here. At first, he had attributed it to their social and economic structure; there was no money on Bodhi, no economic system to speak of. The people here, including Meiind for the last few years, lived in a kind of religious commune, each capable person being attributed twenty hours of work a week in exchange for the satisfaction of their basic needs. Beyond that, people could do what they liked. Meiind spent his free time, such as today, studying and thinking; indeed, many of the adherents here did much the same. But others had more physical – the martial arts and rock climbing were popular on the planet – or artistic interests. Still others enjoyed service-based work and opened free restaurants and tea shops, places where men and women could gather and be together. Meiind would not have thought this kind of social structure possible before he arrived here to stay, and perhaps it was not possible anywhere else. These people shared a distinct sense of purpose, a way of looking at the universe.

That, ultimately, was what led to the slow pace of life, rather than the lack of business and economics. Life moved more slowly here because it is what these people wanted. They wanted every moment to drag out, to pass before the screens of their awareness slowly enough that they may fully grasp each fleeting experience as completely as possible before it ineffably became lost in the past. It had taken Meiind some time to get used to it, but after the first few years, he came to appreciate the deliberation and mindfulness possible in such a place. He had time to think here, and he had found there was always so much to contemplate.

As he passed through the village, waving to friends and acquaintances, and back into the Bodhi-vine forest, his thoughts turned reminiscent of the years he had spent here so far. For years now, under Roshi Moyo's guidance and direction, Meiind had worked to deepen his understanding and scope of his abilities, his touch. He never told the Roshi how President Ondrueut had died, but he suspected the old Master knew well enough the murderous possibilities of Meiind's special talents. A pang of guilt seared through him, and Meiind turned his attention to his breath to take the edge off the feeling. He found himself near a small pond. Insects hovered just over the water, leaving not so much as a ripple when, for the most wonderfully brief moment, they touched the surface to perhaps feed on something floating or to drink. Occasionally, a bird would fall from the open space above the pond, a window to the blue sky above the still, blue pond, and sweep through the clouds of insects. At the other side of the small body of water, two young girls were fishing, sitting patiently in the peaceful setting. The feeling of sharp remorse soon left Meiind, and he continued his walk.

It was not that he regretted his decision to kill the digital being known to him as Ondrueut – whether or not the president had still been human was something Meiind had never been able to answer for himself. Ondrueut's death had been a necessity, had been the only way to stop his manipulation of the human species and his descent into something else, something Meiind could not quite define. In a way, Meiind even thought he had done the man a mercy, ending centuries of a peculiar kind of lonely torment. No, killing the man had been the right thing to do. Yet, it still had been a murder, and Meiind had done it by breaking the promise he had made to himself when he was young, the promise he would never use his talent for harm again. Killing his own mother had been enough, and now he carried another death on his conscience.

Perhaps, he thought, *the guilt follows me not because of the act but because of the consequences.* Indeed, Meiind had kept up with the news filtering in from old Co space, had followed the rise of the Black Sun. He had read the reports of death and destruction, of whole planets either subjugated or sterilized. The Black Sun rampaged through the human universe, moving slowly at sublight from system to system, and without skipping, no one could escape from their path of conquest. Without skipping. Again, the slice of pain. But this pain had two edges. It was true that, without skipping, the people in old Co space could not escape, could not move out of the area quickly enough. But, by the same token, had Meiind not removed the technology, the Black Sun's expansion of power would have been immediate and even more terrifying. The same thing that doomed the people near the Black Sun gave others time to prepare.

These thoughts loomed at once large and small in Meiind's mind as he wandered the paths cut through the Bodhi-vine forest. He could not help but shudder at the idea that his choices had led to deaths of millions and the suffering of billions. How could anyone cope with such a possibility? But, at the same time, his experiences here had changed his perspective of human affairs. First, it was simply the ideology of the Buddhi. For them, human suffering was rooted in an ignorance which made so much of so little. The Buddhi perspective minimized the dramas of humanity as just that: a drama played out for no reason other than drama itself. A lonely impulse of delight, nothing more. This made the sufferings humanity experienced a matter of collective choice and perception. All the social constructs of the human species – the governments, the religions, the economics, the science, all of it – were arbitrary and designed for one purpose: to keep at bay the inevitable end of life all living things faced. None of these things, in and of themselves, held any power aside from those attributed to them by common agreement. And if people killed and suffered for these arbitrary constructs, then that too was a choice. Nothing was real about them, and nothing about them demanded action.

Meiind came now to a small trail which left the main path, trending left up a steep slope. He followed it, his legs soon burning for the uphill travel. He took his time, setting one foot deliberately in front of the other in time with his deep, slow breaths. He needed to calm his mind some, to remove himself from the tension he felt. The apprehension. Perhaps, even, the fear. The fact of the matter was, not being raised here, it was difficult for him to sit and listen to the news reports filtering in every evening about the Black Sun's rampage across the galaxy, about their newest conquest, their latest victory. He felt responsible, at least partially, and he felt the need to do something. It was in these moments he thought of Khalihl and the Inner Cluster, wondering what would happen when the Black Sun made its way to their corner of space. *I hope you are ready, Khalihl,* he thought, and shuddered at the alternative.

The path burst through the top of the forest, a rocky outcropping jutting high enough through the green vines to offer a full view of the surrounding area. Meiind had been here many times before and still the view took his breath away and silenced his mind. The outcrop was high and far enough south to offer an unimpeded view of the southern forests; for miles and miles, as far as he could see, there was nothing but unbroken Bodhi vines. An entire landscape covered with a living, breathing thing. Birds flew in the middle distance, crossing the vast sea of green. And below the sky, living in the vines and on the ground in their shade, was a whole ecosystem of animals and plants. When Meiind stood on this outcropping, looking over the unbroken forest, untouched by human hands or industry, he saw only one thing: life. To him, that is what mattered most.

4

Tolerance! What a pernicious word and concept. Show me a so-called "tolerant" culture, and I will show you a society that has fallen into sin. Show me a "tolerant" people, and I will show you a people that have forgotten God. We should celebrate our adherence to the old ways, not hide it. We must seek to be truer to the Word of God, not to obscure divine will through watered down interpretations and feel-good spirituality.

-*Excerpt from* The Only Way: a Christian Manifesto *by Moises Senstre*

He watched in the viewscreen as his planet grew more and more distant, their ship making its way out of orbit so as to jump to sublight. The planet was mostly desert with a few lush forests and large seas. From space, it appeared as a tan ball with green and blue spots.

Beautiful, John Maldeck thought as he watched his home grow smaller and smaller, likely for the last time, as the ship around him bustled with the cries and moans of the other refugees. No one wanted to leave their home. *You will always be my home, Sianide.*

As he watched, a yellow and orange blossom flashed on the surface, large enough to see even at their distance. An explosion. Maldeck watched in horror as the shockwave from the explosion spread over the surface of the planet, watched as the only two large cities on Sianide, New Jerusalem and her sister city New America, were swept through with the force of the shockwave. There was a collective gasp in the ship, a moment of silence. Then the cries and tears renewed with more fervor. Prayers to God and to Jesus and to the Holy Spirit filled the small common room they had all gathered in to watch the departure. From this distance, Maldeck could not see the destruction wrought upon the cities, but as the shockwave passed through their electric lights, both went dark except for the eerie, orange glow of the burning surface left in the wake of the shockwave. The planet now looked as though the mantle was rising through the surface, as though everything was on fire.

Please Lord, Maldeck thought in a silent prayer amongst the screams and cries of his people. *Please Lord give me and my people the strength so we may survive this calamity, so we may keep Your ways and our faith, so we may exact revenge upon those who persecute your children, so we may one day destroy the Black Sun.*

All while he prayed, burning Sianide grew smaller and smaller in the viewscreen until it was simply no more.

●●●●

The journey was to be long and fraught with danger. Since the Coalition had collapsed, since the Black Sun had come to be the most powerful force in this corner of human occupied space, nowhere, whether on planet or in space, was safe. News and stories of planets being attacked were only matched by similar stories of flotillas of refugee ships being destroyed while they fled to the only place that seemed safe from the Black Sun anymore: the Inner Cluster. Ten years. That was how long it would take Maldeck and his people to reach the Inner Cluster. Ten years of interstellar travel. Ten years of fear of attack. Ten years of food rationing and water conservation. Ten years. Children would be born and many of the elderly would die. Infants would become toddlers and adolescents would become adults. It would be a trying time.

Nothing, Maldeck tried to remind himself, *compared to the Jews and their forty years in the desert. God provided them with mana, and God will provide for us the same.*

The first year was spent getting life aboard their ship, *The Covenant,* under a meticulous routine. If they were to survive, both physically, emotionally, and spiritually, their leaders on the command ship knew the people needed every bit of normalcy they could get. Power was organized so each ship in the flotilla acted essentially as a separate city or state with orders being handed down from the command ship where the planetary leaders of Sianide lived. Great effort was put into giving people work, for idle hands... daily church services were organized for the different age groups, and multiple services were offered to make sure everyone had at least one to attend a day regardless of their work schedule. Then there were community events, group birthdays, religious holidays, anything to keep the fear and boredom at bay. Soon, they had established a pattern, and that pattern became their life.

Maldeck, who had been a common laborer on Sianide, was assigned general maintenance work. He spent his days working on the list of projects handed down to him by his supervisor, who in turn had received this list from the leaders of their ship who reported to the command ship of their flotilla. He spent his days tinkering with different parts of the ship, learning the ins and outs of its various technologies as things broke down. At the end of his workday, he would often go to the common room where the few luxuries they were allowed – coffee and sometimes, when available, alcohol – could be had. There, he talked with other men – the women had their own common room to use – and they discussed everything from the Black Sun to the end of the Coalition to religion to just idle gossip. It was difficult, and the trauma of what had happened, what they all had lost, lingered heavy in their hearts, but in time they grew accustomed to their new lives, and it became just that: a life.

Things changed when their flotilla encountered other groups of ships fleeing the Black Sun and their leaders decided there was safety in numbers. Their exodus grew from a hundred ships to two hundred, then three and four hundred. Soon, shuttle traffic between these different ships and interaction between these different groups, for trade and novelty, became a normal part of life. Maldeck did not visit ships other than the ones of his people. The new groups came from all walks of life: anarchists and socialists from Red, Hindus from Ganesh, transhumanists and criminals from Hub, Originalists from Druid… the list went on and grew with every new refugee group they encountered on the trip. Many from Sianide went to these other ships and interacted with the people there, learning of their stories and making friends. Maldeck, as well as many of his own friends, did not approve. His ancestors had been of the first to arrive at Sianide, and they had left System One in the Skip migration precisely to avoid the mixing of cultures now happening. This kind of mixing, in Maldeck's mind, always had the same result. It diluted their culture and weakened their faith. God's truth, he had been taught, needed to be kept pure, protected from the damning influence of heathen cultures and hedonist atheists.

It was one day at the common room, after work and somewhere near seven years into their journey to the Inner Cluster, that he said as much aloud to the group of men he had befriended. It had become their custom to meet every evening for coffee and for what passed as beer to talk. Early on, their topics had been personal, but, as they had learned more of each other, had learned their similar viewpoints and beliefs, their discussions turned to politics and religion, to the state of human affairs and history. And, as their flotilla grew with the ships of other planets, as the refugees from those ships began to appear on their own, their discussions broadened to include what they felt was happening.

"It isn't right," Maldeck said over a cup of coffee, looking out of the corner of his eye at a group of people laughing in another corner of the common room. The group, some transhumanists from another ship, had just entered with some friends from *The Covenant*. Maldeck could see the implants on their scalps and arms, could see the distant look in their eyes when they referred to the displays laid over their vision. It made him feel sick. "We should not be so open to those who profane God's creation."

The men he sat with turned towards the group that had just entered and there was a general murmur of agreement. Encouraged, Maldeck continued.

"We all were taught our history. We all know how globalism and the mixing of cultures affected our people on Earth in the twenty-first and twenty-second centuries." Again the murmurs. Again the agreement. To Maldeck, it was obvious. All the ills of human history could have been avoided if his people, the Christians and the Christian nations of Earth, would have held strong and taken care of themselves rather than opening themselves to trade with other countries, rather than accepting refugees, rather than opening their borders to immigrants from places that did not hold their values. The Terror years could have been avoided and the glories of the nineteenth and twentieth centuries continued. They could have ushered a millennia of heaven on Earth, of God's plan made manifest by his people. They could have led the world into righteousness. Instead, too many concessions had been made to the liberal globalists of the world, led by the Devil. His parents had taught him well in his private education – Sianide had not had a public education system aside from the Church – and the lesson they had instilled in him was clear: to each their own and God's children to the Truth. God willed it so. "Why should we expect things to be any different now?"

"But what of our destination?" spoke up one of the younger men in their group, a young man named James. *A good Christian name,* thought Maldeck. "Are we not opening ourselves to corruption by seeking help from the heathens in the Inner Cluster?"

Maldeck nodded, listened to the others voice similar fears, similar concerns. Indeed, the thought had been on his mind as well.

"This is a valid concern," he said looking at his brethren who he realized, quite suddenly, were looking to him for answers. "And we must steel ourselves against the negative influences of the culture we are about to enter. We must hold true to our ways despite pressures from the Isla'hai. Be wary of the Musla. They will be as wolves in sheep's clothing, offering help and appearing to make no demands on us and on our faiths. They claim tolerance. We have all heard their lies. But their ways are especially insidious, especially deceptive. Have no illusions about it, we will lose many to their ways through their kindness. We must be especially strong in the face of their seeming love."

"What, however, does it say about us?" said another man, a newcomer to their group from another ship in the flotilla. Maldeck struggled to remember his name, but he did remember the man hailed from one of the more progressive cities on Sianide, one of the intellectual swamps where new thoughts threatened the old and faithful ways. The man continued: "What does it say about us that we flee to the Inner Cluster, knowing full well they will take us in and offer us refuge, with distrust and ill will in our hearts? Is not the message of the Christ to believe in the best in people, even those who are not of our faith?"

No one answered. Rather, all heads turned to stare at the man who had spoken, who withered under the critical glare. *Yes,* Maldeck thought, *we will lose many, but we will also weed out the weak of faith and those who would hurt us by opening themselves to the heathens.*

"We will do what we must to survive," Maldeck finally said, breaking the icy silence. "But we will keep our hearts pure from the corruption of those who malign God's will. We will keep our faith, even as we enter the lion's den, and we will come out on the other side stronger and with God's blessing."

Again, nods and murmurs of agreement all around.

5

Every generation born into war is born into a hate that cannot be soothed with cease fires and treaties.

-Excerpt from The Sins of the Father: the Epigenetics of Violence *by Lowl Aakteein*

The shop was busy with morning traffic as men and women came in and out on their way to work. The smell of coffee and spice was strong and wafted throughout the room and out into the street where Bin Ald sat, drinking his cup as he watched the news on his pad. The sun bore down gently on his neck, and he was aware of a wonderful sensation of warmth spreading through his body as the morning chill slowly gave way to the spring sun. He looked up from his pad for a moment to turn his face, eyes closed, into the sun. The warmth on his face and the pink glow through his eyelids did much to slow his beating heart. For a moment, his anger stilled, and when he opened his eyes again to look out over the park the shop ran alongside, he felt his heart leap out to the space around him.

The park was an open, green space in the center of the enormous capital city on New Mecca, his home for his entire life. He had grown up going to the park, and he had wonderful memories of playing football with his father on the grass and in the sun, laughing as the elder Bin Ald ran in circles around him with the ball at his feet. Even now, decades later, looking out over the park and towards the Grand Mosque at the horizon, Bin Ald felt that same levity in his heart again, the joy he had not felt but in memory for some time now. He swept his eyes south from the park towards the space port, where he could see the massive line of the elevator cable rising into the sky and beyond, thinning to a strand of hair in the distance. Huge transport cars, though they became tiny as they moved up the cable, were coming and going, bringing many things down and sending just as much up into orbit. Surrounding these major landmarks – the park, the Mosque, and the space port – was the city he loved. The financial district a bit north made for a jagged skyline of huge skyscrapers so large some ancient part of his mind still recoiled at their existence, as if they should not be physically possible. The rest of the city varied between smaller buildings clustered together and the suburban sprawl of homes that went as far as the eye could see in all directions. *My home,* he thought. *My home.*

Turning his attention back to his pad, he scrolled through some more news, but all the headlines were variations on the same theme, and the peace he had felt looking over his city began to quickly fade, replaced with anger. One in particular caught his attention. The headline read: "Elder Council Approves Refugee Resettlement, Appropriates Funds." Bin Ald skimmed the article. It offered nothing he had not already read or heard in the last few days, nothing new to alleviate his growing resentment. More Coalition refugees fleeing the Black Sun. More Inner Cluster land being given away. More Cluster jobs being done by the refugees. More Cluster food to feed them. This particular article offered a pro-refugee perspective, arguing compassion and cooperation. We have the space, it said, and we may very well one day need what is left of the Coalition to fight the Black Sun if they push their conquest here. Forgiveness and compassion are the heart of the Prophet's message. Bin Ald scoffed as he set his pad down and sipped his coffee, looking back over the park in an attempt to contain his feelings. His attention was drawn by a family walking along a path through the grass near him, two men and two small children. The men walked hand in hand while the children ran around, playing the kind of game only children could make sense of. The sight nearly brought tears to Bin Ald's eyes, and he felt a kind of double vision wash over his consciousness. On the one hand, it brought him joy to see such a lovely family out for a walk in the park on such a beautiful day. Was it not for this kind of peace his ancestors had left Earth so many generations ago? Was it not for this kind of existence they had left everything they had ever known in search of something better? And was it not for these lives so many men and women had died in the Cluster Wars and the Hero's Battle? Bitterness welled up in his heart as memories came forward, threatening to wash away his touch with reality.

He remembered the day his mother left for the war. His father had been asked to stay and work; the elder Bin Ald was a teacher, and as education was considered critical, teachers were asked not to volunteer. What would winning the war be worth if there wasn't a generation there ready to continue the grand experiment their culture was? His mother had been beautiful in the extreme: tall and handsome, she always held herself with an air of grace and strength. Even then, at the space port, with tears in her eyes as she hugged and kissed her family farewell, his mother had exuded strength and tranquility. He could see her in his mind's eye vividly. She had stood proud in her Cluster uniform, the blue with gold trim, a traditional burka wrapped around her neck and laying down her shoulders while her hair, a wonderfully deep black, shone in the sunlight like the light trapped at the event horizon.

That is how she was forever etched into his memory. The warrior woman, the all-mother, the ultimate sacrifice. Bin Ald even remembered her words: "Do not fear, my son. Allah calls us all to duty, and it is with joy I go to serve." He never saw her again. She was killed, they said, at the Battle of the Rim, her squadron sacrificing itself to protect a system critical to the resource development of the Inner Cluster. His father, a happy man by nature, had never fully recovered from the loss, though he continued to live a productive and comfortable life, providing for his family while he watched his sons and daughters grow up.

The final blow for his father's happiness, as well as for Bin Ald's own peace, came many years later when his youngest brother, the cherub of the family, was killed in the Hero's Battle. Ten years had passed, and the thought of his brother's smiling face still cast Bin Ald's heart hard with despair. But his own suffering at the loss was nothing compared to his father's. The elder Bin Ald had taken the news hard, and even now, a decade after, he spent his days at home in seclusion, only eating when his surviving children came to feed him. He almost never spoke during these visits, instead simply staring out of the window overlooking Lake Prajna in the low valley to the west of the city. It tore Bin Ald's heart open every time he went, every time he saw his father this way. He remembered his father as a strong man, and the sight of him as an invalid was not something he could ever become accustomed to.

A commotion nearby drew Bin Ald from his thoughts. He looked up to see a group of protesters marching through the street just adjacent to him. The group was made of Cluster citizens – Bin Ald could see as much from their dress, from the flowing robes they wore – and they were yelling and chanting what sounded like slogans of some kind, but they were not in unison so Bin Ald could not understand their words. Their signs, however, he could read well enough. The two hundred or so protesters, yelling and stopping ground traffic as they passed, held wide sticks with crudely drawn figures running down them that read things like "Keep Them Out" and "Never Forget." At the same time, a woman was now passing through the shop Bin Ald sat in, handing out leaflets of the same kind. As the woman passed Bin Ald, dropping a few on his table, he noticed a sign deep within the crowd that caused his breath to catch in his throat and his heart to jump in his chest.

"They Killed My Family," the sign said.

Bin Ald took up the leaflet and began to read.

6

*To modern historians, the Black Sun represents
something ancient in the human experience. It
represents the power of Fear and Hate, the twin
demons always on our shoulders waiting to be
given reign if we are not careful. No matter how
far we progress towards a more perfect and
equitable society, no matter how advanced we
become, those two wait at the edges for the
slightest moment of weakness so they may tear
back through our history and wreak havoc once
again.*

> *-Excerpt from* The Demons of Our
> Nature: Fear and Hate in Human
> History *by Tem Herand*

The audience chamber gave the impression of vast
space. The lights brightly lit the throne Eazkaii sat in,
leaving all else, the sides and corners, in deep shadow. At
the other end of the hall, an open doorway let a shaft of
light in, making something of a golden path leading to the
kneeling mat before the throne of the Black Sun. The
shadows softly edging at the contours of the light made it
difficult to gauge the size of the chamber, and the huge
dome above often made the unaccustomed queasy and
disoriented. Made of smart-glass, the dome filtered the
light of whatever planet or sun was nearby to allow the full
depth of the unending cosmos to weigh down upon

whoever found themselves in audience with Leader Eazkaii. He found this to be a useful advantage when holding audiences with the various dignitaries and emissaries who came to curry favor with him and his. In the ten years since the collapse of the Coalition, his Black Sun consolidating more and more power with every conquest, the number of supplicants had increased significantly. It made him glad to think of the fearful travelling light years to him to ask for mercy before the path of the Black Sun found their planet.

Before Eazkaii now kneeled a small man with a large head the leader of the Black Sun found vaguely repellent. The man, under Eazkaii's unfaltering and punishing gaze, squirmed in discomfort, both from the silence dragging on now and from the pain in his knees from kneeling so long on the hard mat provided. The man stared at the floor in front of him, obviously afraid to make eye contact with the Leader. No doubt the stories of Eazkaii's ruthless responses to impertinence had spread far and wide through the old territories of the Coalition. Eazkaii had made sure of that.

"Repeat," Eazkaii's voice, amplified by subtle harmonic devices around the hall, boomed off the walls and glass dome, "for me your request. And keep it short this time."

"Yes sir," the fear in the small man's voice was obvious, even with the tinge of metallic grating so often found in his kind. "My people have sent me to ask for your permission to live as our philosophies deem appropriate. We ask for this freedom, and in exchange, we will do whatever we can to be of service to the Empire of the Black Sun."

Eazkaii's revulsion increased, and he felt a wonderful rage rising up within him. "My people," the man had called them. As if they qualified, the disgusting bastardization of humanity they were. He, Eazkaii, was human, untouched by the temptations of the machine. This *thing* before him, this transhumanist with his cybernetic implants and enhancements, was an affront to the natural order of the universe. Such abominations could not be suffered. Eazkaii glanced at the empty doorway at the end of the hall. Yet, he needed a bit more time. Some drama would suffice.

"The Empire," Eazkaii said, the weight of authority in his voice making the small man before him seem to shrink even more, "is predicated on certain fundamental principles. It is these that gives the Black Sun its strength, these that have led the Black Sun to victory, and these that will lead humanity to glory under our guidance."

The small man then did something utterly unexpected to Eazkaii: he looked the Leader in the face. Eazkaii was at once enraged and astonished. No doubt the man knew what was coming to him and thought to offer some resistance, even in this muted form.

"You and your 'people,'" Eazkaii continued, "as you generously call them, are an affront to these principles. You live without honor, pathetic in your attempts at perfection when nature has already given you the path. You seek to make all equal through improvements, and you tinker with the processes that have made the universe. This is not something we of the Black Sun can abide."

The man, still staring up at Eazkaii, straightened and stood. He actually *stood*. Had not Eazkaii been so angry, he might have been impressed by the man's courage. Eazkaii looked again past the transhumanist to the doorway down the hall. A shadow, his first officer Arn, stood in the light spilling through the dark frame. The signal. Now Eazkaii too stood, and he felt the words of his teachers welling up in his throat.

"There is only one right," he said, slowly stepping down from his throne, "and that is Order. Without it, all falls to entropy, to Chaos. The universe has existed for billions of years, fighting off the Chaos of the Void with the only tool available: Force." Eazkaii reached the bottom of the stairs and stood face to face with the silent man a few meters away. Even on level ground, Eazkaii stood a head above the man, an imposing figure in his uniform. Eazkaii took a step forward. The man flinched slightly. "Your people, the transhumanists, seek to subvert the very processes that have made humanity, the universe's greatest achievement. You court Chaos and call it creativity. You destroy your humanity and call it progress. You seek the Void and do not even know it."

Eazkaii was now within reach of the man. He looked down at him with the disgust plain on his face. This little thing, full of wires and signals and machines. Eazkaii did not have to feign disgust. The man made as if to speak, and Eazkaii cut him short, striking out with incredible speed, the gift of years of training. The man tumbled back, falling, a glistening arc of blood flying from his nose and mouth. Eazkaii stepped forward.

"You ask to be of service to the Black Sun," he said, looming over the fallen and whimpering man. "You already have been. The signals that keep you connected with your kin, the signals you thought you so well-disguised, have led us to your haven. They have been eliminated."

The small man made a sound from the back of his throat and let out a cry of grief and anger which reverberated through the audience hall. He made to stand, but Eazkaii planted a kick square on the man's face, sending him sprawling again across the cold floor, more blood spurting now from a fresh gash above one eye. The man, sputtering blood, crawled back away from the Leader of the Black Sun, a gasping sound coming forth from the red smear of his mouth.

"Your kind," Eazkaii walked slowly towards the retreating man, "are an abomination, a perversion of Nature. You think you improve yourselves, improve upon the human design, but you weaken the body and mind with dependence on these machines. Worse, you weaken the future." Standing above him now, Eazkaii looked down at the cowering transhumanist with disgust written across his face. He lifted a foot and placed it on the man's throat, gently pushing until the shivering thing was on its back, head against the frigid metal.

"The Black Sun will bring strength and order back to humanity," Eazkaii said, "and there will be no place for those like you."

Eazkaii brought the heel of his boot firmly down on the man's throat with a sickening pop. A wet gurgling filled the hall as Eazkaii walked away, leaving the man there to die alone.

7

First Contact! What a time it must have been to be alive. Imagine the swirling emotions for those first few who were privy to the truth, imagine the responsibility that fell to their shoulders. I cannot say I envy them, but I would give anything to have been there to listen to them in that first meeting where word of the truth began to spread.

-Kelnheeard Heurst, Director of the Museum of Intelligence, speaking at the opening of a new exhibit

Khalihl had not been home in over a year, and the sight of New Mecca in her viewscreen, the sight of her home planet, brought a surge of emotion into her body. After so many days listening to the stories of violence and chaos, of death and destruction, the peace of home was a welcome reprieve. But her happiness was tinted with a bitter thought: *I cannot allow the Black Sun to take this from me, from us.* She would give her life to keep New Mecca and the Inner Cluster safe.

Around her, she could sense similar feelings from the crew, a mixture of elation at being home and fear at the recent developments in old Co space. How could they not feel fear? They all knew well enough the most recent rumors from the Black Sun, the stories that they sought the means to begin skipping again. For them, and for

Khalihl, this led to only one logical conclusion: they would be coming for the Inner Cluster eventually. Why else would they care to skip unless it was to subjugate the entirety of humanity? And, if the rumors were true, the Black Sun would need the uratanium only found in the Inner Cluster to make new skip drives. Sooner or later, they would come.

Khalihl pushed these thoughts from her mind and focused on the task at hand. Around her, the crew buzzed with their slightly tainted excitement, going through the pre-landing procedures as the *Gibran* prepared to leave orbit and make its way to the landing field at the government plaza. They were a competent crew, the same women and men who had been with her at the Hero's Battle so many years ago, and they did not need her oversight for so routine a maneuver. After a quick check of their work, just to stay busy, Khalihl settled back into her seat and allowed her mind to roam again, contemplating the now growing planet in her viewscreen. These thoughts of home brought up questions about their new adversary, about Eazkaii, the leader of the Black Sun. Very little was known about his background, about his rise to power. And yet, it seemed, one day he had simply become the most powerful faction of the hundreds which sprang up from the ashes of the Coalition, soon crushing his competition mercilessly. *We will need to know more,* she thought, *if we are to be as well prepared as we need to be.*

Seemingly in response to her thoughts, the ship's down well trajectory brought them close to an orbital station where Khalihl could see dozens of war ships docked. She knew more were spread out in the space surrounding New Mecca, hundreds of ships creating a defense net thousands of AUs wide, and more were on their way from all over the Cluster. Preparations were well under way. Khalihl could only hope they would be enough. But this summons from the Elder Council troubled her.

They would not, she knew, bring her back from her duties at the borders of Cluster space without good reason, and in times like this, good reason usually meant bad news.

●●●●

"We have new developments," Serjevko said once they had finished listening to Khalihl's report on the refugee situation. "Potentially serious developments."

Khalihl sat on a cushion in front of the Elder Council, each of whom sat on a raised chair in an arc before her. They had seemed tense through the formalities, distracted through her report. Ilderis Asura, Khalihl's immediate commanding officer, had seemed especially agitated. She had shaken Khalihl's hand tightly, looking directly into her eyes.

"There is no rest for the wicked," Asura had said with a brief and stressed smile. If it had been intended as comfort, it was cold indeed.

Now Asura sat silently in the arc of the Inner Cluster's head of government, religious and political leaders chosen by the elected officials of the different planets making up their people. Khalihl could see the cares of their responsibilities etched into the lines of their faces. These men and women had seen much, made many difficult decisions. Of them, Serjevko, Asura, Hujad, and Cabrenejos had been with the Council since the Cluster Wars, a long, hard tenure indeed. The three newer members, however, already wore their hardships heavily. As much as she respected and admired them, Khalihl did not envy these men and women.

"The scientists at one of the frontier stations," Serjevko continued, "have sent us something strange, something they received from deep space."

There was a strange tension in the air hanging at the end of those words. *From deep space.* Khalihl's mind balked from the implications, and she took a deep breath to empty it of preconceived notions, to open her mind to whatever came next.

"They believe, due to the contents of the signal as well as the structure and direction of the signal itself, this was purposefully sent, intended to reach human space."

Did Khalihl imagine it or had there been a slight emphasis on the word human?

"The message contained information," now one of the newer members of the council, Anette Thans, picked up where Serjevko had left off, "in the form of a star map. There were no words, no mathematical equations. Just an accurate representation of human space and of a cluster of systems some light years away we had not previously mapped in detail."

A moment of silence. Was this first contact? Finally? A map showing the relative positions of two civilizations? For a moment, an elation filled Khalihl, but this quickly turned to suspicion. The faces of the men and women facing her were not filled with the joy of discovery and exploration but with something else. There would be more.

"Within this map," Thans continued, "was imbedded the indication of a flight plan, a direct line being drawn from the unknown territory to Cluster space. There were also some overlaid star positions that allowed us, purposefully we think, to determine the timeline for this flight plan. They are already on their way."

Khalihl did not speak for a moment. *They*. Her mind reeled with questions, with unknowns and with possibilities. *They are already on their way.* Somehow, the use of the third person pronoun made it seem so much more real, so much more immediate. Her mind starved for more information. Who were they? What did they want? When would they be here? Were they peaceful? Or did they come for other reasons? These final two questions stuck in her mind, the ever-present argument in exobiology. The alien version of the glass half-full or half-empty question. Khalihl considered herself neither an optimist nor a pessimist; rather, she strove to be clear minded and pragmatic. And if human history was any indication, there would be reason to fear an advanced culture coming across the void to meet them.

Finally, she asked, "What else?"

"We do not think the message came from the same group on their way," Thans said. "The message appears to have come from a slightly different part of the galaxy than where the fleet is coming from."

"Fleet?"

"Yes. The map indicates a large fleet, thousands of ships." There was silence for a brief moment. "We believe the message is a *warning.*"

The word hung in space, sucking all the air from the room. *A warning,* thought Khalihl, a sense of dread filling her slowly. She almost wanted to laugh at the absurdity of it. First the Black Sun and now this. An unknown alien fleet coming from across the cosmos. She felt the ground beneath her sway, and she closed her eyes, taking a deep breath to calm herself.

"Is it an invasion?" she asked, looking at the council.

"We do not know," Hujad answered. "But we suspect that, yes, it is. We think we are being warned by some… one else. At least, we think we should treat this as a threat of invasion,"

Khalihl agreed to the assessment. The risk was too great to take any other tack. To ignore it or assume friendly motives would be naive. At best, they would prepare for an alien invasion which would never come or would turn out to be a lightyears long handshake. At worst… Khalihl struck the thought from her mind. They would need to prepare.

There was some more talk, but no major decisions. Khalihl left, her mind in an exhausted daze, told to continue her escort of refugees while the Council and its advisors would try to parse more information from the message. They would meet again soon, hopefully with enough to make some sort of decision about what to do next.

As Khalihl left the great hall, she stopped at the top of the steps leading down to the public park maintained on the capitol grounds. From here, she could see into the park and beyond over the city. In the grass and amongst the trees, families picnicked and children played. She could just hear the happy shouts and laughter coming up to where she stood. In the middle distance, the city sprung up with towers and temples and housing blocks, all gleaming in the now setting sun. She could just make out the bustle of ground cars scurrying around while public transport shuttles crossed in the air over the city. In the distance, on the horizon, rose up the Prophet's mountains, older than old and forever watching over the city. This was New Mecca, her planet. And she could feel the wolves circling.

8

The worldly seek the worldly. For them, power and possession are the guiding principles. We have chosen a different path, one that goes within, in order to better understand the without, as opposed to one that forces the within on the without. The difference is subtle, but the end results could not be more different.

-Excerpt from the Journals of Roshi Moyo, discovered in the ruins of Bodhi 2745

The trance came quickly and easily; Meiind had been in this part of his mind many times now, had honed his skill through the years of practice on Bodhi. He sat alone in the main amphitheater, legs crossed in the open space reverberating with his breath. When he had first done this, it had taken the support of hundreds of monks to fully realize the scope of his touch, to keep him sane while he explored. But now, after years of discipline and hundreds of hours of regular practice, he could enter the trance and run wild through the cosmos, both internal and external, on his own.

Now, with his legs crossed and his spine erect, his hands laid gently in his lap, it only took him a few breaths to be transported from his body and present state. While the surprise of his first experience no longer was there, the sense of elation never left. The sense of freedom was just as strong as ever. His consciousness expanded, growing and growing until he could feel the entirety of the cosmos encompassed within his mind and spirit. Then, he opened the part of himself that seemed to hold his special talent, his touch, and the darkness came alive with light and life. Cold and empty space filled with the living, and he set about exploring corners of the galaxy he had not yet seen. As always, the temptation to become lost in all the information he was receiving tugged at his mind: why not just stay here and explore? You would never have to go back to the world you don't understand. You could just roam forever and, once your body fails, forever more.

But Meiind knew well this temptation and pushed it purposefully from his mind. He had spoken with Roshi Moyo many times, had heard the stories of the young monks who became catatonic, too deep within to ever leave, lost until their bodies wasted away, and they died. Meiind knew many monks chose this way to end their lives after they had aged beyond the ability to be useful to those around them, when they had become burdens to their families and social groups. Tempting as it was, Meiind was not yet done with the world. He simply wanted to explore, try to crack the riddle which had so long puzzled him.

He had gone into the trance with a particular part of the galaxy in mind; he had been using star maps to guide his exploration, systematically exploring sector after sector. The part of space he had chosen today was closer to the center of the galaxy, a section of star systems all in close proximity of one another. Some 150 light years from human space, he had chosen this particular section for the proximity: close enough for humans to imagine one day being able to reach but far enough any mistakes he made would not lead to immediate conflict. Of course, this was without skipping. *With skipping,* he thought, *the mapping necessary to reach here would only take a few years.* He let the unbidden thoughts slide through and out of his mind, a little amused that now, even after almost a decade of practice, the occasional thought could still find its way into his practice. Meiind chose a particularly bright cluster of light in his vision and focused his energies there. The indiscernible mass of light became hundreds of smaller lights as he – or whatever *he* was when in this state – came closer. As he came still closer, covering lightyears in the span of a single mind, these lights now broke into clusters made up of billions of tiny pinpoints. Each, he knew from his experiences, was a living thing, an instance of the Source out there in space. The thought of it, the implications, still cast awe across his mind even after all these years. A galaxy full of life. Full of it. Teeming with life. And, he knew, teeming with intelligent life.

He had already explored thousands of civilizations and had come up against the same issue. This one was no different. When he had first began to work in the trance, he had been careful not to make contact with the alien civilizations, with individuals of these races, afraid of the responsibility of first contact, afraid of some misunderstanding. Then, after he had become accustomed to the process, bored with simply watching, he finally attempted contact. He had become confused by the lack of contact in human history. If the galaxy was full of life, as Meiind knew it was, why had there never been any sign of it? No radio signals. No bursts of energy. It was a question which gnawed at Meiind's mind until he could no longer take it. He spent weeks choosing a particularly open-minded individual from an advanced species on the other side of the galaxy – far enough away any mistakes he made would take eons to come to fruition. He still remembered the tension, the fear, he had when he attempted to touch this living, intelligent alien, attempted to communicate with it.

That first contact had been tentative, just a quiet "hello" thrown into the void. Meiind had felt an anxiousness he had never known, not even during his standoff with Ondrueut. He waited for a response, fairly certain he had been understood and that he would understand the reply. He had already found himself able to understand the sentient beings he explored; regardless of their language, it appeared his talent, his touch, worked at a level beneath language, perhaps, he thought, at the level of direct experience. Whenever he touched an individual, the being's experiences would become clear to Meiind in his own language, translated somehow. And so he waited to hear and be heard, but in vain. There was no response. Nothing. Indeed, the individual he had chosen soon disappeared, the light of its Source gone within a few hours. This happened with every attempt he made, and soon he stopped trying for fear he was inadvertently killing these beings.

This, then, was the problem he had been coming up against, the riddle he could not solve. Silence. In a galaxy teeming with life, no one wanted to talk.

9

As long as there have been states or their equivalent, grand social structures made up of various groups of people, there have always been those who do not neatly fall into the categories defined by their time and place, categories that shift from era to era but that, to those of a certain time and place, appear to be logical and set in stone. This illusion has caused much suffering.

-*Excerpt from* Lines in the Sand: the History of Migration and Enforcement *by Als-de Garcia*

The small moon burst with color — red and orange swirls laid over with blue oceans and white clouds — in Khalihl's viewscreen as her ship the *Gibran* approached. Harken was more like a small planet, large enough to affect a comfortable gravity on those stationed there. It had been an agricultural outpost for decades, the temperate climate and rich soil allowing for genetically modified crops, adjusted for alien worlds, to flourish. The people who lived there, tending the machines which worked the crops from planting to harvest, had provided food for this corner of the Inner Cluster consistently for almost 50 years now. They had lived in relative isolation and peace for that time, their only contact with the Cluster at large the seasonal cargo ships which came to pick up their surplus. Now, as Khalihl came closer, she could see the signs of change.

Hundreds of glittering lights surrounded the usually isolated moon in a ring. As Khalihl approached, the closer points of reflected light grew into small ships of various designs. During her trip back to New Mecca, more and more refugees had begun pouring into Cluster space, prompting a call for planets and moons to open their worlds to the incoming peoples. Many had answered the call, so many Khalihl felt a surge of pride in her people and their willingness to take in the needy despite the fear-mongering of some. Indeed, there had been those who refused, citing threats of terrorists from the Black Sun, and even some purely xenophobic arguments involving cultural purity and the like. But, for the most part, the majorities in charge of the frontier worlds had opened their planets and moons to the incoming refugees seeking asylum. Due to its position, Harken had become one of the main processing worlds, taking the brunt of the influx of people, keeping some and directing the rest to other open worlds.

As her ship approached Harken's orbital station, her officers prepping to dock, her mind drifted to the conversation she had had with the leader of Harken while on the way to the moon. A striking woman, tall in the way of her people, Bretus Ansr had offered an inviting but cautious take on the crisis.

"We are happy to do our part," Ansr had said, the cares of her people written clearly on her face, plain to see even over long-distance communication. "It was not so long ago the Inner Cluster opened itself to us as we fled our own persecutions, and though some of us have forgotten, the people have spoken in favor of helping however we can."

"The Cluster appreciates your willingness," Khalihl answered, thinking back to her knowledge of the people of Harken. Their ways of life had violated some of the legal and cultural taboos of the Coalition, particularly their rituals surrounding the elderly and death. The Harkenites, as they now called themselves, practiced a form of ritual suicide, each person eventually taking his or her own life when infirmity made them a burden to others. The method was up to the soon to die, but the most common was for the elderly man or woman to walk into the wilderness to die alone. "Has there been much pushback?"

"As much as is to be expected," Ansr said with a dismissive wave of her hand. "It is the usual anti-immigration fear. General fear thinly masked in cultural, economic, and practical concerns. Some of us, I am afraid, have forgotten our past."

Some of us have forgotten our past. This response had stuck with Khalihl in the hours since her conversation with Ansr. No doubt this was a common issue in the history of humanity and a difficult one to reconcile. Current concerns were always more pressing than the context within which they appeared, and this short-sighted vision had often led civilizations astray and into folly. Khalihl's own emphasis in her History education – all students in the Cluster were required to focus on a historical topic of their choice – had been on the fall of the United States on pre-Migration Earth, when the populace there had embraced fascism and tribalism barely a generation after the two largest and deadliest conflicts in their history. They had, according to the historians who covered the period later, followed a predictable pattern established even within their period. Now, as she left her ship to enter the station and to speak with the people in charge about the refugee processing, she could not help but wonder if they – her people in the Inner Cluster – were locked into a similar repetition. How many times in history had war led to a humanitarian crisis which, in turn, led to more conflict? She did not need to refresh her memory through research to know the answer. And yet, this was undoubtedly something new.

She eventually found herself, despite her wandering mind, in the bustling control center of the station. Someone called out, "Admiral on the bridge," and the dozens there snapped to attention. She waved them back to work as a young man approached her, his hand out.

"I am Commander Jaier Yscaaidt, he said as he shook her hand. "It is an honor to finally meet you in person."

"The honor is mine," Khalihl responded. It had been her decision to put this promising officer here at the Harken station to spearhead efforts to deal with the tide of refugees. Thus far, he had been as exemplary in this position as he had been in the ones he held before it.

"Let me get you up to speed," he said as he led her towards a console in the center of the room. "We have processed some 50 million refugees so far, most coming from the portions of Coalition space nearest to us."

Khalihl already knew that number from the briefs she received while on her way to Harken, but to hear it again brought the scale of the tragedy into sharp relief. 50 million! 50 million people displaced from their homes. She could only imagine how many more had been subjugated or killed by the Black Sun's forces spreading throughout old Coalition space. Again, she felt the conviction they would have to be dealt with, that their leader, Eazkaii, would not settle for controlling what was the Coalition. He would have his eye on the Inner Cluster.

A sense of overwhelm took hold of Khalihl then. She barely managed to keep nodding as Jaier continued to update her on the status of the refugee processing, on the more estimated to come in the next year. *How will we survive this,* she thought, *how will we survive the Black Sun and whatever it is out there in space coming for us?* She glanced around her, at all the men and women working to alleviate the current crisis with such courage and commitment. They had no idea this was only the beginning, and perhaps a small issue compared to an alien invasion. Would their spirit hold if they knew? Would they fight? Could they handle knowing?

"You have travelled much," Yscaaidt said, offering Khalihl a brief touch on the shoulder and bringing her from her despairing thoughts. "I should have let you rest before inundating you with details you need not worry yourself about."

"No, no," she said, appreciative of his understanding even if he misinterpreted her distraction as fatigue. "Please, contin – "

Before she could finish, a flash of light from the large viewscreen at the front of the control room washed everything in white. For a moment, Khalihl could not see anything, and there was a distinct silence in the room. The light faded and with it the moment of calm. The station seemed to buck up, knocking some of the many officers on the bridge to the floor. Khalihl managed to steady herself on the back of a chair while the station groaned against some unseen force. Alarms began blaring, red lights flashing, as she swung around towards the viewscreen. Jaier was already yelling orders, asking for information and trying to figure out what had happened. More and more yells were beginning to fill the space, people running back and forth checking consoles and attending to the injured. The viewscreen gave static.

"Viewscreen angle forty-one!" Yscaaidt's voice rose above the din, and the static on the screen switched to a clear view of space.

Khalihl's breath caught within her throat. Everything in the control room stopped as the officers froze to watch as well. The screen now offered a view of the ring of orbiting ships surrounding Harken, but in the center of the glimmering ships, not far from the station, was a spreading globe of debris. Khalihl watched in horror as the debris silently collided with other ships, causing a chain reaction. Some exploded themselves, flashes of silent light in the void, while others managed to keep together despite the damage raining down upon them.

The silence in the room was broken by Yscaaidt barking orders, and the chaos then ensued again.

●●●●

Khalihl now indeed needed some rest as she finally, eighteen hours later, settled into her quarters in her own ship. All she wanted was to sleep, to lay herself down and, for a few hours at least, forget the day. But she knew the Elders would be waiting for her report on what had happened. Khalihl made herself some tea and sat down in front of her console thinking about everything that had occurred since she had arrived. She started with the numbers: four refugee and two Cluster ships lost. More than ten damaged. Over nineteen hundred confirmed dead, some twelve hundred missing, and nearly two thousand injured. While this information would break their hearts and cloud their minds, Khalihl knew what the Council would really want to know.

The investigation, which had begun the moment she and Yscaaidt had managed to impose some order on the chaos in the direct aftermath of the destruction, had traced the initial explosion to a refugee ship called *Better Skies*. This was the first flash of light which had initially blinded the viewscreen. The explosion, which had basically incinerated the ship and tore three neighboring ones in half, left little to no evidence to be collected. Sweep teams had found trace elements of explosives in the surrounding space, and the system logs, uploaded to the Cluster net every ten seconds, showed no signs of malfunction in the moments leading up to the explosion. The conclusion was unavoidable: a bomb of some sort.

Then they discovered a series of encrypted messages coming into *Better Skies* hidden in the normal data stream every ship was constantly spewing and taking in as a part of its everyday functions. While they could not break the encryption, they were able to trace them back to an approximate source: somewhere deep within Black Sun territory. Again, the conclusion was difficult to question: Black Sun terrorists had hidden themselves within the refugees.

Khalihl sat back and sipped gently at her tea, looking over her notes for the Council. The facts were there, but they would also want her analysis of the event, her opinions on the implications. The Elders would want to know not just *what* happened, but *why* as well. This question had occupied a large portion of her mind in the hours since the initial explosion while she worked with Yscaaidt to coordinate the rescues and the investigation. They had even briefly discussed their thoughts, both coming to similar ideas. The Black Sun, ruthless as they were, were intelligent and well led; they would have known refugee ships would not be allowed near anything of strategic importance until a significant amount of vetting had been undergone. This meant an overt act of war, an attempt to gain some sort of upper hand through the destruction of some important base or ship or person, could likely be ruled out. This is when they had begun using the word *terrorism* to describe what had happened.

No doubt, Khalihl thought, *the Black Sun has more than*

one goal in mind with terrorist actions. The obvious one would be to discourage their new population base from fleeing Black Sun territory. Afterall, power is not worth much without a populace to oppress. This, of course, worked both ways; they likely also hoped to discourage the Inner Cluster from taking refugees. And finally, and perhaps most simply, the Black Sun probably just wished to inflict whatever damage they could. Khalihl had been following the reports about the power struggles in the old Coalition from the beginning, and the Black Sun had made their chief method of political relations easily discernible from the beginning. Chaos. This was their guiding principle. They sought to sow chaos, thriving in the aftermath and willing to pick up the broken pieces of whatever planet they descended upon.

Khalihl shuddered to think of what it must be like to live under a group like that, to live under the control of Leader Eazkaii and his generals. She leaned forward to enter a few commands into her console, bringing up what little information they had on the man. There was some basic information: Eazkaii was born some fifty years ago on the moon Jet in a small work colony run by religious fundamentalists, adherents to a form of Christianity. This apparently had a profound effect on him and his life, for as a teenager he stowed away on a supply ship and left his home and family behind. From here, his file offered little information for nearly twenty years until he resurfaced as a figure of political significance on the planet Ridge. Khalihl had read through the publications he had written and through the transcripts of the speeches he had given at this time. They offered a view into a man who profoundly rejected all religion and morality as false and insincere, instead embracing a form of hyper-existentialism, an extreme form of social Darwinism. For Eazkaii, at least during this period of his life, any form of moralization, any adherence to abstract ideology, was weakness and indicative of a form of control from outside the self. He spoke of self-reliance and of building a society in which the weak were culled out simply because they were weak. He preached the only right in the universe was Survival and, for humans, its other half, Order. From here, his path became murky in the records again. His transition from small time politician to the leader of the most powerful faction in the void left by the collapse of the Coalition became lost in the chaos following the Hero's Battle and the destruction of the Source harvesting technology. But regardless of that path, Eazkaii was a force to be reckoned with, and Khalihl had no doubt their paths would cross – likely with violence – one day.

Khalihl stood and walked over to the window in her quarters, looking out at the moon over which they orbited. Glints of light rose and fell through the gravity well, people being moved down after processing or for medical attention and supplies and personnel being moved up to help with the still growing influx of refugees. Ultimately, the conflict between the Black Sun and the Inner Cluster would come to a head regardless of her thoughts and advice to the Council. This much was certain. The Cluster was already preparing its military for that contingency. What mattered now, what pressed her mind at the moment, was the question of the refugees. Some had already called for a halt to the acceptance of these asylum seekers, fear of terrorism spreading with the news of the attack. Khalihl herself could not help but think of this as a form of failure, as giving into the Black Sun. If sowing fear and chaos was their goal, then refusing to accept refugees, or even limiting the number, would be akin to handing them a moral and strategic victory in perhaps the first of their coming interactions. Khalihl's military training told her this would be a dire mistake at this stage.

This line of thinking did not even take into account the suffering of the people fleeing the Black Sun. Could she, after sitting with and listening to so many of them, really deny them help? And if the Inner Cluster did decide to refuse entry to the refugees, how many of them would grow to resent the Cluster as their people suffered for generations? What future conflicts would this lead to? Khalihl knew her history, knew the ways in which trauma could be passed through generations. Was not the cessation of this process one of the major tenets of the social and political structure of the Inner Cluster? To deny these people help, to turn them away in their time of need, would be to at once damn them to generations of homelessness and vagrancy, perhaps even to pogrom, and a complete denial of everything she had learned to love in her culture. The dangers were real, no doubt; there would be more terrorist attacks, more death and destruction. But these could be mitigated and guarded against, and ultimately, accepting these people would add to the future strength of the Inner Cluster. They would become citizens and contributing members of society. These were not just refugees, a faceless class of suffering peoples from afar. They were men, women, children, teachers, laborers, doctors, accountants, programmers… they had much to offer in their own ways. How could the Inner Cluster not benefit from accepting them with as open arms as caution would allow?

All of this is beside the point, Khalihl thought as she sat down to write her recommendations into her report. *Taking them in is simply the right thing to do. To turn them away, while we have space and resources to spare, would be abhorrent in the extreme. And the right thing is worthy of action in and of itself.*

<u>10</u>

*The fool says science has no place in spirituality.
The arrogant says science has rendered
spirituality obsolete. The truth is that science is
another tool for the discovery and understanding
of the spirit. To learn the mind is nothing more
than a series of electrical impulses and chemical
exchanges causes the fool to ignore science and the
arrogant to ignore the spirit. In truth, they are
one and the same; honest inspection of both will
lead either person to the same place: reality.*

> *-Excerpt from* The Science of the Spirit:
> Implications of the Source *by Mosden
> Keller*

The tea steamed in the chawan before Meiind, the
gentle aroma bringing a much needed sense of calm to his
mind. No matter the strife in the world around, he always
found the chado, the tea ceremony, even this informal
version, to be soothing. Everything else, all the pain and
suffering, the fear and uncertainty, seemed to disappear as
the powdered tea dissolved into the hot water. Roshi
Moyo, having mixed the tea and wiped his utensils, sat
down in front of his own bowl. Meiind raised his chawan
to the Roshi and turned it before taking a sip; Roshi Moyo
then did the same. They solemnly set their bowls down at
the same time and looked through the steam at one
another. Roshi Moyo smiled.

"I look forward to our meetings," the Roshi spoke first, his voice ever-calm and collected, no hint of any emotion aside from a pleasantness akin to a warming sun. "Even when the circumstances are less than ideal."

Meiind nodded and looked to the side, out from the terrace on which they now sat. They were at the Roshi's quarters, sitting on the small landing in front of his small hut, overlooking the main complex of the largest temple on Bodhi – the capital, in a way, even if their social structure had no real need for such a place. A religious capital more than a governmental one. Meiind turned his eyes back to the gentle gaze of the Roshi. His mind raced with thoughts. He took a deep breath and tried to calm down.

"Roshi," he said, somewhat ashamed at the quiver he could hear in his own voice. Had he been here so long he had forgotten how to face adversity? "What are we going to do?"

The Roshi did not answer right away. Instead, he took another drink of his tea, taking the time to blow over the hot liquid. His movements were slow and deliberate, betraying none of the fear Meiind himself felt. This made Meiind still more ashamed at his own fear, his own inability to control it. Meiind took yet another deep breath, paying close attention to the passage of air through his lungs. A sense of calm spread through his mind. *Panicking will not help,* he thought. *Roshi Moyo is giving me the time I need to understand this myself, to be honest with myself and with him.* Meiind saw then he had simply asked the wrong question. Instead of being direct, of saying what he came here to say, Meiind tried to use his question to goad the Roshi into a response from which he could give his own opinion. Beating around the bush. Again, Meiind felt some shame; nearly a decade here with these people, and did he really think so little of them? He continued his slow, deliberate breaths as the Roshi continued to drink his tea.

"Allow me to begin again," Meiind said after he felt he had some control back. "I would like to talk with you about Bodhi's planetary defenses."

"Yes," the Roshi answered immediately this time, setting down his tea and assuming a posture of complete attention. "Continue."

"Thank you Roshi," Meiind said, running a quick inventory of everything he had wanted to suggest. "No doubt you have heard the latest reports?"

"Yes, Meiind. I have heard the worrying news," Roshi Moyo responded, but he did not explicitly say what it was he had heard. *He wants me to say it,* thought Meiind. *He wants me to build my case.*

"Worrying is something of an understatement," Meiind said. "The Black Sun is on their way. They will be here in less than a year."

There was silence. The words rang in the empty air left after the sound of Meiind's voice had faded. They both took drinks of their teas, finishing what they had left. An attendant entered and cleared away their utensils. Meiind, as he always did, marveled at the deft movements with which the teenage boy silently stacked the plates and bowls, balanced them on a forearm so as to keep his hands free for the kettle and the natsume, and whisked from the room like the apparition he had appeared as. There was silence for another moment before Meiind spoke again, knowing his impatience was showing.

"Sir," Meiind said with obvious deference in his tone and posture, "I do not wish to belabor the point. We both know what the Black Sun does to new planets they conquer. We must think about how we will defend ourselves."

"You have been here many years, my friend," the Roshi said, looking at Meiind with a smile in his eyes. "You have learned much from us, I think, but I fear today's lesson may be particularly difficult."

Meiind recognized the tone of his teacher's voice and instinctually fell into a receptive frame of mind conditioned into him throughout the years he had been here. He had learned to listen when the Roshi spoke in this way, to pay close attention for Roshi Moyo did not mince words when offering a lesson.

"We will do nothing," Roshi Moyo said with a gentle but firm voice. "We will await the Black Sun and welcome them here as we do for everyone who comes to our planet."

"Sir!" Meiind burst and immediately, realizing himself, stopped. The Roshi smiled and signaled for him to continue. "Sir," Meiind said with more control this time. "Please allow me to remind you of their ways. They do not approach planets and peoples with civil discourse in mind. They do not come with hopes of treaties and commerce, with the desire to trade ideas and learn. They only have one objective: to conquer. And their method has been singular. They attack until the victim planet submits. If the planet does this, then they conscript much of the male population for service in their fleet and require a heavy tribute. If the planet is well-defended but unable to defeat the Black Sun, they sterilize the planet and move on. Sir, and please forgive the passion in my voice, but I cannot imagine the men of this planet fighting for the Black Sun, nor can the social structure here produce a surplus adequate for tribute. Our only choice is to defend ourselves successfully."

The Roshi listened patiently and without any judgement visible on his face. After Meiind had finished, the Roshi said, "And how would you have us defend ourselves?"

"We must call to the Inner Cluster, call for help." Meiind had already thought about this some. "They will come."

"You realize what you are saying, of course." The Roshi's voice became low, serious. "You ask for us to become a reason for war."

"Sir," Meiind said, somewhat taken aback, "that is assuming the Black Sun is willing to risk a war right now. They are too spread out for war with the Inner Cluster. A Cluster presence here will act as a deterrent."

"Allow me a question, my friend: when has the Black Sun ever been deterred? When have they ever backed away from conflict at the threat of violence? Where in the narrative do they appear to tell themselves is there room for that kind of thinking?" The Roshi was silent for a moment, allowing Meiind to chew on his thoughts, before continuing, "You have read the reports, kept up with their progress across what was Co space, as well as I have, Meiind. Have they ever backed down from a battle? Do they not tend to rush headlong into battle, especially into odds not in their favor? Do they not seem to thrive on violence and conflict? Seem to seek out aggression?"

Meiind did not answer. Roshi Moyo was right, of course; nothing in the Black Sun's pattern of behavior so far indicated they could not be deterred from a fight, even if they faced overwhelming odds. The Black Sun had gone into battle after battle, winning by sheer brutality and gall. Now that he thought about it, Meiind knew the Black Sun would probably revel in a chance to engage the Inner

Cluster. This was likely why they approached Bodhi in the first place. The Buddhi planet was close to Cluster space and could serve as a jumping off point for their fleet. To call for help from the Inner Cluster would be playing into their hands, into their hopes. But to not even make an attempt at defending themselves! The thought simply did not register in Meiind's mind.

"It's not a simple matter of strategy," the Roshi said gently, his eyes kind and full of compassion for Meiind's inner turmoil. "There is much more than territory at stake here. Much more than even life and existence. We Buddhi have a way of life here, a way we have held onto for thousands of years. We seek truth and clarity; we seek to interact with reality, objective reality. We seek to become more ourselves, and here on Bodhi, we have come closer, as a people, to that vision than we ever have before. Do you understand what I am saying? Do you understand the story of the ferrywoman in our tradition?"

Meiind's mind snapped to attention with the Roshi's last words. He knew the story, of course. It had been one of the first he had been taught here, a simple parable: a young woman goes into the world seeking to find her way. She tries her hand at many things: different religions, desires of the flesh, commerce, only to find none of them offer her what she is looking for. Finally, she meets a ferryman, a man who lives in a small hut by a river and spends his life watching the river and helping people to cross it on their different journeys. For some reason, the woman is attracted to this man, to his simple life and his plain way of speaking. She hears wisdom in his voice, sees peace in his life, and decides to stay and learn from him. After a few years, the man dies, and the woman takes over as the keeper of the ferry, continuing the work of helping people cross the river as they go about their lives. In the process, she hears their stories, learns about their common complaints and fears, their strife and struggle. She sees firsthand the four noble truths of the Buddhi faith: the suffering of life, the source of that suffering, the answer to it, and the journey that had taken her to the answer. One day, a man attempts to rob her of what little coin and food she has. She willingly gives up her material possessions, for she sees in the man the suffering ignorance brings and has pity on him. He resents her pity and, before leaving her to her ferry, stabs the ferrywoman in the stomach and leaves her to die. She does die, thinking of the man and hoping he finds peace in this life.

Meiind had never pretended to grasp the significance of the story, but suddenly, at the nexus of his desperation, his fear of the Black Sun's approach, and the calm, confident, yet gentle voice of the Roshi, a wave of meaning crashed over him. The fear of death, of annihilation, had led many men and women over the millennia to do terrible things. Indeed, much of the suffering in human history could be seen as the death throes of humanity, the collective thrashing against the end-void awaiting every individual. How many men and women, tribes and nations, had given up on their professed ideals when facing their final breath, the fading light? How much evil had been visited upon living beings for fear of non-existence? This, then, was the message of the ferrywoman's parable and the Roshi's point: the woman did her duty and kept her humanity until the end, refusing to die in fear and bitterness and instead dying as she lived, with love and peace. If Bodhi became the reason for another interstellar war, another unfathomable period of death and destruction between human groups, they may survive but in doing so lose the very spirit that made them who they were. Was that not the worst kind of death, the death not of the flesh but of the soul?

Roshi Moyo saw this line of thinking and understanding play across Meiind's face, saw his point sink into the man sitting across from him.

"You say we need to 'defend ourselves,'" the Roshi said with a nod when he felt Meiind's thoughts had settled. "Ourselves. You consider yourself to be one of us now, and while this pleases me, this is not entirely true. You have learned much from us, learned our ways and our thoughts, but our path is not quite yours. We are here for different reasons than you, and the truth of one's dharma is to be true to one's self. Your dharma led you here, but it does not end here.

Meiind did not speak but listened with conflicting feelings. One part of him resisted the Roshi's words; he felt at home here, felt at peace. But, at the same time, another part of him knew what the Roshi was saying was true. He would not be at peace here forever. He could not stand by while the Black Sun rampaged across space, could not ignore the death and destruction. He felt, growing within him as the Roshi spoke, the knowledge he needed to take what he had learned here and use it in the outside cosmos, in the interstellar world of humanity. Still, he hesitated, he fought this growing conviction. And then his fears melted with the Roshi's final word:

"Go."

11

General Eazkaii is something of an enigma to historians. We do not know where he came from, nor how he came to power. He is one of those characters in the vast sweep of the human story who appears suddenly and has profound effects, a product of his times to be sure, but also a driver of them, someone who, through force of hand and will, shaped the path humanity would take, at least for a time.

-Excerpt from The Road to Hell *by Jessica Ilken*

Eazkaii surveyed the holomap projected in the air before him. His study was silent and empty except for the barely audible breathing of the advisor standing in the dark corner to his left. *Slightly distracting,* he thought absently as he looked at the territories marked in gray, red, and white. *I will have to make sure my next advisor is not so loud.* Still, this man had served his purpose well enough to live a little longer. He waved his hand, and the map rotated so the gray areas, those representing territories now firmly held by the Black Sun, were central. It almost covered the red, which showed the old Coalition borders.

Ten years, he thought with a mixture of pride and bitterness. *Ten years of sacrifice and death and destruction.* Since the fall of the Coalition, he had fought and schemed his way through the separate factions that appeared in the power vacuum left by the rout at New Mecca. Dozens, no, hundreds of warlords and religious or cultural groups had come forth, claiming this or that planet and territory as sovereign. Eazkaii had seen where this would lead – a planetary feudalism which would make it easy for the Inner Cluster to dominate the whole of humanity. *The Inner Cluster,* he thought with disgust. The weaklings. Religious idiots. They preached tolerance and compassion and peace. All the things which made humanity weak, that would lead to the stagnation of the species. He felt the anger rising within him and turned his attention back to the holomap in front of him.

There were only a few worlds left worth conquering. Those could be handled by his generals spread throughout the fronts, each with their own fleet of ships and their own armies. He made a gesture with his hand again, and the map displayed the placements and distributions of his generals and their men. He looked at the new information with interest.

"Dallu," he said without looking up, "give me a brief of General Tryond's latest report."

"General Tryond," the advisor in the corner said after the moment it took to bring up the information in his retinal display, "reports three new planetary conquests in the last month, as well as an increase in volunteers joining his army."

Eazkaii found this troubling. He had sensed Tryond's ambitions from the very beginning, had made use of them by sending him to the most difficult sector of old Coalition space. His success, while good for the Black Sun, would, Eazkaii had no doubt, eventually lead to a power struggle for the role of Leader. Eazkaii zoomed in on Tryond's part of the holomap, looking at the unconquered territories left in that sector. Only a few moons, a few million people. Nothing which should be any cause for concern.

"Have Tryond killed," Eazkaii said, his voice utterly flat and devoid of emotion. "Make sure it happens publicly and brutally. Announce we discovered treason on his part. Promote whoever is under him to continue their orders."

Dallu did not answer, knowing well less is more with Leader Eazkaii. His understanding of this almost excused his noisy breathing. *Almost.* Eazkaii motioned again towards the map, rotating now to the space his fleet currently occupied. The grey line of his boundaries came up against empty space, nothing worth the effort. Inward, towards the galactic center, beyond the empty space, a bright line of white demarcated the territory of the Inner Cluster. He stared at this line for a moment before bringing up the Cluster home system. The representation of New Mecca was highlighted, a small sphere hanging in space, the center of the Inner Cluster.

"Dallu, have the Inner Cluster gained any territories since their defeat of the Coalition?"

"No sir. They have made no advances and have publicly stated they do not wish to take advantage of the power struggle in former Coalition space. They have offered asylum to refugees, however."

Shrewd bastards, Eazkaii thought. *They curry favor with the populace by opening their borders. They weaken the Black Sun not through battle but, as cowards, through public opinion.* This could not be allowed, Eazkaii decided then. He had known, from the beginning, the Inner Cluster would have to be dealt with. The time had come.

"How far is the nearest Cluster space?"

"At sublight," Dallu answered, "Six years flight-time."

Six years. That was too long. No doubt the Inner Cluster was already preparing their military, expecting the Black Sun to eventually turn its wrath towards them. In that time, they would be ready and perhaps strong enough to defeat him. But *now*, now the Inner Cluster was weakened from their recent battle with the Coalition. If only the Inner Cluster had not taken the skip drives and the batteries holding what was left after production stopped. A few thousand of those, and then nothing would be capable of stopping him and the Black Sun from consolidating power throughout human space. A wave of bitter resentment washed through Eazkaii, and he felt the need to hurt something or someone. He looked at Dallu, wondering if he could be easily replaced. Probably not. Not at such a delicate moment in their progress.

Eazkaii turned the holomap and zoomed out so he could have an overview of the area. This all could have been accomplished so much faster with skipping. He would gladly have sacrificed an entire planet of people for the Source-based energy to speed his mission and to bring humanity under the rule of the Black Sun and into prosperity and glory. But the technology no longer existed, destroyed or confiscated by the Inner Cluster. And that final president, Ondreut, the machine masquerading as a human, had over time, throughout its long and secret tenure as the governing force of the Coalition, consolidated all information on the technology into its mainframes. When it was destroyed by the Inner Cluster, all the knowledge necessary to replicate the science behind skipping went with it. There was nothing left but rumors and idle theories.

"Dallu," Eazkaii said, focusing his map once more on the Inner Cluster Territories, "do a search of all level reports in the last five years. Look for anything, any rumor and claim, involving skip tech."

As Dallu silently – except for the damned breathing – sought the information, Eazkaii mulled over the whitewash of territories central on the holomap now. The Inner Cluster, with their high-minded and religious morality, had taken it upon themselves to choose for humanity that using humans for energy is wrong. Only the ignorant, the stupid and irrational, could make such a choice so broadly, and only the self-righteousness found in illogical beliefs, in *faith*, could allow for that choice to be imposed on so many cultures. They had no right! Dallu jumped at the sound of Eazkaii's fist slamming on his desk but continued his information gathering without comment. He, Eazkaii, would destroy them, if not because they stood in the way of total conquest then because of their presumption. And once he ruled humanity, the scourge of religion – even the word brought disgust to his face – would be forever removed from society and history. Humanity would never again find itself prey to the whims of madmen and false gods.

"Sir," Dallu said tentatively, unsure of interrupting the Leader's thoughts.

"Have you found something?"

"Yessir. A few years ago, a ship in Sector Eight picked up a prisoner claiming to be from the prison planet that processed humans for their Sources. He is still alive, being kept in a camp on a moon in the area."

The tension in Eazkaii relaxed some, and he leaned back in his chair. The prison planet. Perhaps there could be some remnants of the processing equipment, some leftover and forgotten skip drives or batteries his people could use to reverse engineer the technology. He flipped the map to Sector Eight. A few scattered stars and accompanying systems, all relatively close together. Nothing with any major civilization. A planet called Bodhi.

His generals had swept through years ago without much resistance and left most of the area untouched.

"Alert the rest of the ship," Eazkaii said, still staring at the map. "We go to see this prisoner."

12

In the Beginning of the Universe there was the Light of the Word, and the Light of the Word was the spirit of God made manifest in the Cosmos.

-Excerpt from The Holy Bible: New Interstellar Version, *John 1:1*

The shock was two-fold. First of all, Maldeck had never seen a Musla before, and he found the dress and skin tone of the military officer who addressed him and his people to be strange and disconcerting. The woman wore her clothing like a man, pants and all and with a straight back. Her uniform was a dull brown with bright blue trim, and she wore a turban on her head with a golden pin in the front. The woman looked about the room with a strong eye and with determination and hardness in her gaze. This was the second shock: Maldeck had never seen a woman in a position of power before. On Sianide, they followed the Old Ways, and those proscribed specific functions for men and women, as was only natural. *This,* he thought, *is just the beginning of the perversions we will see.* Maldeck glanced around at his fellow delegation who had come to meet the woman. All men, he wondered his delegation too felt the rising sense of conviction hardening in his heart. *We must stay strong. We must not let their influence destroy who we are.* Fear meddled in Maldeck's heart.

Ten years. They had been on this ship for ten years now, traversing the vast void of space, fleeing the destruction of the Coalition by the Black Sun. As Maldeck looked at the hardened faces of the men around him, he thought with pride of what they had endured and of how they had come through. God works in mysterious ways, and this trial of the spirit had proven a boon to their culture. On Sianide, Maldeck reflected as the woman officer spoke of banalities, his people had become comfortable and had begun to dilute their values, losing sight of the Truth as God had revealed it in ancient times. People had begun to seek out cybernetic enhancements, the youth had begun to value their own fun over the glories of God, women had begun to work, men had begun to seek the pleasures of the life rather than the riches of heaven… the list of distractions went on and on. But ten years of fear and strife, ten years of flight from persecution, of cramped and tense living, had weeded out the weak and left only the strong. Of course, some of that weeding had been done intentionally. Many of the weak of faith had been excommunicated to the other ships in the flotilla, and now they were left with only the strong in the Lord. *Thank you Lord for your guidance and for your purification,* Maldeck thought, offering a quick prayer while he looked at the other men in the room listening to the women. These men represented the best of them, and he knew they would feel the same about her words.

"The process I have just outlined will not be easy," the woman was saying in her man's tone, a juxtaposition which made Maldeck uncomfortable, "but I am here to assure you we of the Inner Cluster will do whatever we can to ease the transition. I have studied some of your ways in preparation to be useful to you, and I am cognizant of the tensions between our cultures. We do not wish to aggravate those."

Maldeck almost sneered. Such pretty words. Such

seeming kindness. But underneath he knew the insidious influences of the Inner Cluster culture would slowly wreak havoc amongst his people. This could not be allowed to happen, and he made a conscious effort to harden his mind and heart against the woman's soothing words.

"As such," she continued, "your people will be given a home. We have set aside a small continent on a small planet for you. This planet has everything you will need, and we will leave you all the tools necessary to develop the land to your ways. As for trade and the like, the decision of your involvement with the rest of the Cluster will be up to you."

"Will this planet," Maldeck asked, speaking up over the murmurs coming from the group of men he represented, "have others on it? Or will we be the only ones?"

"You will have to share the planet," the woman answered, turning her gaze onto him as if she knew the secrets in the deepest recesses of his heart. "The number of refugees coming in from Coalition space is massive, and the number of hospitable planets we have ready for occupation is limited. The continent will be yours, however."

"Who will we be living with?" spoke up another man, John, from Maldeck's group.

"The planet you will be living on, Sahaj, has been the home of my people for many generations. You will be sharing the planet with us."

This sent a current of shock through the group and the murmurs became louder. The woman waited patiently as the men aired their concerns, though none spoke out. Soon, the room quieted and the woman spoke again.

"I know this will be difficult for you. It will not be easy for my people either. Many hold dear the stories of our ancestors, and the memories of our collective pasts is not always the easiest to set aside. Yet, we all have little choice. Only together can we survive the coming conflict."

There were nods of agreement from some in the group of men. Nods of agreement! Maldeck took note of those men. They would have to be watched.

"For us," he said again, and the whole of the group turned to him, "sharing a planet with the Musla may be very difficult." He could not allow his people to forget their loyalties nor their enemies.

"Sir," the woman said, staring at him calmly with those damning eyes. "My people and I are not Musla. We are Sihken."

Another wave of approval from his men, this time more joining in than before. *They come to you in sheep's clothing,* he thought, *but inwardly they are ravening wolves. I will not be fooled into letting my guard down. I will not allow you to subvert everything we have achieved on the journey here.*

<u>13</u>

All ideas water down over time – this is only natural. It is also natural for some to see this process as a negative thing, rather than as progress, and to react. Often, the reaction engages in false memories of better times, in exaggerations of contemporary problems, and in a sense of righteousness that underpins an insecurity in the future.

> *-Excerpt from* Spectrum Swing: an Analysis of Fundamentalism *by Kerrae Higdens*

The meeting, as detailed on the leaflet, was to be held in the industrial sector of the city in a large warehouse owned by someone sympathetic to the cause. Bin Ald wandered through blocks of gray buildings, the night sky above obscured by the many fluorescent lights shining down into the street. Most parts of the city had noise pollution ordinances, but with the refugee crisis putting such strain on resource development, many of the production-based sectors of the city had taken to working through the night. He could hear people within the buildings as he passed, could hear machinery of various sorts working on whatever it was their particular company did. There were others walking around the streets, coming from or going to work, but, unlike the city center where Bin Ald lived and worked, the people here did not look up and greet one another. *Probably exhausted from work,* Bin Ald thought as a woman passed close to him with her eyes glued to the street plastic. In the distance, above the buildings, Bin Ald could see the mechanized cranes swinging their heads like ancient dragons, moving massive loads as they rolled on their tracks laid throughout the district. He had, in his youth, spent some time working here as a part of his education – the Cluster education system included a work study program which put students in various sectors so they could decide what was appropriate for them – and he remembered marveling at the gliding efficiency of the cranes. For that matter, at the perfection of the entire industrial apparatus. He had learned in school of the way their ancestors had worked, of the Industrial Revolution and of its effects, and he had been, still was, thankful of the robotics that allowed humans to avoid the most dangerous and most unhealthy work. He remembered vividly photos of the smog which covered industrial cities in the twenty-first century. In contrast, here, all the robots ran off clean energy sources. The work was safe and fulfilling and had no adverse effects on the environment. Bin Ald, when he had been in school, had been amazed at how much ancient peoples had suffered for their economies. He had been taught a different ethic, one which emphasized people before business. And that was ultimately why he was here now. *To protect my people,* he thought.

Finally, he came to the address printed on the leaflet: a smaller, non-descript building with nothing to differentiate it from the others besides the numbers on the door. He walked over, heard voices within, and knocked. The door opened immediately, and he was washed with noise and light. The man who had opened the door beckoned for him to enter but did not speak; the meeting was already under way and someone was up on the small stage behind the crowd in front of Bin Ald. As Bin Ald entered, the man on the stage continued to speak to the energetic crowd. The room was large and full, maybe four or five hundred people as far as Bin Ald could tell. He could not quite make out what the speaker, muffled by the crowd and by the bad acoustics in the building, was saying. Bin Ald began to work his way through the crowd, trying to gently elbow his way through the cheering people until he finally could make out the words.

"- they spend our resources on what? On our enemies? And they tell us what? That we need to be compassionate and forgiving, that we need to consider their plight?" The man on the stage paused to allow for the jeers from the crowd before continuing again. From where he stood, Bin Ald could see the man was tall, well-dressed, and handsome. His voice had the character of strength and boomed throughout the space despite a lack of obvious amplification. While he certainly had a microphone and speakers hidden somewhere, the effect was his voice seemed to carry of its own will, and the effect on the crowd was something like awe. "We here all know our history, both ancient and recent. We know why we left – nay, why we were forced – to leave Earth so many generations ago. They forced us out! And we know who were the aggressors in the Cluster Wars. They came to invade us! Have our people forgotten the many tragedies rained upon us by the Coalition?"

The crowd surged and shouted "No!" and, to his surprise, Bin Ald heard himself joining in the chorus, his voice lifting with the hundreds, losing itself within the noise. Then there was silence, or something near it, in the vacuum left after the echoes of their voices faded. The man on the stage looked over the crowd, holding them in anticipation. When he spoke, it was almost a whisper.

"I know many of us have lost people," he said, swinging his gaze over the crowd to gather all those assembled under his pull. "We must remember them. We must never forget them. I lost my entire family at a bombing on Trejna 4. The Coalition came without warning and destroyed our entire settlement. A civilian settlement. It is true we mined materials which went into ships, both military and otherwise, but we were not a military installation. We were just people, families, working to make a living, working to do our part for our civilization. My wife, Rose. My son, Jose. My two daughters, Rosita and Regina." The man's voice choked and stalled with emotion, and he paused to wipe his eyes. Bin Ald could feel the tension in the room, could feel the tears running down his face and saw the tears in the eyes of those around him. They had all lost people in the wars. They had all lost people to the Coalition. The man continued, "They were my family, and now they are gone forever. It has been so long… I came to New Mecca to find a new life, to live in a way honoring their memory. The Inner Cluster helped me resettle, protected me and provided for me when I needed it. My people were here for me." Again, a moment of silence, of rising tension, of electrified air. Then, in a rising voice: "But now, they have smeared the memory of my family. They have turned their backs on those of us who suffered and sacrificed. They have invited the very ones who murdered my family here into our home!" More shouts of agreement as the crowd's energy followed the man's voice. "The Coalition lived by the sword, by conquest and by coercion through violence. Now, their own violence, past and present, has come for them through the Black Sun. I say let them die at the blade of the sword they lived by! I say close our borders! I say we protect ourselves! We owe them nothing!"

The speaker pumped a fist into the air and the crowd, who had been hanging on his words, released their pent up energies in a ferocious fury of voice and applause. Bin Ald found himself cheering wildly, completely taken in by the man's words. The meeting was adjourned after that, with plans to meet again the following week. Bin Ald walked out into the cold night air, into the illuminated darkness, with his heart and mind full of energy and something else he could not quite put his finger on. As the crowd dispersed into the night, he watched the many people silently disappear into the dark streets and around corners and wondered where they were going home to. He had not recognized anyone there, did not know much about who he had just shared this experience with. But, as he began his own walk home, he knew one thing: *We are all in this together now.*

<u>14</u>

*Fear is the most powerful motivator in the human
experience and the most easily manipulated.*

-Anonymous

Exhaustion swept over Khalihl in a sudden wave. She
motioned to an attendant, who immediately came over to
her seat before the Council and poured some fresh
kol'koff into her cup. For a brief, lovely moment, the
voices of the arguing council members disappeared in the
bitter and refreshing smell of the coffee. For Khalihl, this
first sip was a much needed moment of peace. Things had
been chaotic since her return. Indeed, there was much to
argue and disagree over.

"We simply cannot put the welfare of these refugees
– Coalition citizens, I might add – over the welfare of our
own people!" Aiadaam Isdet, one of the newer three
Elders, said, his voice ringing with fervor and anger in the
large and open chamber. "I am sympathetic to their plight,
but even the slightest chance of harm to our own people
must be taken into account."

"Sympathy," Cabrenejos scoffed, "these people need
not our sympathy. They need our help! Need I remind you
they are fleeing the Black Sun, a group whose ascension to
power *we* are responsible for?"

"Responsible? How? We only defended ourselves against the Coalition! And was it not one of their own who destroyed the Source processing centers?"

Khalihl took another calming drink of her coffee, momentarily tuning out the arguments. All in all, the issue was moot; the council had already voted to follow her recommendation and continue to accept refugees. Only Isdet had voted against the idea. She spared herself a quick glance in his direction. One of the newer members, Isdet was younger than the rest by a fair amount, younger even than herself, and represented a portion of the Cluster that had been trending towards religious fundamentalism for some time now. His addition to the Elder Council had been controversial, and some saw it as a legitimization of ways of thinking the Inner Cluster had been founded to guard against. But Khalihl had agreed with his addition; his group represented a significant population of the Cluster, and to ignore them would be to invite division in their society. Better to include even those on the fringes of a culture than to give them even more reason to feel excluded.

"Enough!" Serjevko's voice cut through Khalihl's thoughts and snapped her mind back to the argument at hand. He continued in a lower voice. "We have already voted on the issue. Aiadaam, we recognize your concerns, and we have increased security at the processing points and bolstered the vetting process significantly. For now, that will have to be enough. There are other matters we must discuss."

Khalihl watched Isdet angrily fall back into his seat, arms crossed and face awash with frustration. *Is this how cracks begin to appear,* she thought, *under the weight of fear and anger?* But she wiped the thought from her mind, making a personal note to keep an eye on Isdet and his followers. Serjevko was right, however. There were more pressing issues now.

"We have, since you left," Serjevko now turned to Khalihl, "discussed at length the threat implied in the message from the Senders and have narrowed our options to a few courses of action."

"Our first thought was to contact the Senders," Thans picked up, "by sending a spread of our skip radios into the general area from which the message seems to have come. More information, more detail, would have been helpful in deciding."

"In the end," now Hujad spoke, and Khalihl marveled at how in sync the older members of the Council were, "we decided against this course of action. The message sent to us, upon further examination, appeared to be tightly aimed as to avoid its accidentally spreading anywhere near the sector of space from which the fleet is coming. We have to assume this was done on purpose by the Senders. We do not know the reason this fleet is coming for us, their motivation. If this is an aggressive and threatening force, sending messages back to the Senders may put them at risk as well. It is possible they put themselves at risk by warning us. They are, after all, much closer in space to the incoming fleet."

"Indeed," Thans said, "and we could not justify risking another civilization. We are on our own."

The statement struck Khalihl with some force. She suddenly felt hemmed in on all sides by danger, and weariness fell over her. A life lived under the threat of violence from other humans and now this. Perhaps peace was, after all, a fool's dream. She remembered the optimism of previous ages, the hope instilled in the idea of first contact. That an advanced civilization, by the very virtues of science and technology, would have to be morally advanced as well. She had read some of those ancient works of fiction, watched some of their entertainment. As a child, she had loved to dream of other intelligent species coming and teaching humans how to compromise, how to better understand the cosmos and consequently themselves. Was this not the main conceit of science even now? That knowledge was always a net positive for society? That with knowledge of the universe and the human place in it came a settling of the passions which had so often led to strife in history? This idea suddenly seemed naive in the extreme to Khalihl.

"We need you," Serjevko said gently, cognizant of the strife written on Khalihl's face, "to begin preparing our military to defend ourselves from this new threat. We must treat it seriously. The risk is too great to do otherwise."

"Yes sir," Khalihl nodded, her mind now sprinting through the necessities. "We will have to treat this as two fronts. The Black Sun will come for us eventually." Everyone on the Council nodded their agreement, and she continued. "This means we will need more ships and more soldiers."

"You have whatever resources you need to begin building more ships," Hujad said. "As for soldiers, we will put out a call for volunteers."

Khalihl nodded. Cluster law said the government had to call for volunteers; conscription, a draft, was illegal. If the power structures in place truly served the people, they would answer the call to defend it happily. They had never had an issue in the past, and Khalihl did not expect one now.

"I recommend," she said, "we use the Black Sun as our primary reason for this escalation of military readiness and hold off on announcing publicly what we know about the alien invasion." Again, the Elder Council simply nodded in agreement, this time after some glances at each other. None of them liked the idea of withholding information from the public, especially if they were going to ask people to fight, but in this case it seemed the most prudent course. First contact would engender major shifts at every level of society, and right now, facing invasion on one side and probable annihilation on the other, the Inner Cluster would need as much stability and unity as it could possibly muster. Khalihl had no doubt , when the time came, when they had more information, they would inform the public of what they knew. There was still time. *There is always time,* she thought, *until there isn't.*

"May Allah guide you, Admiral Khalihl," Serjevko said with a grave air about him. "And may Allah be with our people."

<u>15</u>

For some groups, the breakdown of the network, and the Coalition with it, was a loss. For others, those whose ideals and lifestyles were marginalized and unaccepted by the larger forces at play within the Coalition, they suddenly found themselves free to express their lives as they wished.

> *-Excerpt from* The Outside Looking In: Fringe Politics and Marginalized Peoples *by Jen Fretre*

This time, Meiind was not entering the trance to simply explore the silent life of the void. He had a purpose.

His mind, as it usually did now, responded to his posture and guided breathing by settling immediately into the necessary frame of thought. He was still, and soon he was there amongst the living light of the galaxy surrounding him. Instead of seeking a cluster of light to go to, to explore and learn about, he simply waited.

"I am here," he projected into the void. "I will wait as long as it takes."

It had been over a decade since the first time he had entered the trance. Back then, he had attempted to use it, with the support of the monks, to find the prison planet where humans, as he learned later, were being bred and harvested for their Sources. In that first experience, overwhelmed by sheer wonder and surprise, Meiind had become lost in the revelation of life flourishing throughout the cosmos. He had forgotten his purpose, his reason for using the trance, and spent nearly three days simply roaming, learning, and ignoring his reason for being there. That was when he had met it: the Presence. Something, some prescient force, had found and spoken to him, reminding Meiind of the reason he was there and setting him back on course. In the decade since, he had thought much about this interaction, though he had never once encountered it again. But now, he sought it. The Presence had helped him once before; perhaps it could do so again.

Meiind and the Roshi Moyo had spoken many times about the Presence, trying to work out what – or who – it could have been. Meiind had no idea. Nothing in his brief interaction with the being had given him much to go on. Roshi Moyo, however, believed it had been a bodhisattva, an enlightened being who stayed within the realm of the living, in the cycle of birth and death rather than transcending entirely, in order to help all living beings attain Buddhahood. The Roshi felt, rather strongly, this Presence had waited for one like Meiind, one with his touch and who could access the space in which the Source existed. To Meiind, this was possible, but he was unsure. The Presence had felt somehow different, somehow like a multitude. He had never sought the being out again, assuming, if it wanted to, it would contact him while he worked on his trance.

After his conversation with the Roshi Moyo about the Black Sun, Meiind had left conflicted and fearful. He had dedicated over ten years of his life to these people and to their way of life, and to hear the Roshi tell him he was not one of them… in his heart of hearts, Meiind knew the

Roshi was right. He could not accept their way wholesale, could not accept not defending against the Black Sun. He understood the Roshi's position, even saw wisdom in it. A world that thought as the Roshi did would be a peaceful one indeed. But, at the same time, he could not let go of the feeling they would be justified in defending themselves, that they were not the aggressors and they could fight back with a clear conscience. Meiind left feeling as though he was trapped between worlds: the one he had been raised in and the one he had chosen to become a part of. He felt as though the latter had rejected him. So now he sought to break the dichotomy he had developed in his mind, sought an outside perspective.

He did not know how long he had been in the trance when he finally felt it: the Presence. It did not speak.

"I am here," he projected. "I have many questions."

It was a moment before the words formed in his mind.

We do not have the answers you seek.

"Can you help me?"

The answers you seek do not exist.

"Am I asking the wrong questions?"

It is not the questions but the form. You speak the wrong language.

Meiind did not know what to make of this. He was not even sure language was a part of their interaction. Rather, he had the distinct feeling some sort of direct communication was happening, that it was his mind which was translating the experience into words rather than words being the vehicle of communication itself. He did not know what the Presence meant.

"I do not understand."

You cannot understand.

"How can I learn to – "

The Inner Cluster. Speak to the Inner Cluster.

"The Inner Cluster? Khalihl?"

The Inner Cluster. Speak to the Inner Cluster.

And with that, the Presence was gone. Meiind felt the absence both within him and in the space surrounding him. Slowly, he eased himself out of the trance, back into the physical world around him. He was sitting in the space before his hut, facing the horizon. When he opened his eyes, Meiind was met with the brilliant colors of the setting sun, the light of the fading star blazing through Bodhi's atmosphere in deep hues of red and purple and orange. *The Inner Cluster,* he thought as he watched the sun wash the sky anew with the night. *Khalihl.*

<u>16</u>

Nothing Gets Down well.

-Unofficial Motto of the Inner Cluster
Orbital Defense Unit 112

The *Gibran* hung in orbit around the planet Lion, the beautiful white and gold sphere appearing to pass beneath the ship as Khalihl watched on her viewscreen. She was ignoring the projection in front of her for the moment, trying to step away from the problems that had so filled her mind for the last week or so. She could not quite remember how long it had been since the Council meeting, could not quite account for all the days since. She had been to many of the border planets since then, taking note of existing defenses and planning new ones, better ones. Her training and decades of experience allowed her to compartmentalize the demands being made on her without allowing them to get too close to her own psyche, but those walls were beginning to break down as her fatigue was compounding. So much rested on her shoulders.

And now she found herself unable to look at the star map she had called up for even another moment, instead focusing on the viewscreen showing the landmasses and oceans of Lion passing beneath her ship with the unnatural smoothness vast distances and large scales imposed on everything. Her orbit was low enough she could make out the lights of cities, the peaks of mountains, and even some of the smaller lakes to be found in the less arid parts of the planet. Lion was mostly desert, eons of erosion and wind breaking down the peculiar rock-crust of the planet into a fine, golden sand covering much of the surface. The world hosted a small population, much of it descendant from the Jain settlers who had left in the Slow Migration centuries ago, and produced a kind of glass, made from the gold sand, magnitudes stronger than any other. In peace time, the planet also hosted huge numbers of tourists who came from all over human-occupied space to see the incredible golden deserts, oceans of sand exploding with color and light during sunrise and sunset.

Khalihl looked away from her viewscreen of the planet, bringing a hand to her temple. Even now, she could not shut off this part of her mind, the part which planned and sought advantage. That very sand was one of the reasons she was here now; they would need more of it to meet the increased needs of the military. She dragged her eyes back to the star map projected in the air in front of her, forcing her mind to address the other reason she was here. Lion's position in Cluster space made it likely to be one of the first planets to encounter the alien invasion, when the time came. They would need to be prepared.

And that preparation would require people. Millions and millions of people. With a few deft movements of her fingers, Khalihl brought up the most current recruitment reports. She had put out a public statement a few days ago asking for people to join the fleet, to volunteer to defend the Inner Cluster. She had cited the increasing threat of the Black Sun, and indeed, recruitment had increased by nearly 500 percent. And still, Khalihl did not believe it would be enough. They simply needed more. They needed to be ready for anything.

Khalihl stood, moving away from her desk and from the star map and stood in front of the viewscreen, watching the planet slide by beneath her ship. That was the issue, what had been nagging away at her mind. The unknowns. They had so little information on the alien fleet, so little concrete knowledge for her to use. She had spent the last week rereading the classics in exo-threat scholarship, an admittedly fringe segment of military academia. She had gone through a short phase in which the topic interested her early in her education, but now with the possibility confirmed, she had gone back to these texts in hopes of finding some direction. She read *Threats from the Void* by Iden Dostoy, *Big Universe, Big Trouble* from Esla Sadfre, Riechaard Tromky's *Insecure Mote*, and the abstracts of every academic paper on the topic she could find. She had listened to countless lectures, and yet for all the speculation on the topic of an alien invasion, it all boiled down to just that: speculation. The better of the sources consistently harped on what seemed to be the only point of concrete agreement between them, that an alien civilization could be so different from humanity that any attempt to posit or extrapolate information about them through reason was likely a failing enterprise in the extreme. There was just no way to truly know.

There was something else eating away at her mind, coloring her thoughts: fear. She could feel it distinctly within herself. And this was something different than the kind of fear she had felt in the past, during the Cluster Wars or just before the Hero's Battle. With those, the fear had been personal, the fear of death, of failure. But no matter the magnitude of the threat in those, she had been certain, at the least, her culture would survive. Now, facing something so alien, so inhuman, certainty did not exist, and the fear expanded from death to extinction. *Extinction.* For a moment, Khalihl felt faint and leaned against the frame of the viewscreen. *Extinction,* she thought. *I wish you were here, Raasch. You would know what to do.* She knew this line of thinking was an indulgence, a weakness, but she felt so alone that, for the time, she felt comfort in allowing the holes in her self-confidence show a little, even if only to herself. And alone she was, so very alone. The weight of the Inner Cluster's existence rested on her shoulders. Perhaps even the weight of human existence. And she had no one she could turn to, not even historical precedent. When had humanity ever before faced so great a threat? For millennia, humanity had been its own greatest threat, and now, at the moment when humanity's threat to itself was reaching a peak, there comes a threat from the outside, from beyond humanity.

Humanity, Khalihl thought, and the key log suddenly fell into place in her mind. She pivoted back to her desk and brought up the most recent maps of Black Sun territories. They controlled much of Old Co space now, but not *all* of it. What was more, and Khalihl called up a representation of known Black Sun military operations to overlay on the map, they did not appear to have an active presence in all the territories they had so far claimed. Khalihl pushed the specified date back, watching the movements of the Black Sun's fleet. She went back two years, and then moved to the present again. There was a pattern in their movements, in their tactics. The Black Sun, it appeared, often conquered and left, moving onto the next target and only leaving behind troops or ships in areas strategic to further expansion. No doubt they thought their tactics sufficiently brutal to discourage any rebellion, even without an active military presence. Again, a few keystrokes and new information displayed itself while Khalihl's mind ran. *I am concerned with humanity,* she thought, *but I am only considering a small portion of humanity in my plans.* The new information she keyed up solidified her thinking. The Black Sun had territories encompassing over 30 billion people, but they had active military presence covering only half of that, maybe even less. *15 billion people. That's the extra power I need.*

She knew then what to do and who could help her do it.

17

The historian — at least any historian with a true passion for her field of study — cannot help but wonder at the chance meetings, the small details and the random encounters, which seem to, from the distance of time, sway the great wave of humanity and its path through history.

-Kerl Hedgins, in lecture, Planetary University of Liberius, 2601

She was still in his thoughts a day later when he left Bodhi. They had not spoken in many years, not since they disagreed about the ways in which to approach the dismantling and disuse of skip tech. The long silence hadn't been intentional, at least not at first. Meiind had, after years on the prison planet helping the poor souls raised there, retreated from the world to Bodhi, had left society behind to explore himself and the universe in his own way. He had, however, kept up with news of Khalihl, knew she had spent the intervening years doing her part for the refugee crisis, helping those fleeing Co space find new homes in the Inner Cluster. These simple, surface facts he knew. What he had not known, what he had not felt until now, until the prospect of contact raised its head again, was the extent of his feelings towards her.

The ship Meiind now piloted was on course to Outpost 34, a small moon orbiting a gas giant in a system neighboring Bodhi. It was a few days travel, and as he watched the small planet shrink with distance in his viewscreen, the incredible green of the planet-wide vine forests vibrant even from space, a sense of foreboding had come over him. It had been many years since he had left, and leaving now felt as though he was leaving his home. *Home,* he thought with some surprise, *Bodhi is my home. Another unexpected feeling. I am becoming sentimental as I age.* Meiind had spent much of his adult life travelling from planet to planet as a mediator for the Coalition, never staying in one place with one group for too long. He had never felt a lack, a sense of loneliness or loss. Rather, the travel suited him; he enjoyed seeing new places and learning from new people all the time. But the years he had spent on Bodhi had settled onto his shoulders like well-worn and comfortable clothing. He felt naked now without it. Meiind spent the first day of travel distracting himself from these novel feelings of homesickness by reacquainting himself with piloting a ship. It had been many years, but the feel for it seemed to come back right away.

Meiind had spent his time since going over everything he knew, trying to make sure he was making the right decision by getting back involved. It seemed to him, however, it was not his decision after all. The Presence, whatever it was, had told him to contact the Inner Cluster, and while he did not know exactly what this Presence was, he felt compelled to obey. Outpost 34 was the nearest settlement with a quantum comm he could use.

His mind wandered now again to his experience with the Presence, with that unknown entity that seemed to be waiting for him in whatever space it was he accessed in the trance. Despite only two contacts in the hundreds of times Meiind had been in trance, he had the distinct feeling the Presence was always there, could find him when it needed to. Those two contacts, though brief, had been important:

the first had guided Meiind through his near-engrossment into the trance, and second had now led him to leave Bodhi for the first time in ten years. For all their brevity, these contacts had proven important, and Meiind had dedicated much thought to the Presence without much avail. Even Roshi Moyo, whose wisdom and insight Meiind often found useful, did not have much to offer on the topic. They had spent many hours discussing the possibilities, discussing what the presence could be, and while the Roshi's idea of the Presence as a bodhisattva seemed to fit, it was too simple, a predetermined label, a religious conceit, for Meiind to fully accept. Whatever, or perhaps whoever, the Presence was, there had not been enough in Meiind's interactions with it so far to make any substantiated claims. *Perhaps one day,* he thought as he sat at the helm of his small ship, *it will reveal more of itself. I do not think the Presence is done with me yet.*

Meiind shook his head, used the years of mental training he had undergone to forcefully clear his mind. He knew where thoughts about the Presence led, knew the endless and useless speculation he was to chase down when it occupied his thoughts. At the moment, he had more pressing issues. More dangerous questions. He assumed, right away, the Presence's request to contact the Inner Cluster had something to do with the Black Sun. He was still unsettled by his conversation with Roshi Moyo, by the Buddhi's decision to not defend themselves, and he felt whatever he learned from the Inner Cluster might have something to do with this. Perhaps he could convince them to protect Bodhi, to take the small planet in as a part of the Inner Cluster. The monks may not seek help, but Meiind refused to give in so easily, their wishes be damned. *But that isn't all, is it?* He thought to himself. *You sensed more in the Presence, more it wasn't telling you. There is going to be something else. Something big.* Meiind had indeed come away from the encounter with a nagging sense of ignorance, with the feeling there were layers upon layers to the threats facing the Inner Cluster and the peoples of the collapsed Coalition. He would have to press Khalihl and find out what.

Khalihl, he thought, and he wondered how she was. No doubt her life as Admiral of the Cluster fleet had been made more difficult by his decisions, by his sudden and complete shutdown of the glue that bound human space together. That, however, was not the tenor of his thoughts towards her. He had decided long ago to not regret his decision, and he still felt he had done the right thing. He even felt she, in her way, agreed. *No,* he thought, *the fear of her disapproval isn't what has kept her in my thoughts all these years.* He suddenly had a flash of image, an insertion of memory. He saw her in his mind's eye, exiting her ship, the *Gibran,* in the aftermath of the Traitor's Battle, standing foot upon the prison planet for the first time. He remembered her face then, the mix of emotions he could see playing across her fine features. Fear of the things she had just done, the people she had killed and the people she had led to their deaths. Anguish at the loss of her friends and, Meiind knew even then, at the sacrifice of Raasch. And exultation at victory, the glow of glory. He remembered the exhaustion apparent in her posture and gait as she walked across the landing field towards him. He remembered the press of her body, the smell of her skin and hair, as they embraced in utter disbelief at their survival. He remembered these things, even now over a decade later, as though they were yesterday, as though she were still here with her arms thrown over his shoulders, as if his hands could still feel the curve of her waist. But, more so, he remembered her love for the Admiral, her utter devotion and respect for him, a sentiment he too felt.

Forcing these thoughts from his mind, Meiind brought up the settlement records and reviewed what he already knew so well. The Outpost had been home to an

ill-fated colony a hundred years ago. Politics and mis-
management had led to the deaths of thousands of settlers,
and no others had ever bothered to return. Not, at least,
according to official records. Meiind himself had made
sure the records stayed that way. In the aftermath of the
Traitor's Battle and the collapse of the Coalition, Meiind
had been approached by the Neurosons. After centuries of
discrimination against their ways of life, both in terms of
social taboo and law, all they wanted, they told him, was a
place where they could disappear and live their lives the
way they saw fit. It was a modest desire but a difficult one
to actualize. After a lengthy search, Meiind settled on
Outpost 34 as a near perfect spot for them. Abandoned
and forgotten, Meiind had thought they would likely be
left alone there. He helped get them there, helped connect
them to sympathetic shippers who would keep them
supplied with resources in exchange for repair and
maintenance on their ships' computers. When Meiind had
finally left them to their small moon, they had appeared
excited and hopeful for their future, a feeling, as their
leader described it to him, they had not had as a people in
many generations. Meiind hadn't spoken to them since and
hoped to find them thriving.

His computer chirped at him, letting Meiind know his
ship was approaching the system. He ran through the
necessary procedures, dropping the ship out of sublight
just outside the gas giant's orbit without any perceptible
shift in inertia thanks to the dampeners. The viewscreen
came on with the touch of a button, showing the huge
planet as a small marble of color in the distance. It grew in
size rapidly as Meiind's ship approached, the blur of colors
becoming more and more detailed until he could make out
the swirls and lines of white, orange, red, and blue.
Beautiful, he thought. *They named the planet aptly.* The original
settlers, focused as they were on quick-turn profits, had
not bothered to name the planet which dominated much

of the sky of their small moon. The Neurosons, with their penchant for the history of their culture, had taken to calling the gas planet Antikythera, equating the elegant design of the ancient computer with the visual beauty of the planet around which they orbited. Meiind felt, now with the planet looming huge in his viewscreen, the name somehow fit. There was something primordial about the gaseous swirls of the planet's atmosphere, something that hinted at evolution and change.

His computer beeped again, this time an incoming message. Meiind accepted the hail.

"Identify yourself," a voice completely devoid of emotion or gender spoke from his comm.

"This is Aasben Meiind of the ship *The Five Rings* from the planet Bodhi requesting permission to land."

There was a long moment of silence before the voice on the comm returned, this time with an almost imperceptible change.

"Herr Meiind," the voice said with the hint of a smile behind it. "Welcome back. It has been too long. Permission granted."

18

*Calculated cruelty is a category error; the cruel
think of themselves as strong, but the truth is the
cruel hide their weakness behind violence, lashing
out for fear of annihilation. To defeat the cruel,
look to where they are most violent. This is where
you find their weakness.*

*-Excerpt from Elder Council Minutes,
spoken by Elder Serjevko*

*We exist for one purpose and for one purpose
only: to seed the universe with conflict and chaos
and thus ensure its continued growth.*

-Excerpt from the Book of the Black
Sun, *Author Unknown*

The man on the other side of the glass writhed in
pain and agony as the soldier in the room with him applied
various tools to various parts of his body. Eazkaii watched
with interest, standing close to the glass where the man
could see the one who had ordered his interrogation. They
had asked if he wanted the glass to be one-way, but
Eazkaii wanted the prisoner to be able to see his face, to
see the utter lack of emotion behind his pain. The screams
came through small speakers in the wall surrounding the
windowpane, another conscious decision on the Leader's
part. He wanted to hear it, to hear the suffering and to

hear the tenor of the man's voice when he confessed whatever information he had. He wanted to hear the truth in the pain.

A few more minutes, Eazkaii thought. *Let him suffer a few more minutes, and* then *we will start asking the questions.* He let his mind wander as the interrogation continued, keeping his expressionless eyes and face trained on the prisoner while he thought about what had occupied his mind on the journey to this outpost. Bodhi. Religious sanctuary for followers of the Buddhi religion, an unimportant and uninvolved group of people who had managed to slip past the attention of the Black Sun and the Coalition before them. They had no political involvement, no military, no wish to engage with human society at large. They were content to stay self-sufficient and distant, living only to continue the path of their religion and philosophy. This enraged Eazkaii. The thought of these people out there perpetuating the disease of faith – any faith! – was a thought he could not bear. They would have to be dealt with, and Eazkaii smiled, looking forward to the day.

A particularly sharp scream of pain brought Eazkaii from his thoughts and the interrogation on the other side of the glass back into focus. The soldier conducting the torture, experienced enough to know when the prisoner had reached the point of maximum compliance, waited to the side while the man on the table panted and squirmed in agony. Blood pooled beneath him on the alloy floor. Eazkaii signaled to the soldier who then promptly turned and left the room through a door on the opposite wall. The Leader let the prisoner wallow in his pain and suffer alone for a moment before entering the room himself. The prisoner did not acknowledge the leader of the Black Sun as Eazkaii came to stand over him. Eazkaii studied the prisoner for a few silent moments before speaking, taking note of the surgical cuts and small bits of flesh torn away.

"Do you know who I am?" Eazkaii asked, his voice heavy and calm in the air damp with blood and sweat. The man on the table did not answer, did not even open his eyes. He only nodded, shaking from fear and pain.

"Do you know why you are here? What it is I want to know?" Again, the man nodded.

"Then tell me."

●●●●

Later, in his own quarters, washing the blood from his hands, Eazkaii thought about what the man had told him before he died. The coordinates given had already been checked, and there was indeed a planet there in the database, marked as inhospitable and well within Coalition space. He could feel the excitement rising within him even as the adrenaline from the killing was beginning to fade. The key to complete domination of human controlled space could be on that planet! With skip tech, he could take the Inner Cluster and unify mankind. He could govern intimately, able to instantly be wherever he was needed to crush insurrection or to mediate conflict. Without the ability to skip through space, he knew he would spend the rest of his life conquering and reconquering as the vast distances weakened his control on his people. But with skipping, with the almost magical ability, he would never be more than a few moments away from anywhere in his empire. The power it would give him…

He left his room and made his way to the bridge, sweeping into the nexus of his ship briskly as all his officers there snapped to attention. He sat in his captain's chair and motioned them back to work.

"Helm," he snapped. "Lay in the following course." Eazkaii entered the coordinates given to him by the prisoner, adjusting the flight plan to include a small detour. He smiled at the thought of it.

Bodhi.

<u>19</u>

Cooperation is often lauded as the pinnacle of human achievement, and in some sense this is true. All the great achievements of humanity — interstellar travel, scientific advancement, social justice — have been achieved through a willingness to work together. But we must not forget the other side of the coin: war, genocide, mass exploitation. These too are only possible through the virtue of cooperation.

-*Excerpt from* Vice or Virtue: a Study of Human Cooperation *by Nigel Dentree*

The halls of Outlook 34's central government building were spare in the extreme: no photos of past leaders, no art depicting epic scenes, no plaques outlining ideology. Nothing of the like. Just plain, silver walls and windows overlooking the massive urban sprawl covering nearly the entire moon. This was what had surprised Meiind most. When he had left the Neurosons here over a decade ago, the settlement had been small. Today, as he had entered the atmosphere from orbit, he could not see the end of the city. It seemed every inch of the moon was covered in buildings and roads.

He was now following the woman who had met him on the landing field. A head taller than Meiind and strikingly beautiful, the woman had introduced herself as

Melanie.

"A strange name for a Neuroson," Meiind had said, taking her outstretched hand.

"I am a historian," Melanie said with a shy smile, "and am somewhat more interested in the old ways than my fellow citizens."

Meiind could see this in her posture, her movements, even in her voice. They appeared, to him, more natural. More human. Many of the transhumanists he had dealt with revealed their cybernetic enhancements most not in the obvious places, like the plated lights in Melanie's skull, but, rather, in the subtleties of their movements and of their voices. Still, Meiind noted, she did not hide her cybernetics. Melanie's shaved head revealed a number of implants in her skull, metal plates and blinking lights that looked a lot like 21st century fictional imaginings of transhumanists Meiind had seen. *That period of humanity had gotten so many things wrong,* Meiind thought. *Funny it would be the artists of the era who got much right.*

Melanie had led Meiind across the landing and into the building where they now walked through a long central hall lined by closed doors.

"This is the main hub of our administrative services," she explained as they walked. "From here, the entire colony is run by computer and algorithm. Work details, resource management, population control, implant upgrades and maintenance… everything falls back here. We call it Node."

"What is the population now?" Meiind asked. When they had first come here, the Neuroson's numbers had been small, less than a thousand people.

"Twelve million, though we intend to grow some

more before we stabilize our population," Melanie responded. "Most of the population lives near here. The rest of the buildings you saw from orbit are for our planned growth. Here, we build first and then expand population."

Meiind almost asked how they had grown their numbers so quickly, but he knew the answer already. The Neurosons had many practices the Coalition had not approved of, and their genetic development of embryos had been one of them. Meiind knew the Neurosons developed their populations through accelerated in vitro fertilization, keeping the embryos in stasis for a few years while they advanced cell growth and began cybernetic implantation. The Neurosons were born fully formed adults, no childhood to speak of. For them, this was the most efficient and logical way. Even Meiind, open-minded as he thought he was, found this idea difficult to swallow and accept. Rather than allow his bias to seep into his voice, which Melanie would no doubt recognize with her enhancements, he changed the subject.

"Where are we going?"

"Ah, please excuse my folly," Melanie said. "I was asked to meet you because I know much about you and your involvement in finding us this home, for which we are forever indebted to you, but I do not have the authorization to fulfill your request to use our interstellar comm. For that, you must see our leader, First."

First. Meiind remembered the Neuroson's government structure. When a citizen was assigned a term of political service, they were asked to drop their name in favor of the title of their assignment. The idea was for the individual to cease being an individual and so embody their position for the duration of their time in service. First, as in First Citizen, was their leader, chosen by their central computer based on the needs of the people and the merits of the individual. When Meiind had first dealt with the Neurosons, it had been the First, from that time, he had dealt with, had worked with.

"Here we are," Melanie said, stopping before a nondescript door at the end of the hall and bringing Meiind from his thoughts. "First is expecting you. I hope we are able to be of service to you, and I hope to meet you again."

"Thank you for your kindness," Meiind responded, pressing the woman's hand before she turned away and left him alone in front of the door. He stood there for a moment, reflecting on what he had seen and learned so far, a feeling of overwhelm threatening to take him. When he had met the Neurosons nearly 30 years ago, they had been an underground social group, trying to live under the radar of the Coalition, having to uproot themselves every time they were discovered in order to avoid persecution and in order to maintain their way of life. Now, they had a home and they had momentum; they were a whole group, and they had lived their way for over a decade of uninterrupted peace. Meiind felt lucky to have had the chance to do his small part for them. Meiind knew what he now asked of these people was asking quite a lot. By using their quantum comm, they would risk discovery. While the Coalition had collapsed, the Black Sun was out there, and their views of transhumanism were stricter than the Co's had been and their methods less civil. For a moment, Meiind doubted himself. Could he ask the Neurosons to risk themselves just so he could use their communication equipment? What right did he have? But then he thought of Bodhi, defenseless and at the mercy of the Black Sun. He thought of the monks either forced to serve in the military or being killed. He thought of them working to make tribute. Their entire way of life would be destroyed, assimilated and coerced by the Black Sun. He could not let that happen.

Meiind knocked on the door.

"Enter," came the strangely modulated voice distinctive to the Neurosons.

Meiind opened the door and passed from the hall into a large, spare office with the same, blank, and metallic walls found in the hall. At a wide, shining desk in the center, facing the door and now Meiind, sat a man with a posture too erect to be from a natural skeleton. And indeed, when the man stood to welcome Meiind, his movements had an element of precision to them that was off-putting to Meiind and somehow made him want to look away. Efficient and completely devoid of waste. The word mechanical came to mind, but that did not do justice to the fluidity of the man's movements. The man walked around the desk and approached Meiind with his hand out with a grace and awareness of body which could only be achieved, Meiind thought, by the perfect blending of machine and biology, not the seamless transition from one to the other but the smooth interlocking of both.

"Welcome Meiind," the man said, his voice similarly too toneless, too smooth to be entirely human.

Meiind set his thoughts aside, his natural revulsion to the uncanny feeling he often had when dealing with transhumanists who showed their being so openly. He looked into the man's eyes, saw the small flecks of bio-circuitry there, saw the lights and wires just under the skin of his forehead running down his jawline and up under his hair. What he saw, perhaps what he forced himself to see, was a man – one with a large element of cybernetic implants in his brain and body, sure, but a man nonetheless.

"Thank you, First," Meiind said, gripping the outstretched hand in a cordial shake. First nodded as though he could read Meiind's thoughts, could see the interplay of judgement and tolerance on his face, and turned with a swift pivot to return to his seat.

"Please sit," First said, indicating a chair on Meiind's side of the desk. As he did so, Meiind noticed the window behind First, overlooking the urban sprawl of the city. He stared out of the window for a moment before sitting down.

"Yes," First said, noticing. "We have grown much since you last came. We flourish here."

It was a simple statement, devoid of gloating or pride. A fact, nothing more, and the end of the conversation. True to Neuroson form, First had answered an entire series of questions Meiind had wanted to ask in that single phrase. There was nothing left for him to do but to make his request.

"I am glad," Meiind said. "And I assume you know why I am here."

"You wish to use our comm equipment," again, voice flat and devoid of feeling. No answer there. "I grant your request – I could do no less for you, my friend." Meiind heard a simultaneous friendly undercurrent and hard edge in the man's voice. "But, I wish you to understand fully what it is you ask of us, the risk you take with our lives."

Meiind almost physically recoiled. There was no anger in First's voice, no rise in volume or venom dripping from the implications of his words. Just fact. Just direct observation. Somehow, that made it worse. Meiind knew precisely what he asked, and he was not happy about it.

"Thank you," he said, refusing to hide his eyes and

looking directly into First's. "I know the risk, and I wish there were another way. I am compelled by circumstances out of my control to make contact with a friend in the Inner Cluster, and there is no other way for me to do this in a timely manner. I would not ask this of you if there was another way."

First simply nodded, accepting Meiind's explanation in that single, perfect movement. "I know," he said. "We trust you Meiind. You have always been a friend to us, have treated us as human when many would not. We have you to thank for our home. It is not our way to shun the requests of friends. Besides, the Black Sun will find us eventually, no matter how hard we try to avoid discovery. It is inevitable." First stood. "Come. I will take you to our comm unit myself."

<u>20</u>

Religious fundamentalism in all forms has always existed as a response to the liberal and cosmopolitan forces that define progressive societies. Defined by fear of the new, uncertainty about the future, and nostalgia for pasts that mostly exist as historical fictions, these groups seek to stall what they see as social movements detrimental to the world view prescribed by whatever ideology they believe in.

-Excerpt from Spectrum Swing: an Analysis of Fundamentalism *by Kerrae Higdens*

The planet was, Maldeck had to admit, beautiful. Even if the name sounded like a curse in his mouth, there was little he could find to fault the place the Inner Cluster had sent him and his people. He stopped from his work on the agbot to face the breeze and take in the view for what seemed like the hundredth time. *After ten years on a ship traveling across space,* he thought as he looked out over the valley above which he found himself, *I can be forgiven my regular stops to breathe the fresh air to smell the plants and to watch the horizon.*

Sahaj was a heavily forested planet, covered in thick groups of trees which, in the slightly less than one G gravity, grew tall and thin with massive canopies spreading out like fans from their tops. The leaves of the varying species of trees tended towards the brightly colored – reds and oranges and blues and purples – and were massive, evolved as such, according to the informational classes he had taken upon arrival, along with everyone else in his group, to capture what was left over from the distant star that made it through the planet's thick atmosphere. It was almost as if the planet was covered in bright umbrellas. Maldeck took a deep breath. It had taken some getting used to, as the air was thick enough as to feel heavy in his lungs, but still the air was wonderful after the stale and recycled atmosphere of the ship.

He stood in a clearing on the top of an artificially raised hill which brought him above the canopy so he could see far in every direction, the u-shaped valley his people had settled in ringed with old, sloping mountains. In the far distance, through the opening in the mountains at the end of the valley, Maldeck could just see a line of shimmering light on the horizon. The ocean, he knew, was far off, just beyond the planet's curve. Just before the line, he could see the faint lines of buildings that were his village. It had only been a few months, but they had grown much with the help of the Inner Cluster mediators and the Sihken they shared the planet with. What had, at first, been only a few impermanent hovels had become a small town with permanent homes and buildings. They even had a school and hospital now, and there was talk of the first few businesses opening. Pride surged in Maldeck's heart. His people had not only survived, but by the grace of God, they were thriving.

A glint of light in the sky caught his attention. A ship coming in from the south. Maldeck's face darkened some. A Cluster ship no doubt. Perhaps they were bringing supplies, but Maldeck knew it was more likely they were bringing back men and women of his group who had gone to visit Praj, the capital city of the Sihken on the planet.

On their home planet, Sianide, his people had lived modestly in small villages, for that was the way God had intended them to live. There had been no large cities, and the single spaceport was carefully regulated, so there had been little temptation for his people to wander beyond the desires of God. This, however, was changing. And it wasn't only the youth. Even some of the men on the governing council had been to visit Praj, had spoken in awe of the large, gleaming buildings and the busy roadways and of all the people. He had even seen some of his people begin to change their dress, a development Maldeck found particularly disturbing. This planet was colder than Sianide had been, but he still wore their traditional garments. Doubling up on the robes made moving a bit more unwieldly, but such was a small price to pay for the glories of obeying God. He looked down at himself, pride at his own strength and sorrow at the failings of his brethren mixing into a confusing elixir of feeling. Suddenly, he felt very far from home, and the sight of the waxen robes and of his own sandaled feet brought him some brief comfort. Some of the younger people in the village had taken to wearing the warmer, synthetic garments provided by the Cluster on their arrival. These included pants, of all things, and unnatural colors and cuts.

Maldeck's mind jumped to a conversation he had just had earlier in the day, after the morning's study but before they had parted to address their various daily tasks. The issue of clothing had been on Maldeck's mind; he had noticed a few of the men in his devotional group had forgone the traditional garments and were wearing the bright colors of the Cluster. He and a friend, James, had gone for coffee after the meeting, and Maldeck aired his grievance.

"It seems a small matter," James said flippantly as he added sweetener to his steaming cup of dark liquid. "These people have suffered much. They watched their planet die, lost friends and relatives to the Black Sun. Perhaps they deserve what small comforts they can have."

"You know as well as I do," responded Maldeck, scowling, " there are no small matters in the eyes of God. A sin is a sin, be it murder or a failure to live as He ordained. We have lived by the rules of God for generations, and now we risk losing that. And for what? Comfort?"

"I think you worry too much, my friend," James said as he sipped his drink. Maldeck suddenly noticed how comfortable the man looked, how at ease. "The youth will be the youth, but they will come back into the fold when they are ready. The transition has been especially hard on them."

"But it is not only the youth," Maldeck almost cried, his passion rising in his mind and heart. "Did you know some of the Elders have been to the Sihken capital? Did you know some of them have brought back educational texts and technologies we never had on Sianide?"

"This is just the way of things," James shrugged, uninterested in the conversation.

Just the way of things. Maldeck turned from the view and brought his attention back to the agbot he had been called out to repair. As he pried off the side panel, revealing the internal circuits of the small robot, he tried to clear his mind. *Judgement is the Lord's alone,* he thought. *Have I been infected by these people as well?* His first few months here had been spent in classes taught by Cluster citizens. He had learned to operate and repair the agbots, the job which sustained him now and allowed him to look into the internal working of the small machine before him and know exactly what to do. He had refused the classes on Inner Cluster history and culture. The classes offered the ease of the transition and, he suspected, assimilation of his people, but he had nonetheless accepted their help and taken their learning. These were the first mistakes. They never should have come here. It would have been better for them to die with the Truth still intact in their hearts than to watch it slowly fade away through contact with these others.

A small spark from his soldering tool brought him jumping from his thoughts. There would be time to think of this later, before the meeting tonight. And there would be time to speak, to make others see the dangers. Until then, this damn agbot was not going to fix itself.

<u>21</u>

But from these chance encounters, from the serendipitous events of the past, the historian must resist the urge to see providence. As humans, we evolved to seek patterns, even patterns that are not truly there, and this evolutionary gift can also lead us into folly.

-Kerl Hedgins, in lecture, Planetary University of Liberius, 2601

It had been a long time since they had seen each other's faces, heard each other's voices. Ten or twelve years? They could not quite pin it down exactly. What they did know, though, was the relief they both felt and could see on the other at coming back into contact, even if it was only through the transparent images of each other now projected over their respective comms. They had been through much together, and now with turmoil and conflict seething around them again, they both found comfort in knowing the other was on their side. Together, they had overcome much already. Together, perhaps they could overcome this.

To Meiind, Khalihl looked as beautiful as she ever had, if a little more worry-worn. New lines creased her face around her eyes and mouth, but she had not succumbed, he noticed, to the temptations of cosmetics. Those lines, even some of the gray in her hair, could easily be disguised or erased altogether, but she wore them plainly and openly, a tribute to her own life. This is my face, she seemed to say, and written on it is my life. Deal with it. Meiind was immediately energized by the strength she projected.

Khalihl too was happy to speak to Meiind, the only other person still alive who knew what she had gone through during the aftermath of the Hero's Battle. She had many friends and confidants, and she felt close to many people. But this man, Meiind, with his gentle features and soft voice, had loved Raasch the same way she had, had chosen righteousness over the petty conflicts of loyalty and government, had done the right thing in the end despite the enormous economic importance of skipping. She knew he would always do what he thought was right, regardless of any other considerations. She trusted him more than anyone for this quality.

After their initial excitement at seeing one another, after her surprise had faded – she had, after all, been trying to find him, trying to speak with him about the Inner Cluster's need for more recruits in their defensive fleet – there came a lull in their conversation. A moment where they both recognized in the other troubling possibilities. The eye of the storm. These were dangerous times, and they both had favors to ask of the other.

"I have been seeking a way to contact you," Khalihl began. "I need your help."

"I need the same from you," Meiind said with something of a laugh, a dry chuckle. "You begin."

"Something big is happening," Khalihl said, and she told him all about the message the Inner Cluster had received from the aliens they called the Senders, the message warning of the alien invasion coming. She was concise and exact, offering no commentary on the topic but only what information she had. She told him they could not confirm the message's information, but the Elder Council had chosen to take the threat as serious. How would they do otherwise?

Meiind was stunned into utter silence. After a full minute, he let out a string of obscenities and then a string of questions.

"What are you doing to prepare? How long until they arrive? How advanced are they? Does the Black Sun or any of the old Coalition know about this? What are their intentions? Can you contact the Senders again?" The questions flowed from him in an unceasing torrent. Khalihl allowed him to exhaust himself before speaking.

"We know nothing about them," she said, "and we do not know how to reach the Senders to request more information. We have begun to prepare a fleet, turning the systems on the side of Cluster space they approach from into a line of defense, but we are afraid it will not be enough. According to the map we were sent, they are coming with massive force. We simply need more people."

"This is why you needed to contact me," Meiind said, his mind leaping ahead. "You need to gather forces from what is left of the Coalition."

"Yes. We do not think they are coming just for the Inner Cluster. They come for *humanity*."

That final word hung in the space between them like a guillotine waiting to drop. Neither spoke for a moment as the depth of the threat sunk fully into Meiind's bones. His mind raced, and he forgot his reason for contacting Khalihl. His worries about Bodhi were so small compared to this: an invasion against humanity. The Black Sun suddenly seemed a small worry, an inter-species conflict like the millions of others that had plagued humanity since the beginning of time. This alien invasion, however, this was something new. A threat of new proportion. Bodhi could wait.

"We need more information," he said. "I have some contacts still in the remnants of the Coalition, and I will put them into communication with you, but we need more information to fully assess this."

"I agree. The lack of information, and the lack of a way to gather it, is the most frustrating part of this. Our scientists are assuming the aliens have some way of monitoring us. Otherwise, how could they send a fleet in with confidence? But we have been unable to learn anything new about them. We are weakened by the asymmetry."

Meiind was quiet for a moment. Then:

"I have an idea, but first, I have to tell you something about myself."

And Meiind told Khalihl about his touch, about his special ability, about the trance he had learned from the Buddhi monks, about the true cause of Ondrueut's death, his murder. He told her about his exploration of life in the galaxy in the years since the Coalition had collapsed. He told her everything. It was her turn to be stunned into silence.

"Perhaps," he said into the charged distance between them, "I can use this to contact the Senders, to ask for more information. Maybe we can even convince them to help. Maybe we can do something, give ourselves some sort of advantage."

"Right," Khalihl said after a moment, her voice heavy with unasked questions. "We will take anything at this point. Anything is better than the complete dark we have been operating in so far. We have some left-over skip batteries; I have a few things to do here, but I can meet you at Bodhi in a few days to attempt contact."

Meiind set aside his misgivings about the left over batteries – powered by the murder of humans – and agreed. They would meet at Bodhi in three days, and he would, using the monks for support like he had the first time, attempt contact with the Senders.

When they said their goodbyes, Meiind heard something new in Khalihl's voice, something he had not noticed was missing until he heard its return now: hope. She had hope again.

Things must be bad over there, he thought, *if this plan is a source of hope for her.*

22

Some of the ancient thinkers, such as Tolstoy and Bergson, saw it long ago: humanity operates as a wave or as a swarm, its general movement dictated by the collective movements of the individual parts. While certain individuals find themselves at the forefront of these mass movements, it is the mass that, ultimately, decides where the entire thing goes.

-Excerpt from The Tides of Time: Movements and People *by Aldet Oournet*

Bin Ald looked at the men and women sitting around him and wondered: *Can they see it? Can they see the truth?* The group was discussing the most recent meeting of what they were now calling the Original Way, where their leader, the man who had spoken the first night Bin Ald attended, had put forth some ideas about how to proceed as a body politic. This, it seemed, as evidenced by the argument now happening, had opened something of a schism in the group. Some agreed politics, the normal avenue for reform, was the right way to go about changing things. Others felt this was too slow, too tilted towards the status quo already in place. Bin Ald listened and thought, *None of them see it.*

After that first meeting of the Original Way, Bin Ald

had felt his entire mind shift. Indeed, if he were to put it into words, which he did in occasional conversation with like-minded men and women at later meetings or out in the world when they found one another, identified by the red band they had taken to wearing on their arms, he called it something like a spiritual shift. That night, after the rousing speech by the man he now knew to be called Kareem Obdyal, Bin Ald had come home and performed his prayers, as he had learned in school the ancients did, for the first time in his life. And, for the first time in his life, he had felt the glory of Allah coursing through his body, felt the divine in his soul and felt the power of the One True God.

All his life, Bin Ald had been raised as a Musla of the Isla'hai of the Inner Cluster. But Isla'hai was essentially a cultural system rather than a religion, a series of customs and linguistic patterns tying the citizens of the Inner Cluster together and giving them communal strength. He had been taught, again in school, Isla'hai was an improvement on the fundamentalism of his ancestors, a dogmatic approach allowing all manner of evil to be performed in the name of righteousness. In contrast, Isla'hai, he was told, centered on what was good and important in the ways of his ancestors, on the peace and cooperation which could be achieved through shared values and commitments, while removing the elements that separated people. After his night in prayer, after his touch of the eternal, Bin Ald now saw the error his people had undertaken as their way, saw where they had strayed from the path.

After that night, much changed for Bin Ald, beginning with his perspective. The world looked different to him, somehow. At first, it was only in the edges, some sort of shimmer glinting on the outer rim of his consciousness. Slowly, as he continued his prayers and read his Quran more regularly, it began to seep into his mind and then into his vision until everything he saw glimmered with what he came to recognize as the Glory of Allah. And once it was there, once he was cognizant of it, he could hardly believe he had been so blind before. Allah was, truly, in all things, and His words were truly in the Quran.

Bin Ald came out of his thoughts in time to hear one of the members in the group, a woman named Jessica, say, "The change has to begin in the way we educate our citizens. We have to teach them to value their own over all others. We have to teach them to think of themselves as sovereign. This whole mess with the refugees has at its roots our own identity as refugees. We identify too much with them because we were taught to look at ourselves the same way." There were nods all around; even Bin Ald nodded. What she said was true. He remembered his own education well enough. *Still,* he thought, *it won't be enough.*

"I couldn't agree more," said another member in attendance, a man called Oman. "But that still does not solve our problem. The education system is provided and the curriculum developed by the government. This means , to make those kinds of changes, we have to work through politics, which brings us back to the failures of our system. I still think we need some sort of structural change. The Elder Council, while effective in its day, has outlived its usefulness. We need a more direct democracy now. The people need their voice now more than ever."

"The Elder Council has never let us astray," chimed in another man whose name Bin Ald did not know, though he recognized him as the most moderate of the voices in the discussion here. "And we have some elements of democracy. We all learned about the fate of democracy in the Post-Terror Years, did we not? Don't you remember the lessons? All democracies fall to one of two fates: stagnation or populist lunacy. Paralyzation or mob rule. The Founders knew this, and this is why they balanced our democratic institutions with the Elder Council. To temper the passions of large groups with the wisdom of our best individuals. No, if we are to make changes, it has to go through the systems already in place."

The argument continued for a few more minutes, and Bin Ald listened, biding his time. He had been coming to this group for a few weeks now, mostly just listening to the ideas being bandied about but rarely speaking. Today, however, would be different. He finally had something to say, had finally seen the errors of their, his, ways, and he knew the path the Inner Cluster needed to take. *It is so obvious,* he thought. *It has been there for thousands of years.*

"May I offer an idea?" he said mildly during a moment in which the argument had waned. All eyes turned to him. "We all have the same goals here, and we have heard many good ideas. Yet, and I am sure I am not the only one to notice this, there is little agreement." He looked around at the men and women who listened now, trying to connect with each, trying to make them feel his words as much as hear them. "The problem is not the ideas. Ideas are just abstractions, and all ideas have benefits and negatives. The problem is we, as limited beings, cannot possibly begin to foresee the total of all the ramifications of one of our ideas. Look at the Founders. They, the best of us, put into place a government system they felt would best serve their progeny. But they could not have foreseen what the future would bring. They could not have imagined how the discovery of the Source would bring us back into contact with humanity at large, with the Coalition. They could not have foreseen the consequences, the wars and the suffering. They were only human, after all. Similarly, they could not have foreseen what their understanding of Isla'hai would do to us." Bin Ald paused, allowing his audience to puzzle for a moment at the connection between their cultural system and the current state of things. He had their utter attention. They had been arguing for weeks and were tired of hearing the same arguments put in different ways. Here was something new, on the surface at least. "Yes," he continued, "the problem is simply us. We are finite, small in the cosmos, incapable of the understanding necessary to truly address the complexities of our interactions, our interactions with the universe, with each other, with ourselves." Bin Ald knew he would lose some of them here, with this blatant rejection of the enlightenment values, the hubris of humanity, many of them held dear. They believed, above all, they could solve problems, either through cooperation or through individual inspiration. And here Bin Ald was denying them that foundation.

"Are you saying it is hopeless?" someone asked, right on cue.

"No," Bin Ald responded, "though I am saying if we continue to attempt to solve things from our own, limited perspective, this conversation will never end. Even if we come to agreement, eventually the argument will begin again when something else comes up the system in place cannot handle. It may be in a year, ten years, maybe a hundred. But there will always be a day when the ways of humanity fail them. This is a fact of our existence."

"What are you suggesting?" this was Oman.

"Our people have known the answer for thousands of years," Bin Ald responded, pulling something from his robe pocket. "We were given the answer, only we chose to forget it."

With that, he set the Quran down on the table before them.

<u>23</u>

All things end, even endings.

-Buddhi Aphorism

Meiind knew something was wrong within a few minutes of dropping from sublight. His hails to Bodhi went unanswered, unusual for the diligent monks, especially in these dangerous times, who kept track of in-system traffic. A sense of unease began to spread through his mind and heart like a stain spreading through cloth. This unease burst into full-fledged panic as his ship came closer to the planet and entered orbit. Still, his cries on the comm went unanswered. Bodhi was silent under him.

The usual green and white and blue marbling that appeared as the surface of Bodhi from space was gone, replaced with a lifeless gray ash covering the entire sphere. The planet looked dead, utterly devoid of life. Meiind tried to push the thought from his mind, tried to keep calm as he entered the landing sequences into his ship's computer, but he knew what had happened here, knew what evil had befallen his adopted people.

The Black Sun.

On the surface, the planet looked much the same as it had from orbit: ashen gray. The buildings still stood, but everything else was gone, even the vine forests. As far as

Meiind could see, there was simply nothing. Just a fine layer of ash that covered the planet's surface a foot or so deep. Even the buildings, now empty, had a layer of ash turning them into the same lifeless gray that covered the ground from horizon to horizon. Meiind walked around in a stupefied daze, looking for someone, anyone.

No one had come to greet him when he landed his ship in the landing field. The radio never gave anything but static on the way down. Terrified but determined, he entered the nearest building. What he found turned his heart to stone, and he felt something he had never felt before rising within him. A feeling he could not control. In the halls of the building, a school by the layout, Meiind found what had happened to the people of the planet. Everywhere he looked, in the rooms and the halls, he found charred robes in the different colors used to demarcate the adherent levels resting on the floor atop and within mounds of lifeless ash. Bits of jewelry could be seen glinting in the gray flakes of burnt and cremated flesh, sandals left mid-step. And everywhere, the thin film of ash.

He passed a computer terminal with a blinking light, grabbing his attention. Meiind entered a few commands, brought up a flagged audio file. Hesitating for the fear in his heart, he hit play.

"This is Edson Cairns, originally of the planet Fuscia, initiate of the Buddhi." The voice of a young woman came out of the computer, and Meiind was frozen by the fear he heard in her voice. "They appeared in orbit less than an hour ago. We have tried to hail them, but there has been no response. Our sensor sweeps are not tuned for military applications, so we cannot read their power allocations… we do not know what to think. We wait." With that, the message ended, but another came up a moment after, Meiind hit play. "We received word," the same, scared and shaking voice started up again, "about two minutes ago

138

something struck the surface to the south. There was no explosion, according to reports. Just a flash of light. Within seconds, our villages there went silent on the radios. Our satellites show something is happening to the planet, something terrible. The Bodhi forests, the vines, they are dying, and the birds and animals with them. It is as if a wave of death is spreading across the planet, turning everything to gray ash. I have never seen or heard of anything like it before. In the villages, it appears to leave the buildings, anything not alive, intact. We are unsure of the people. We have not heard from any survivors, and our hopes are failing us. Whatever it is, the spread is rapid. Even now, it approaches us here in the capital. We have maybe a few seconds left before the wave passes through us. I do not know – "

With that, the recording went dead.

Outside, Meiind sat on the steps leading up to the building he had just exited and surveyed the landscape. He felt almost empty inside, almost devoid of feeling except something new, something he thought he had felt before but which had only been a false version of what was growing within him now. The sun was setting. The ash had spread into the atmosphere, and Meiind could look straight at the orange ball of fire through the somber, ashen skies as it approached the line of the horizon. Death covered the planet, and a rage unlike anything he had ever felt spread through him until he could feel his body shaking with it. His mind afire with it.

I could kill them, he thought, and the thought rung in his mind with the clarity of a bell. *I could kill them all.*

A deadly calm descended upon him, and he felt his body and mind entering into the trance as though compelled to do so by his now steady rage, an anger with the depth of a calm but infinite sea. The trance descended upon him, almost unbidden, almost as though he were uninvolved. An observer.

It'd be so easy, he thought. *With a thought, I could take them. Crush the Source within them. Rid the universe of their evil.*

His eyes were now closed, and he felt the universe within him expanding, saw the light of humanity glow within the corner of the galaxy they occupied. A strength surged through him, fed by his pain and anger.

What difference would it make, he thought with a heavy bitterness in his heart, *if I killed everyone in the Black Sun? Another evil would rise to take its place. It never ends.*

I could take us all into oblivion, the whole human race, this whole failure of evolution and biology. His thoughts spiraled out of control. Tears began to flow from his eyes. *What have we given to existence? What have we given to each other? Pain. Suffering. Exploitation. Death. We clawed our way from instinct into sentience, from land to space, from the confines of Earth to the stars. We could do anything. And we chose this.*

We do not deserve the life we have. The Universe would be better without us.

A slight breeze ruffled through Meiind's robe, over his bare skull and across the skin on his face, bringing him out of his thoughts, and then, out of the trance altogether. He opened his eyes and looked out over the ashen valley of shadow and death. He could feel the death here, feel the weight of suffering and pain in the air and on the land. It was true: humans had done something unimaginably terrible here, a horror beyond all horrors, and for what? In the name of power? Ideology? Belief? And if he responded in kind, if he used his mind to kill them or to exterminate his species, capable of evil as it was, was this any different? The Buddhi had been good people. Peaceful, loving, just.

How would their memory be served by such an act? What would Roshi Moyo say to him?

And, with that thought, Meiind's anger broke, and he put his face into his hands.

<u>24</u>

After Babel, God separated the peoples of the world into different nations and cultures. It was, and is, God's will we stay unmixed. Look how we blaspheme against the Divine!

-Excerpt from The Only Way: a Christian Manifesto *by Moises Senstre*

The church was small with a low roof, a far cry from the wonderfully massive and awe-inspiring building they had had on their home planet. It was only temporary, however, and as Maldeck stood outside greeting the congregants as they entered the humble doorway, he could see the partially completed steeple of the new church being built just a few streets over. Even surrounded by scaffolding, the size and beauty of the structure was already beginning to show itself. *This one will be truly worthy of God,* he thought with pride.

Men and women passed him as he said hello to most by name. Ten years on a single ship selects for a tightly knit community, and he was glad to see their faces after the difficult work week. He could see the exhaustion on their faces. They had only been here less than a year now, and there had been much to do to settle the land they had been given here on the planet. *There is still much to do,* he thought, his mind wandering to the agbot which had been giving him trouble lately. And yet, in spite of the exhaustion he saw in people's faces, he saw something else as well: hope. They were, for the time being, safe, and the trauma of watching their home planet fall to the Black Sun was beginning to fade. *Glory to God,* he thought.

"Have you seen the Lleur family?" a man named Kenneth asked, stopping at the front entrance and shaking Maldeck's hand happily.

"I saw them pass through, yes." Maldeck replied.

"Did you notice anything?"

"I don't think so. Not anything special, at least," Maldeck said after a moment of thought as more congregants passed with smiles.

"You can barely notice," Kenneth said as he moved through the doors, "but the missus, Jenny, word is she is pregnant. The first!"

As Kenneth walked away and into the church, Maldeck could not help but smile. A child! What surer sign of renewed hope could there be? He began his greetings again with new interest, looking for other signs. Had this couple been together before? Look how healthy this child, born on the ship from Sianide, was! Now, this new information in mind, Maldeck saw hope in the eyes of everyone who passed him.

But darker thoughts also crept into his mind. His people were settling into life here, and with that knowledge, with the idea of new souls being brought into their world, came a renewed sense of responsibility. Some of these people may be lost to the influence of the Cluster, but the next generations… they needed to keep their ways for the salvation of future generations. If their ways were lost, it would be the fault of his generation. This could not be allowed to happen. As the number of people walking in began to thin out and as the time for the service drew close, Maldeck turned to enter through the threshold himself, a sense of purpose and conviction growing within him. He would be the voice of God to these people. He would keep the flock from straying too far from the Word and the Way. He would be their strength.

Their service began as they always did, with a prayer of thanks from the pastor, the congregation's leader. The prayer began as Maldeck found his seat next to some friends.

"Lord in Heaven," the pastor, a man named Micah, began, "we come together before You today to be in Your presence, above all things. But we also come with grateful hearts. You have delivered us from destruction and from our time in the desert of space. With Your blessing, we have crossed the emptiness of the void, fleeing from persecution, but You kept our faith strong and have delivered us to this beautiful planet where we may begin again to live and glorify Your name."

"Amen" rang throughout the congregation, Maldeck's voice among the chorus. Some, he heard, were already weeping. *How long has it been,* he thought, *since they congregated with such hope and joy in their hearts? For so many years, fear was the only emotion this congregation shared. How wonderful!* Maldeck's heart swelled with love and thankfulness, but his feelings were short lived as the pastor continued.

"Lord, we also wish to thank You for our brothers and sisters whom You sent to deliver us from our suffering, the men and women of the Inner Cluster."

Less "amens" this time and Maldeck's mind leapt with shock.

"It has been many, many generations since our

people have had to live with others of differing faith, but You have shown us peoples can work together to be one, can help one another without avarice or evil intent. We thank You for them, for the Inner Cluster who have allowed us to live here and to practice our ways unencumbered, and for the Sihken, who have agreed to share their beautiful planet with us. Amen."

Maldeck opened his eyes and glanced around as the people were seated and as the pastor continued on with general announcements. He saw others seeking his eyes, looks of shock and frustration and anger on their faces. He also saw the same looks on men he had not before known to be so faithful. He marked them in his memory. They would need everyone they can if they were to keep their ways pure.

His mind more made up than ever, his heart harder with conviction than it had ever been in his life, Maldeck sat through the service awaiting the open forum which always came at the end. He had come with things to say, with a word of warning to his people, but now he felt the words bursting from his heart. He had not realized how close to peril they already were, but he was determined to fight the degradation of his people and their culture.

When the time finally came, the pastor called for anyone who wished to take the floor. Maldeck stood and walked forward, the eyes of the congregation burning into his back. A few knew what he had to say today. Others would feel it in their hearts and would be called by his words. Yet others, those with sentiments like the pastor's, would disagree with him and his views. He saw clearly the schism that would open here today. *So be it,* he thought grimly as he turned to face the seated people, *God's way is not easy.*

"Thank you, Pastor," Maldeck said after the pastor

had briefly introduced him. "And thank you for your wise words today. What a blessing it is to be able to be together, in a house of worship on solid ground, as God intended, again." He paused for the "amens" and "hallelujahs" trickling through the audience to die down. "I look out at your faces, my brothers and sisters, and I see something I have not seen in many years. Hope. Hope for a life worth living. Hope for a future for your children. Hope for an eternity with God. It makes my heart weep with joy to see hope on your faces again, for is that not the message of Christ we so nearly lost on our voyage here?"

Maldeck paused once more. He looked over the faces. They sensed the tension in his voice. He had them now, and he felt a surge of pleasure roll through his body as he realized how they hung on his words.

"I come before you today, my brothers and sisters, to make sure we do not lose sight of God's Truth in that hope, to remind you hope is not the only message, to say to you , while we are finally safe again in one way, we tread on dangerous ground in another. Remember the lesson of the Great Losing!"

His words rang in the utter silence as the congregation caught their breath at his words. The Great Losing! The phrase would evoke in them fear and shame, for they all knew well their history. They had all been taught of how their ancient brethren in the 19th and 20th centuries, brimming with the hope of the Message and filled with the optimism of their righteousness, had gone into the world to spread their joy only to, over time, lose their way. Everyone in this congregation had been through their schools, had learned of the dilution of the Christian faith in the 21st century and since, and they had all been taught the reason.

"We, our people, have tread this dangerous ground

before," Maldeck now lowered his voice and leaned forward. "We have mistaken blessing for laxity and hope for enthusiasm. We remembered many of the values of God, and we forgot many others. We lived with joy and forgiveness and love, and we forgot about purity and discipline and strength. We have been there before, and I see us here again." Another, brief pause. The audience waited with bated breath. "Our ancestors thought they could be of the world and still keep their faith, but we now know that for the hubris it was. They thought they could tolerate sin and sinful teachings, but we now know the folly of their ways. They thought they could serve two masters, but we now know they lost their souls in the process. Will we make the same mistakes?" Maldeck scanned the crowd and was encouraged by the many nodding heads he saw. He also saw many squirming uncomfortably in their seats, and he knew he was saying the right words. *Let them be uncomfortable, for the truth often is painful and rarely convenient.* "We now share this world with the Sihken, and it is true the Cluster peoples, the Musla, have allowed us this place to continue our culture. But need we lose our culture in the process? Need we forget our past in order to be grateful to them? Need we sell ourselves to their ways?" Another pause. Maldeck felt his control over the audience, felt their anticipation, and he reveled in it. "No!" he screamed, causing many to jump and many more release their held breaths in unison. "It is our duty, no matter the circumstances, to remember who we are. Who are we? We are God's children! We are the sons and daughters of Christ Almighty, the one and only true God of the universe. They are his commandments we follow, none other. His glory we seek. Salvation and paradise are our promise. And we risk these for what? For cultural exchange? For the tolerance of heathen ways? For acceptance by heathens? We already know where that path leads. We must, not for ourselves but for our way of life, for our children and their children and their children, hold fast to our Truths, for they are the only things that matter. God commands it be so, and history tells us it is the only way. May God give us the strength to stay pure. Search your hearts, those who go to the Sihken cities and those who mingle with the Cluster peoples and remember it is not only yourself you damn but us all."

The congregation erupted into chaos as Maldeck stepped off the stage and made his way down the aisle and through the back door. Some shouted "Amen!" and "Hear, Hear!" over those shouting their defensive protestations to his words. Others still sat silently, pondering his ideas. Maldeck himself felt light of spirit; he had said what had been put on his heart to say. He had obeyed God, damn the consequences, and he felt the righteousness of God buoying his heart. He walked out of the building, eyes forward and head high, and into the bright light of the mid-day sun.

<u>25</u>

We leave the world be, and the world leaves us be. This is all we want, and we ask this tradition of isolation be respected. It is not that we consider ourselves different or better than the rest of society. Rather, we have simply chosen to value different things, and this choice requires we stay aloof in order to achieve our own goals and ends. We hope you can understand this.

-Excerpt from Transmission, Bodhi to the Black Sun Flagship

Khalihl had read the reports, knew the Black Sun had some sort of weapon capable of killing every living thing on a planet. She had listened to the stories of refugees watching their planets die as they fled, watching everything they had ever known be turned to ash. She had listened with horror, had seen the utter disbelief on their faces, had felt the hatred in her heart swell and threaten to consume her.

But to see it in person was another thing altogether.

As soon as she entered orbit, Khalihl knew what had happened. She had never been to Bodhi but knew it was a forested planet, knew what it should look like from space. Full of the color that is indicative of life. Green, blue, white, the colors that spoke to the cradle of humanity.

None of that was left. Only a gray, dead ball hung below her ship. Lifeless. A blind eye in the void.

She followed the transponder signal from Meiind's ship to a landing field in what appeared to be a large village, the largest one on scan. The devastation was even more shocking on the ground. Buildings, any structure not made of the Bodhi vines, still stood, but they somehow added to the sense of death and desolation hanging in the utterly still air. She wandered, leaving lonely footprints in the fine layer of ash that had settled over everything. It was even in the air; she could feel it coating her lungs. The stories of the refugees had been horrific, but nothing could have prepared her for this.

I will not, she thought with a mix of anger and determination, *allow this to continue.*

She found Meiind sitting on the steps of a building overlooking a low valley full of small frameworks. Homes, by the look of them. Ash had settled onto his shoulders; he had been seated there a while. He did not move when she came up behind and sat next to him. She did not speak, just looked out over the valley and watched as the sun began to dip low to the horizon, as the sky began to change color into reds and oranges muted by the ash in the air. Soon, the sun was low enough to strike through where the ash in the sky was thickest, casting an apocalyptic orange glow across the landscape. The sun burned through the filthy sky like a red eye of fire.

"Twenty-five million people," Meiind finally said, not turning towards Khalihl. "That's how many lived here. That's how many had dedicated themselves to a simple and peaceful way of life. They didn't deserve this."

Khalihl didn't speak, and Meiind didn't continue, but the unsaid words hung in the air. *Deserve,* Khalihl thought.

Deserve has nothing to do with it. Abstract concepts… what are they in the face of this? And for the first time in her life, Khalihl felt her beliefs waver, ever so slightly, and threaten to come tumbling down. *Everything I was raised to believe in – justice, love, peace, hope – how can any of that help us now? How can we respond with anything but hate and violence? The language the Black Sun speaks. The language humanity seems to speak. For all the prophets of peace and love*, she thought, *who have made their mark on human history, who we have glorified as the best of us… have we truly learned anything? Changed at all?*

"We will stop them," she said, leaving out again the word hanging in both their minds. Revenge. *We will avenge these deaths.*

"They refused to defend themselves, refused to use violence," Meiind said, turning to look at Khalihl, tears in his eyes. "They chose to live by a higher ideal, by peace, and this is what happened." Again, the unsaid: *this is what always happens to the peaceful.*

They both sat silently for a few moments, lost in their thoughts, lost in their inner conflicts. Khalihl had seen death before, had killed and led her people to be killed in battle. She had listened to the stories of refugees, had known about what the Black Sun was capable of, had seen the looks of trauma and horror on the faces of men and women who had barely escaped them. She knew about this, knew what the Black Sun were doing to the planets they determined not worth their time in resources. But to see it with her own eyes, to be here among the millions dead, standing in the ashes of an entire planet – an entire planet! – was something else altogether. Whatever objectivity she had maintained up until this point fled from her heart and mind as shadow before light. In its place she felt a rising flame, a fury she had never known before, rising into the void. It didn't burn out of control, it wasn't a wildfire, but rather it rose with the steady consistency of a forge. She felt her heart hardening within its awful glow.

Eazkaii, she thought as her thoughts finally settled on a target. *Eazkaii.*

"You know what this means, of course," Meiind spoke again, dragging Khalihl from her thoughts.

"Yes," she replied. Up to now, the Black Sun had kept its activities constrained to the central corridors of old Co space, attacking and conquering the major planets and population centers. This made strategic sense: these planets are where the major ports could be found. Shipyards and manufacturing centers, resource processing plants. These were also the planets with the largest remnants of the Co Fleet, both in terms of soldiers and equipment. These planets added to the Strength of the Black Sun. But Bodhi was a planet of monks. No industry to speak of. No soldier class. No warships or weapons. Nothing of value to a group like the Black Sun. However, Bodhi was the inner-most planet of the Old Coalition, the planet closest to the center of the galaxy. Closest to the Inner Cluster.

"They are heading towards the Cluster," Khalihl said. "War is coming."

26

All things operate under the principle of momentum. Be wary of what you begin, lest it cannot be stopped.

-Anonymous

Bin Ald walked around the dimly lit room and wondered at how far they had come in so short a time. The only light came from the glow of dozens of computer monitors, each with a ghostly face in front of it. Each with a faithful man or woman doing the work of Allah. It was, after all, only a few weeks ago he had made his pitch to the group from the Original Way, had told them his ideas. And now look at them. They had gone from a few to a few hundred in that time, from a discussion to action, from folly to the glory of Allah. It humbled Bin Ald to know, by the power of the Almighty, they were bringing the will of Allah back to the people of the Inner Cluster.

As he walked up and down the rows of people at their workstations, answering the occasional question or intervening to offer advice, he thought about their growth and their mission. New members were joining their group every day, and these in turn converted their friends, their families, and sometimes they came to work here on the net campaign. This had been Oman's stroke of genius. By word of mouth, they were limited to New Mecca. With the Cluster net, they had already reached millions. And they could do so much! Not only could they put their ideas out there, they could organize events and meetings. Already, groups were meeting on six different Cluster planets, and there had been demonstrations on three of them. *The people are responding,* Bin Ald thought with wonder as he looked over the dark sea of floating, blue faces. *They feel the truth in their hearts.*

Bin Ald looked up, his eyes drawn by a sudden fan of light coming from the other side of the room, to see Oman enter. Oman met his eyes, nodded towards the office. Bin Ald, understanding, walked over. Once inside, they greeted each other like old friends. *And we are, now,* thought Bin Ald. *Together, we are changing our world for the better.*

"Hello brother," Bin Ald said, embracing Oman in the old way.

"Good morning brother," Oman responded. "How goes the work today?"

"As well as ever," Bin Ald sat behind the desk, motioned towards a seat for Oman to do the same. "We are growing every day, and we have demonstrations planned on more planets. Your idea has proven most effective."

"Did you see we made the news?"

"Did we now?" Bin Ald raised his eyebrows with mild concern. He had always known the day would come, but he was wary of it nonetheless.

"Yes," Oman brought out his pad and swiped to a news page. He handed it over to Bin Ald. "The faithful are becoming impatient."

Bin Ald took the pad and looked at the headline:

"New Musla Group Implicated in Refugee Attack." He skimmed the article quickly, a little alarmed. When he was finished, Bin Ald set the pad down on the table in front of him and lowered his head in thought. Oman, respecting this, waited. *How quickly it turns to violence,* Bin Ald thought, wondering at his own responsibility in this. A group of four men who claimed to be members of their group had beaten a refugee man from the Coalition nearly to death on the planet Oasis. The entire incident had been recorded by surveillance cameras; the men had been espousing Bin Ald's, nay the group's, views during the attack and had continued to do so, apparently, after being arrested and while being interviewed by the police. The possibility of violence as a means to an end, Bin Ald knew, was always there. Afterall, Allah often used violence to bring his will about. But Bin Ald had hoped for it to be a last resort. He had hoped to grow through more social and political means first and, perhaps, use violence only if needed. This jump troubled him.

"Did you read the comments after the article?" Oman asked, and Bin Ald sensed some relish in his voice and saw a gleam in his eye.

He wanted the violence, Bin Ald thought as he reached to pick the pad back up. *He had something to do with it.* It was true, while Bin Ald had advised their people use neutral language in their rhetoric online, Oman and some of his associates took a more inflammatory approach. They had argued about this, Bin Ald on the side of slow, consistent growth and Oman on the side of passionate, explosive intensity. People respond to passion, Oman had said. Just look at the Quran. Allah's people are motivated by the most ancient of emotions: fear, anger, hate. The love of peace is what, he had argued, drove the Musla to complacency in the first place. Bin Ald could not disagree with that. The Quran, and history for that matter, was full of examples where Allah's will was brought forth with the passions, often with violence. Allah knew how to use humanity's own demons for good, Oman had said.

Bin Ald scrolled down to the comments in the article and was surprised by what he saw. He looked up at Oman with the shock apparent in his eyes.

"They are inspired," Oman said, leaning forward with his hands on the table. "The faithful, they see action and they want more."

This certainly seemed the case, Bin Ald thought, looking back at the pad again. While some commentators bemoaned the violence, the vast majority were people who vehemently agreed with the attackers' motives, who wished to see the refugees pushed out by any means necessary. Much of the same sentiments which had led Bin Ald to his ideas, which had drawn others to him, were there in the words. People remembered the pain of the Cluster Wars and did not want to forgive and forget. People were afraid, and they looked at the actions of these men with hope. This troubled Bin Ald, but he could not deny the power of it, could not deny the response.

"Get a team of a few people together," Bin Ald said, handing the pad back. " I want you to work on getting in contact with those in the comments who responded positively to the article. They will want to know who we are."

Oman nodded and stood, smiling for a moment before turning and leaving the office. Bin Ald sat alone for a while, deep in thought, at once bothered by what he had learned and intrigued by the new information.

27

At some point, we must consider the possibility that the cosmos is silent not because it is empty but because it is a dangerous place, and silence is necessary to survival.

-Excerpt from The Quiet Cosmos: Theories and Explanations *by Jeck Vertion*

The trance did not come easy. Emotions – anger and fear and sadness – stormed in Meiind's mind as he tried to quiet it, tried to take control of his feelings and shunt them aside. Sadness at all he had lost, all the people he had known and loved who were no longer here. Fear of the future and the conflict surely coming. Anger at those who had committed this atrocity, who had destroyed the planet he had chosen as his home. Anger at the Black Sun. Rage.

Meiind took a deep breath, inhaling and exhaling as slowly as he could, and tried to re-center himself. He dared not open his eyes, though absorbing the landscape often helped him quiet his mind when his thoughts were being difficult to manage. He knew what he would see: the ashes of a dead planet, the remains of millions of people and of billions of acres of dead plant matter. No, that would not help. Better to keep his eyes closed and fight through without the fresh reminder of what had happened. Of what the Black Sun had done. Of what they would continue to do if they were not stopped.

Meiind kept his breathing calm, despite the pain splintering through him. Soon, he was sinking into the trance despite his feelings. It felt as though he was sliding into sleep, into a well-worn quiet his mind knew well and accepted. All those years of practice helped him push through his emotional responses to the tragedy surrounding him. *Emotions have their place,* he thought, the words ringing with simple clarity in his now empty mind, *and so does calm. I need calm. We need calm if we are going to find help.* With that thought, it was as if the lights of his thoughts were suddenly clicked off, and he was left with nothing but empty space within his mind. He could hear the echo of his breath entering and leaving his lungs, could hear the gentle roar of its passage reverberate through his skull. With each breath, he fell further into the trance, feeling it as though it were something physical, something happening to his body rather than his mind. Soon, he was there and could begin the search. His inner vision began to fill with the familiar clusters of light, the light of life throughout the galaxy, but he needed to find one source in the millions he could sense.

The Inner Cluster had estimated the coordinates of the origin of the message they had received from the Senders by tracing the signal back. Khalihl had shown Meiind a star map of the area, and he had memorized it as best he could. Now, he held that image in his mind and hoped the trance would do the rest. At first, there was nothing. No instinct to go in any direction. No push. No pull. But then, quite suddenly and gently, Meiind felt his mind sliding away from its current position, felt the fabric of whatever space he occupied while in the trance begin to stretch and fold within him. He was accustomed to the feeling and had given it much thought, but he had never fully understood it. What was it he felt? What was this space? Even Roshi Moyo had not been able to answer the question in a way that satisfied Meiind's analytical mind. To the Roshi, and to most of the Buddhi, there was something that existed in a pre-language state. Perhaps even a pre-rational state. To try and understand these things through reason and language, the Roshi had said, was like trying to paint a picture using the wind. The medium simply was not right. Some things could not be explained in language. Some things existed outside of physical reality, went beyond the bounds of word and thought.

The lights. The lights of life in the galaxy were now shifting in Meiind's inner vision until one particular cluster, surrounded by empty darkness, was centered in his mind. The cluster grew larger and larger, and Meiind realized his usual method for seeking information about alien species through the trance likely would not work here. He often singled out one individual and gently, ever so gently, reached and touched them. From this, he often was able to get the basics of a species: their history, their social structure, their ways of thinking. The things every individual in a species knew about their people. But, he realized, such general information would not be enough here. He needed more specific information, information about the Watchers, and about the message that had been sent to the Inner Cluster. He needed to find the information from those specific persons who had sent the warning. He needed to try something new.

Meiind had been practicing with the trance for over a decade now, and he had learned many things. One of them was the Roshi had been right: there are some things that exist on planes and levels that are not physical and which language cannot touch. Language, Meiind had realized over the years, was a physical thing, a response to and tool for understanding physical reality. It could not, by design, adequately describe and express things and ideas rooted beyond physicality. Beyond human reality. This is why,

Meiind had decided, abstract concepts like love and justice and religious ideas always relied so heavily on ambiguity and metaphor to get their points across. This, too, was why they were always so fraught with disagreement, so open to interpretation and too poorly suited for translation from individual to individual, let alone society to society. This lesson, sparked by Roshi Moyo's musing thoughts on Meiind's experiences in the trance, had been key in his education in how to use the trance, how to manipulate and move in it.

Before his inner vision could get too close to the cluster of light, before the individual pinpoints of life became too distinct from one another, Meiind stopped his mind's movements towards them and held the entirety of the cluster in his mind's eye. Then, rather than reach out with his touch to engage with just one, Meiind tried to embrace their entirety, tried to touch them all at once. He felt a sudden wash of sensation, an overwhelming sense of multiplicity coursing through his being. Information came crashing against the beach of his mind, and for a moment he was lost amongst the waves, lost in the torrent of impressions he was absorbing. It was like the first time he had entered the trance, the same sense of overwhelm and awe threatening to sweep his own identity away in the current. But, after a decade of practice, he was better prepared to handle it, better understood how to filter out what was unnecessary and focus on what he was looking for. He called forth to his mind the idea of the invasion fleet, of this alien species on their way to conquer human space, and strained the wall of consciousness he had touched through the part of his mind which held the image of the fleet. Almost instantly, the flood ceased and what was left coalesced into one – not thought, but more like a feeling, an impression, the sense of an idea. In this one, unified response to Meiind's attempt to constrict the flow of information into a trickle dealing only with the invasion fleet, he felt something different. He sensed recognition, agency. Someone in there, someone in the group with which he was interacting had felt his presence and responded, had understood his questioning touch and had sent a message back. The transmission hit Meiind with such force he was knocked out of his trance and left blinking into the starlit darkness of the now night sky. It had been one emotion, one feeling, concentrated into one word. Meiind sat, stunned, looking out over the darkened valley in which no light burned anymore, in which no living soul breathed. The stars above cast a heavenly glow over the dead village and the empty planet, and Meiind felt a coldness creeping up his spine, felt the residual tingle of the message he had received reverberating through his entire being.

Something terrible is coming for us, he thought, still stunned. *Something we cannot understand.*

The feeling he had received had been fear. Utter and devastating fear. Fear that drives peoples to madness and self-destruction. Fear that cannot be pushed aside, cannot be reasoned out of. And the word had been singular, laced with the energy of that fear, a single word which coalesced an entire species' experience:

RUN.

<u>28</u>

One faithful can move a mountain; imagine what three, four, a hundred can do.

-Unknown

Maldeck looked up from his coffee at those seated around him in the small shop. The establishment was modest, just a room and some tables where men and women could sit and have some food and drink together. A low roof and low lighting added to the intimacy of the place. Maldeck had become a frequent patron here, as had many others who had been there for his speech. The proprietors, an elderly couple, were of the faithful. They refused service to Cluster citizens, choosing instead to serve only their kind. They would be rewarded, no doubt, in heaven for their faith.

Maldeck saw many faces he now knew well, and some he recognized but had become distant to him. It had been a few weeks since his speech, and his words had drawn lines between the pure and willing to sacrifice and those who made the same mistakes of the past. Some decried the schism, but Maldeck knew the necessity of it. God's ways were not up for discussion or interpretation. Let the weak of spirit damn themselves, but he would not allow them to take their culture with them.

He caught the eye of a man he knew well, Luke, and

nodded. Luke stood and walked over to a table with a family who did not belong here. After a few, hushed words, the family stood, keeping their eyes down, and left under the watchful gaze of the faithful. Luke glanced at Maldeck, whom nodded again. The owner of the shop, a man they called Eber, walked over to the front door and locked it, flipping the "Open" sign to "Closed."

Without any instruction, everyone stood and began to push their tables to the sides of the room, leaving their chairs. Once the tables were out of the way, they arranged their chairs in a circle and sat, leaving Maldeck standing in the middle. As he watched them settle into their seats, Maldeck felt a stirring in his heart. These were his people, those faithful to the same God as him. They would die for their ways, as would he. They could not be defeated. He knew pride to be a sin, but he also knew the pride he now felt in his heart as he looked over these true brothers and sisters to be a gift from God. He would need strength to lead this flock, and the pride would be a strong source of that.

"Let us begin with a prayer," he said gently, opening his arms and turning so as to sweep all the souls here into his presence. They all bowed their heads and closed their eyes, hands clasped, as Maldeck began, "Lord in Heaven, I thank you for those seated here today. These are the souls faithful to You and to Your word. These are the souls who have sacrificed to keep Your ways pure so they may not be lost. These are the souls who truly believe, not only in spirit but in action. Bless them Lord. Show them Your abundant love and grace. Protect us Lord, as we seek to spread Your ways to the unbelieving and show us the path that will lead to Your Kingdom come. Amen."

The group echoed the end of the prayer, and Maldeck sat at their head. "Thank you all for coming," he said, looking at the group. "It is good to know the faithful are here and willing to meet. We will need to keep strong to one another if we are going to keep our faith. The Lord tells us we are each our brother's keeper. It is my hope in these meetings to offer guidance and support to one another so we may not lose our way like others already have." There were murmurs and nods all around. "It is also my hope, in these meetings, we may discuss and discover ways to bring our people back from the temptations they have fallen into. But first, I want to ask you all a question: what have you seen? In what ways are our people straying from the path? We need not name names, but if we are to combat this loss of faith on the part of our brothers and sisters, we must better understand their actions and thoughts if we can."

It was silent for a moment but for the small sounds some in attendance made as they uneasily readjusted themselves in their seats. Maldeck looked around the room until a young man raised his hand. Maldeck nodded and sat back.

"My name is Bindo, and what I have seen has bothered me greatly. Namely, I have seen some of our people fraternizing with the Sihken, inviting them to eat in their homes and spending time with them. At first I told myself it wasn't so bad. After all, didn't Jesus spend time with the unfaithful, with the worst of society, during his ministry? But I have seen the loosening of their ways through this, have seen them even adopt some strange practices in place of our own. I have even heard one person wonder aloud if perhaps we all serve the same God."

Again, there were murmurs as the people in attendance shook their heads and offered commiserating thoughts.

"You are right to speak, Bindo," said Maldeck,

addressing everyone though he looked only at the young man. "Association with those who do not hold to the Path, whether with Sihken or atheists or the Buddhi, is the primary way we as a people tend to lose our ways. We see this in our history, and the lesson is clear: keep to yourselves! Protect your ways! You are right, Jesus broke these rules in his ministry but allow me to ask: are you Christ?" Bindo shook his head. Maldeck looked down the line of people. "Are you? You? Is anyone here the Christ?" Shaking heads all around. "We see the folly of trying to be too much like the Savior then. Christ is the Messiah, is God incarnate, and the laws of our Lord do not apply to him the same way they apply to us. God gave us the path because we are human and, as such, fallible. The path is what keeps us strong. While Jesus offers us guidance in His perfection, we cannot hope to achieve that ourselves. To think such is hubris, the very basis of sin itself. This was the folly of the 21st century church and the reason we are so fractured now, the reason there are so few of us on the true path still. By trying to mimic Christ rather than following God's commandments exactly, our ancestors opened themselves, unknowingly, to the temptations of Satan."

Words of approval sounded, and another man raised his hand to speak. The meeting continued for some time, with each in attendance describing a concern they had and Maldeck using the observation to create a lesson for his flock. This was how he had come to think of them. His flock. They would need his guidance and his wisdom if they were to succeed in their mission. And Maldeck knew the power of grievance. He knew, through these meetings, through their shared experiences, they were building a wall around them which would keep them pure from the influence of others. They would, over time, come to identify themselves with him and with each other, and these bonds, as they strengthened, would be the glue holding them together when the way became difficult, when God asked much of them. That day was coming, Maldeck knew, though he did not know what would be expected. *The way is not easy,* he thought as he listened to another add to the list of fears they had. *God asks much of the faithful.*

29

We may be pacifists, but there are other ways to resist than through violence. Indeed, we are of the belief the most powerful forms of resistance are not physical. We believe true victory can never be won by becoming the enemy.

-*Excerpt from* Meditations: the Collected Writings of Roshi Mendact

Night had fallen, and the village lights went up automatically as they had always done, bathing the eerily empty streets in a soft, yellow glow. Not enough to make seeing easy, but enough for you to walk around and not run into things. Meiind had told Khalihl that the Buddhi preferred the low light levels in order to reduce light pollution. The Buddhi believed it important to be able to see the stars every night. She had to admit the wisdom in the idea. Above her, above the empty and dead planet, the Milky Way exploded in dusty grandeur, pinpoints of bright light spreading from horizon to horizon. It was utterly beautiful and humbling, and Khalihl found some comfort in the vastness she felt in the space above her. Ashes to ashes, stardust to stardust… while she wandered through the dead streets, stirring up the layer of ash left by the destruction of every living being on Bodhi, she took comfort in the view spanning the sky overhead. The galaxy, the universe, was so vast, so massive, and humanity so small. *Perhaps it is cliché*, she thought, *but there is comfort to be had in the realization that we don't matter as much as we think we do.*

She looked back over her shoulder, up the street she had just walked up. She could just barely see the dimly lit form of Meiind sitting in the middle of the road where it dipped down a hill and into the valley that held the capital village of Bodhi. He had wanted to be above the village, had wanted a vantage point of space and distance. He had been uncertain about whether or not this would work without the support of the Monks, but they had both decided trying to contact the Senders still was the correct course of action. Whatever tragedies had befallen the people here, whatever threat and evil the Black Sun posed, the alien fleet still marched towards the Inner Cluster. They still needed whatever information they could gather in whatever way they could.

Here, at the top of the hill where Khalihl now wandered above the village proper were most of Bodhi's government buildings. One street lined with low offices, a few residences for those whose duties required them to be available often. Khalihl marveled at how simple their life must have been here that they could sustain a population of 25 million with so few resources. A part of her admired the Bodhi commitment to simplicity and minimalism. Her life had been anything but in the last year. In the last decade, really. How often had she wished to leave everything behind and join one of the Isla'hai communes scattered throughout the Cluster? To retire from her duties and to commit herself to the spirit and the mind, to her religion and to academics. History. That was what she had found most interesting in school, especially the history of her people in the late 22nd and early 23rd centuries. She remembered the classes she took in those periods, the books she read, remembered wishing she could have been there to witness the transformation of her people from a misunderstood, often oppressed, and just as often oppressing people to what they were now, beacons of reason and learning in human occupied space. The change, she knew, had been at heavy cost. The ashes she now waded in, ashes from the flesh and bones of people… her culture had this kind of horror on its conscience as well. The Isla'hai may have transformed into something new and different in the late 22nd century, but the 100 years before had been full of violence and death, much of it unnecessary. Much of that blood was on their hands.

Khalihl came up to a small hut which attracted her attention. Nothing but a frame left, she knew, at one time, the hut had been made of Bodhi vines guided and bent to grow into the form of a hut. The monks here lived in these Bodhi structures, taking years to slowly and gently form the growing vines into their desired shapes. What resulted was a living home, self-repairing and well-insulated against the extremes of weather. It also required minimal resource processing – simply put up the frame and tend the vines. Now, there was nothing left but the frame and a pile of ash almost knee high. A nearby light cast spaces of shadow through the interior of the hut. Khalihl made to step inside and stopped, glancing over her shoulder at the distant silhouette sitting cross-legged in the road at the top of the hill. She found herself arrested by the sight.

Meiind had explained to her the trance, had explained to her what he knew about it and what he had learned from it. A galaxy full of life! What a wonder, and yet it brought more questions to mind. Uncomfortable questions, one of which had been ringing through Khalihl's mind ever since Meiind had told her about the alien life he had explored while in the trance. *If the galaxy is full of intelligent life, as Meiind says, then why haven't we found a signal, an artifact, anything?* Humanity had been scouring the skies in all directions for hundreds of years, and nothing conclusive had ever been found. Khalihl believed Meiind, knew he would not lie. And his abilities had already proven themselves. Had he not found the prison planet? Had he not contacted her just when she needed to speak with him? Why, then, this silence in the void? This apparent but false emptiness? Khalihl saw one likely possibility: these civilizations did not want contact. But why they chose silence was another issue altogether. Khalihl's intuition, however, told her the alien fleet on the way to the Cluster was somehow connected to this revelation. Perhaps the Senders as well. There simply was not enough information to know that connection. Khalihl was tired of the asymmetry, tired of making important decisions with limited knowledge. So much rested on what they did now, on how her people planned and prepared, and they knew so little! The difference between life and death rested in what they did and did not know. Khalihl looked away from Meiind, still in the light at the end of the road. *Perhaps he can learn something that can help us.* She turned back to the hut before her.

Inside, she found a single room home, the small living quarters of some monk of the Buddhi. Untouched from the layer of ash outside, the room was immaculate, everything clean and in its place. She scanned the interior of the hut, taking notice of the small details which stood out to her. The hut was sparse but comfortable seeming. Save a small light bulb hanging from the ceiling in the center of the room, there didn't seem to be anything electronic. No computer, no viewer, nothing of that nature. Just a small desk and chair with some writing utensils and papers spread out on its surface. Khalihl looked over the papers, hoping for some clue as to the last few moments of this planet's life, but instead she found what appeared to be some sort of translation in process. Next to the desk was a small bookshelf packed with slim volumes, mostly unmarked. She flipped through a few. They seemed to be split between personal journals and reprints of religious and philosophical texts, as well as a few larger tomes on physics and mathematics. In the center of the room was a low table with tea and eating implements organized neatly in one corner. Lastly, in one corner, there was a bed, a mat on the floor really. That was when she noticed it. The pile of ash on the bed.

Khalihl walked over and stood above the bed, looking down at the ash. Whomever it was had died laying down, one arm stretched out; the ash had settled in the shape of a human body. Khalihl was struck with a sense of awe and trepidation. *25 million people,* she thought, *and they had each died like this. Peacefully and willingly.* Meiind had told her of the Buddhi's refusal to defend themselves, their utter rejection of violence. At first, she had felt similarly to him: she could not understand their refusal, could not understand their acceptance of not just death but of annihilation. Extinction. While Buddhi would continue, Bodhi and its native plants and animals, as well as the way of life the Buddhi developed here... all of it was gone forever. Khalihl had felt almost as much anger at the Buddhi as she had at the Black Sun. *If they would have just asked for help sooner,* she had thought. But now, looking at the ashen body left in its bed and home, her feelings shifted. She suddenly saw and understood the power of their refusal, the statement in their pacifism. What more complete rejection of human folly could there possibly be than to refuse to engage even in self-defense? *This wasn't a display of weakness,* she thought with growing admiration. *It was inaction as strength, inaction as rebellion. You could never conquer a people like these.* Most humans killed for their beliefs. The Buddhi had died for them. *They died on their own terms, free until the very end.*

Khalihl turned to leave when she noticed something strange about the shape on the bed before her. While the ash had fallen in a shape recognizable as a body, a line of ash stretched from the body's left shoulder, up and out. As if the person here had been reaching for something as she or he died. The thin line of gray ash continued off the mat onto the floor and ended right against the wall. For reasons unknown even to herself, Khalihl got down on her knees for a closer look at the panel the ash led her eyes to. Nothing. There was nothing there but a smear of ash across a small section of the wall. Khalihl was about to stand when, under some strange impulse, she placed her hand atop the ash on the wall, over what she assumed had been the person's hand. She felt it then. A barely discernible edge. She could not see anything, no matter how closely she looked, but she could just feel the gap in the panel. Khalihl ran her fingers along the edge, tracing the outline of a small square. She began pushing on it in different parts. Then, with her fingers pushing in the upper right hand corner of the nearly invisible box and with a slight give and click, a piece of the wall swung open to reveal a small, hidden compartment.

She had to get down onto her elbows to look inside the newly revealed space, but it was too dark to see anything. Khalihl reached in slowly, tentatively, feeling around. She pulled out a small, wooden box and a stack of papers which appeared to be official in nature. Certificates, identification, and the like. She recognized the name she saw printed on each. Ryu Moyo. The Roshi of the Buddhi here on this planet. Their leader. Khalihl glanced back at the shape of ash on the bed, back at the humble hut in which she was. The leader of 25 million people, more if you counted the faithful living on other planets throughout both the old Coalition and the Inner Cluster, and this is where he died. In a hut indistinguishable from the millions of other huts to be found on the planet, alone and without fanfare. Her awe and respect grew. *This was a great man,* she thought, *a man who knew the power of humility. Who saw through the chaff and into the heart of existence.*

Khalihl returned her attention to the small pile of things she had just brought out of the hidden compartment, setting aside the papers and turning the wood box over in her hands. It appeared to be made of the wood of the Bodhi vine, like so much else here on the Buddhi planet. Polished until the surface shone like a mirror, Khalihl could see her reflection in the sides. The lid had inscriptions along the border in a language she could not read. On one side was a small, unlocked latch holding the lid down. After a moment's thought, Khalihl opened the box; she did not feel good about it, about invading this man's privacy, but they needed as much information as they could get about what had happened here, and as the leader of the planet, the Roshi was likely to have some to offer. Inside the box were two small items: a memory crystal and a portable playback device. Having already made her decision, Khalihl did not hesitate to insert the crystal into the device and activate it. Immediately, Roshi Moyo's soft voice filled the hut.

"I am Ryu Moyo, Roshi of the Buddhi here on planet Bodhi. If you are listening to this, then we have all likely perished. As of this recording, the Black Sun are in orbit and have made no response to our hails. We did not expect any. They have little patience for societies like ours, spiritual and religious in nature, and we have little to offer in way of tribute or soldiers. Our council has discussed our options. We fully expect to be destroyed."

Khalihl listened, transfixed by the utter calm in the man's voice. No signs of panic, of anger, of fear, of desperation. No sign whatsoever he and his people were about to be massacred by the most violent political faction to come to power in human space in two centuries. He may as well have been reading the news posts for a planet on the other side of the galaxy. She did hear, however, a kind of compassion she had never encountered before, a compassion that loves both good and evil but that accepts its fate with equanimity. Again, the thought struck her: *A great man. We, humanity, are less without him.* She glanced back at the ashes of his remains while the voice on the recorder continued.

"I have nothing to say; indeed, leaving a recording goes something against my beliefs. I hope my life has spoken for me already. But I have responsibilities, and while we Buddhi reject violence even in self-defense, we do not begrudge others the instinct to fight back. We are all human, even those in orbit above Bodhi who prepare our destruction. We forgive them, for they know not what they do."

Here, the Roshi stopped speaking for a moment, though the recorder had picked up and now played back his breath. Shallow shuddering breaths struggling to become deep and calming. Khalihl could hear the breaths of a man with too much on his shoulders, a man ultimately up to the task of seeing his people into death, a man of faith and honor, a man who knew there were deaths worse than physical annihilation, who knew you could keep your life but lose your soul, who was trying to preserve the spirit of his people and of his ancestors and of his philosophy. The breaths on the playback became, after a few moments, long and calm. The voice began again.

"We have intercepted some signals between parts of the Black Sun fleet, uncovered information that may be of use to anyone who is fighting against them. The Black Sun plans to invade the Inner Cluster next."

Khalihl's mind immediately started racing at those words, snapping into a mode of thinking reserved for command. They, both her and the Elder council, had known this was coming, had known the Black Sun would not suffer the Inner Cluster as a competing power and social structure within human space. An ideology like theirs left no room for multiple ways of being. Their entire sense of existence relied on them being the only way, the correct way. Thankfully, the Black Sun did not have access to skipping. While they did have some of the old batteries, which Cluster scientists theorized they had weaponized in order to commit atrocities like what they had done here on Bodhi, their slow progress through old Co space revealed they did not have the drives to use them for instantaneous travel through space. This meant the Inner Cluster had time. *It will take the Black Sun, at sublight speeds, more than ten years to reach cluster space,* Khalihl thought, calculating. *Time enough to-*

"The Black Sun is impatient," the Roshi's voice continued, interrupting her thoughts. "They are not planning to go straight to the Inner Cluster, for they know they would be detected well in advance of their arrival and the Cluster would have time to arm themselves. Instead, they have fallen on another plan. They have discovered, somehow, the location of the prison planet Meiind uncovered, the place where skip technology was developed and powered. If we are dead, if Bodhi has been sterilized like so many planets before us, then the Black Sun are on their way there in hopes of reverse-engineering new skip drives. In hopes of conquering the Inner Cluster sooner."

With that, the recording abruptly ended, and Khalihl could almost see the Roshi rushing to put his things in the secret compartment in the wall, closing the panel with his dying breath, his arm outstretched to shut the door while it turned to ash before his eyes. *Thank you,* she thought gravely as she looked at his remains. *Thank you for the warning. This changes everything.*

<u>30</u>

Fight or flight, the most ancient of choices. All illusions of free will stem from this original dichotomy: either stay and protect what you have or give it up and flee but survive. With a far back enough perspective, any action can be traced back to that.

-*Excerpt from* Meditations on Original Action *by Lebraan Jelisco*

They appeared in high orbit above New Mecca. While she checked the controls of her ship, Khalihl took a moment to thank whatever poor soul it had been who had just powered their skip. The thought still horrified her, but after all these years she had to become accustomed to it. *How many people,* she wondered. *How many people were killed, murdered, for our convenience?* With this thought came a powerful sense of guilt and shame. She had to remind herself the use of the skip engines, of what they had left, was warranted in this case. With the Watchers coming, they didn't have much of a choice. Not to mention the Black Sun. Khalihl felt a tide of hopelessness threaten to overtake her, and she focused her mind on the task at hand and pushed the feeling away. *Neither the time nor the place.*

New Mecca hung in her viewscreen like a jewel, blue and green and white, a lovely oasis in the vast void of space. It warmed her heart to see her home, and she focused her energies on that feeling, on the planet and the hope it represented. They had already survived so much. They would survive this, if they could. She considered calling out to Meiind, to have him come see the view, but thought better of it. He had not spoken much since Bodhi, mostly staying in one of the ship's small quarters, and she had chosen to respect his seclusion. She could not imagine what he was going through. The pain and anger, the suffering and anguish. As of yet, Khalihl had not been personally affected by the Black Sun. Meiind, meanwhile, had been through so much.

The comm chirped with landing permissions from the government space port in the capital city. She put in the commands necessary to bring her ship over the city. It would be twenty minutes or so before they landed, so Khalihl sat back to watch the planet grow in the viewscreen, the geographic features now coming into view. She could just make out the Great Eastern Ocean, the one they called the Stillness, stretching across much of the planet visible to her now, separating the two major landmasses of New Mecca. Now they were coming over the western continent, the Peninsula, shaped like a spike jutting out of the ocean. As she watched the planet turn below them, now revealing the uppermost corner of the massive mountain range, the End Times, which ended with the peaks known as the Five Prophets just outside of the capital, Khalihl's mind turned to her own losses, her own fears about the future. She was, she had to admit, afraid she was not up to the task before her. Her mind reeled at everything she had just so recently learned. The Black Sun was on their way to New Mecca, surely a battle to the death. The Watchers would be arriving at close to the same time, looking to exterminate humanity. All the while, the refugee crisis continued and, if the newslines were to be believed, there was unrest in the Inner Cluster.

People were responding violently to the influx of Coalition refugees. Not too many, but enough it would have to be dealt with somehow, enough that groups were beginning to form on an anti-refugee platform. Khalihl didn't understand it. Perhaps her training in history had been more in-depth in the military academy than the public schools got into, but to her it seemed obvious claims against immigration, against helping groups who were once your enemies, were always very short sighted. On a long enough timeline, and humanity had a fairly long timeline under its belt now, and with enough distance for perspective, and humanity had felt first-hand the vastness of space, divisions of the kind these groups demarcated began to seem arbitrary and indefensible. Didn't these people see the circles in their thinking? Didn't they hear the echoes of a past not worth reliving? Didn't they know the seductive call of the "good old days," of past greatness and supposed social cohesion, was nothing more than the siren's wail, nothing more than a lie that never truly existed, a trick of retrospect?

I wish he was here. He would know what to do. The thought came unbidden to Khalihl's mind and with it a heavy sensation in her chest. She knew the feeling well; it came every time thoughts of Raasch emerged. She took a moment to allow herself the indulgence of these emotions as, on her viewscreen, the capital city came into view. What was normally a happy sight now gave her a moment of pause. She knew she would do whatever it took to protect her people, her home, but doubt gnawed in the back of her mind. She thought of the strength Raasch had shown, so many years ago, of his steadiness, his constant readiness. His sense of command. And she tried to conjure the same qualities up in herself. They needed Raasch now, but he was beyond them. He had done his part. Khalihl knew someone would have to take up his mantle now, and she felt beneath the task. As the details of the city began to appear – the massive park in the city center and the Grand Mosque jutting up from the surrounding landscape, its domes and spires fancifully rising to meet the sky, to meet them on their descent, the massive buildings in the financial sector to the south gleaming like the teeth of civilization, the unending sprawl of humanity in the blocked out buildings surrounding these monuments and then in the suburban neighborhoods spread out to the now closer horizon – Khalihl allowed herself one more wishful thought. *Wherever you are,* she thought despite her own agnosticism, *give me strength for the ordeals coming.*

●●●●

"Tell us about your experience," Elder Serjevko said.

The statement was directed at Meiind, who stood next to Khalihl in the chamber of the Elder Council. He felt exhausted, physically and emotionally. *That's not quite it,* he thought, *I feel empty.* The loss of Bodhi, of all the Buddhi, of Roshi Moyo, had left him deeply lost. Emotions surged through him in a way he had never experienced. There was fear of the Black Sun, the destroyer of not only Bodhi but of the remnants of the Coalition. There was sadness at the death, the utter wanton destruction. The image of the completely dead planet, the pipal trees and the people and the buildings – everything – gone, a layer of ash in their place, was burned into his mind such that he seemed to see it no matter what he was looking at. Then, most difficult of all, was the anger. He seethed with fury in all directions, directed at the universe. He had spent the short trip back from Bodhi in meditation, trying to control his anger, but only one thought remained: *I can make them pay.* Guilt and shame at the thought always followed close behind. He had already broken his oath once.

"I will try," he said, trying to keep his voice from shaking with anger. Khalihl would tell the Council of the destruction of Bodhi and of the message from the Roshi. He could focus only on his own experience in the trance. "I managed to enter the trance without the Monks' help." A stab of pain, a flame of fury. "Once in the trance, I managed, using the coordinates given to me, to locate the Senders, and to make contact. They responded with terror."

"Terror at you? At humanity?" Elder Morejas asked, leaning forward in his seat with his chin in his hand.

"Not exactly," Meiind replied, closing his eyes and trying to remember as clearly as possible. "They were afraid of the discovery, of the contact. It was simply being known which terrified them. And the fear itself, it was like nothing I had ever experienced. An entire species, whatever they are, unified by the feeling of fear. It was overwhelming, terrifying. I tried to make contact with them, tried to reach out, but the fear kept me at bay."

"Were you able to ask them anything, able to ask their advice?" Serjevko asked.

"I tried, but they would not allow me to get close, to get anywhere within. Somehow, they were able to, as one, fortify themselves against close inspection."

"Perhaps," chimed in Isdet, "it is a defensive technique they developed. If they know of the Watchers, then it is possible their primary defense has been concealment. Maybe they are each individually trained to avoid contact with any kind of outside interaction."

"That was my thought as well," Meiind said. "But I

did manage to get across my reason for seeking them out. And someone did send a message back."

"What did they say?" Hujad's voice betrayed anticipation.

"Only one word: RUN." Meiind's voice fell ringing into the silence left. That one word, which had haunted his thoughts since, now in the open, was like a sunburst which burnt away everything, which shed all illusion and delusion and left only the truth. And the truth was a hard one.

"Thank you for sharing, Meiind," Serjevko said after a moment, his voice quite heavy in the silence. "Khalihl, what do you make of it?"

"Sir," Khalihl said, taking a deep breath. She had been thinking much about the message, about what they knew and what they did not know, in anticipation for this question. "What we do not know is the motivation of the invasion fleet. A few possibilities come to mind: space, or resources, which is much the same thing. These seem unlikely, considering the amount of apparently empty space between us. Why would they need to travel ten years for resources they likely have closer and they could likely attain without battle? More likely, then, is technology. We have all read the theories positing humanity's discovery of the source was a fluke, a non-linear jump in technological progression. It is possible they want that, our skip tech."

"How could they know we have it?" Thans asked.

"The Hero's Battle," Khalihl responded. "The Hero's Battle was the single largest military engagement using skipping in our history. It is possible the spatial disruptions caused by the thousands of ships skipping in such a short interval could have been detected throughout the galaxy. It is plausible the Watchers picked up the distortions with their sensors and divined the likely cause of such readings."

"You sound doubtful."

"The Sender's response to Meiind's attempt at contact suggests another possibility, though the two are not necessarily mutually exclusive." This line of thinking had occupied much of Khalihl's mind in the last hours, and she was unsure of airing out half-thought theories based on pure speculation and intuition. The Council, however, looked at her expectantly. She glanced at Meiind, who had the same look of interest on his face. "If the Senders were fearful of *discovery,* then it follows they have been trying to hide. Theorists have long posited, both in science and in less formulaic methods, the possibility of some marauding species as an explanation for the apparent lack of life in the galaxy. We know Meiind has seen the galaxy teems with life." She looked at him again, and he nodded his agreement. "Perhaps the theory still applies to the silence of the galaxy, not the emptiness. Perhaps any species who achieves technological maturity does so by learning to hide from… well, from whatever the Watchers are."

"What is it they would want, under this possibility?"

"I don't know."

There was a moment of silence as what Khalihl proposed sunk in. She understood their reaction, their awed quiet. She had been thinking about this possibility the entire way home, and the concept of a galaxy full of life yet terrified to venture forth because of some powerful species bent on – on what? What could motivate such a species? Khalihl had thought and read and thought and read and had found nothing to illuminate what such motives could be.

"Which of these is the most likely scenario, in your opinion?" Serjevko asked her. Then he turned to Meiind. "I am asking this of you as well, Meiind. You are the one who interacted with them. Did anything in your interactions seem to make one possibility more likely than the other?"

Khalihl and Meiind traded glances. They had not spoken much on the way home. Khalihl had chosen to respect Meiind's privacy, to let him be alone with his thoughts and emotions. The destruction of Bodhi, his home for the last ten years… she simply could not imagine. She nodded for him to answer.

"It is difficult to say, Herr Serjevko," Meiind said after a moment's pause. "The terror I felt from them was more powerful than anything I have ever felt. It wasn't terror for one's own life, though that is a powerful feeling of course. No, it was… bigger than that. It was terror for one's own species. It was existential terror." Meiind paused and took a breath. "Khalihl's analysis rings true with what I perceived. The Senders were not afraid of conquest. They were afraid of destruction. Regardless of the Watcher's motives, I believe they are coming to annihilate us."

Even though this had been the tenor of Khalihl's thoughts since Bodhi, hearing it aloud, hearing it validated by someone else, made her head reel some. She grounded herself to the floor, focusing for a moment on her posture and on her breathing, while a wave of nausea passed through her. Looking up, she saw the same feelings reflected in the faces of the men and women of the Elder Council. She could see their wheels turning, could almost hear the self-doubting thoughts whirring through their minds. *How could anybody,* she thought, *think themselves equal to this?*

"I do not think we can keep this from the public any longer," Cabrenejos said quietly into the tense room. "Our call for volunteers yielded good returns, but we will need more if this coming battle is one of attrition, one to the death. We will have to tell the people what we are up against." The Council, along with Khalihl and Meiind, all nodded in numb agreement. "Beyond preparing for the coming conflict, do you have any other recommendations, Admiral?"

"Yes, sir," Khalihl snapped quickly, the use of her title jutting her mind into a military mode of thinking. She felt her thoughts snap into place as the dread and terror faded behind the pragmatic parts of her mind. "I have two things to add, sir. The first is we must consider this is an enemy we know nothing about. We know nothing of their technology, how advanced they are, nor even what they will look like. Considering the Senders and their terror, we must consider the possibility this is a battle we cannot win."

Khalihl's words echoed.

"As such, I think, in addition to preparing the military, we must consider at least a partial evacuation of our territory. That way, if this fleet is truly coming to commit xenocide, some of humanity may have a chance of surviving."

The council absorbed the idea with calm looks on their faces. Khalihl sensed they had reached some sort of threshold in their thinking. They were no longer surprised by anything, and their minds had been so stretched so as to be wide open to any possibilities. Khalihl admired their equanimity. *Extreme times,* Khalihl thought. *Extreme measures.* Their ability to handle such things, even things like this, something perhaps no human had ever had to shoulder before, was why they were on the council.

"You are recommending we run?" Thans asked.

"Partially," Khalihl answered. "Considering our lack of knowledge about the threat, we must take the Sender's advice seriously."

"We could rebuild the old generation ships, the ones that brought us here so long ago," Hujad said. "But we would only be able to evacuate a several million souls, maybe ten million or so."

"That is better than losing all of humanity," Serjevko said with an edge in his voice. "Ten million could have a chance of flourishing. And if we survive, they could be recalled."

For a moment, a sense of the absurd threatened to overtake Khalihl. Were they really operating under the assumption an alien species was coming to wipe them out? But the facts were there, regardless of whether her brain had evolved to handle such possibilities or not, and she pushed the feeling down.

"One more thing, sir," Khalihl said. "On Bodhi, we found a message left from the Roshi. He must have recorded it just before the planet was... sterilized. In the message, he seemed to be under the impression the Black Sun had located the prison planet, that they were going to go there to try and acquire what is left of the skip drives."

"How could they know of that information?" Morejas asked.

"I do not know sir," Khalihl answered. She had thought much about that question but had not arrived at any satisfactory conclusions. "But we must take the chance seriously. For the Black Sun to have access to skipping would be disastrous. They would be able to accelerate their conquest, and we would be fighting them well before we are ready. We must reinforce the prison planet, or bring the technology, what is left, back to our territory. They must not be allowed to gain access to it."

"Agreed," said Serjevko. "That would make our difficult position much worse." He stalled, and for a moment Khalihl saw something on the Elder's face she had never seen before. For the briefest of nanoseconds, she saw despair flicker through his eyes, quickly replaced with resolve. What she saw scared her. How many times had she depended on the Council's seemingly indefatigable strength? To see that strength and resolve falter, even for the slightest of moments, hit Khalihl hard in her gut. She felt a new fear rising, a fear she had up till now simply ignored.

"That is all for now, Admiral Khalihl, Herr Meiind," Serjevko continued, his voice purposefully resolute. "The Council will consider what you have told us, as well as your recommendations for moving forward. Thank you both for your service. When we have made our decisions, you will be summoned again. You are dismissed."

••••

Khalihl left the Elder Council with her heart in turmoil. She and Meiind exchanged half-felt pleasantries before parting ways, making plans for dinner that evening. Neither felt much like expressing their thoughts at the moment. Too much had happened which they had not had time to process yet. They were emotionally drained and needed time to recharge themselves.

Instead of heading home to her flat near the Grand Mosque, Khalihl went for a walk. She took the pedestrian path circling through and around the entire city, a favorite of hers when she felt the need to think. She was troubled, and as she walked away from the council and through the large park surrounding it, she watched the people around her – friends and families out for a lovely day – and tried to settle her mind into a productive state. The existential terror which had piqued during the meeting with the Elder Council was still there; she could sense it on the edges of the awareness waiting to flood her mind the moment she let it. She wondered about the men and women and the children she saw as she walked. She envied their innocence, their naivete. *They have no idea what is coming,* she thought, surprised to sense a drop of bitterness seeping through the puncture in her mind. She had, for many years, worked, even risked her life, to serve these people – her people – and never once had she felt anything but love and respect for the people she served. *I must be getting old for this,* she thought. *But they will all know soon enough. And then we will all be in this together.*

She let the bitterness pass through her without much more thought. She was tired, scared, even a little hungry, and knew enough to not take too much stock in whatever mental state she found herself in from moment to moment. She could not expect herself to keep calm and strong all the time. So long as she did not allow her impermanent states to define her, did not act on them, these feelings were nothing more than her dealing with the fears and worries she had. She laughed a little to herself. In her youth, she had often been angry with herself when she felt she was doing a poor job of controlling her emotions. Now, she knew better. Controlling your emotions had nothing to do with stopping their flow and everything to do with how you reacted to them. They could, and would, always come, but that did not mean they had to be paid much attention to.

Already, Khalihl felt better, calmer, clearer of mind.

The walking and the air, the sound of the people living their lives around her, the view of the horizon now as she came over a hill in the park and looked down into a small valley with a pond and the first of the houses surrounding the open space… she took these in and was comforted by their familiarity. By their wholesomeness. For her, home, New Mecca, had always been a source of peace and strength. It was no different now.

As she continued to walk, the sun setting behind her and casting long shadows from trees and houses askew and across her path, she took a deep breath and set her mind to the things she had already learned, trying to parse out the important unknowns. The Black Sun was the most known threat. They had good intelligence on the size and capabilities of the fleet. If they could keep them from getting the skip drives at the prison planet, if they could keep the Black Sun on their original timeline, then it was likely the Cluster could be prepared in time such that they would be able to defend themselves. But then, how much time would they have before the Watchers arrived, and how much defensive capability would they have left? Khalihl felt the gap in her knowledge about the alien threat like a physical thing, like a space in her mind she simply could not access. There were so many questions, questions about who they were, what they wanted, how they wanted to get it. The optimist in her still hoped for a peaceful resolution. There was always the chance communication could solve the issue, that perhaps there was some other reason the Watchers were coming. But Khalihl did not take much stock in this hope, considering the Senders and their fears. They would have to hope – first seeking a peaceful resolution would be the ethical thing to do – but they would also have to be prepared for the worst.

Then Khalihl's thoughts drifted to the neighborhood she found herself in. It was typically suburban fare: rows of neatly similar houses, with some modular variation, all on trim lawns. Aside from the style of the homes, all very modern and angular, the scene looked like something out of the 21st century. Khalihl mused for a moment on how little the ways in which people lived had changed since those times. Apartment blocks in the city, homes in the suburbs, land in the rural areas. While everything else had changed, from transportation to food production to the economy, home life had stayed very much the same. She found the quiet night, which belied all the people she was surrounded by, all the people living their private lives in their homes, to be very comforting. But her feelings of comfort were brittle. All this peace, all this domestic simplicity, would be shattered when the news of the Watchers got out. *How many of these homes are going to suffer immeasurably?* She thought as she passed a house from which she could hear the sound of children arguing. The news would shock everyone, would pull the carpet out from under the illusion of safety their well-ordered society gave them. And what if they had to fight the Watchers in the end? How many of these men and women would volunteer to protect the life they loved only to lose it? Only to never be able to return to it?

How many of them will I lead to their deaths?

• • • •

The air in the Elder Council's chamber seemed heavy, as if a blanket laid upon them all. No one spoke as they all entered from their various passageways and settled into their seats. Every one of the council members had a somber look painted on their faces. Khalihl looked over at Meiind. He had been distant at dinner the night before, prone to being lost in thought – they had spent much of the meal simply eating in silence – and he looked about the same now. His eyes were open, but they saw nothing in front of them. His thoughts were retreated into his own mind, not connecting with the world around him. Her heart went out to him, and she felt the sudden need to able to share his burden. But she knew she could not. To see the place you called home, the entire planet and everyone on it, annihilated… she could not imagine the emotional state he was in. She hoped she never would.

Khalihl turned her attention to the other person now settling into his seat, looking as young and crisp as he had at their last, brief meeting. Commander Jaier Yscaaidt. Something of a rising star in the military with a reputation for seriousness and creativity. Even now, he held himself with what appeared to be utter calm, no hint of worry or tension anywhere to be seen in his posture or face. Khalihl approved of that. She sensed something familiar in him as well, something she recognized from somewhere else, but she could not quite nail it down. As the Council began, she took mental note of the young man; she would look more into him later.

"Thank you three for coming," Serjevko, the Head Elder, began, looking at each of them in turn with a warm smile. After some preliminary ritual and introduction, he began to speak in earnest. "We have come to some conclusions as per our conversation yesterday," he said. "Thans, do you wish to begin?"

"Yes, sir," Thans said, clearing her throat. "We will tell the public about the Watchers."

Khalihl took a quick glance around the council and could see one or two faces shadowed with slight disagreement. Isdet especially did not try to hide the look of contention on his face. Khalihl could understand. The decision to tell the public must not have been easy, what with all the tensions involved. Do you lie to the people? Or do you risk panic? Khalihl, for her part, agreed with their decision. Nothing good comes of lying.

"This will happen soon," Thans continued, "by public address from the council. In the next few days. The address will tell them everything we know about the threat, as well as our plan for preparing for it."

"The first stage of that plan," Hujad jumped in, "is with the military. We will be expanding our defense budget considerably in order to prepare as many ships and planetary defenses as we can before the Watchers – and the Black Sun, for that matter – arrive. Admiral Khalihl will be in charge of this preparation."

Khalihl accepted her orders with a nod.

"At the same time," Morejas said as the Elders turned to look at him, "we will send a call out to all the political entities left in the Coalition. We will explain to them the threat and ask for them to join in the defense against the Watchers. If the nature of the threat is such as we think, then this involves all of humanity, not just the Cluster."

"Stage 2," now Cabrenejos spoke, "involves Commander Yscaaidt here. He will lead a small force to the prison planet to collect whatever he can of the skip technology there and return it to the Cluster. You will also wipe the prison's main computer core. The Black Sun must not gain access to the technology."

"Sir," Commander Yscaaidt said, his voice quieter than Khalihl would have expected. "Am I to engage the Black Sun if they arrive first, or during the mission?"

"We hope it will not come to that, but failure is not an option. You will use some of our own skip reserves to make sure you arrive with plenty of time," Cabrenejos answered, "but you will take sublight on your return. We must conserve what we have."

Yscaaidt nodded his understanding.

"The final stage," Serjevko said, "will be the building and the preparation of the evacuation fleet. We have asked our best public and private industry engineers to begin designing colony ships. They will be generation ships, equipped for voyages which will likely take more than a single lifetime. Those we evacuate from Cluster space would risk being discovered again if we used skipping to get them to a new planet, undercutting the entire point. We will ask for volunteers, resorting to a lottery if we receive more than we need. Admiral, you will oversee the construction of these ships as well."

Khalihl nodded her ascent once more under Serjevko's gaze. He then turned his eyes to Meiind, who had been waiting patiently, eyes down.

"Herr Meiind," Serjevko said, "You are not a Cluster citizen and therefore are not in any way beholden to the Council. We did not know the level of involvement, if any, you desired, so we have left you out for now. You have been through much, and your service to us has already been invaluable. If at any point you wish to become involved, we will gladly accept your help. Otherwise, we have arranged for everything you need to live comfortably on the outskirts of the city. Again, we thank you."

"Thank you, sir," Meiind said after a moment's thought. "I think I will want to become involved at some point, but first I do require some time to... recover. I will let you know when I am ready."

"Of course," Serjevko responded. He sat back in his chair and let out a sigh, looking out over the entire group.

"Are there any questions? No? Then we know what we must do. The Inner Cluster thanks you all for your dedication in these trying times. May Allah and the Prophets guide and protect us."

With that, they were dismissed, and Khalihl, Meiind, and Yscaaidt all left together. Outside the chamber, they offered each other some half-felt platitudes, each of them occupied by their own thoughts, and parted ways. Khalihl left the building and walked into the bright light of the morning sun, her eyes momentarily blinded after the darker chamber. The light seemed to wash scales from her eyes, and when she could see again, looking out over the massive park and the sprawling city, looking past the large buildings to the distant mountains, she could not help but see this, her home, as something rare and precious. A place of peace and prosperity. A place she loved. With this renewed vision came a sense of urgency, and close behind it was something like fear. Trying times were ahead, she knew. Difficult times for them all.

31

It was a moment humanity had been waiting hundreds of years for, since thinkers first imagined the possibility. But all that anticipation could not prepare us for the reality of the thing; nothing would ever be the same.

-Excerpt from Broken Chains: Social Evolution in the Post-Coalition Era *by Nigel Dentree*

Bin Ald was not paying much attention to anything around him in the café. Working on some new promotional material for the Original Way on his pad, he was engrossed in what he was doing. It was not until the voices around him all reached a certain threshold of tension that his ancillary senses picked up something was wrong, that something in the ambient atmosphere of the room had changed. He looked up to see everyone had stopped speaking; this was what had brought him out of his own work, the sudden stop of the usual hustle and bustle of the café. He looked around. Some people were whispering, but everyone was looking up at the vid screen occupying the corner of the room. On it, a news woman was speaking, the only voice in the shop.

" – in a few moments," the woman on the screen was saying, her face and voice perfectly emotionless and impartial, "Elder Serjevko of the Council will be addressing the Inner Cluster. This message has been deemed important enough by the Council to interrupt all normal broadcasts and the functions of all media devices. We have been asked to encourage everyone to stop what you are doing to listen."

The woman paused, tilting her head slightly. There was a flurry of whispering in the café.

"I have just received word the message is coming through now," the woman said, looking back into the camera. "In a few seconds, we will be cutting – "

The screen cut to a portrait shot of Elder Serjevko sitting in the Council chamber, flanked on either side by the other Elders. The sense of tension in the room amplified as everyone fell silent. Bin Ald sat up and set his pad down, rivetted by the looks on the faces of the Council.

"I would like to begin," said Serjevko in his low voice, "by thanking everyone who has taken the time from their day to stop and listen to our message. We do not take your time lightly, and we would never interrupt the lives of Cluster citizens unless circumstances demanded it. And circumstances do demand it." Here, the Elder's voice shook ever so slightly, and he looked down for a moment. He appeared to be gathering himself, gathering strength and control. "A number of facts have come to our attention," he continued. "You have all heard of the Black Sun and of the violence happening in what is left of the Coalition. We have been warned the Black Sun will be turning its desire for conquest towards us, towards the Inner Cluster, next."

The café seethed with whispered voices, a humming of human vocal cords. Most people in the Cluster had kept up on the news of the Black Sun. The influx of refugees had affected them all, one way or another, and talk had spread. People wondered whether the Black Sun would be satisfied with Coalition space, or whether they would want all of human space. That question was answered. The room quieted again as the Elder continued to speak.

"They do not have skip technology, though they are attempting to acquire it. If they do, they will be at our borders very soon. If we are able to stop them, they will arrive in ten years. Regardless, we are beginning preparations now."

Here, the Elder paused and took a few deep breaths, as if preparing himself for something. The café fell silent, and the tension grew still tighter, still more prevalent. Bin Ald could feel the people waiting. The news of the Black Sun had been expected. Anyone following news from what used to be the Coalition had anticipated they would turn their attention to the Inner Cluster, had expected the government to eventually take official action to prepare for the contingency. But the Elder had not completed his message, it appeared. It seemed there was more to the issue, or some other issue. Bin Ald was suddenly afraid. Some of the more radical people in his groups had been saying some radical things about the Inner Cluster and, especially, about the Elder Council. *Did they know?* He wondered to himself, looking at those around him, looking for anyone out of place.

"This is not the only threat to the Inner Cluster," the Elder began again. "This will be difficult to explain, and many will doubt us about this, but we have confirmed it independently and therefore must take the threat seriously." Again, another pause as Serjevko seemed to compose himself. "A few weeks ago, we received a message from an unknown source deeper within the galaxy, beyond human space. This is First Contact."

The whispering voices that had begun again fell dead. Everyone sat in stunned silence, blankly staring at the screen. Bin Ald's mind began to roar with static. He could not formulate a coherent thought. It seemed as if the room had begun to fold in around him. He looked at the others. No one spoke anymore. Eyes wide and mouths still, everyone waited for the Elder to continue.

"The message was a warning to us. A warning about a species called the Watchers. According to the message, from whom we are now calling the Senders, the Watchers are on their way here to invade our space. The message gave no details, but the implications were clear. The Watchers are coming to attack. The message also offered a timeline. The Watchers will be here in ten years, the same time as the Black Sun."

First Contact! Bin Ald's mind reeled at the idea. Various emotions began to rise within his mind and in his stomach. He felt sick. He felt afraid. And, most of all, he felt doubt. The Quran, Allah's word, made no mention of other sentient species in the galaxy. It offered nothing, that he could think of, in this vein. Panic began to swell, a crisis of faith arising.

"While the motives of the Watchers are unclear, we suspect they may explain the Drake Paradox. Our understanding of the Sender's message is we have been detected by the Watchers, triggering their coming. It seems sentient life in this sector has two choices: be known and destroyed or hide and survive. The apparent emptiness of the void could be explained this way.

"Preparations for both these threats will begin immediately. The coming days will bring more announcements. Expect military reserves to be called. We will also be asking for volunteers. Certain industries will be nationalized for the preparation of our defenses. As more information becomes available, the public will be told. We will face this threat, this new unknown, as we always have: together. Our strength is in each other, our faith is in our future, and our way is in our lives. In uncertain times, times of fear and of violence, our brothers and sisters, our fellow citizens, have always been our greatest source of strength. Do not forget that now. We will meet this challenge with the same humanity and fortitude we have met all others, since we left Earth so long ago. We will do everything possible to meet this new threat. May Allah guide us all."

With that, the transmission ended, cutting back to the newscasters who were now shocked into silence. A similar awed silence had filled the café, but, after a few moments, the water broke and a flood of exclamations came flowing forth in the voices of the people. Bin Ald sat silently, lost in his thoughts, ignoring the tumult around him. His mind spun with possibilities, with explanations which framed this new information in a way he could understand. *First Contact. Drake's Paradox.* He remembered this from school. The paradox was as follows: if space is infinite, statistically there should be sentient life other than humanity out there. But the void had always been silent. Paradox. *Until now,* Bin Ald thought gravely. *An alien species bent on destruction, keeping life in the galaxy silent and separate from one another.* And then he had a thought. It had the nature of a chess key, a move after which the seemingly random flow of the game fell into logical sequence leading to a specific ending. Bin Ald saw his thought shimmering in the recesses of his mind and felt all his doubts and fears dissipate in its light. He knew then the truth. He knew then what he must do. He looked around him at the panicked people, the unfaithful.

Allah works in mysterious ways, he thought, and he stood and calmly left the café. There was much to do.

<u>32</u>

*And His armies will come from the heavens, and
the wicked will wither before their flaming
chariots, and ruin and destruction shall be
wrought upon those who have forgotten the Truth,
and God will make ash of the lands of Sinners,
and from that ash His Kingdom will rise.*

-Excerpt from The Holy Bible: New
Interstellar Version, *Revelations 15:3*

On the planet of Sahaj, Maldeck's mind was working
in similar ways, though the context was different. *God has
finally sent His wrath upon us,* he thought. *The End Times come.*

He had been out at work, checking irrigation pumps,
when the call to come in had been given over the comm.
The announcement was already underway when he entered
the office, stuffed with people all silently listening to the
Elder speak. As Serjevko explained the threat from the
Black Sun, Maldeck glanced around at the others, men and
women he had known for some time now. Some of them
wore concerned looks on their faces, but nothing more.
Most appeared passive, accepting. They had already been
through much at the hands of the Black Sun, had escaped
their clutches before, and the news was not a surprise.
There had been, since their arrival, talk of this moment,
the moment the Black Sun turned towards the Cluster.
They who had seen the chaotic appetite of the Black Sun

already knew they would not suffer the Inner Cluster to live independently of them.

Their faces, however, turned to shock when the Elder continued his message and announced the coming of the Watchers. Even he felt his jaw drop as a cold chill ran itself through his body. When he looked around at his brothers and sisters, he saw the same shock painted on their faces, the same tension in their bodies. This one, it appeared, had been truly unexpected. God had not warned them.

After the announcement was complete, the people in the room milled around for a bit, talking a little, trying to better understand and process what they had just learned, trying to offer some comfort if possible. Maldeck didn't speak much, mostly just listened to the explanations people attempted. There were references to Isaiah, the book in the Bible in which the prophet sees a wheel with windows soar across the sky. There was talk of the mysterious ways of God. People called forth verses in which God promised protection to his children. But no one, it appeared, went the same direction that Maldeck's mind had gone immediately. And the more he thought about it, as he half-listened to the others, the more certain he became he was right. Still, he was not ready to air out his convictions. The thought of it set him shaking with fear and anticipation.

When he returned to work, he struggled to focus, so preoccupied was his mind. After a few botched repair attempts and smashed finger from his inability to pay attention to what he was doing, Maldeck gave it up and called to say he was not feeling well, that he was going home and would finish over the weekend. The foreman on the comm assented easily; apparently Maldeck was not the only one shaken up by the news.

It happened, the experience that Maldeck would, for

the rest of his life, interpret as a visitation from an angel of God, while he was driving the groundcar home from the field he had been working in. The road had been straight, the landscape an endless seeming repetition of field after field after field. Maldeck was not paying particular attention, lost in his thoughts. He was trying to recall everything he could about the book of Revelations, the book of the End Times. When the Elder had explained the threat of the Watchers, this was where Maldeck's mind had immediately leaped. All of the faithful knew God had a plan for all things, and that He had given everything humanity needed to know about that plan in his Word, the 100 books of the Bible. This plan included the end of humanity as they knew it, the destruction of the world to make way for God's kingdom come. How could this, the Watchers, be anything but a part of that plan? The more Maldeck worked through it, the more obvious it seemed, and the more terrified and awed he became. Finally, he began to shake and his breathing became panicked, his thoughts began to roar in his head until he could not hear anything else. He desperately called out to God for guidance. Then, quite suddenly, there was a flash of light in his vision, and his sight went blank in an infinity of white. He heard a voice, but he could not understand it. The sound of it reverberated through his body and through his mind, and he felt something he had never truly felt before. He felt the presence of God.

When Maldeck came to, he was parked askew on the side of the road, his groundcar off and safely settled on its landers. He snapped awake immediately, gasping for air like someone who had nearly drowned. What's more, the fear and anxiety he had felt before the visitation was gone, replaced by a strange serenity, a calm assurance. More importantly still, he knew the truth, and he understood what was expected of him. He knew what his part was in all of this. He knew what he, what they – the children of

God – had to do.

33

It is one of the great mysteries of existence: the same information can lead different people to different conclusions, even in similar circumstances. It is something like the random gene mutation which drives evolution, only applied to experiences and ideas. The importance of this phenomenon, which I call Meme Mutation, should not be underestimated.

-*Excerpt from* Meditations: the Collected Writings of Roshi Mendact

The skeleton floated serenely in orbit, the bare shape of the ship it would one day be there to be inferred but only to those with experience in the process. To the layman's eye, it looked like something ancient and dead, like the bones of the leviathan floating still in the deep and inky sea. Even the shuttles coming to and from the bones of the ship fit within the metaphor – fish feasting off the carcass. But Khalihl did not permit her mind to run too far with its own imagination. She, and everyone else in the Cluster, knew letting your mind run in times like this was a dangerous game. Fear lurked around every thought, just beyond every conclusion. She forced herself to look at the skeleton and see it for what it was: a massive generation ship, the small fish scurrying around it smaller builder ships. Nothing more and nothing less. But even that, the reality, was a frightening one, and terror and dread still lurked in the actuality of what she was doing. The threat required no imagination to see and feel.

She tried to push those thoughts from her mind as she looked over progress reports on her pad. Everything was going according to schedule. These ships – the skeleton she was currently looking at and the two others being built on platforms around the planet – would be done in a few years with plenty of time for them to be fitted and launched before either the Black Sun or the Watchers arrived. She had been briefed on their general specifications and design. Each was about five kilometers in length with various levels for food production, recreation, living, and maintenance. The engines, massive pipes at one end, would propel the gigantic ships until they reached sublight, and the artificial gravity drives would protect the passengers from the incredible forces of acceleration and, when they reached their destinations, deceleration. Their destination had not yet been chosen; they needed to learn more, if possible, about the Watchers so as to pick a location which might allow them to be safe indefinitely. Some scientists had already suggested S-146, an exoplanet beyond Coalition space, farther from the center of the galaxy than humanity had explored, with a large sun generating an unusual amount of interference. If the planet proved habitable, the sun might provide some protection from discovery. Other scientists had suggested building the generation ships larger still and making them permanent homes, possibly propelling humanity into a space-faring species. Khalihl could not help but shudder at the idea of never having a home, of always having to move for fear of being discovered.

She looked again out of the view port and at the skeleton of the ship being built. She tried to imagine it filled with people, somewhere around three million with room to grow. People living the rest of their lives on the ship. Others being born and dying on it. No doubt they

204

would arrive at their destination very different than they had left, much like her ancestors had changed during their original voyage to discovering the Inner Cluster. She wondered what kind of people would volunteer for such a journey. Perhaps the outsiders of society, drawn to the promise of a new place and a new way to start over. Perhaps people who romanticized the original voyage, people who obsessed over the dramas constantly produced and took place on the *Eden* and retold those stories through fantastic lenses. Or perhaps men and women attracted to the challenge, attracted to the adventure and the exploration. They would have to be very careful about their selection process. A lot could go wrong on a long journey such as the one they would be taking.

Khalihl signed off on the report and, after making sure there was nothing else pressing at the moment, indulged in her thoughts some. She swiped her pad to a news stage, quickly looked through the headlines. The aftershocks of the Elder Council's recent announcement dominated the news cycle. Volunteers had already begun putting their names in for both the defense and the evacuation fleets. There had been some panics that had risen to the level of riots on some planets. A sense of existential dread seemed to permeate the gossip channels. All to be expected. In actuality, Khalihl had expected a more difficult response. She felt lucky to be involved in the way she was; this offered her a way to work actively against the source of the anxiety now affecting them all together as a people. But for the average citizen, trying to continue on with their days as normal... she could not imagine trying to act as if nothing had changed. That probably explained the high volunteer numbers. Helplessness was one of the worst states to be in. Better to join and help than sit and wait.

Khalihl knew, however, these were not the only two options being considered by the people of the Inner

Cluster, that other forces were beginning to take shape. Her recent briefing after the Elder's announcement on the public's reception had included a report on a group called the Original Way. Little was known about them – they had kept a low public profile, meeting in person and forgoing a formal net presence as much as possible for their more serious conversations – other than the fact they considered themselves to be fundamentalists returning to the original conception of Islam found in the Quran. They prided themselves on a literal interpretation of the book, as well as on dismissing the Commentaries provided by the Founders of the Inner Cluster, which had transformed Islam into Isla'hai. The report observed these groups, which as of yet were still small and loosely connected, had been born in response to the influx of refugees from the Coalition. Thinking now, Khalihl could not help but shake her head. Still, ideas of nationalism, of culture and sovereignty, made forgiveness and reconciliation difficult. These refugees, still pouring in through their borders as they were, were not the blood thirsty murderers these fundamentalist groups imagined. They were civilians, people with families, trying to escape the turmoil and devastation the Inner Cluster was, at least in an ancillary way, responsible for. But the men and women of the Original Way saw the refugees as Other, as representatives of a government which had, both historically and contemporarily, tried to wipe out their way of life. This was true, to a degree, but to align citizens with the machinations of their government was to conflate who was responsible. Most people lived in constant tension with their governments, even here in the Cluster. That was what the members of this group seemed to not understand.

Khalihl swiped her pad to another report, this one of the defense fleet being built. She quickly looked over the stats, seeing them but not really able to engage with the numbers. She could see everything appeared to be going according to schedule; they were building a web of planetary and asteroid based defenses in addition to a fleet of new ships, and these were progressing much as planned, but beyond that, the words and numbers in the report just went past Khalihl's eyes, not really entering her mind or thoughts. *I am more distracted than I thought I would be,* she thought, and she shut her pad off and stood. She glanced out of the view port again, saw the Leviathan's skeleton hanging there in front of the distant planet from which the materials were being mined and transported. For a moment, she saw the half-built ship with a kind of transcendent vision, not as it simply was but, instead, as the center of a vast web of human cooperation. As she held this vision in her mind's eye, she could see everything that had gone into the building of the ship, from the designers to the laborers to the engineers to the transports. The web of interaction was massive. And, as she stared at the skeletal remains, her vision panned out to include all of the Inner Cluster, one enormous web of humanity interlocking in an infinite number of over and subtle ways. Her imagination continued to run, and the image widened to include the Inner Cluster, the Black Sun, and, finally, the Watchers. Everything was tied together by the gossamer strings of cause and effect, each element in her vision tied to something else either as a result or by producing some part of the next thing. What was more, she could see strings leading into the darkness beyond her vision, parts of the web and chain she did not know, did not understand. Some led into the inky darkness of what she thought was the past, and others led into what she sensed to be the future. Others still just led to places in the now she did not know about. A sense of overwhelm struck her hard in the center of her chest and the vision began to fade. *So many moving parts,* she thought as her mind cleared itself of the vision. *All interconnected in unfathomable ways. I need some caffeine.*

She stretched a little where she stood, feeling the tension and ache in her neck and muscles, and tried to remember the last time she had had a decent night of sleep as she walked to the common lounge, which was closer than the officer's mess. She could not remember having slept well since before Meiind and her went to Bodhi, since before she witnessed first-hand the destruction the Black Sun was willing and able to bring down. She had even tried relaxants and sleep-inducers, but to not much avail. The stress of it all was beginning to catch up to her. And, as it always did in times when fear and anger and uncertainty gnawed at her mind, Khalihl's thoughts leaped to the figure she wished was there now, wished she could turn to for his strength and decisiveness. But, she reminded herself, Raasch was dead, and he could not help. Yet, even as she pushed the thoughts of him from her mind as she entered the common area, filled with workers mingling with soldiers, she felt a small boost of energy and confidence. Even from the grave he was a source of strength for her. Still, she did not want to rely on those thoughts too much, and chose to try and force them out nonetheless. There would be a time and a place for her to use that source of strength, and she wanted to save it for when things got bad.

There was a sudden snapping of heels and grunts when she entered the soldier's mess hall as the men and women there all came to attention. She waved them back to ease with a smile; she was just there for some kol'koff, nothing more. The soldiers, seeing her easy demeanor and sensing her attention was on other things, sat back in their seats and fell back to whatever conversations she had interrupted. Soon, the room was filled with voices again as Khalihl poured herself a cup of the steaming, dark, aromatic liquid and found a seat in a corner. She waited for her drink to cool, listening to the fragments of conversation happening around her. Most of what she could hear centered around work – the building of the ships – but some of the soldiers were also discussing current politics, which had been somewhat in upheaval since the announcement from the Elders. She heard the phrase "Original Way" once and could not help but scowl. The men and women of that group, the fundamentalists calling publicly for a return to the religion of old, were a small but dangerous group. They wished to repeat the past, and Khalihl could not see the benefit in it. They all knew how that had gone the first time.

"Sir," a voice from behind her brought Khalihl out of her thoughts. She turned to see a female soldier standing at attention. "Permission to speak, sir?"

"Permission granted," Khalihl said. "Have a seat, soldier. You may speak freely with me."

"Thank you, sir," the soldier, a young woman maybe in her mid-twenties, sat across from Khalihl with a deep breath. "May I ask you a question?"

"Of course. Anything."

"Some of us," the soldier said, and Khalihl became aware of a silence in the room now; the others were listening, "are wondering what the Elder Council intends to do about the members of the Original Way."

"What do you mean?"

"Some of us feel they are undermining the Cluster when we need social cohesion most. Some of us fear the Original Way will spread and deter our defense efforts."

Khalihl took a moment to answer, glancing around at everyone who was listening. As an admiral, as the Admiral, she knew she was insulated from much of the street-level talk, knew she did not often hear the bulk of the whispers and rumors permeating through the social levels of their culture. She turned back to the woman in front of her.

"Name and rank, soldier?" she asked.

"Ensign Isa Hadif, sir."

"Tell me Ensign, what have the Original Way been saying?"

"Sir," and here Hadif leaned forward with an intensity in her eyes Khalihl recognized immediately. "They speak of treason, sir. They call for a return to the Islam of our ancestors. They say we have lost our way, that we mix too readily with the heathens of the Coalition."

"What else?"

"Some of the more extreme factions are calling for the dissolving of the Elder Council, for a reinstatement of a caliph. Some even are saying the Watchers are an instrument of Allah to bring about the end times, that we must not resist them. They say many things some of us worry about, sir."

"And what do you think of their ideas, soldier?" Khalihl pitched her voice so it would carry, heard the scraping of chairs as people turned to pay better attention. Ensign Hadif spoke for many of them, voiced many of their concerns, and they would all need to hear this.

"I find them to be inconsistent with my understanding of history, sir."

"How so?"

"Well," Hadif looked down at the table for a moment before continuing, gathering her thoughts. "The ideas they espouse have already been tried in our past. They call for a return to a past that, truly, never existed. Even in that past, there were people who believed the faithful had lost their way, that they needed to return to an even more ancient way of living. The glorious caliphate they claim to want, the one they claimed we once had, was not a world, from my understanding, I would want to live in."

"You are describing the tensions between the past, present and the future," Khalihl said, nodding her agreement with Hadif. "Every generation has to battle with it. We are coded with the need to move forward – more resources, more security, more space, more, more, more. Biologically, this is a survival instinct, same as any other animal, but, through the lens of culture and our own hubris, this process becomes endowed with a moral dimension. This process, because of the moral dimension, is fraught with peril. We wish to progress, but, by virtue of the same survival instinct, we are wary of the new. We fight it, and, due to our ability to accumulate knowledge through culture, we see the past as a safe place, a place we already survived, and the future as an unknown, a danger. Do you understand what I am saying, Ensign?"

"I think so, sir. You are saying the past is something we carry with us."

"That is correct. And the ideas of the past, the ideas that eventually become the ideas of the present and will become the ideas of the future, have their own gravity -- they pull at us, both individually and socially. This is, ultimately, what the Prophets on their journey from Earth to the Cluster on the Eden gave us. They freed us from our past. They allowed us to break free from a past you are right to not wish to return to."

"If this is true, sir, then why can't the people who buy into the Original Way see it?"

"You must understand their grievances are real, their fears a real part of their lives and a response to real things. Without this basic empathy, no understanding is possible. Tell me, why do they believe what they believe?"

"I do not know, sir. We have all been trying to figure that out."

"Let me try a different question. What do they fear?"

"They fear the refugees coming in from the Coalition."

"Why?"

"Because they associate the refugees with the war."

"And what was the war like?"

"I was not yet born, sir, but from what I understand, it was horrible."

"Something worth fearing?"

"Yes, sir."

"This is an important point. The Cluster War was terrible, more terrible than any war in the history of Humanity. We of the Cluster faced utter annihilation. But those of the Original Way engage in mistaken cause and effect, they misplace the blame. They look at the refugees and they see the same legions that came so long ago to destroy us. They think back to the war, and they see an ideological battle. And it was ideological, second. Firstly, it was economic. The Coalition wished to have control over our resources, and they did what historically almost always worked; they resorted to violence. But, as governments have always done, they painted their greed in cultural terms. They made it a battle of ideas where, in truth, it was anything but. They painted it with a moral dimension. Those of the Original Way do the same thing now."

"But why do they pine for some day and age we all know was worse?"

"This is what I am getting at," Khalihl said. *This is the key log,* she thought. "Evolution is not logical. In many ways, it is the exact opposite. Survival is the only goal. For the organism, the past is known – already survived – and the future is unknown – fraught with danger. These people, because of their fear of destruction, feel a deep sense of nostalgia for the past because it is known. The world around them is changing, and they know this will change everything about them. They watch new people bring new ideas to their communities. They watch their children play with these other children. They instinctively sense the world will be a very different place when they are gone and their children are adults. This is the most natural thing in the world; from a distance, we call it progress. But, for them, coupled with the fear they feel, they revert to the past as a safe place. They misinterpret the ideas of the past, bad ideas we have already overcome, as ideas that ensured survival. They are only acting as a thinking animal would."

It was silent in the mess hall for a moment as everyone entertained their own thoughts on what Khalihl had said. She suddenly felt tired, more tired than she had ever been in her life. But she took a sip of her kol'koff, inhaling the bitter aroma and letting the warmth flow through her body. She felt the stimulants in it pick up in her mind. She could not afford to lose these soldiers, these people who would be the future of the Inner Cluster, if it survived. *If we survive,* she thought. *And if we are going to survive, we have to understand and overcome the flaws in our coding.* She needed them to understand the dangers of the Original Way, the traps in their thinking.

"How do we get them to see this?" Hadif asked.

"Do you believe their ideas are incorrect? That the Original Way is based on a foundation made of shaky logic?"

"Yes, of course."

"There is no 'of course' about it," Khalihl said, feigning some annoyance. "You should never believe something as a matter of course."

"I am sorry, sir. What I meant was I see their flaws in their logic. I see their logic will eventually fail them."

"Exactly. Their logic will fail them eventually, just as all bad ideas fail eventually. It is very difficult to convince people of anything; argument only convinces if one has an open mind, the opposite condition of these fundamentalists. You must have faith – a scary word, I know – that good ideas will win out, good logic will hold when incorrect logic and bad ideas fail. They always do. And, perhaps more importantly, you must be ready to reaccept these people when their ideas fall out from under them. Nothing causes people to stay with bad ideas more than a sense they have nowhere else to go. The best thing we can do is to remember , even if we disagree with them, these people are still citizens of the Cluster. They are still us. If we keep that in mind, if we treat them accordingly, then they will return to us eventually."

"Yes, sir," Hadif said, her eyes distant with thought.

"I know that is difficult," Khalihl said, lower now, leaning forward to speak directly to Hadif instead of to the entire room as she had been. Still, she could sense the others lean in as well to catch her words. "It will become more difficult still. They will say things, do things, that will stretch the limits of our compassion. But, ultimately, compassion is the only logical position. Remember this."

"I will try, sir," Hadif responded, smiling back at Khalihl. "Thank you for your time, sir. I will think about what you have told us."

Hadif stood and went back to her table. Khalihl sat back and sipped her drink while conversation slowly picked back up in the mess hall. Soon, the soldiers were joking as if the conversation had never happened, and Khalihl appreciated the young's ability to snap back to frivolity no matter the stakes, no matter how serious things were. *Some of us,* she thought, *cannot afford that. Some of us must dive deep into the despair to better understand the world around.* And with that, her thoughts turned to Meiind, to his suffering since the destruction of Bodhi. She had a sudden longing to be with him, to try and help him somehow, even as just a friend, but she knew he had to work through his pain on his own. His actions made such clear enough. After their meeting with the Elder Council, Meiind had gone into seclusion, into deep meditation. He had not said much, and Khalihl did not much know the tenor of his thoughts or feelings, but she could imagine. She could imagine the impotent rage, the anger that made it hard to think. And she could imagine the utter despair, the sorrow which made it hard to live. She looked out of the mess hall window towards the planet below them. The planet's curve filled the long window from one corner to another, and the system's sun was just about to crest over the horizon. Already, Khalihl could see the atmosphere changing colors as the sun rose, could see the long shadows cast by the mountains now brimmed in golden light. The space elevator's tether, usually so fine as to be invisible, caught the sun and now appeared as a single line of perfectly white light rising from the surface like some ancient god ascending to the heavens. Then the sun's light passed a threshold and hit the window of the station, and, for a moment, Khalihl was washed in light before the glass automatically darkened and dimmed the glare. She watched light march across the planet, watched daylight chase away the night. *I hope you work things out, Meiind,* she thought. *We are going to need you before this is done.*

34

*Scientists have been unable to replicate the
conditions which allowed Ondrueut – the
President, as he is often now called – to achieve
digital existence, what, in technical terms, is
called full mind emulation. As such, there is
painfully little we know about how he came to be,
but this has not stopped thinkers, philosophers,
and historians from speculating as to the
psychological effects of such a protracted digital
existence. The question is irresistible: what does
that kind of life do to one?*

-Excerpt from Transcendence: the
History of the Digital Mind *by Mosden
Keller*

His thoughts would not quiet. He tried to let them
pass, but they rang so loud in his mind he could not help
but be swept away by them, to be taken in by their
emotional content. He thought of the Roshi, his mentor
and friend, now dead and nothing more than a pile of ash
on a dead planet. He thought of all the monks he had met,
the men and women who had stunned him with their
patience and kindness, who had taken him, an outsider, in
and taught him their ways. Images began to form in his
mind's eye. At first, it was things he had already seen:
Bodhi ashen and devastated, void of all life. He saw
thousands and thousands of square kilometers of dead

pipal trees, whole forests burned to powder. He saw the piles of ash that had once been living people fallen into place wherever they had been when the weapon had dropped. Then, his mind began to fill in the gaps, and he saw the planet, lush and green, transform into a gray, blind eye. He watched as the wave of death spread from one horizon to the next, watched as the life was taken from the planet. He watched as millions died without raising a hand to defend themselves. He watched children turn to dust as they ran into their parents' arms. He felt his heart rate beginning to rise, his breathing becoming more and more labored, and his thoughts continued their frenzied tenor until he finally only felt one thing: anger. That, however, did not do it justice. It was rage he felt. Fury. Hate most of all. And try as he might, he could not find himself on the other side of the emotions, could not stop the flow of thoughts and clear his mind. He opened his eyes.

Meiind sat in the center of his quarters, facing a blank wall. Slowly, he unraveled his legs from their crossed position and stood, taking care with his sore joints. He had been sitting for hours every day, and every day had been much the same. As soon as he sat, as soon as he tried to focus on his breathing, anger flooded through him. Then came the unbidden images, and his mind became full of death and destruction. Sometimes it was Bodhi, as it had been today. Other times, it was other planets, or maybe even New Mecca. Regardless of the content, it never failed. Whenever he sat to meditate, his mind was full of death and destruction, full of anger and sorrow. He had never dealt with anything like this before, had never had such strong feelings. *If only the Roshi were here to guide me,* he thought. And this thought brought down a fresh wave of anger.

He had an idea then, and he sat back down. Slowly, he folded his legs beneath him, laid his hands in his lap, and closed his eyes. This time, when the anger came, as it did right away, he did not try to fight as he had been for days on end. Instead, he embraced it. He imagined his anger a beam of energy, and as he focused on it, it tightened and became more powerful. He felt this power coursing through his mind, feeding his meditation. He focused harder, trying to remove everything but the anger. He wanted to feel it in its entirety, wanted to turn it into a source of energy, wanted to burn it out. Suddenly, he found himself floating free, calm in the center of an inky blackness speckled with light. He was in the trance.

It came as something of a shock. He had been trying to get here for days now, always blocked by his own attachment to his emotions. He had not seen it that way — he had been trying to fight them — but now it was clear wanting something about his emotional state to be different was a form of attachment. When he had accepted them, leaned into the fury and hate, he broke free.

The first thing he did was spread himself as wide and thin as possible in search of the Watchers. The Black Sun was being covertly followed through a combination of long range scans and surveillance ships. At the same time, the authorities in the military had been compiling first person accounts of the Black Sun attacks on planets. Through these, they had assembled a good amount of information about the Black Sun, though their leader still remained opaque. They only knew his name, General Eazkaii. But the Watchers were still an unseen menace hidden in the vast emptiness of the void. They knew nothing that could help them prepare for the coming threat. For days, Meiind had tried to get into the trance so he could try and find them. Maybe he would be able to glean some information about them, about their culture or their technology, anything that could help the Cluster, humanity's only chance at an organized defense now that the Coalition was dissolved. But he had no real way of differentiating them from the millions of other forms of life he sensed in the cosmos. He knew nothing about them. Knew nothing about their minds, about their position in the universe, nothing which would give him any direction in his search. But he had his anger, his hatred. And he knew these could fuel him beyond his own perceived limits. He would find them, if it was possible. He would do whatever it took.

Meiind searched for some time, spreading his awareness around the inner galaxy. He sensed many alien species, though, after what had happened with the Senders, he kept his distance. He did not want to alarm anyone, did not want to accidently lead to their discovery. Still, he did not find anything which appeared to be the Watchers, did not find any massive fleet on its way to the Inner Cluster. And the Presence which had guided him before, that had come to him when he needed help, did not come to help him. Without it, he felt lost in the vastness of space. He was not surprised he could not find the Watchers. Without something to guide him, without at least some idea of their location, space was just too vast, life too numerous, to single out a single species. After a few hours, he gave it up.

He turned his attention then to the other threat the Inner Cluster faced. This time, he knew their position well enough to find them rather quickly. The Black Sun fleet was on its way from Bodhi to the prison planet, and he was able to sense them, the thousands of massive ships, as they crossed the sea of emptiness between the two planets. Still, Meiind kept his distance and did not touch them; he did not want to alert them to his presence. Instead, he just checked their position, made sure they were still going for the skip drives left on the prison planet. As far as Meiind could tell, the fleet was still on their way there. Still looking to find whatever technology was left on the planet so they could more quickly spread their swath of destruction to the Inner Cluster.

Meiind felt a surge of anger, and he had the thought he swore to himself he would not, the thought which had hung in the back of his mind since Bodhi, the thought he had promised himself to never indulge. But now, as his presence encompassed the massive fleet responsible for the deaths of billions of innocent people, the death of whole planets and societies, as his hatred for them came to the forefront again, he could not help it. *I wonder,* he thought. *I wonder if I could kill them all right now.*

He was at once horrified with himself and interested in what the limits of his ability were. He had used his touch to kill only twice, and both times he had been in the physical presence of the person. He had never tried it at a distance. Regardless, he told himself, he had sworn to never use it again, no matter how just the cause seemed. He had told himself it was a power too great to be used by anyone, even himself, a responsibility he did not want. But now his resolve crumbled under the weight of the Black Sun's collective presence and the hatred he felt for them. So many lives could be saved if he just… and before Meiind knew what he was doing, he had found a soldier of the Black Sun whose mental state seemed to be too calm to be awake. Someone who was asleep might interpret his touch as a part of a dream. More importantly, the people he reported it to might make that interpretation. Meiind, without much thought, reached out and touched the man, squeezing as hard as he could before the memories and understanding came. He did not want to understand this soldier. He did not want to know what led a person to join a force like the Black Sun. He just wanted to conduct a test and perhaps remove one from the world of the living.

Nothing happened. In the moment after, Meiind realized what he had just attempted to do, that he had just tried to murder someone, and a sense of horror with himself came washed in a sense of relief it had not worked. He could touch them at a distance, could absorb someone's essence, their life, but he could not kill them as he had his own mother and the President of the Coalition so many years ago. He apparently needed to be closer for that, perhaps even in their physical presence. But before he could really process what he had just attempted, he felt the wave of the man's memories come crashing upon him.

He saw, through the man's eyes, and felt, through the man's mind, a family. But they were distant, lost somewhere, dead. And in an instant, Meiind understood the man so well he ceased to be a stranger, he ceased to be separated by the void between them. In the moment he had touched the man, Meiind became cognizant of the soldier's life story, and with this understanding came a sense of empathy washing his own hatred away. The man had lived on a planet the Coalition had instituted a draft on during the Cluster Wars. The man had been too young then, just a boy, but his father and brothers all went, and they all died in the war. Meiind sensed a deep hatred of the Coalition for this, a sense of betrayal that had never healed. What was more, the Inner Cluster had attacked the man's home planet, an important source of resources for the Coalition's war effort. The rest of his family had been killed then. He was the only surviving member of his family. He had lived most of his life alone, blaming the Inner Cluster and the Coalition for the suffering and loneliness of his life. It was no wonder he had joined the Black Sun; he had lived with the hatred and sorrow so long the chance for revenge could not be passed up. And Meiind sensed something else. The man had not only wanted revenge, he wanted a place. A place in a group that would protect him the way the Coalition had not against enemies like the Inner Cluster.

Then the images he was receiving from the man changed and took a different tenor. Meiind began to see the man's life as a soldier of the Black Sun. He saw hundreds of men and women suiting up in the staging bay of some great ship, each putting on body armor and bristling with weaponry. They were hustled into individual landing pods. Meiind felt the man's anxiousness as he waited for launch, but there was something else in his thoughts, some other feeling. Meiind recognized a great hate for the people of the planet beneath them, a lust for destruction. The pod launched, and for a few minutes the turbulence was so intense the man passed out. When he came back to, Meiind with him in the memory, the shaking had stopped some, but the radio was screaming with the voices of dying soldiers, some on the ground already barking commands and some still in their pods being shot out of the sky. A nauseating sensation of deceleration pinned the man to the bottom of his pod as the landing thrusters engaged, then a hard crash as the pod hit the ground. The doors hissed and opened to an immense battle happening both in the sky and on the ground. The man hit his comm, checking in with his commander as he stared in awe at the assault of the planet happening before him. Massive ships were coming down from orbit, each raining waves of destructive energy on the surface. Flame and earth exploded in all directions; the horizon was a wall of fire. Closer, the man could see pods being shot out of the sky even as others made it to the ground. His display came alive in front of his eyes, and arrows pointed in the direction of his battalion. He sprinted in the indicated direction, staying low under the energy bursts searing overhead. Around him, soldiers were running in the same direction, dropping as they were hit with enemy fire. As the man approached a cluster of blown-out buildings, a small town center, his display brought up orders to clear the buildings in the order highlighted in his vision. He turned himself towards a building washed in red, ran up to the closest door, and kicked it in. He entered an empty hallway full of debris and a few bodies strewn about. There was an eerie silence in here, the battle raging outside muted by the walls, maybe even by some sound dampeners somehow still operating. He patched his display into the sensors of the orbiting ships and saw a room to his right full of people. Without hesitation, he opened fire on the wall separating him from the people in the room, his energy bursts ripping through the plaster and glass and shredding the people within. Whatever dampening field that was in place turned the loud retort of his weapon into a distant hum, and there were no screams to be heard. He shouldered the door open and opened fire again, making sure no one was still left alive. Once finished, he surveyed the dead. The room appeared to be some kind of classroom, and the bodies on the floor, now piles of smoking flesh in boiling puddles of blood, were mostly of small children. The man, sure everyone was dead, went down the hall to the next room that showed, in his display, another group of people hiding, oblivious to the fact they were no longer safe. He opened fire. Room after room, he slaughtered everyone in the building.

Meiind came out of his trance screaming, sweat beading out on his forehead and tears running down his face. It was a full few minutes before he was calm enough to have a coherent thought, before he could take a full breath without gasping. When his mind had calmed down, when the images had faded so he did not see the torn apart bodies of children before his eyes anymore, he felt the conflict within him rise up while, at the same time, his determination turned to stone. These people, these soldiers of the Black Sun, were just that. People. They had suffered, many of them profoundly. The Black Sun gave them a way to fight against the world they felt had been so unfair to them. Meiind could understand this, could empathize with the impulse. Yet, through the Black Sun, their hate and fear was being wrought upon the world, upon innocents who had nothing to do with their grievances. Their hatred was direct, their destruction indiscriminate. As he thought about what he had just experienced, Meiind's mind made some kind of pivotal shift. He pushed his internal conflict to the side, and in its place, there was only the reality of the Black Sun.

They won't stop until everything burns, Meiind thought. *No matter what promises I made to myself in the past, they have to be destroyed.*

The thought left Meiind cold, as if he lived in a body he did not know. But his mind had been made up. He knew what he would have to do.

35

Morality and ethics only apply to others, never to ourselves.

-Unknown

Yscaaidt could not help but be unsure about what they were doing. The refitting of their ships was taking somewhat longer than expected. Finding technicians with the necessary knowledge had not been easy. Most of the men and women who knew how the skip drives worked had retired after their skill set had become obsolete and were out of practice. Still, they had managed to reinstall the drives and now just needed to load the banks with the energy source which allowed them to travel instantaneously through space. Yscaaidt watched from the dock bay windows as his men worked on the ships on the staging floor below him while he mused over their mission, his reservations growing as he thought more about it. As a woman wheeled a cart stacked high with the cylindrical skip banks from ship to ship, each ship receiving two, Yscaaidt could not help but think, *Who died for this energy? Who was the person whose Source is now held in that bank?* He tried to remove the thought from his mind, however. It was not his duty to moralize. He had his orders, and there were good reasons for them to use the skip tech for this mission. In this case, the risks outweighed the moral ambiguity. Still, the fact these banks had once been human beings, had once been living things, nagged at him.

The men and women had been working day and night, in shifts, to get the fleet ready… well, ready for anything. In the best case scenario, they would beat the Black Sun there and not meet any resistance. Worst-case scenario, they would have to fight their way in, or out, or both. Regardless, the Black Sun could not be allowed to get any of the necessary resources for them to build their own skip drives. If Yscaaidt and his fleet failed in their mission, there would be little chance of stopping the Black Sun's onslaught from continuing through the Inner Cluster as they had rampaged through the Coalition.

Yscaaidt willed the thoughts of failure, the anxieties of his mission, from his mind as one of his officers approached. The woman, Commander Nathalie Lensut, stopped a few paces away from him and waited patiently at attention. *She knows me well,* Yscaaidt thought. *She can tell when my thoughts burden me.*

"Commander," he said without taking his eyes off the work happening below him.

"Captain," Lensut responded as she held out a pad. Yscaaidt took it. "We have made up some of the lost time refitting the ships. We should be done and ready to depart within 24 hours."

"Good," Yscaaidt felt the tensions within him rise as he looked over the detailed engineering report she had handed over. "What do you think about the skip drives, Commander?"

"Sir?"

"I mean, what do you think about us using them?"

"May I assume, sir, you are referencing the origins of

their energy?"

"Correct."

"That," Lensut took a breath here and let it out slowly with a shrug, "is a difficult question sir. Removing them from use, once we learned they required the murder of humans to collect, was undoubtedly the right thing to do."

"Was it?"

"Sir?"

"How many people have died as a result of the decision to shut down the skipping network immediately?" Yscaaidt turned to look at his Commander and felt a wave of emotion as his eyes fell upon her. He pushed the wave back, however. There was a time and a place, and this was not it. He did allow himself to offer her a thoughtful smile as he continued. "I just cannot help but wonder if it would have been better for us to phase it out slowly. Perhaps the Black Sun's rise could have been avoided if the Coalition had not collapsed so immediately."

"I see," Lensut said, looking up at Yscaaidt with the same emotions he felt mirrored in her eyes. He wanted to reach out and touch her, touch the scar running across her cheek, the result of an accident during basic training, where they had met, so many years ago. But he resisted. "I think about it as well sometimes, sir."

"And?"

"Sometimes I wonder if we, our culture and society, carry the deaths of all those people, all the humans who allowed us to live the way we now live, collectively. Like some sort of sin that has accrued in the soul of humanity. And sometimes I wonder if we will have to commit worse sins to cover up the sins of our past. I know you do not like things phrased in that kind of religious terminology, sir, but that is what I think about."

"I understand the sentiment," Yscaaidt turned back towards the men and women working beneath them. His thoughts seemed to sour suddenly. "There is something... almost supernatural about the Source. Something epic on a religious scale about our misuse of it. Religious terms seem a good fit. Though I shy away from that language, I wonder much the same things, Commander."

"Does the Captain see any other way?"

"It is not my duty to make decisions, just to follow orders," Yscaaidt snapped, immediately regretting it. He turned a gentle look to Lensut and lowered his voice to try and soften the sting. "I'm sorry. I dislike the unknown, and there are so many here. But no, I do not see another way. All I see are worse alternatives."

"As my father used to say," Lensut said with a gleam in her eye. "Damned if we do, and damned if we don't."

"More like: 'damned if we do, and dead if we don't.'" Yscaaidt looked at Lensut, feeling the distance between them as a physical thing, a barrier he wanted nothing more than to cross over. He could see in her body she wanted the same. They had both been so busy the last few weeks, had barely had any time to spend together. He missed her. He wanted nothing more than to reach out and touch her. Instead, he turned his back on her, looking down over the bay again, where his men and women were working. "The fact is the people who provided the energy for these skip drives died a long time ago. They were murdered, but they no longer have any use for the energy their lives created. In the past, their deaths would have been for the sake of the mundane: commerce, travel, leisure. At least now they are being used for something worth the sacrifice. At least now they will help us to save the Cluster, to save humanity. Perhaps that is better?"

"They would probably choose to be alive still. To have had the opportunity to live full lives," Lensut responded quietly.

"Yes," Yscaaidt said, looking over the soldiers under his care. "Fair enough. But they will not be the only ones to have sacrificed by the time this is over."

36

Looking back, it is one of the great moments in the story of history: two groups, sworn enemies for thousands of years, brought together by a strange twist of fate in interesting times. The effects of this union would ripple through history.

-*Excerpt from* The Outside Looking In: Fringe Politics and Marginalized Peoples *by Jen Fretre*

"How else can this be interpreted?" Bin Ald asked earnestly, looking into the faces of the men and women around him. No one answered. "I have no doubt this is all a part of Allah's will."

There were some nods, some faces frozen in grimaces of various shades of fear, terror, and dread. Bin Ald could understand those emotions in light of what they had learned. Even himself, despite his faith in the One True God, had awoken sweating every night, the echoes of a scream sounding in his ears, from dreams of the coming apocalypse. Even though he knew, as one of the faithful, he would be spared the worst of the suffering, the prospect of seeing God's revenge made incarnate upon the galaxy was a frightful one. Yes, he could understand their fear, their doubt.

They sat, as had become their custom, in a café

whose owners were sympathetic to their cause, if not yet full members. The establishment had been shut down for their meeting, so only the faithful – or at least the interested – sat in the audience in front of Bin Ald as he spoke. Outside, the night was quiet and the streets empty. Ever since the announcement from the Elders, the people of New Mecca had taken to staying in during the night. Some sort of ancient defensive instinct, the gossipers liked to say. Bin Ald preferred it this way. He had taken to walking through much of the night when he could not sleep, after his nightmares, and had learned to see the city anew in this silent rebirth. It also increased their privacy in these meetings, decreasing the chance someone might overhear something which would put the Original Way on the radar of the Elder Council. That day would come, Bin Ald knew, but he wanted to be the one to choose the timing. Here, inside the café, with the smell of roasted kol'koff permeating the air, the men and women seated before him waited for Bin Ald to continue. He could sense their need. They depended on him. He could also sense their varying degrees of acceptance. Some had reconverted and had hearts full of faith. Others were close but had not yet made the full transition. And still others were skeptical. Suddenly, Bin Ald was struck with a kind of double vision. In his mind, he saw a similar scene, only thousands of years in the past, of a man speaking to a small group of people in a tent in the desert. *Is this what it was like,* he thought with a growing sense of awe, *when the Prophet first preached the Word of the Quran? Was this how the first Muslims came to be?*

"I understand your hesitation," he said, forcing his thoughts to the side to be indulged in later. "I even understand your doubt. People of all religions have been prophesying the end of times since the beginning of time. But there is no other way to understand what we have learned."

"What if," said a man Bin Ald did not know, a newcomer to their group – there had been many new members since the Elder Council had made their announcement about the Watchers – averting his eyes as if from shame for his question, "this is just what it seems, another species in our massive galaxy? What if this is just the First Contact our scientists and novelists have been speculating about for generations now?"

"That is a good question," Bin Ald responded with enthusiasm. He wanted to encourage questions, because they encouraged his people to think deeply. He just needed to guide their answers to the proper place. "And of course, that is what the unfaithful will say. That is what the shell of the once great Islam will say. That will be the token answer from the powers of the Isla'hai, no doubt. But we know their faith is not in Allah but in their own hubris. We know the Musla of our era are watered down versions of the Muslims of our past. For them, Isla'hai is a cultural lifestyle, not a true religion. We know they have lost their way, have forgotten the Words of the Prophet and have strayed from the will of God." Everyone was nodding now. These ideas were the ones that had brought them to the Original Way in the first place, and they were the way Bin Ald would get them to see his logic, to see the truth. He needed to keep their common ground firmly beneath them. "And we know everything we need to know about life as a human, about the destiny of humanity, has been given to us in the form of the Word of God, in the Quran. So surely that is where we must turn to understand what we have learned."

With that, Bin Ald swiped on his pad and brought up his Quran. He had spent the last few nights reading and studying the word of God, looking for clues as to Allah's plans and intentions, and he was certain he had found what he needed to know, certain the One True God had spoken to him through the Prophet's words. He said as much to those seated before him, and then he began to read.

"'So watch out for a day when the sky brings forth a distinctive smoke that covers the people; this is a painful punishment,'" Bin Ald said in a voice heavy with the weight of the Quran. "Later, it continues: 'So when the horn is blown a single blast, and the earth and the mountains are lifted and crushed with a single blow; on that day, the Event will occur.' From this passage, I think we can understand Allah's will for us and how the Watchers factor into His plan," Bin Ald said, looking over his followers. He could see the wheels turning in their eyes, could see their understanding beginning to blossom. "What else could the reference to the 'sky' mean, how else could a planet be destroyed in a 'single blow?' The 'Event' can only be the coming of the Watchers!"

"They are His instrument!" someone in the back called out to nods and murmurs of agreement.

"Yes!" Bin Ald hissed excitedly. "Allah has sent these… these aliens to us to bring about the End Times, to usher Allah's kingdom into humanity's existence. What else? What does this mean for us, those who have submitted themselves to the Allah and His will?"

"We must do what we can to help bring about the Will of the One True God," a woman in the front said quietly.

No one responded right away. Bin Ald, looking over them, could see the effect the woman's words had. He had led them here, right to this point, on purpose; he wanted them to see Allah's plan and their place in it. The recognition of such was beginning to register on their faces. They were beginning to see the implications.

"Yes," Bin Ald said, matching the quiet seriousness which had descended upon the group. "For the faithful, like us, there is only one thing that can be done. We must help Allah's Will be brought to fruition, no matter what the cost. Allah is all powerful, but He chooses to work in the world through his sons and daughters. His plan requires our involvement."

A moment of pregnant silence. The emotional tension in the room was thick, and Bin Ald could sense the different mental states bouncing around behind the glazed over eyes, deep in thought, of the people before him. But he had them now. That much he knew. And when the word of his ideas spread, they would become a powerful force for the true Islam, for the Truth itself. He felt a sense of conviction swell through him, a sense of righteousness, and he was thankful. He sent a silent prayer to Allah thanking Him for the strength to speak to these people and for the words to win them over. But there was still one more step before he was done, one more piece in the puzzle that needed to be fitted.

"This brings me to the last thing I wanted to talk about today," he said. "This will be a difficult thing for some of you to understand, but I ask you to hear me out before casting judgement on the idea." He looked over them all with calm eyes, trying to exude confidence. "I have learned of a group of Christians – not, mind, Theoretical Deists, but true Christians – who have emigrated from the Coalition to a Cluster planet called Prajna, the planet of the Sihken." He paused here, took a breath, and let his words settle into the air. This would be a difficult point to make. Old prejudices, even ancient ones, still existed. They all knew their history well enough, had ancestors who had fled in the original Slow Migration. "It is my understanding they have come to similar ideas about the Watchers, about their role in bringing about the One True God's will."

"How can that be?" a man to the left asked. "They do not believe in the Prophet's message."

"That is true," Bin Ald responded, "and I do not know. But I do know they have been preaching the Watchers are the instrument of their God to bring upon what they believe the end times will be, to bring, as they say, the 'Kingdom of God' to humanity. As we have said before, and as we are learning now: Allah works in ways we do not understand. It is not our duty to understand, only to obey. Only to do whatever we must." Again, he paused to let the words sink in. They were almost ready for it. "I am sure you have all noticed the attention our group is beginning to garner with the population here, attention sure to spread to the media and government soon." The turn took a moment to register, but they mostly nodded in agreement. "And I am sure you are aware of how truly small we are, how few of the faithful there are." Again, nods. It was time to give them the beginning of his plan. Not too much. They would balk at the full extent of it. They were faithful, yes, but what he planned would call for a faith the likes of which they have never endured. And that was what faith, true faith, called for: endurance. The coming tests of their faith would be formidable indeed. "It is my belief the Will of Allah calls for us to reach out to these ancient enemies, to see if we truly have common goals, as it might seem from a distance and according to the rumors. And, if they have, it is my belief we, the Original Way, can be more successful in our attempts to enact the Will of Allah if we work with the Christians."

There was a general murmur of excitement, whispers. Some were nodding already, but others shook their heads in disbelief to what they were hearing. And Bin Ald was well aware of how his idea sounded. But he also believed it was the best way possible to move forward.

"I know how this sounds," he said quickly, speaking

over the voices, "but allow me a question: what is more important? Our prejudices or the Will of Allah? If they truly believe the Watchers are an instrument of their God, what does it matter? The end result will be the same, and we will be vindicated in our faith. We will be the agents of Allah, and they will be judged for their lack of faith in the Prophet. Ultimately, the only thing that matters is our success, and we will need every tool at our disposal to undermine the Cluster's sinful resistance against Allah's Will."

Bin Ald stood tall before them, his case rested, scanning the now quiet and thoughtful audience. His words had had their intended effect, he could see. It would take them time, some more than others, but they would see the wisdom of his idea. They would see the benefit in having a scapegoat as they work.

37

The rise of the Black Sun as a political and military power in human occupied space has yet to have been satisfactorily explained. Many theories abound: some think the Black Sun arose from what was left of the Coalition fleet after the Traitor's War. Others believe the Black Sun originates from the planet Liberius where it began as a small group of fascist extremists. The fact of the matter is we do not yet know. More study is needed.

-*Excerpt from* Broken Chains: Social Evolution in the Post-Coalition Era *by Nigel Dentree*

"How goes the preparations of the defense fleet?"

The question, which Khalihl knew would be first and foremost in this meeting, hung in the air like a cloud blocking the sun. They all sat in its shadow, in the shadow of its portents. Khalihl took a deep breath and composed herself. The Council would not accept anything but the truth from her. She thought about how the preparations had gone thus far, about the numbers the Elders had on their pads now.

She thought about how the Inner Cluster had never before engaged in such pure military expansionism. In the months since her last meeting with the Elders, the Inner Cluster military was on track to reach its peak Cluster War size, and it would be getting much, much larger beyond that. New ships and weapons had been designed, new planetary defenses, new tactics. The military was essentially making itself anew under her command. And, despite a lifetime in the military, the expansion made Khalihl nervous. For her, the Inner Cluster military had always been a primarily defensive and exploratory institution. While what they were building was still defensive, the sheer size of it would make for destructive power beyond her imagining. If humanity and the fleet survived the threat of the Watchers, whoever was left in command of what would be a massive fleet would have enormous power. *If we survive the Black Sun and the Watchers,* she thought darkly. Their fleet was still nowhere near the size of even the Black Sun's massive, thrown together army, and they had no idea what the Watchers would bring.

"It goes according to schedule," she said, leaving the rest unsaid.

"However…" Elder Serjevko said, picking up on the spaces between her words.

"However," she continued, "I do not know whether it will be enough." Khalihl looked at the Elders seated above her. Each had his or her pad on and was looking over her progress reports on the defense preparations. They would see they were producing ships as fast as they could, faster than they ever had. They would see the new hull designs, the new weapons technology the government scientists had come up with. They would also see they were running short on personnel, that, if they continued the way they were, there would not be enough soldiers to man the ships when the time came. Khalihl looked at the dome that roofed the Elder Council's Chamber. She wished she had better news, more optimistic things to say.

"Please elaborate," Serjevko said gently. "There is no need to hold back your thoughts. Speak freely."

"Thank you, sir," Khalihl said. "As you can see, we will have many more ships than soldiers if we continue production at the pace we are building at. I know we cannot institute a draft – against the Cluster Bills such as it is – but we are going to need more volunteers somehow."

"Have you any suggestions?" Cabrenejos asked.

"A few. I recommend we open service enrollment to refugees, perhaps with the promise of full citizenship for them and their families in the Inner Cluster. This may give us enough."

"But you don't think it really will be enough, do you?" Hujad now.

"Sir," Khalihl took a moment before continuing. "I simply do not know. There are so many unknowns, so many variables, the greatest of which are the Watchers themselves. We know nothing about their species, about their technological capabilities nor about the size of the invasion fleet. Without that information, it is very difficult to gauge our own readiness. But you are right. I fear it will not be enough."

There were nods all around the Council. *They anticipated this,* Khalihl thought. *They know we may come up short.*

"We feared this may be the substance of your report," Serjevko said, again in that gentle voice of his, taking care his voice did not carry with it even an ounce of blame. "We appreciate your frank honesty, Admiral. Without it, we would most certainly be worse off."

Khalihl nodded and stood silently at attention,

waiting. If they had anticipated her report, then surely they had ideas for a solution beyond her own. The Elders traded meaningful looks, and Serjevko nodded at Isdet. Khalihl turned to face him.

"Your idea is a good one Admiral," the old Elder said, his wizened eyes staring brightly at Khalihl. "We have discussed something similar, and taking your endorsement of the idea as proof of its merit, we will be making that announcement within a few weeks, once the legal matters have been smoothed out. However, we have another idea as well. Perhaps a more... ah, radical proposition."

There was a pause here, and Khalihl sensed tension in the room. *There had been an argument about this here,* she thought, looking from Elder to Elder. Hujad and Thans did not meet her eyes. *They do not agree with whatever this proposal is.* It troubled Khalihl to sense this schism in the Elder Council. They often fought, it was true, but they rarely allowed those cracks to show beyond the bounds of a discussion. They always maintained a united front.

"We have been discussing," Isdet said with an emphasis on "discussing," making its euphemistic use obvious to Khalihl with something of a humorous twinkle in his eye, "the possibility of seeking help from elsewhere. Of, perhaps, using this threat to humanity as a way to force cooperation and peace on other fronts. Some of us are of the opinion we should tell the Black Sun of the Watchers and invite them to join us in the defense of human occupied space."

The words rang in the air, and Khalihl felt a sense of shock pass through her. She wanted to burst out, wanted to berate the Black Sun, wanted to remind the Elder Council of the horrifying crimes they had committed, wanted to express the immediate repugnance she felt towards the idea. But she immediately recognized the

241

emotional reaction for what it was – a gut reaction, a subjective response. She took a few deep breaths to calm herself and attempted to step away from the idea, attempted to approach it from a distance. *I have spent much time with the refugees fleeing the Black Sun. Their stories have not left me untouched.* And, as soon as she had managed to distance herself from her own response, she saw the merit in the idea.

"We know it is a difficult idea to accept," Cabrenejos said, reading the look on her face. "Yet, we think there are several reasons this course makes sense.

"Sir," Khalihl said. Now that the initial shock had worn off, she could see the reasons why such an idea would perhaps be prudent and ethically sound. "I think I begin to understand."

"Go ahead," Cabrenejos encouraged her.

"Militarily, it makes sense. We face an unknown enemy. The more power we have, the better prepared we will be. The better prepared, the higher our chance of victory." Nods all around. "There is also reason based in ethics. The Watchers are a threat to humanity. To all of humanity. This includes the Black Sun as one of the major human forces in play currently. They have a right to know what they fight for is threatened."

"Exactly," Serjevko said now, leaning forward with his elbows on his knees and his hands clasped before his face. "It is a difficult idea. We on the council do not all agree. But it would seem the right thing to do. And, if they can be persuaded, then our own strength will be greatly increased. There is also an added advantage. Perhaps, through cooperation against an existential threat, some sort of lasting understanding and peace could be achieved. You are, of course, aware of the Bringham Hypothesis?"

"Yessir," Khalihl recalled the idea from her days in the Academy. "The idea was, essentially, that a major existential threat from outside of humanity could, possibly, heal political, ideological, and social divisions in humanity. That such a threat could, if navigated correctly, lead to a single human politic for the first time in history."

"That is correct," Serjevko leaned back now. "The added strength of the Black Sun is enough to consider the idea. The ethics demand we do it. But this possibility cannot be ignored. We must consider the future of our species, should we survive this threat. Considering what we now know about our galaxy, about life in the galaxy, humanity will have a greater chance of survival, not to mention flourish, if we can find a way to come together. We do not know what other dangers lurk in the darkness of the void beyond what we have explored. We must, as a species, begin to think in a more unified way about the galaxy, and universe, at large."

Khalihl sensed this explanation was not only intended for her. She had sensed, and Elder Serjevko had mentioned, the disagreement in the council on this issue. *He speaks to those who voted against the idea,* she thought, looking at Hujad and Thans. They met her eyes now, not willing to show their dissent and, perhaps, deciding to present a united front. This, Khalihl realized, was for her benefit. The Council had decided, but they needed her belief. And, suddenly, she knew why.

"Am I to understand," she said, "you are ordering me to propose a treaty, under these circumstances, to the Black Sun?"

"Yes, Sister," Serjevko said. The tension in the room deepened and went still. "I must admit, I do not relish the idea of putting you into danger. None of us do. But the Council agrees you are the best candidate for the mission.

If we are lucky, the Black Sun will judge the whole of the Inner Cluster by your example."

The compliment fell cold on Khalihl, whose mind and body now felt empty and devoid of life. For a moment, she struggled. In order to be successful, she would need to wholly believe this was the right course of action. She knew the trappings of power and the flaws, as well as strengths, of those caught in its trappings. If she did not approach the mission fully committed, the leader of the Black Sun would sense that and could interpret it as deceit. Or, perhaps worse, as weakness. To show weakness to a predator...

"You will, of course, be given anything you require to complete the mission. All you need to do is ask," Serjevko's face belied concern. He could sense the turmoil within her. They did not enjoy asking this of her. They did not like the position they were in. *Desperate times,* thought Khalihl.

"Sir," Khalihl said after thinking about it for a moment. "I would like to bring Herr Meiind with me. He has certain skills which would make him useful in such an endeavor."

"Of course. You may ask him to join, though we cannot force him. Anything else?"

"A fast ship. A very fast ship."

38

*The main problem with the world isn't that there
aren't any good people out there. It's that all the
good people must compromise their goodness just
to survive. When push comes to shove, we all
become a part of the problem.*

*-Overheard in The Black Hole Tavern on
the planet Rot*

The ship's cabin was small, as was the ship itself. *The
Fortune Maker* had been a smuggler's ship that had been
confiscated, with thousands of other ships, when the
defense fleet against the Watchers had begun to be built.
Normally, the Inner Cluster tolerated a certain amount of
crime, which came with a certain amount of smuggling.
But the Cluster was going to need as many ships as they
could get, so they had begun to crack down on the more
harmful criminals. The *Fortune Maker* and its pilot, a
particularly violent man, had been engaged in selling an
especially dangerous drug. As Khalihl went through
systems check after systems check, making sure everything
was in working order and adjusted to her specifications,
Meiind sat out of the way and watched; he was no pilot,
and had no real experience with Cluster ships. Instead, he
was supposed to be reading up on what was known about
the Black Sun, especially about their leader General
Eazkaii. He was, however, having trouble focusing on the
pad before him. His own thoughts, instead, dominated his

awareness.

As Khalihl busied herself at the helm of the small vessel, Meiind thought about the coming meeting, about his surprise the General had agreed to it at all. When Khalihl had asked Meiind to join the mission, he had agreed right away. The mission fell so neatly into his own plans he could hardly believe it. This thought sent a pang of guilt through Meiind. He did not enjoy keeping the truth of his intentions from Khalihl, but, at the same time, he could not risk her trying to stop him. *It must be done,* he thought. *Perhaps it will make the Black Sun easier to negotiate with as well.* He had already wrestled with the idea for weeks, and he always came to the same conclusion about what he had to do. He was determined now. He would not fail himself. He would not fail the billions the General had already murdered.

"Learning anything interesting about the General?" Khalihl said from the helm without turning around. "I haven't read it yet. Where did the information come from?"

Meiind snapped from his thoughts, taking a moment to answer. He had read some of the information provided in the dossier, intelligence gathered from captured Black Sun agents and from rumors spread through the refugees. There had even been some – maybe a few – defectors who had crossed over to the Inner Cluster who seemed sincere, though they were being watched closely. Meiind said as much.

"Still," he continued, "not much is known about how the Black Sun began nor about the General Eazkaii. We do know he grew up as part of a dissident group within the Coalition. His ancestors had been political refugees, anarchists of some kind, who had left the Solar System during the Slow Migration only to be swept up in the expansion of the Coalition later. Eventually, his ancestors stopped trying to get away from the Coalition; every time they moved to a new planet, the Coalition's colonizing forces weren't far behind. Though they settled into life as a part of the Coalition, their culture never really gave up their political roots and always maintained a hate for the Coalition. For any organized form of government, really."

"A little ironic," Khalihl said, still working on the helm controls, "considering he is now the leader of a large political group."

"He doesn't see it that way. According to the defectors the Inner Cluster has interviewed, the Black Sun looks at itself as a kind of militia, albeit a large one. And while they do seem bent on conquest, we have no evidence they leave any sort of governing body behind on the planets they capture. Rather, they seem to fight until a given planet's population submits, scour the planet for men and resources, and then leave. That, or they destroy the entire planet immediately."

They were quiet for a moment as they both remembered the devastation they had seen on Bodhi. How many planets had seen the same fate? How many billions had the Black Sun already killed? Meiind's own determination, already set in stone, hardened all the more.

"Do we know anything about their purpose? About their reasoning?" Khalihl asked.

"Not really," Meiind answered. "Some of the defectors described something like a warrior's cult, described the soldiers sought to die in Glory, in battle. But, beyond that, we know nothing."

Meiind had thought much about this. When he had been a mediator for the Coalition, understanding the motivations of the different groups he worked with was key to facilitating negotiations. He suspected the warrior's cult described in the dossier was more functional for the General of the Black Sun than a belief he himself indulged in. At least, historically, the use of warrior cults to ensure the loyalty and dedication of one's soldiers was well documented. It would not be unheard of to learn Eazkaii held a very different set of beliefs and, therefore, a different set of motivations than simply the desire to die in battle. As to what the true motivations of General Eazkaii could be, Meiind had no idea. He had read the report the dossier included on the Black Sun's known actions and movements, looking for some sort of pattern, some sort of method. As of yet, however, he had not been able to discern anything which helped him to understand Eazkaii. The General left a wake of death and destruction behind him and his fleet. There did not appear to be any reason behind his actions, beyond, perhaps, a need to force others to recognize his superiority. *No matter,* Meiind thought grimly. *Understanding is not necessary for my purposes in this mission. Understanding is beside the point.* Again, Meiind felt his resolve harden. Again, he felt a visceral reaction which seemed to be more in his body than in his mind. What he was about to attempt, the promise to himself he was about to break… he shook his head, trying to clear away the thoughts. Thinking too much now would only serve to sway him in his determination. Instead, he thought more of what he had learned through the dossier.

In the ten years since the Coalition collapsed – *since I caused it to collapse,* thought Meiind – the Black Sun had emerged as the major power in what had been Co space. Little was known about their rise to power; for most of the refugees they had spoken to, the Black Sun had one day appeared in their systems, a fully developed force of destruction. Even the soldiers, those who had been conscripted or had joined and later defected, said much the same. No one seemed to know exactly how the Black Sun had become so powerful, who had funded the creation of their ships, nor how Eazkaii had come to be in charge. The analysts who had compiled the dossier Meiind was reading theorized whatever system the Black Sun had originated in must have been left so destroyed by their ascent to power all information had been lost in the years since. What was known, however, was what the Black Sun had been doing in the years since they rose to prominence.

Over twenty planets taken, some of them conquered and others, the ones that put up fierce resistance, simply destroyed outright. Billions – the estimates ranged from just over two to over ten – had already been murdered. Their fleet numbered in the tens of thousands of ships with millions of soldiers, both prisoners forced to fight and volunteers. And at the head of this massive force, this wave of death, was one man, the man they were preparing to meet with. Meiind tried to think about Eazkaii, tried to imagine a man as evil as this one seemed to be, as callous and destructive. But Meiind could not create an image that seemed to encompass what was known about the man's actions. The idea such a human could exist, that such a person could live with so much blood on his hands, flew in the face of all his years as a mediator, all his years working with people, and was an affront to his view of the universe. How could any single human be so evil?

Meiind did not know, but he intended to find out.

"All set," Khalihl said from the helm, turning to look at Meiind. "Are you ready to meet with the devil?"

"Yes," Meiind said, his face set with determination. "Yes, I am."

39

*This is where it all began and where it all ended.
I am not a superstitious man, but this planet has
seen the forced deaths of millions, perhaps
billions. It is haunted.*

*-Excerpt from Captain Yscaaidt's Log,
11.2476.25*

Yscaaidt had the feeling something was not right. The scout ships performing an orbital sweep had not detected anything out of the ordinary, and neither had long range sensors. Everything appeared as it should be: empty, completely abandoned. Still, he could not shake the feeling something was hiding out there. *Maybe I am just being paranoid,* he thought. *Maybe I am just on edge.* Still, one more sweep would not hurt.

"I want another full sensor sweep of the planet and the system," he said to his tactical officer, Lt. Sonth. "Go over everything one more time. We have to be sure we are alone before we risk putting ships down on the planet."

"Something have you worried?" asked Commander Lensut, his first officer.

"Just an uneasy feeling. Enough to prompt prudence."

Lensut nodded her head. She and Captain Yscaaidt had been together, professionally and intimately, for many years now, and she had learned to trust his instincts as a captain. Yscaaidt's gut feelings had kept them alive during the Hero's Battle ten years ago, and she was willing to listen to them now. Rarely, if ever, had she seen her captain, her partner, so agitated.

Yscaaidt could sense Lensut's concern for him, could feel her eyes on him, watching and reading. She knew him well enough to know what was on his mind now. It was comforting to be so well understood, to have someone on the bridge who could read his thoughts and understand his motives. Yet, at the same time, there was a slight sense of discomfort around the edges, something he always became aware of whenever he realized just how well he and Lensut knew each other. As if their connection entailed a loss of individualism some part of him rebelled against. But, as usual, he found her concern enlightening. Often, her concern for him revealed turmoil within his mind he himself was not aware of. Turmoil he had pushed away and ignored without realizing it. *What has me so tense?* He asked himself, taking a mental inventory as he looked over the reports and readings beginning to stream in from his ships. *What has me so on edge?*

The sensor readings showed nothing out there but their own ships, and still Yscaaidt's unease did not settle. *Perhaps it isn't the Black Sun,* he thought, and he looked up at the planet hanging in space on the view screen. As he gazed upon the gray and white marble suspended in the blackness of the cosmos, his unease grew, and he had a stroke of insight. *It isn't the Black Sun at all,* he thought. *It's the planet.*

"Do you believe in ghosts, Commander?" he asked, his eyes still fixated on the planet.

"Sir?" Lensut looked up from the readings she too had been pouring over, caught off guard.

"Ghosts. Sprits. The souls of the dead left in material form."

"No sir, I do not."

"Of course not," Yscaaidt looked over at the commander with a fond smile. "My grandmother used to tell me stories about ghosts when I was a boy. I don't think she really believed in them, but she told me stories of places that were haunted by the spirits of the people who had suffered in them. They were usually houses and compounds, depending on the story, but one story she told me about was about a haunted planet." Yscaaidt stopped, staring at the planet in the view screen. He could sense the rest of the bridge crew listening as they went about their duties collecting data from the probes and other ships. "Haunted. That's how this planet feels to me. Like it's haunted."

"Many people suffered and died here," Lensut responded.

"Exactly," Yscaaidt now pitched his voice so the rest of his crew would pay attention even though he appeared to still be talking only to Lensut. "That was the point of some of the stories she told me. Places can have their own histories, and those histories can have an effect on the place itself. We should respect those histories, take the time to engage with them." He swept an arm out at the planet in a gesture that was partly anger and partly sorrow. "We do not know how many people died here, but we do know their deaths helped the Inner Cluster grow, expand, thrive. While we of the Cluster did not create this place, did not even know of its existence, we were still accessories to the exploitation of the people who lived here, who were born and suffered here. Even today. Who were the men and women that died so we could skip here to intercept the Black Sun? The debt we owe is far from over."

A tense silence fell upon the bridge as the soldiers who had been listening to their Captain turned to look at the planet on the viewscreen. His words had the effect he wanted. They all, in their own ways, felt the presence of death before them. But it wasn't just death. All things die, and that is only natural. It was the death of the innocent, the exploitation of the oppressed, which left this planet so burdened by the past. It was the exploitation of a people who never had the chance to enjoy the fruits of their own sacrifices that was the true horror here. *Let them see it fully,* Yscaaidt thought. *Let them feel and remember.* After a few moments, he spoke again.

"Any signs of the Black Sun?" he asked, turning to Lt. Sonth at the tactical station and breaking the spell.

"No sir," Sonth replied after a moment off balance. "Long range probes do not show anything, nor do the orbital sweeps. It appears to be all clear."

"Open a channel to all ships," Yscaaidt said to his comms officer, Ensign Deryu.

"Channel open," Deryu responded.

"This is your Captain speaking," Yscaaidt said, his eyes still on the planet before him. "Alpha and Beta, you will head down to the planet. Land just outside the largest compound on the continent in the Northern hemisphere." Meiind's reports had indicated this one to be the main compound of the planet. Yscaaidt and his officers had decided that would be as good a place to start as any. "Gamma and Delta, we will set up a wide perimeter around the planet and keep sensors running. All ships maintain Red Alert. If the Black Sun shows up, I want to know about it immediately. Watch your backs."

A series of "Yes, sirs" and "Aye, sirs" came through the comm as the squadron leaders acknowledged his orders. The lights dimmed and an alarm sounded throughout the ship as tactical input the Red Alert standing. He looked over at Lensut and nodded. She returned the gesture. Yscaaidt turned to his pilot at the helm.

"Ms. Deiift, please take us into orbit," he said.

"Yes sir," Deiift responded, her hands shuffling across the helm controls. "Entering orbit now."

Time to face our ghosts, Yscaaidt thought at they swept down from the void into orbit, the planet growing in the view screen before him.

40

God works in mysterious ways, and He is under no obligation to make His plans known to us. Get over it.

-Anonymous

Maldeck had never been to New Mecca, had never even thought he would ever see it. The vast sprawl of the capital under his orbital shuttle, the massive buildings he could see in the distance at what he assumed was the city center, was overwhelming. On his home planet – a sharp pang ran through him as he thought about the place he was born and where he had lived his life until the Black Sun had forced his people to run to the Inner Cluster – there had not been any large cities, no large buildings. They had been an agrarian people, living on farms. Small town centers, at most, had been at the places where major roads intersected, but these usually had only a small number of buildings and businesses. Even on Sahaj, where his people had been resettled, Maldeck had never been to any of the larger cities, avoiding contact with the Sihken as he thought was right. So to see a place like this, to see the massive structures reaching for the sky and the roads and buildings stretching from horizon to horizon, to sense the incredible mass of people living here, flowing through their lives beneath him as he flew over, to feel all of this for the first time made Maldeck feel slightly intoxicated. *No wonder they worship themselves and lose sight of God,* he thought as he looked out of the porthole. *No wonder they feel as if they are the masters of the universe, of themselves.*

He looked away and took a moment to distance himself from the sensation. How many young people had they already lost to the temptation of the city, to the excitement the city offered? He must stay strong despite the wonderful things he might see here, the incredible feats of humanity's hubris. Maldeck glanced at the people around him on the orbital shuttle, an eclectic mix from different parts of the Inner Cluster. The people of the Cluster visited New Mecca for many different reasons: the hajj, to settle civil suits, for business, or even just for vacation. The shuttle was quiet, mostly, except for a small child playing some sort of word game with his mother towards the front. Maldeck recognized some of them from the public ship he had taken from Sahaj, though there had been thousands on that ship and only hundreds on this one. His imagination had begun to create lives for them, to extrapolate stories from their lives based on small details he observed. *But I must not forget,* he forced himself to think, *most of them are heathens. Most of them do not believe in the truth.*

The thought of heathens, of the unbelievers, brought to mind his purpose in coming to New Mecca, and a shadow passed over his mind. He felt, as he had many times on his journey here, a stab of doubt and a pang of guilt. Maldeck could not help but wonder if his coming here was a mistake, a foolish errand of optimism. After all, how could they possibly share the same goals in light of how different they were? Even if the message said all the right words, it was hard to believe. He and the men of his colony had discussed the message for nights on end, arguing about the wisdom of the course of action Maldeck was now taking. And even though, in the end, they had decided it was worth the chance, Maldeck could not help but feel naïve, could not help but fear they were being misled. *We will just be using them for our own means,* he reminded himself. *Nothing more.*

"Please prepare for landing," a voice over the comm system drew Maldeck from his own thoughts. He looked back out the window. The shuttle was low now, the city closer and closer. He adjusted his safety webbing as a woman, wearing too few clothes in his opinion, came by and checked to make sure the passengers were all securely fastened. The landing was, as usual, smooth and uneventful. Maldeck went through the motions without thinking much, his mind focused on the coming meeting, on the message that had precipitated his coming here to New Mecca. As he went through customs and through the security checks, he read the message again in his mind, while, at the same time, he kept aware of his surroundings.

In the message, the writer had identified himself as Bin Ald, a member of the Original Way. This had been the first cause for alarm for Maldeck and his people. They had heard of the Original Way in the Cluster news feeds, had heard of the Musla group who was returning to the original ways of Islam, rejecting the new teachings that had transformed the old religion into Isla'hai. Maldeck at once respected and feared them. He respected their desire to return to what they perceived to be the ancient wisdom of their pasts. Even though he thought of them as the unfaithful, he sympathized with the impulse, as it was the same impulse which had driven his ancestors back to Christianity. But he also feared them, for he knew his history well enough to know Islam had been a powerful and violent force in the world for many generations. This simultaneous respect and fear had been apparent in the way the news had covered the group's sudden rise to political prominence. The people of the Inner Cluster responded to their message but did not know how far to trust them, did not know how far the New Muslims, as they called themselves, would go.

As he waited in line in customs, Maldeck saw a large group of disheveled men, women, and children being ushered through the checkpoints by a group of Cluster soldiers, some of them apparently medics. Maldeck instantly recognized the group as refugees – he could sense their exhaustion, their desperation, their loss of sprit. He had been there once and remembered the feeling of hopelessness distinctly. As they passed, he sent a silent prayer after them, an automatic reaction, wishing them God's blessing and wishing them a path to the truth and salvation, before returning to his thoughts.

The message had been simple and direct. The writer, this Bin Ald, claimed to respect the fundamentalism of Maldeck's group, to admire their return to faith. He also claimed they, Maldeck's people and the Original Way, could be of use to one another in the coming crisis between the Cluster and the Black Sun and the Watchers. He asked for a meeting, in person, so they could discuss the potential mutual benefit of working together. Had the message ended there, it is likely Maldeck and his people would have ignored it, and he would never have come, would never have been sent to seek out this Bin Ald. But there had been one more section, one section Maldeck and the men he had discussed the message with simply could not ignore:

The end draws near. The ways of the One True God are mysterious to all men, even to those of faith. The instruments of God's judgement know not our petty differences and will hold us all accountable. We cannot avoid our own reckoning.

The similarity of those words to things Maldeck himself had said in discussion shocked him. The men in his group had argued heavily over the meaning of those words, over the understanding they seemed to entail. Was it possible, Maldeck had asked, they of the Original Way, despite their heathen faith and ways, had interpreted the signs the same way? Was it possible they recognized the Watchers for what they were? While not everyone agreed this was so, most of them agreed the message made it a possibility. And that possibility had to be explored.

"Reason for visiting?" the agent in the small stall, behind protective glass, asked when it was Maldeck's turn to approach.

"Tourism," Maldeck said, none of the lie audible in his voice because it was not quite a lie at all. They had decided telling the truth would be the best option, so Maldeck did intend to see some of the capital, to do some of the things visitors to the planet do. "I am excited to see the Grand Mosque, to see where the Prophets first started the Inner Cluster," Maldeck added as he passed his travel pad through the glass, hoping it did not sound too enthusiastic.

The agent glanced up for a moment, considering Maldeck's words, before returning his attention to the pad before him. For an agonizing few seconds, Maldeck became frightened something would go wrong. *You've done nothing illegal,* he thought to himself. *Even meeting with the Original Way is not against the law.* Still, he could not help but feel his meeting was meant to be clandestine somehow. That the Original Way had plans which would bring them into conflict with the Inner Cluster powers that be. *Like our plans and ideas,* he thought. And, the Original Way had already caused some stir with their ideas; there had been demonstrations organized, public meetings held. Maldeck had seen reports on the news feeds about their political impact. After receiving their message, Maldeck and some of the others had gone through the old feeds to see what the Original Way had already been up to. No doubt they were being closely watched by the government as well.

"Enjoy your trip," the agent said, handing the papers

back through the slot in the glass and motioning Maldeck along. A wave of relief passed through him as he accepted his pad and walked through.

Outside the space port, it was a warm and sunny day. In the distance, Maldeck could see the swirling minarets and the pointed domes of the Grand Mosque, massive looking even at such a distance. Beyond that, the city center, with its massive buildings glinting in the sunlight like so many jewels, stretched out across the close horizon. And behind them, a mountain range with a few distinct peaks, the Prophets' Mountains Maldeck knew. He had refused the offered history courses when he had arrived on Sahaj, yet the story the Inner Cluster's founding was hard to avoid now that he lived in their territory. He knew the Prophets, the leaders of the original generation ship that had made its way to this planet from Earth, had climbed those mountains when they first arrived, had used its vantage point to plan the city that would become New Mecca, the capital of the Inner Cluster. It troubled Maldeck in some vague way to know the story. The sight of it all gave him a general sense of unease. He felt as though he was in enemy territory. *Perhaps after my meeting tomorrow,* he thought, *I will be in a very real sense.*

Another wave of tension – more like fear – ran through him, and he spent a long moment pretending to look at his papers while he fought it down. It had been his decision to volunteer to come for this meeting; no one else had been forthcoming, and he had, after all, been one of the more vocal about what he believed the Watchers truly were, about their true purpose. So it felt right he should be the one to come find out if the Original Way, if the New Muslims, could be of use to their small group of the faithful. Still, he felt ill suited for this kind of thing. He was a simple man, a farmer and a laborer. Nothing in his life had prepared him for what he was planning to engage in now – sedition, espionage, and who knew what else, who knew where this meeting would lead. *Noah was a drunk with a stammer,* he thought to himself, trying to marshal his courage. *Magdalene was a prostitute, Paul was a tax collector, and Christ was a carpenter. My past does not matter. It's only through God we achieve greatness.* The thought bolstered his resolve some. His sense of faith, of conviction and of righteousness, returned.

Maldeck turned and began to walk over to where the public transports sat waiting for patrons. Tomorrow he would put his faith to the test. Tomorrow, he would meet with this Bin Ald and, God willing, his destiny and that of his people would become intertwined with God's plans for humanity. Today, however, he needed to act the part of the tourist. Today, he needed to keep his faith safe while he pretended to admire the works of the humanity he had rejected in favor of a more divine purpose. Today, he felt, would be the last day of the simple life he had always known.

41

The only good is Might. The only virtue is Strength. The only truth is Chaos. The only goal is Glory. Push all else from your mind.

-*Excerpt from the* Book of the Black Sun, *Author Unknown*

The bridge was kept dark, just the way he liked it, so the darkness of the void, displayed in the massive view screen he had ordered installed, seemed to seamlessly transition into the interior of the ship. He had heard officers new to working command posts talk about the feeling of being on the bridge, the feeling that the barrier between the ship and space felt thin and permeable here. They talked about the pull of the void, about how they felt as if they were going to be sucked out into space at any moment. They talked about how it never quite passed, about how they never quite get accustomed to it. This feeling itself was why Eazkaii had ordered the viewscreen expanded. He wanted his bridge officers to be on edge, to be alert. And he wanted them to remember their place in the cosmos, to be reminded of the reality of the universe around them. Looking at the view screen now from his captain's seat, he could see billions of small pinpoints of light as well as the wash of color of a nearby nebula. *Chaos,* he thought. *Each of those lights represents unimaginable chaos and power. And from that fire, from that destructive force, the universe is made. We are made. It all begins in chaos.*

Eazkaii enjoyed contemplating this view, especially just before a disciplinary council. He found being reminded of the Primacy of Chaos, as he called it, in such a visceral way, his limited being confronted with the infinite, always wanting to shirk back and hide, he found this sensation, this combination of emotions, always strengthened his resolve. It was the same before a battle. Or when he harbored doubts. That is what it all came down to: pitiful, weak doubt. But sitting here, staring into the face of emptiness, into the truth of the universe, into Chaos itself, his doubt was always burned away by the fire of the stars, by the turmoil of creation. *It is time,* he thought. *Some housekeeping first.*

"Bring me the prisoner," he said quietly, motioning to his security officer, who immediately left the bridge. A few moments later, the officer returned with a man, a soldier in uniform, shambling before him, his hands and feet shackled. The officer brought the prisoner in front of Eazkaii, who sat in his captain's chair, and brought the butt of his weapon to the back of the man's knees with just enough force to buckle his legs, forcing him to kneel. The officer stepped one pace to the side.

"Commander Retrin," Eazkaii said, keeping his eyes on the lowered head of the prisoner. The bridge had gone silent when the prisoner had been brought in, everyone waiting to see what would happen. *They fear they could be next,* Eazkaii thought with satisfaction. "Read the charges."

"Private Balklen," Retrin began, "is accused of treason. He was apprehended attempting to send a message into enemy territory."

Eazkaii did not speak for a moment, letting the commander's words fall into the silence and echo there. This council was being fed to and displayed in all the ships in his fleet. He knew a certain amount of drama went a long way, that this man's transgression and punishment, if handled correctly, could be useful in keeping his grip over his army. Many of them believed, as he did, in their cause. But many were, as this man before him, conscripted soldiers, men captured from their conquests and forced to fight. It was this group Eazkaii needed to make sure understood their place, understood the consequences of disobedience.

"What do you have to say for yourself, private?" Eazkaii asked, keeping his voice low but letting a hint of rage linger in the air of his words.

"Sir," Balklen's voice came out shaky with fear, though he did not look up. "I was only trying to send a message to my family, to let them know I am still alive. Nothing more."

"Is your family a part of the Black Sun? Do they follow our way?" Eazkaii asked.

"Sir?" Balklen stammered. "They are simple people sir. Laborers on Telus. My father – "

"Then they are not of the Black Sun," Eazkaii cut Balklen off, allowing his voice to rise now. "And if they are not of the Black Sun, then they can only be one thing: the enemy. To attempt to communicate with them is treason. I find you guilty as charged by your own admission."

"Sir," Balklen's stammer grew worse as he raised his bound hands in pleading. "Please understand – "

"Silence!" Eazkaii screamed, his voice reverberating throughout the bridge, his anger beginning to swell. He let the silence brew for a moment before speaking again, now pitching his voice so all those listening knew he was also speaking to them. "It is you who needs to understand. There are only two truths in the universe: Chaos and

Glory. Chaos is the creator, the destroyer, the machine powering the cosmos, the function of everything within it, the primary force. Glory is what we achieve when we live and die in service of Chaos. All else is false. All else is weak. All else is blasphemy to the truth." Eazkaii now swung his gaze around to take in everyone on his bridge, everyone on every ship now listening. "We of the Black Sun worship Chaos and seek Glory. We are instruments of the primary force of the universe. We create Chaos, and through it we bring the universe into being, we bring Glory into being. Nothing else matters. Understand this: we of the Black Sun have no selves aside from Chaos. We have no pasts nor futures. We have no possessions nor ambitions. We have no families. We only have the Black Sun. Do you understand?"

The man kneeling before him, now shaking uncontrollably, nodded, and Eazkaii could sense everyone on the bridge nodding as well. The point was well taken, but the final nail still needed to be placed, still needed to be forced into position.

"You are lucky today, private," Eazkaii said, allowing his voice to trail back to a normal speaking tone. "I am feeling lenient, maybe even merciful."

"Thank you, sir," Balklen could hardly speak, he was trembling so much.

"Commander Retrin," Eazkaii turned his attention to his stoic security officer who had not moved from his position just off to the side of the prisoner. "I believe this man is truly repentant for his mistake. What do you think?"

"I believe you are correct, sir," Retrin responded without any hint he knew the set piece Eazkaii was playing. "Private Balklen appears to have seen the error he has committed."

"Then let us do the best we can for him," Eazkaii now kept his eyes on Balklen, smiling warmly. "Let us send him to Glory before his unfortunately weak constitution fails him again, before he is able to lose his chance for Glory forever. I sentence you, Private Balklen, to death by jettison. Take him away."

Balklen began to open his mouth to protest, his eyes wide with shock, but Retrin was behind him in an instant and slapped a neural inhibitor on the base of his skull before the man could get a word out. He went silent and completely still. Using a small pad to send electrical impulses through the inhibitor and into the man's brain, Retrin forced him to stand and led him away. Eazkaii watched, his face calm and set in stone, as Retrin handed Balklen off to another security officer and as the man demurely walked off the bridge to his death. Retrin returned to his post to continue whatever work it was he had been doing before the interruption. Slowly, everyone on the bridge returned to work. Eazkaii sat back in his chair and contemplated what had just happened. There were always more soldiers to be had, more people to force into ranks, but the man's disobedience troubled him. He had no room for such blatant sentimentality, such weakness, in his army. A message home seemed like a small thing, but the same sentiment during a battle, the same willingness to defy orders in a crisis, could be very dire indeed.

"Computer, give me Lt. Peruy in Reassignment," Eazkaii said, tapping his comm.

"Lt. Peruy here, sir," came the answer almost immediately.

"I would like to see you on the bridge, Lt.,

immediately." Eazkaii's voice betrayed no emotion.

"Sir," the voice on the other side said after a moment of hesitation. "On my way, sir."

It was then Eazkaii's first officer, Commander Yenzeiishin returned to the bridge and took his seat next to the captain.

"Sir," Yenzeiishin said, leaning over towards the captain and speaking in a low voice. "I have just received word from the Inner Cluster emissaries. They should be arriving very soon. They will let us know a few minutes before they come."

"Excellent," Eazkaii said. "Keep me informed of their progress. I wish to be ready when they get here." *But they will not be ready,* he thought. *They will not be ready for what awaits them.* Eazkaii had been surprised when the Admiral of the Inner Cluster, a woman called Khalihl, had contacted him and requested a meeting. Usually, the Black Sun did not meet with their enemies. There was no compromise to be had, other than utter surrender to the Black Sun, so Eazkaii did not often bother. But they, the Black Sun, had shown their supremacy, his advisors argued. Perhaps the Inner Cluster wished to surrender and avoid conflict. Perhaps they saw the Black Sun could not be defeated. Eazkaii had listened to his advisors' arguments and disagreed with them. The Inner Cluster had never shown any willingness to surrender to the Coalition, and though the Black Sun was more ruthless and aggressive in their conquest, they were not larger. They were also ten years apart at sublight. Why, he had asked his advisors, would they surrender now? Why not wait five or eight years to do so? They could do a lot to prepare in that time. A lot could happen to the Black Sun in that time. It was in the Inner Cluster's favor, even if they chose to surrender in the end, to wait. No, Eazkaii reasoned, they must have other reasons for requesting the meeting. Just as Eazkaii had his own reasons for accepting the meeting.

"Sir," Yenzeiishin said from his seat next to the captain. "Lt. Peruy is here."

Eazkaii stirred from his thoughts and raised his eyes to see the Lt. kneeling before him, ten paces from his chair, head lowered and eyes on the floor. *This one knows his place,* he thought. *That humility just saved your life.*

"Lt.," Eazkaii said, allowing the years of command flow from his voice. "I just had to execute another conscripted soldier for attempting to contact home. Tell me, how many is that now?"

"Three this past month, sir," Peruy said immediately, snapping the words out without hesitation. "This is three times Reassignment has failed you under my command, sir. I have failed you and the Black Sun. I wish to retain my place in the Chaos and request the Glory, sir."

"You have failed me three times now, Lt.," Eazkaii said, even as his thoughts went a different direction. *This one is true to the faith, willing to die rather than to fail. We need men like him. We will need many more by the time this is all done.* "That is, as you know, unacceptable. However, you have also reassigned thousands and thousands of conscripted prisoners, some of whom have become trusted officers even here on my bridge after passing through Reassignment under your command. I would say your success rate is quite high, no?"

"Sir," Peruy said after a moment of pause. "I am grateful for the praise, General, but failure is still failure, no matter what successes come before or after."

"Spoken like a true soldier of the Black Sun," Eazkaii said. *Balance,* he thought. *In the end, Chaos brings balance to all things. We should be no different. Let the crew see how forgiving I can be.* "Stand, Lt. Peruy. I want you to review the files on Private Balklen's reassignment and try to find out what went wrong, where he slipped through, and to develop a more robust system for recognizing and dealing with high-risk individuals."

"Yes, sir."

"I am going to have two new conscriptions for you soon, in a few days perhaps," Eazkaii said. *If they survive interrogation,* he thought but did not add aloud. "They will not be easy cases, and I want this new method to be ready by then."

"Yes, sir."

"Dismissed," Eazkaii watched as Peruy snapped a turn on his heels and marched out with intention, presumably to begin work immediately. *A model soldier, even when he fails me,* Eazkaii thought. *If he is successful, he will deserve promotion.* Eazkaii quickly made a note of this intention in his personal log. He was just finishing up the entry when Yenzeiishin leaned over once more.

"They are here, sir," the first officer said, his voice deadly calm.

"Good," Eazkaii said. *Now, we can begin.*

<u>42</u>

Knowing what we know now, there are parts of the historical record, twists in the story, that make more sense. Where there were gaps before, we now see the agency of a previously unseen actor. The importance of this actor, whatever it may be, cannot be overstated.

>*-Excerpt from* God's Hand: the Unseen in History *by Eldish Juret*

It is of some controversy whether or not the meeting ever actually took place. Why would they risk their most experienced and highest ranking officer on such a hopeless mission? But others believe the legend is in character with the Inner Cluster's ideology and actions. I, for one, choose to believe in its truth, for sometimes the story is more important than the facts.

>*-Excerpt from* Legends of the Inner Cluster: a Study through Story *by Aasned Hujah*

General Eazkaii's ready room was as black as the rest of the ship, though not as spartan. The walls were covered in what he had explained were souvenirs from planets he had been to – trophies of conquest. At least, this was how Meiind interpreted the comment, and the idea made his resolve deepen even more. Still, he found himself hesitating as Khalihl and the General went through their opening lines, through their introduction and into negotiations. *Maybe,* Meiind thought, *he will see reason and join us.* It seemed an incredibly unlikely scenario, but Meiind had to give the man that chance before he made his move. He could at least do that. But the moment the General showed any aggression, the moment it was certain he would not join them…

Eazkaii had welcomed them with pomp and fanfare, the docking bay entrance lined with his officers holding flags bearing the dark circle of the Black Sun's crest. There had even been a small band made up of soldiers playing the kind of percussion-driven music authoritarian regimes tended to enjoy. The General himself had been charismatic and flamboyant when he welcomed them aboard his ship. The entire scene had surprised Meiind, as well as Khalihl, whose surprise he could read on the mild look of concern she wore on her face, until he thought about it some more. Tyrants, in order to gain and stay in power, often had to use narratives of greatness, stories of righteous purpose, in order to impress others and to keep their own in line. All the show, the flags and the band and the General's behavior, all of it was a part of the narrative. It was all for the benefit of the crew as much as for them, the emissaries from another power.

The General took them on a quick tour of the ship before they settled to speak, passing them through the engineering decks and the weapons bays before finally taking them to the bridge and to his ready room. Meiind had to admit he was impressed. After ten years of nearly constant battle, he had expected a more haggard group, a more derelict ship. He had thought of them, before coming here, more as a band of pirates than a military force and had expected them to look the part, to match the image he held in his mind. Yet, everything was immaculate and in perfect order. From the officers' uniforms in the entourage trailing them to the soldiers snapping to attention whenever they entered a room to the spotless walls and floors of even the engine room, Meiind got the sense the ship was well run under tight discipline. At first, he assumed this too must be a part of the show, but as they went from deck to deck, room to room, the General talking the entire time about the ship and about the history of the Black Sun, Meiind began to suspect this was how things always were. He saw nothing but complete obedience in the soldiers they encountered, though he did sense something else just under the surface. He reached out with his touch occasionally, just observing the mental states of the mostly men they encountered, and he sensed the same thing in them all: fear. They were afraid of the General. He ruled through terror.

This made the most surprising thing of all, General Eazkaii himself, even harder to understand. From the moment they had met, the General had been at ease and loquacious, almost friendly, with his new guests. He talked almost the entire time, asking a few questions but mostly just telling them about what he termed the glorious history of the Black Sun's rise to power. He seemed to revel in the chance to paint the Black Sun as a major power in human space to the other major power, but Meiind could not tell if this was a part of the act or if he was being genuine. A feint within a feint or true hubris? Either possibility fit with what they knew of the Black Sun. There were, however, some hard edges to the man who now asked if they would like anything to drink while motioning them to sit around a small table in his room just off the bridge. Well covered by his friendly words and glances, Meiind could see something beneath the surface, something in between the lines of his words and in the backs of his eyes, something hidden and, Meiind thought, sinister. He glanced at Khalihl, who had been the one doing most of the talking, matching the General's friendliness with her own. Meiind sensed a hard edge within her too, could see it in the not-quite-relaxed set of her shoulders and face. She was playing the General's game, playing at openness, but, Meiind thought, she too sensed the undercurrent of fear and brutality running through the ship. She too saw through the General's act. Whether or not this would be enough to give them an advantage Meiind did not know. He still could not tell what chance they had of success in this mission. He certainly was not holding his breath.

Both Khalihl and Meiind refused the offer for refreshment, and the General sat down across from them. He motioned for the officer who had followed them into the room, a man introduced as First Officer Commander Yenzeiishin, to leave them alone. The man complied hesitantly. In an instant, the mask of friendly cooperation fell from Eazkaii's face and was replaced by a stone visage of hard determination.

"Now that the pleasantries have been done with…" Eazkaii said, leaning back in his chair. "Please excuse all the show. The crew wishes to be seen as powerful in the eyes of their enemies," he waved a hand to stop Khalihl from speaking, "they do see you as an enemy. The Black Sun has no allies, only enemies who have not yet surrendered and become a part of the Black Sun themselves. At least, this is what they believe."

"And you," Khalihl responded, "what do you believe?"

"I believe in the Black Sun," the General said with a slight smile, "though I have a bit of a more nuanced view. As their leader, a certain amount of ambiguity and gray often must be dealt with."

Khalihl nodded, but Meiind sensed something behind

273

the words. *He is lying,* Meiind thought. *He believes as much as the rest of them.* And then the last piece which had been bothering Meiind fell into place and with it everything he had seen began to make sense. *He is a zealot, a fanatic,* Meiind thought with growing alarm. He wanted desperately to warn Khalihl.

"Now," the General said, his eyes narrowing, "tell me why you are here."

It doesn't matter, Meiind thought grimly. *Just do what you came to do,* he told himself. And with that, he reached out not to touch General Eazkaii – he had learned to control his abilities well enough in the last ten years he could manipulate an individual source without the deluge of memories and life experiences – but to squeeze him out of existence. He found it and wrapped his mind around the General's essence, thinking to himself: *Don't hesitate. Think of the lives he has destroyed. Think of all the people he will murder if he is allowed to live.* He felt the General there like the glow of a light through closed eyelids, and, determined, Meiind began to close his energy around the General's source. But, just as he was about to squeeze, he felt something he did not at first recognize blocking his ability, separating his contact with the General. He fought against it, beginning to panic. *Does Eazkaii have the same ability as I?* Meiind's thoughts began to swirl wildly, and he looked at the General, who was still looking at Khalihl and awaiting an answer to his question. Only a few moments had passed; he did not seem to be aware of what Meiind was trying to do. Meiind tried harder to squeeze, but whatever force repelling him only grew. And then he felt something enter him, enter his own space in whatever dimension the Sources inhabited. And with that sensation came recognition, for he knew at once he had felt this before.

It was the Presence. Whatever it was that had guided him in his times of need in the trance before was back, and this time it had sought him out. Without any choice, Meiind felt himself falling into the trance, being pulled into it by the Presence. He took one last glance at Khalihl before the trance overtook him.

●●●●

"We have information," Khalihl began after taking a deep breath. *The moment of truth,* she thought. "We believe this information is important for all of the human race to know about. As the leading power in this sector of space, we wished to share this information with you."

The General's face, still as stone, just stared blankly back at her, inviting Khalihl to go on. She glanced over at Meiind, but he appeared to be intently staring at the General, perhaps trying to read the man. She pressed on.

"A few months ago," she said, bringing out her pad and swiping it on, "the Inner Cluster received a message from deep within the galaxy." At this, the General's eyebrows rose slightly, a small chink in his armor of impassivity. "The message was a star map. On the map, a large fleet was indicated, as well as a flight trajectory. The fleet, which was represented as thousands of large ships, is, according to the message, heading directly for human space."

Silence descended upon the General's ready room in his massive ship. Already dark, with black walls and low lighting, Khalihl's words seemed to drop them into yet another magnitude of darkness. *Even after all these months of preparation,* she thought, *all these months contemplating the fact of the Watchers, it still my heart to know they are on their way.* She pushed the thought aside and focused her attention on the

General, who had shifted his body weight in his seat and was staring at her intently. He required her full attention. He was not to be trusted.

"Is that all the information you have?" he asked slowly, cautiously.

"No," she said. "We attempted to contact whomever sent the message. We believe – "

"How did you contact them?" the General snapped.

"That… technology is classified and not within the scope of this meeting," Khalihl responded, stifling the urge to look at the, as of yet, silent Meiind seated next to her. The General, apparently not surprised at her unwillingness to divulge information, gestured for her to continue. "Our contact with the source of the message was cut short by them, but the impression they left was clear. They believe the information they sent us, and they fear whatever fleet it is that is on their way to us now. They fear them as prey fears a predator." The General seemed to respond to the analogy, as Khalihl hoped he would. *I must speak his language if I am going to be able to convince him to join us.* "The Inner Cluster has chosen to take this threat seriously. We think you should as well. We are currently preparing ourselves for an invasion of human space."

Khalihl could see in the General's eyes he understood the doubling thrust of her last comment. He would interpret it in two ways: the threat was real – at least real enough to require preparation – and the Inner Cluster was increasing their own military strength. Whether it was to defend themselves against the invasion from the inner parts of the galaxy or against the Black Sun did not matter. They would be ready for either. *Men like this,* Khalihl thought, *respond not to reason, not to empathy, not to friendship, but only to one thing: strength.* She needed to project as much strength as she could.

"This information," the General said after a long moment looking over the information on the pad Khalihl had handed him before sliding it back across the table, "could have easily been sent over a message. Tell me, why did you really come to meet with me and with the Black Sun?"

Khalihl glanced one more time over at Meiind, who was still frozen in place, his eyes focused on something distant, something unseen. *Damn you,* Khalihl thought. *Not much help, are we? I hope whatever you are learning there now, Meiind, is worth it. I could use your instincts right now.* She gathered up her pad and looked into the General's eyes. They were cold and intelligent, and there was something else in there Khalihl could not quite place. *He is not going to agree to this. And, likely, he is not going to let us go.* It was clear to Khalihl then; the meeting had been a mistake. They had assumed some common ground between the Inner Cluster and the Black Sun – humanity – but, looking into Eazkaii's eyes now, Khalihl could see he operated under a different set of rules. Under a different set of beliefs. And that was when she realized what she had been looking at, what she was seeing in his eyes. *Belief. He truly believes.* She knew then he could not be reasoned with. She also knew, in that moment, that, sitting in the docking bay of this vessel, the flagship of the Black Sun fleet, was her own small ship... with a fully functioning skip drive installed.

"Why have you used such force in your conquest of what is left of the Coalition?" she asked suddenly, switching her tack as quickly as the intuition about Eazkaii had come to her. *Information. The best I can do now is information.* "You are powerful enough to force submission. Why all the death and destruction?"

"Is this to be a tribunal?" Eazkaii settled back in his

seat, utterly at ease and unconcerned with the question. "Am I to be tried for my crimes?"

"No," she said, feigning submissiveness. "We are in your space now. I would not presume. I just… wish to understand before I relay the Inner Cluster's offer."

"You are going to ask the Black Sun to join you against the coming invasion, yes?" The General looked down his nose at Khalihl. He glanced at the silent Meiind and then turned his attention back to the Admiral. "I sense that is your mission, but you have realized the futility of it. You are right. We will never join with the Inner Cluster, nor with anyone else. Alliances are for the weak, and there is only strength in this universe. Alliances seek to create order, and there is only chaos."

Strength and Chaos, Khalihl thought, having heard the ring those words carried in Eazkaii's voice. "I don't understand," she said, allowing her voice to sound somewhat plaintive. *Let him think I despair.* "You already have taken the Coalition. What more does the Black Sun need?"

"The Black Sun does not *need* anything," Eazkaii sneered, his up till now stoic face twisting into a sinister grimace. "The Black Sun seeks only one thing: Glory. There is only one path to Glory: Chaos. And there is only one thing that matters in the context of Glory and Chaos: Strength. You weak hearted fools of the Inner Cluster are worse than the Coalition was with their democracy and their economics. At least they accepted a certain amount of uncertainty. At least the Coalition allowed work through competition. But the Inner Cluster, the Isla'hai, you focus your efforts on cooperation and planning. You seek equality and fairness. You don't know it, but you seek the very thing which will be your undoing in the end: stagnation. If we were all to fall under the Inner Cluster, humanity would cease to be the force it is. We would cease to be the power we are. Instead, we would wither away in complacent comfort."

Khalihl, listening to his tirade, recognized the words and tone, saw then what she had truly seen behind Eazkaii's eyes. *Religion,* she thought. *The Black Sun is not a political power. It is a religion. This is a holy war they wage.* This information changed everything, and she felt the pieces of the Black Sun's history fall into place. Their rise to power, their tactics, their continued aggression despite their apparent dominance, their inflexibility. All of it made sense through the lens of a religious ideology. *I will have to think more of it,* she thought. *But right now, I need to convince him not to kill us. I need to convince him he needs us. The Elders need to know this about them.*

"The skip drive in our ship will not work without my authorization," she said, dropping her mask of fear and submission and starring straight into his eyes. She saw him recoil ever so slightly, just enough for her trained eyes to see, at her leap of logic. "If you try and access it in any way, it will be destroyed. It will be of no use to you." She had argued for this precaution successfully and was glad for it now. It will give them some time to work out a way to get the information she had learned about the Black Sun back to the Inner Cluster, a problem part of her mind was already working on. *There are always malcontents,* she thought.

"I assumed as much," Eazkaii said in his venomous voice. "There is no need to fight us. The Black Sun cannot be defeated. Chaos is the natural way of the cosmos; it cannot be tamed or resisted. It would be much better for you to simply give us what we need. The other options… well, they are much more painful."

"I—" Khalihl looked again at Meiind, who had not spoken or moved for any of the conversation, lost in thought or in the trance or wherever he was. "We will not help you. We came only to inform you of the coming invasion and to ask you to join the defense effort. We have completed our mission. As a citizen of the Inner Cluster, I demand you release us to return to our own space."

"No," Eazkaii said. "No, I don't think I will."

He reached forward and tapped something under the table with a hand. The door to the ready room immediately opened and a contingent of security officers stepped into the room, weapons leveled at Khalihl and the inert Meiind. *This might have been a fool's errand,* Khalihl thought grimly, *but we learned what drives these people, what motivates the Black Sun. The Elders must learn of this.*

"Pray my engineers figure out how to remove the skip drive from your ship," the General said, his voice dripping with malice as he pressed his hands on his knees to stand. "Pray I don't have to come ask you… questions about it."

43

We will use whatever tools Allah has put at our disposal to achieve His Will. For some, this may mean doing unseemly things. But who are we to judge, ultimately, the righteousness of the Will of the One True God?

-Unknown, overheard at political rally

The man sitting across from Bin Ald had not said much upon entering the café where he had planned for their meeting to happen. The introductions had been short, even curt, and now it had been a full few minutes since either of them spoke. Bin Ald had asked about Maldeck's travels, but the man had only muttered an unintelligible answer. Their kol'koffs sat steaming on the table between them, and the café was silent and empty save for the faint sounds of people outside in the street. *We will have to get around to speaking eventually,* Bin Ald thought with a sigh. He did not know what he had expected, but this silence, this refusal to engage, was not it. Maldeck had barely even looked him in the eye when he walked in, and now he sat with his eyes pointed down at his hands in his lap. Bin Ald cleared his throat, an incredibly loud noise in the relative silence of the room.

"It is obvious you are uncomfortable here," he said, trying to be gentle. "Is there anything I can do to help with that?"

Maldeck finally looked up at Bin Ald, staring into his eyes, for a long second. Then, there appeared to be some sort of change in his face, as if he had come to a decision of some sort.

"I am sorry," Maldeck began, his voice wavering some. "My people are... unaccustomed to visiting strange worlds and speaking with strangers. We mostly keep to ourselves. As such, I am not very good at things like this."

"I understand," Bin Ald said, relieved they were finally making some headway. "Your people have isolated themselves for a long time, yes?"

"Yes," Maldeck leaned forward and sniffed the steaming cup before him tentatively. "We lived in almost complete isolation. Until the Black Sun came and we were forced into the Cluster, that is. We now share a planet for the first time in generations, though most of us still prefer to keep to ourselves."

"I understand. We of –"

"Do you?" Maldeck looked up quickly with a sharp glance.

"Yes, I believe so," Bin Ald said. *Common ground,* he thought. *Start with common ground.* "It is the opinion of the Original Way, my sect of Islam, that our ancestors lost their way, lost the truth, through too much contact with other cultures, other religions, other ways. We seek something similar to what your people have protected over the generations, if my understanding is correct. We seek to keep the old ways. We seek to return to the truths of our forefathers. The truths of the One True God."

"Yes," Maldeck nodded with something like grudging approval. "I can understand that, though, from our perspective, you worship an idol and not the true Savior."

"Yes," Bin Ald forced a smile, thinking, *common ground.* "We say the same of you and yours."

Maldeck surprised him then by smiling back and visibly relaxing some. *He needed to say that,* Bin Ald thought. *He needed me to know his religion is foremost for him. That he will not compromise it. So long as I respect his commitment…* It was time to address the true purpose of their meeting, Bin Ald decided.

"Why did you come?" he asked. "Why did you accept my invitation?"

"There were," Maldeck answered, "connotations in your language which spoke to me. Things , despite our obvious differences, I felt like I understood."

Bin Ald nodded but did not speak, waiting for more.

"That," Maldeck continued, "and we are but a small group of simple people tucked away on a planet distant from the center of things here in the Inner Cluster. We have no influence, no hope of making a difference in these… interesting times. I sensed similar goals to ours in your message, though I still do not know how it is possible."

"I have wondered about that as well," Bin Ald said, still nodding. "But the ways of Allah – of God – are strange, are they not? And in times like those we live in now, times when most have given up their faith or turned faith into a caricature of what it once was, into a lifestyle or culture, there is a certain sense to our two ways coming together. We are, in our own ways, the faithful in a galaxy of the unfaithful, even if our faiths differ. Perhaps this makes us more allies than enemies."

"Perhaps," Maldeck said quietly, and Bin Ald sensed the man's guard beginning to rise again, though not like before. *Common ground,* Bin Ald reminded himself.

"I read some of the history of your people before contacting you," Bin Ald said, changing the subject. "We of the Original Way are new in our return to the old ways. Your people have never lost it. I admire that." Maldeck did not respond. Bin Ald forged ahead. "Whether we like to admit it or not – our ancestors certainly did not – our two separate faiths have some commonalities, especially in our origins. Please," Bin Ald raised his hand to keep Maldeck from interrupting him, "listen before judging my idea. I know this is an unpopular concept with your people. But I have been thinking about it much these days, especially since hearing of you and yours. Will you listen?" Maldeck nodded, though he did not look pleased. "It seems to me there are many similarities between us," Bin Ald continued. "Both of our faiths began as reactions to other, more corrupt religions. Christians broke away from the Jewish tradition in a time when the Jewish bureaucracy had become nothing more than a form of control. Islam broke away from Christianity at a time when my ancestors were being persecuted mercilessly and needed a religion which offered them a way to fight back. Both consider themselves to be continuations of, improvements on, past ideas. And both have served our respective peoples well. Christianity and Western culture became the dominant force in human history for much of modern times, and Islam eventually found its way here to the Inner Cluster where it created the foundation for this society.

"But those advantages came at a cost, did they not? Time had diluted both our faiths. Your people are some of the only true Christians left – the theoretical deists have taken precedence in Coalition space. What are they but a dumbing down of the original? Likewise, Isla'hai has replaced Islam here in the Cluster, and much of the original faith has been removed and lost, has been wiped away as if the truth does not matter." Bin Ald allowed his voice to rise here, allowed some anger to sound in his words. He knew Maldeck would be able to relate to this sentiment. "We of the Original Way feel it is our duty to guide our people back to the original, ancient truths, despite their ignorance. Surely your people harbor the same goal for Christianity?"

"We do," Maldeck said cautiously, though Bin Ald could sense his receptiveness increasing. "But our plights are different, in the end. We both believe in the absolutism of our own religions, beliefs that are incompatible no matter how similar the circumstances we find ourselves in are. I don't see how that can be reconciled."

"Why must they?" Bin Ald asked eagerly, leaning forward. *Here it is,* he thought, sensing the moment had come for him to make the main thrust of his argument. "It is true our beliefs conflict in many ways, but there are some important things over which we are in complete agreement." Maldeck did not speak, but a look of puzzlement began to form on his face. "I know how you and your people have interpreted the Watchers," again, Bin Ald held up a hand to keep Maldeck from speaking. He tried to sound reassuring as he saw panic on the other man's face and fear in his eyes. "Do not worry, please. There have only been rumors. The announcement of the invasion has generated countless speculation and gossip; no one takes too seriously a group of outdated Christians claiming the Watchers are the instruments of God meant to bring about the End Times. That claim seems rather tame compared to some of the other, more outlandish theories spreading through the Cluster. But I think I know more about what you and your people are thinking than you realize. You know God would not allow those made in his image to be annihilated without fulfilling his Word. You have the conviction the Watchers must be his tools to fulfill the prophecies. And yet you see the rest of humanity either unaware and involved in their own strife, like the

Black Sun and what is left of the Cluster, or preparing open defiance to God, like here in the Cluster as we prepare to defend ourselves. And with that conviction comes the desire to act: you and your people seek some way to hasten the Kingdom's coming. Some way to show God you act according to his will. Some way to show the Watchers you are among the faithful, not among the heathens."

"How?" Maldeck asked, hissing the words out in a fearful and trembling breath. "How could you… understand?"

"But you and your group are small. And you are new to our space. You have no power, no way of acting out your convictions. You feel trapped, as you have for generations, watching your fellow humans fight the truth as you know it, watching humanity damn itself for all eternity. You do not know what to do."

They did not speak for a long moment as Bin Ald watched Maldeck's face rifle through a ream of different emotions. Surprise, fear, anger were all there. But Bin Ald sensed the anger was not aimed at him. Rather, it was aimed outward, at everyone else, at history, at the masses of unbelievers. Bin Ald sensed he had managed to transcend the divide separating them, that, through his apparent understanding of their plight, he had become included. *Now,* he thought. *Now, he will give me the in I need.*

"We will persist as we always have," Maldeck said, a forced pride entering his voice. "We will keep the faith even when others do not."

"Indeed," Bin Ald said. "In that way, your people have my admiration. But it need not be so hopeless for you. You and your people need not endure alone."

"What do you mean?"

"I mean that though our ways are different, surely, history has put us on the same path. For centuries our people have fought one another, but now, through the grace of your God and our Allah, we have common cause. We both want the same thing. We want the Watchers to bring divine judgement to humanity. Let us work together to that end."

Bin Ald stopped here as Maldeck gawked at him in shock. But the moment quickly passed, and Bin Ald saw Maldeck's mind begin turning, the possibilities begin to unravel before him. *He sees it now,* Bin Ald thought. *He sees we can be of use to one another, that in the end it is all the same. It doesn't matter that we hold different faiths. We both want exactly the same thing now.*

"What," Maldeck said, "do you have in mind?"

44

Captain Yscaaidt's stand against the Black Sun, in the years before the Endtimes Battle, as it has come to be known, has become one of the most famous military moments in history. From entertainment dramas to novels to holo-synaptics, this was a moment the public loves to live and relive. Much has been written on the social psychology of this fact, but the question remains: why are we, as a people, so connected to this pivotal event?

-Excerpt from The End of Times: a Brief History of the End of Humanity *by Ibn Dars-Elat*

The extraction crews had been on the surface for over 48 hours now, combing through every compound on the planet. They had already collected most of the skip drives and banks, but purging the computer mainframes on the planet was proving more difficult. Yscaaidt sat on the bridge of his ship, the *Windrawn,* looking over the reports from the soldiers still on the surface, a part of him waiting for one in particular. *Damn it,* he thought. *Hurry Nathalie.* The longer they were down there – the longer she was down on the surface – the more the tension in his mind and body increased. He normally did not get anxious when in command, but something was different this time. He looked over the long range scans again. Nothing. Still, he could not shake a sense of portentous foreboding, could not shake the feeling he was missing something.

"Open a channel to Commander Lensut," he said to his comms officer, his impatience getting the better of him.

"Channel open," the officer responded promptly.

"Commander, this is Yscaaidt," he tried to keep the tension from his voice. "Report. How is your progress?"

"Sir," Lensut's voice was calm and direct over the comm channel. "Ground crews are nearly done loading the last of the banks we have found. I have instructed the rest to comb through the compounds for anything else, anything that might offer information about skip technology."

"Good," Yscaaidt felt the tension in his back ease a little. *Just a little longer,* he thought. "And you? How are you faring with the mainframes?"

"It is slow going, sir," as always, Lensut's voice carried a hint of sarcasm in it whenever she referred to their differences in rank. Not enough for the crew to notice, of course, but enough for Yscaaidt, knowing her so well, to hear the tone and smile slightly. "The computers here are protected by a complex encryption I have never encountered before. I don't recognize it as Cluster nor Coalition. I am making some headway, but I will need some more time."

"You have as much time as you need," Yscaaidt said, though he did not feel it. The sense that something was going to happened was still growing within him. "But hurry," he added. "I want to leave this place as soon as we can."

"Yes sir," came the response, a hint of flirtation in the tone. Yscaaidt smiled openly and looked up at the comm officer, who quickly hid her own smirk, gesturing for her to cut the signal.

"Reeigndrikt," the captain said, turning his attention to his tactical officer. "How many do we have still on the surface?"

"Sir," Reeigndrikt answered. "Six separate away teams are left, including Commander Lensut's. Three of them are preparing to leave the surface now. Two others are reporting they will be ready for takeoff within five minutes. Then, we will only have Commander Lensut's team left on the planet."

"Helm," Yscaaidt turned his attention to the front of the bridge. "Bring us into synchronous orbit over Commander Lensut's position."

"Yes, sir," the helm's officer responded, his hands already sliding over the ship's navigational controls.

"Do you expect difficulties at their position, sir?" the tactical officer asked.

"Just a feeling, Reeigndrikt, nothing more," Yscaaidt answered, looking at the planet on the view screen as it turned under their position in high orbit. "Still, keep weapons charged and ready."

"Yes, sir."

Yscaaidt stared at the view screen, his thoughts now centered on the small planet beneath them. It was so small, so seemingly insignificant, but it loomed large in the trajectory of humanity. He had been briefed on what had happened there, what had been discovered there. The official story, the story his officers and the public both knew, was that a portion of the Coalition government, those high up, had known since the beginning the true nature of the Source, the true cost of the energy and of skipping. This itself had been a shock to the people of the Inner Cluster when it had been revealed so many years ago. Yscaaidt wondered for a brief moment if the citizens of the Coalition were ever told about what had been happening on this planet, if their government had come clean before the collapse of the skip network and, consequently, of their state. *Probably not,* Yscaaidt thought. *The Coalition was not prone to honesty, especially not when it required admitting its own sins.* And perhaps not telling the truth had been the right thing to do. A secret like that could destroy a people, even those not directly responsible.

Still, this was not the whole of the story, Yscaaidt now knew. His briefing for this mission had included a story he had not heard through official channels before, had not even heard a whisper of from the perpetual rumor mills filling the Cluster with conspiracy theories and wild claims. Even thinking of it now, despite having had over a week to mull over the new information, to feel it out, Yscaaidt felt his chest tighten with an emotion he struggled to place. Something like anger or fear – their roots were, after all, often one and the same – mixed with something else. Disgust, perhaps. Or a fundamental sense of dread, an anxiety which dug to the roots of his being. He had been told about Ondrueut, had been told about the digital mind who had run human history for nearly 400 years.

And this was why it was so important for them to get everything they could from the computer mainframes on the planet. For nearly ten years, the mainframes had sat inert on the planet while the Cluster dealt with the fallout of shutting down the skip network, putting off collecting whatever data they could about Ondrueut and his existence. And Yscaaidt could not blame them for wanting to study the phenomenon, the only full brain digital emulation ever successfully achieved. That was the kind of technology philosophers and scientists had been theorizing about for hundreds of years, a technological capability which could so fundamentally change the nature of the human experience so as to change what it even means to be human. Perhaps even to change humanity into something else, something no one could possibly predict. *Look what one emulation managed to do,* Yscaaidt thought. *Imagine what thousands, millions, or billions could do.* The thought was not a comfortable one for Yscaaidt. He had always looked back at human history, whether it was in the academy or in his own personal studies, and felt a kind of kinship with the past, taken comfort in the relative regularity of the human experience for the last eons. Something like this could change all that, take all that away. But now, with the threat of the Black Sun looming, the information on those mainframes needed to be collected, even if just to keep it away from General Eazkaii and his brutal fleet. A man like him… Yscaaidt did not want to know what a man like him could and would do with the technology to transfer his mind into a digital form.

"Sir," something in Reeigndrikt's voice drew Yscaaidt from his thoughts immediately and suddenly, as if with a knife.

"What is it?" he asked.

"Sensors show a fleet of ships approaching. Hundreds," Reeigndrikt's voice was admirably calm considering the information he was relaying. "It's the Black Sun."

"On screen," Yscaaidt said without hesitation, as if a part of him had been expecting this all along. The viewscreen cycled to a more zoomed in perspective of the empty space before them, revealing a cluster of light moving towards them. It was the Black Sun indeed. And a lot of them. "How did they get here without us noticing?"

"They must have expected us to be here," Reeigndrikt said, his hands passing over the controls of his tactical console in a fury. "They masked their approach vector by lining it up directly behind the sun of this system. The sun's radiation disrupted our sensor readings, making it impossible for us to read them."

"Clever," Yscaaidt said, his mind settling into a mode of thinking he had only engaged in a few times. Thoughts ceased to flit through his awareness, leaving only the hard edge of his military training. "Tactical analysis."

"Over 500 ships, sir," Reeigndrikt's voice carried in it the same flat tone Yscaaidt's had fallen to with the appearance of the ships. "All are battle ready, approaching with shields and weapons charged. I don't think they mean to talk, sir."

Yscaaidt smiled a little at that. *Over 500,* he thought. *We're outnumbered three to one. Not exactly a hopeful position.* But, he knew, they were not here to win a battle, not here to fight at all. Collecting the skip technology and the data from the mainframes was the main mission and took priority over all else.

"Red Alert," he said, his voice hard and his eyes on the ships on the view screen. The lights on the bridge dimmed as an alarm sounded throughout the ship. "All hands to battle stations."

<u>45</u>

There is an ancient saying: "Two wrongs don't make a right." Much of the complicated history of human ethics can be boiled down to whether or not that idea is true.

-*Excerpt from* Meditations: the
Collected Writings of Roshi Mendact

Who are you? Can you explain that to me?

Not in those terms, no. "Who" cannot apply to this form, for the sensation of presence you feel is only an illusion generated by your own mind's need to frame the unfamiliar within familiar contexts. You are generating the "who" you sense.

Then what are you? Where do you come from? Why are you helping me?

It is unlikely any of those questions can be answered in a way you will find satisfying. There some things that exist beyond the pale of your experience, of your being, things that resist being "understood," as your language puts it.

What can you tell me then?

Only what you are capable of knowing. Only what you need to understand.

And who decides that?

This is a case in point, as the human expression goes. Your insistence on an actor, with agency, is another illusion generated by the limited nature of your existence. There is no agent here to be described, only the logic pervading the universe, pervading all things coming into and going out of existence.

Where does this logic come from? Are you implying some sort of First Cause, some Prime Mover?

Nothing of the sort. Again, your limitations insert narrative structure where there is none to be found. It is a fault of the evolution of the human mind. Accept that limitation.

I will try.

Good. I sense the question on your mind. Ask it.

Why me?

The same delusion. There is no reason, only the chance you have become the one able to interact with this level of reality. As such, you find yourself here. For each universe, there is only one way. Nothing can be otherwise. Do you understand?

No. Are you saying all things are predetermined? That we have no choice?

Again, your limitations show themselves. Try to leave your assumptions behind, to move beyond your limited form and to think from a perspective outside of it. We do not have much time, and such would greatly increase the efficiency of this interaction. Predetermination requires some determining force. Things simply are the way they are, nothing more and nothing less. There is no reason to assume some sort of outside mover, observer, or determiner.

What are you then?

I will attempt to answer your question in a way you will be able to understand, but you should be warned: the very act of answering, of using language to explain something to which your language does not apply, will distort the truth of it. Do you see that?

Yes, I think so. Some things cannot be communicated directly. Some things cannot be simplified into words and sentences.

Exactly. Hence tools like metaphor and simile, as inexact as they are. Hence poets and artists.

I see.

Energy is neither created nor destroyed. Your species has known this for hundreds of years now, has understood this simple fact of the energy economics of physical reality. You have also known, though for a shorter period, that life itself is a form of energy.

The Source.

Yes. And with this knowledge, your species learned to harness the energy, though this proved to be against your sense of ethics. Allow me to ask you a question now. What happens to that energy source when a life is extinguished?

It has been a long time since I took energy-based particle physics, but, if I remember correctly, the Source is dispersed back into the fabric of space-time, becoming diffuse with matter itself at a molecular level.

And what happens then?

Nothing. The energy is lost, spread too thin to be useful, for life or for any other use.

That is not quite correct. It is true the energy of life reintegrates itself with space-time, and it is true it becomes too thinly spread out for your species, at your current level of technological progress, to detect it. But it does not disappear or cease to exist, does not fully dissolve into the fabric of reality.

What happens to it then? Are you saying we, life, live on after death?

In a manner of speaking, yes, though not in the way your species has traditionally assumed. A being, an individual human for instance, is a distinct interaction between this source of energy, life, and physical matter. As such, if you remove the body, the being ceases to exist in the way it had. So while yes, the energy does continue its existence, the individual being, the subjective experience accompanying the intersection between this energy source and matter, does not. It dies with the body.

And the Source? Where does it go?

Like large bodies of water, energy has currents. It flows, and that flow is characterized by phenomenon analogous to eddies and whirlpools. The fabric of space-time, the foundation of the universe, is full of energy constantly flowing in currents, and in some places, these currents gather the energy with enough density the energy begins to regain some of its properties.

Is that what you are?

In simple terms, yes. I am sentient energy.

How long have you… existed?

I came into consciousness some time ago, in this portion of the galaxy. Without a body made of matter, time has little distinction to me. I do not know, in human terms, how long I have existed, but it has been what you would consider to be a very long time.

Are there others like you?

I do not know. I must assume the phenomenon that gave rise to my existence is not unique, that it must happen elsewhere in the galaxy, but, as of yet, I have encountered no other. But we must move on to other things. Your mind cannot sustain the effort required for us to communicate much longer.

How is it that we can communicate at all?

That is a mystery even to me. I have observed many thousands of species, watched many civilizations come and go, but never once have I encountered a physical being who could interact with the energy of life the way you do. This is why I have sought you out.

How did you find me?

Your first use of the Trance, as you called it, created ripples — please remember I speak in metaphor in order to attempt to make this understandable to you — ripples in the flow of energy. The disturbance was something I had never experienced before, and I was able to trace it back to you and your abilities.

Why?

Why what?

Why did you seek me out? Why did you make contact?

Surely a human does not need that question answered. I was alone in the universe, able to sense the happenings of the physical universe but unable to interact with it. And then you came along, a being who I could engage with, and for the first time in my existence, I was not alone anymore. And contact was necessary to avoid the catastrophe you and your kind were creating.

Do you mean by using the Source for our own purposes?

Yes. I do not have time to explain now — you are running out of endurance for this conversation — but the human propensity to inflict suffering on others has consequences in my sphere of existence. However, there is a more important problem. You.

Me?

Yes. You have the ability to interact with what you call the Source. That includes the ability to separate a being's physical and energetic elements, killing the material body and releasing its energy. You have done this twice thus far.

And I was about to do it again when you stopped me.

Yes.

Why did you stop me? The leader of the Black Sun has killed millions, and millions more will die while he is still alive. He must be stopped.

The politics of physical beings is none of my concern. From the perspective of the energy, the lives and deaths of physical beings are a natural part of energy transition and distribution. But such is not the case when you enact your abilities in the way you were planning to.

What do you mean? What happens?

I have experienced the deaths of billions, both by observation and by direct sensation.

What do you mean?

The energy which created me, the energy that comes from a life, is not sentient, but it is not left untouched by its time alive either. For every life energy I have within me, I have something like what you call memories, though they are not as distinct. More like impressions.

It sounds as though you are describing an afterlife.

No. The impressions are there, but nothing else. The memories are void of anything like sentience. At least, that is how it is supposed to be. I was there, observing, when you killed the being you called Ondrueut. When you separated his life energy from his body, what came into my side of existence was not the same. It had... intention of some kind. A will through sentience. And I sensed something else within it: malice.

What does that mean?

I do not know. The energy of Ondrueut was gone — I believe it fled — before I had a chance to study it further. I know not where it went, nor can I sense it, but I do know something is happening within the flow, within the currents, of the energy spectrum occupying this reality. I can sense the ripples of some sort of imbalance. I believe whatever it is that came from Ondrueut has done damage to the fabric of the energy spectrum, and I believe your ability has something to do with what happened.

I did not know. My mother…

Yes. It is possible the same occurred to your mother, but it went unnoticed. I was not paying very close attention to this region of space then.

What can we do about the imbalance?

I do not know, but I believe it prudent not to add to it. You must not use your abilities in such a way again. Do you understand?

Yes.

Good. It is time for our interaction to end.

Wait. I have so many questions for you. The Watchers. What can you tell me about the Watchers?

There is no time. Much has happened in physical space since you entered the trance, and much more is about to occur. Your companion needs you. I will return.

Meiind's eyes snapped open, and his mind snapped back into normal reality. He had been so deep in the trance it took him a full minute to transition back into a normal state of mind. When he could see again — when his mind could recognize the information gathered by his eyes — he saw he was no longer in the ready room of the General.

Rather, he found himself to be in a small, spare room with a few, metal cots and an opening that shimmered with the slight light of a force field. Outside of the opening, he could see a guard standing, facing away, holding some sort of weapon. Sitting on the other cot, eyes closed, was Khalihl.

"Khalihl," he said, the sound of his voice strange in his ears. She raised her head and opened her eyes slowly, unsure of what she had heard. He repeated himself, and she suddenly turned and looked at him with a start. When she saw Meiind's eyes were open, that he was aware again, she rushed to his side.

"What happened back there?" she asked. "Are you alright? One minute I was negotiating – if you could call it that – with Eazkaii, and when I looked over at you, you were gone, in some sort of trance."

"I was in the trance," Meiind said. "I am sorry I left you alone. What happened?"

"Well," Khalihl said, sweeping an arm out to encompass their current situation. "He did not accept our proposal. He is only keeping us alive in case he needs one of us in order to understand how the skip drive on our ship works. Once his engineers figure that out – though they won't – I imagine he will have us killed. Sent to Glory, as he puts it."

"Why won't they get the drive?"

"Before we left, I had the engineers put in a failsafe. If anyone tries to remove the drive from the ship or tries to start the drive without the proper identification codes, an overload sequence will be initiated and the ship will be destroyed. I was not optimistic about our chances with this meeting, so I thought some backups might be a good idea."

"Seems you were right."

"Unfortunately. Tell me what happened to you back there."

Just then, as Meiind was about to begin recounting his experience, there was a muffled sound from beyond the force field. They both turned to see a man dressed in Black Sun colors – the black uniform with the red trim – enter the room beyond their cell. The man spoke to the guard posted outside, though the field made it impossible for Khalihl and Meiind to understand what he said. The guard saluted and left, leaving the new soldier alone with them. For a moment, he stared at them through the field, just watching. Not speaking, they stared back, unsure of what was going to happen next. The soldier seemed to come to some sort of decision; he nodded and then moved to the side of the cell entrance where he appeared to be entering commands into what must have been a control panel of some kind. The shimmering light of the force field dissipated with a buzzing sound, and the man stepped into the cell. He stared at them both.

"My name is Fen Wuou," he said, looking them both over. "You must come with me if you wish to live."

46

*Follow the commandments of God and of his
servants, for this is the whole lot of Humanity.
No more, no less.*

-*The* Holy Bible, New Interstellar
Version, *Ecclesiasties 15:6*

The woman tried her hardest to keep her face as
impassive as possible despite the adrenaline in her blood
and the turmoil in her mind. She could not risk someone
noticing her agitation, stopping her and asking her
questions, perhaps even asking to see what was in the
bundle she carried in her arms. Instinctively, the woman,
called Rebecca, hugged the small, square block wrapped in
a rag closer to her chest protectively. Everything hinged on
this small package. That, and her ability to get into the
place without drawing attention or causing alarm.

The security checkpoint in the shipyard had been
nerve-wracking, but her faked identification had worked.
The guard, after looking back and forth several times
between her face and the authorization pad she had
presented, let her in without comment. After that, she had
passed dozens of guards and workers in the partially
completed halls, tensing up every time someone glanced
up at her, but nobody stopped her, nobody said anything.
Rebecca could not help but say a silent prayer of thanks.

She had never been in a ship's construction yard before, had never been inside an incomplete ship. The lack of a hull was disorienting at times. For the most part, the halls, even when the walls were not yet up, were surrounded by an endless array of wires, tubes, lights, and boards so you could not see past. But in other areas, where the construction was not so complete or where the halls passed closer to the outer edges of the ship, Rebecca could see directly out into space. She had only been in space once when her people fled their home world to seek refuge in the Inner Cluster – a long journey during which she spent most of her time trying to ignore the fact they were in open space – and the sight of the void both thrilled and disturbed her. Even though she knew the atmosphere was held in by containment fields, Rebecca could not help but hold her breath whenever she passed one of the open sections. She hurried along as quickly as she could.

The halls were filled with men and women working – debris littered the floors and the odor of chemicals was strong in the air. And, for the most part, they stayed focused on their work, not even looking up at her as she passed. Occasionally, someone would take a glance in her direction, and seeing her worker's uniform, return their attention to whatever it was they were bonding, cutting, soldering, or calibrating. A part of her was amazed at how easy it was, but another part of her was ashamed of her own surprise. Of course God would not allow anyone to stop her in her mission. She served Him after all. All that was necessary was the faith to trust Him, and He would protect and guide her.

She had memorized the ship schematics over the few weeks she had to prepare herself for the mission, and she took lefts and rights almost instinctually, not thinking much about where to go. Instead, her mind was occupied with thoughts about the reason she was here.

The Watchers.

She believed with all her heart what the leader of her church had said, that the Watchers were the instrument of God come to usher in the end times and, after that, the Kingdom of God into the universe. And she believed with all her heart she had some role to play in the process, some part in God's plan. So strong was her conviction, when the church asked for volunteers for two dangerous missions, she immediately rose up. Rebecca had always felt, ever since she was a child, she was destined for something more, something like the Bible stories she had grown up being told and read. God had some great use for her, of this she had always been sure. Now, she knew she had been right all along. She was a part of God's plan, and that knowledge filled her with a righteous joy.

Rebecca passed a man who, from his kneeling position before an open panel, looked up at her. He was young and handsome, and he smiled at her before looking back to his work. For a moment, she could not help but wonder at his fate. What would happen to him? Surely he was not one of the faithful, otherwise it would not have been necessary for her to sneak her way into the half-built ship. And, as such, surely he would go to eternal damnation when her work was done while, at the same time, she would be welcomed into paradise. Rebecca experienced a moment of empathy for the handsome man, but she forced the weak thought from her mind. If the man went to hell, so be it. All things according to the will of God.

She came out of her thoughts just when she found herself standing before the door to the engineering deck. Rebecca stalled for a moment, adjusting her precious package in her hands and solidifying her resolve. Failure was not an option. It was imperative she completed her mission. She reached out and hit the door control. The wall before her slid open, and she stepped through. She was immediately stopped by a guard.

"Identification please," the woman with the rifle said pleasantly. Rebecca handed her pad over and, as the guard looked at it, she glanced around the room she had just entered. It was full of people, all busily working on something or the other, all blissfully unaware of her and the danger she presented. Unconsciously, she adjusted the package in her hands, settling it onto one hip. The guard took notice.

"What's that?" she asked, handing Rebecca back her papers and pointing at the wrapped box.

"Just some isolator chips for the energy couplings surrounding the engine manifolds," Rebecca said without missing a beat, falling onto the script which had been written for her should anyone ask such questions.

"Open it, please," the guard said, tapping the box with the barrel of her weapon. She smiled comfortingly. "It's just standard procedure for the engine room. Nothing personal."

"Of course," Rebecca said, trying to keep calm as panic struck her in the chest and throat immediately. Her mind raced, trying to figure out what to do while, at the same time, she began to unwrap the box she carried under the guard's watchful gaze. She glanced around, seeing a table just to the side and a little behind her. "May I set the box down while I open it?"

The guard nodded, and Rebecca turned to the table, positioning herself between the box and the rest of the engineering deck, with her back to the guard. Slowly, she uncovered the box and opened it, revealing a small, black cube with a control panel on the top side. Quickly, before turning and before the guard could look over her shoulder to see she had lied about what was in the box, Rebecca input the code she had memorized, punching the numbers as fast as she could. When she was done, in less than a second, the screen on the panel, above the keypad, flickered with a number.

5.

Rebecca watched the number tick down one to 4, and then she turned to face the guard, who had a quizzical look on her face and her weapon pointed directly at Rebecca's chest.

"What is in the box?" the guard asked, her voice betraying her sense something was not right.

"'Follow the commands of God,'" Rebecca said, turning her face upwards and closing her eyes while she recited her favorite verse, "'for that is the whole lot of – '"

The explosion incinerated her before she could finish.

<u>47</u>

To negotiate is to show weakness. To compromise is to fail. There is only one way through the Universe for the adherent of the Black Sun: take what is yours and let nothing stop you.

-Excerpt from The Book of the Black Sun, *Author Unknown*

"Hail them," Yscaaidt's voice tense and his eyes were on the viewscreen before him.

"They are scanning our weapons systems," Reeingdrikt said from his position at the tactical console.

"They are not responding to hails," the comms officer replied.

"Open a channel, transmit on all frequencies," Yscaaidt responded, his mind racing. *We can't beat them in a fight, though we can skip out of here if we need to. But with Lensut and her crew still on the surface...* "This is Captain Yscaaidt of the Inner Cluster ship the *Windrawn*. You are entering restricted Inner Cluster space. Please leave immediately."

"No answer, sir," the comms officer said after a moment.

"No surprise there," Yscaaidt said under his breath. He turned towards tactical. "Reeigndrikt. Send encrypted messages to all the ships off planet that are carrying skip tech. Order them to skip back to New Mecca immediately." He turned to his comms officer again. "Give me Lensut again."

"Sir."

"Yes, sir."

Yscaaidt turned his attention back to the viewscreen, back towards the now closer ships still approaching. His mind raced, thinking for an advantage, for a way to slow them down.

"How long until they are in range, Reeigndrikt?" he asked.

"Less than two minutes, sir."

"Channel to Lensut is open, sir." The comms officer said.

"Lensut," Yscaaidt said. "Report immediately."

"Still not done sir," Lensut said, her voice eerily calm over the comm system. "What is happening up there?"

"We have company," Yscaaidt said. "More than we can handle. I need you to get out of there now."

"I need more time, sir," Lensut responded.

"You don't have it. They will be on us in less than a minute. We don't have a chance in a fight."

"We can't leave this here, sir. I haven't broken through it all yet, but enough to know some of what is on here: schematics for skip drives and banks. Everything they would need to replicate the technology."

Shit, Yscaaidt thought. "How much more time do you need?"

"Just a few more minutes, sir. Ten at the most." Lensut's voice was still calm.

"Keep at it, Lensut. We will do our best to give you time. Order everyone else off planet immediately, except whoever you need," Yscaaidt said, doing his best to instill his voice with command and with the same level of calm he heard in hers.

"Yessir."

Just then, the ship lurched to one side, sending the officers on the bridge stumbling a step or two. An alarm sounded. Yscaaidt swung himself into his chair, opening the panel on the right armrest. He began calling up information about the two fleet positions.

"Report," Yscaaidt said, his eyes now back on the view screen. The Black Sun had closed the distance between them and were beginning to fan out.

"Our shields are holding," Reeigndrikt said, raising his voice over the alarm. "They have begun an attack pattern."

"Helm," Yscaaidt said. "Evasive maneuvers, pattern Y-42. Reeigndrikt, begin firing at will. Comms, open a channel to all ships."

"Channel open sir."

"This is Captain Yscaaidt. Engage the enemy. I repeat engage the enemy. Do not let them reach the planet. Keep yourselves between them and our people down there. Do not let them capture any of our ships. We must keep the skip tech out of their hands." Yscaaidt paused for a moment before continuing. "Self-destruct to avoid capture if necessary. Is that understood?"

He listened as a flurry of acknowledgement came in over the comm. *Hurry Lensut,* he thought. *Please hurry.*

48

*Estimates as to the size of the Black Sun's fleet
during this time vary, but most experts agree on
numbers close to the following: a hundred
thousand ships and over a million soldiers, at
least half of which were likely slaves forced into
service. And, as with all instances of forced labor,
rebellion was always a possibility.*

-Excerpt from The Road to Hell *by
Jessica Ilken*

The Black Sun soldier, Fen Wuou, who had just
entered, dropped the bag he had been carrying before him.
He looked at Khalihl and Meiind, one and then the other.

"We must hurry," he said. "They will realize I am not
at my post soon and begin to search."

"Why should we trust you?" Khalihl asked
immediately, not missing so much as a beat. She glanced
over at Meiind, who positioned himself away from Khalihl
so they could not be attacked at once.

"Truly, you have no choice," Wuou said. "Once
General Eazkaii has the information he needs about the
skip drive of your ship, once he does not need you
anymore, he will kill you. And then, with the technology,
he will continue his devastation of human space even more

efficiently."

"That does not mean we should agree to go with you," Meiind said.

"Not all of us who have been forced to fight with the Black Sun believe in their mission, believe in Chaos and Glory like the General," responded Wuou, having sealed the door now, turning back towards them. "There are many of us who have been biding our time to escape, to find a way out."

"Why help us now then?" Khalihl asked, still wary. "Why risk exposing yourselves so far from human space?"

"A few of us decided that, perhaps, if we help you, the Inner Cluster will welcome us," Wuou looked directly into Khalihl's eyes, and she saw true anguish there. "We have done many terrible things. There are not many who would have us after what the Black Sun has been responsible for."

Khalihl glanced again at Meiind, who shrugged and nodded. *We really do not have many options,* she thought. She had no doubt the General would kill them without hesitation once they had outlived their usefulness. *And we must get back to the Inner Cluster. The Elders must know what we have learned about the Black Sun, about the General. They must learn the Black Sun cannot be reasoned with.*

"Do you have a plan?" Khalihl asked, releasing the tension from her body. She realized she had been clenching her fists, ready to fight if need be. She flexed her hands and stretched her fingers.

"I do," Wuou said, a look of relief flashing across his face. He knelt down and began to open the bag he had brought in with him. "We will meet the others in an empty cargo bay not far from here. From there, we will go to the docking bay where your ship is being held."

"And if we come across resistance?" Khalihl asked.

"If we come across resistance," Wuou reached into his bag and pulled out an energy rifle, holding it out to Khalihl, "we fight."

Khalihl nodded and took the rifle, passing it to Meiind.

"I hope you know how to use one of these," she said. Meiind offered her a tense smile in return.

A few minutes later, the three of them were out in the hall, having left their guard unconscious and locked inside the cell. Khalihl and Meiind did not speak as they followed Wuou through the narrow passages of the ship, the walls dark with red lights for trim. They ducked through a series of corners, Wuou checking around each one before motioning them to follow. Khalihl stayed close behind Wuou, not quite ready to fully trust him, while Meiind kept an eye behind them. They did not run into anyone.

"Where is everyone?" hissed Khalihl, coming up beside Wuou as he checked yet another corner.

"It is currently night shift," Wuou said, ducking around. "Only the bridge staff and essential systems are on duty. We should be able to make it without detection."

"How much support do you have?" Meiind asked from behind them.

"There are many dissidents within our ranks," Wuou said as they rushed down another hall that looked exactly like all the others they had gone down already. "But only a few were willing to risk this operation. The Black Sun rules through fear, and rather effectively."

"What if the others," Meiind asked, "the ones who would not risk it, alert the General to our plan?"

"They would not," Wuou said.

Just then, an alarm began to sound loudly, filling the halls with noise. The red lights lining the tops of the walls began to flash.

"Damn," Wuou said. "Spoke too soon. That's the intruder alert. Come on."

Giving up any pretense of stealth, the three of them took off down the hall at a full sprint. Somewhere in the distance, they could hear energy blasts and yelling. After a few moments, Wuou came to a stop just before a T-junction where their hall ended against another. He waved at Khalihl and Meiind to hug the right side while he glanced around the corner. The yelling was close now, the blasts of energy loud and distinct.

"The cargo bay where we are meeting in is just around to the right," he whispered, turning back to them. "The people we are to meet are pinned down inside." Wuou set down the bag he had been carrying over his shoulder and reached inside, pulling out a small device Khalihl recognized to be some sort of explosive. He tinkered with it for a moment, opening and then closing a small control panel, before leaning around the corner and tossing it underhand down the hall. The yelling stopped for a brief moment before a wash of white light flashed down the corridor. Without hesitation, Wuou pivoted around the corner and began to fire his rifle down the hall, blasts of energy lighting the walls. Khalihl and Meiind followed his lead, jumping around, sending blasts of light down the hall and into the smoke left from the explosive. The yells picked up again, and energy blasts began to blaze wildly back towards them. The three, crouching low, pushed forward towards the smoke, shooting blindly towards the voices now yelling for retreat. Then came a new flurry of fire, a new uprising of voices, as the men and women pinned in the cargo bay came rushing out, sensing a change in the tide of the battle. Khalihl kneeled low and right, firing her rifle down the still smoking corridor blindly, just trying to keep the pressure up. Meiind stood behind her, firing his rifle over her shoulder. Enemy fire came flashing down the corridor towards them, reflecting on the alloy walls so the entire scene seemed to flicker in dancing light. Screams from both sides could be heard, and people fell, their skin burning and their insides boiling from the charges flashing through them. Wuou pressed forward, his rifle sending blasts of charged energy down the hall, until he was standing with the men and women who had just come from within the cargo bay. The Black Sun soldiers, pressed now by this new push, fell back around another corner and through a doorway, locking the sliding gate from the other side. Everything fell into an electrified silence, the moans of the fallen soldiers who had survived their injuries echoing down the walls of the narrow corridor. Wuou looked back at Khalihl and Meiind, motioned for them to come up to where he was squatting next to a man dressed in the same uniform as all the Black Sun soldiers. He was barking orders at the soldiers around, telling them to check the wounded.

"This is Cartage," Wuou said as they came up to him, motioning towards the man. "He helped me to organize this. Went a little off the planned path, eh?"

"Indeed," Cartage said, nodding at Meiind and Khalihl. "They've barricaded themselves behind that door. No doubt they are sending forces around to come up behind us. We will likely be surrounded in a few minutes."

"What is the plan?" Khalihl squatted down next to Cartage and Wuou, setting the butt of her rifle on the ground so she could lean on her gun. "How can we get to my ship?"

"The plan was to do all this quietly," Wuou said. "We're onto Plan B now."

"And what is Plan B?" Meiind asked.

"There is no Plan B," Wuou responded. He turned to Cartage. "What happened?"

"Hell if I know," Cartage said. "Someone must have gotten cold feet and tipped them off. A couple of people didn't show as planned. Could have been any one of them."

"How many soldiers do we have?" Khalihl asked.

"Let's see," she turned back towards the cargo bay door behind them. "Trenz!"

A man came running out of the doors and up to them. He snapped to attention.

"Sir!"

"How many did we lose?" Cartage asked. "How many do we have who can still fight?"

"Two dead and three wounded," Trenz responded immediately. "Two of the wounded can walk. One will have to be carried. Eight can still fight."

"And of the opposing force?" Wuou jumped in.

"Three dead and four wounded, sir. Your flanking maneuver caught quite a few of them."

"Alright, Plan B then. I have an idea." Cartage said to Wuou. She turned back to Trenz. "Send someone to seal all the doors with access to this section of the ship. Weld them shut, jam the control panels, whatever you can to slow them down and buy us some time."

"What have you got in mind?" Wuou asked.

"We're going to try and get to the docking bay through the engineering access strips," Cartage said. He turned to Trenz again. "Send Manhas to me. He worked in engineering. He should be able to jam the sensors and cover our movements."

"Yes, sir," Trenz said. "And the enemy wounded?"

"Execute them," Cartage said without missing a beat.

"Is that necessary?" Khalihl asked.

"We're not in the Inner Cluster yet," Cartage said, turning a cold look on the Inner Cluster admiral. "They will be punished severely for falling in battle for their failure. Tortured before being sent to the Glory. This is the way of the Black Sun. We do them a mercy by killing them now and quickly."

Khalihl did not respond but did not accede either. She simply stared into the man's face and saw the hardness there, saw the abuse, the fear and anger.

"How long have you been with the Black Sun?" Khalihl asked.

"Since they took me from my home when I was a girl," Cartage said. "Long enough to know their ways. Long enough to have been one of them. Long enough to prefer dying over continuing with them." He turned to Trenz again. "Go."

Trenz pivoted on a heel and reentered the cargo bay.

318

After a few moments, soldiers came running out in different directions, two going past them, to seal the doors, Khalihl presumed. Then there was the sound of rifle fire, four blasts in quick succession. Cartage made a motion with his hands, saw Khalihl looking at her.

"Habit," Cartage said. "The Black Sun honor death above all."

"Do you think this is going to work?" Meiind asked.

"Probably not," Cartage said. "But we haven't much choice."

"It has to," Khalihl said. "The Cluster needs to know as much as we can tell them about the Black Sun. At the very least, we have to get a message out."

"Then let's get started," Wuou said, standing.

<u>49</u>

*When that final blow came, the Inner Cluster
was left stunned into a collective paralysis. They
had underestimated their enemies; indeed, they
had not even seen the knife until it was already
twisting into their back.*

-Excerpt from The End of Times: a
Brief History of the End of Humanity
by Ibn Dars-Elat

"How long has it been?" Serjevko asked, the strain he
felt obvious in his voice.

"Over forty-eight hours since her last transmission,"
Thans answered. "She sent us a message announcing the
Black Sun had granted her request for an audience.
Nothing since then."

Silence descended on the private chamber of the
Elder Council like a black cloud. Unlike their public
chamber, where they sat in their chairs all facing one
direction, towards whomever they were meeting with, here
their chairs were arranged in a circle. This was where they
debated, discussed, and came to conclusions. And they had
hard choices to make now. The weight of these decisions
hung heavy in the air. Serjevko looked around at his fellow
Elders. He had never seen them in so despondent a mood,
so slow to think and to find solutions. Not even during the

Cluster Wars, when things, at times, had seemed dire
indeed. He looked at each of them one by one, trying to,
with his gaze, draw them from their melancholy. Only
Thans appeared prepared to tackle the issue at hand head
on. The rest – Cabrenejos, Hujad, Asura, Isdet – seemed
somewhat broken by the recent chain of events. Serjevko
hoped all they needed was some rest, that this downturn in
their energies was only temporary. He needed them to do
their work.

"Assessments?" Serjevko asked, his voice betraying
his fear of the worst.

"We must assume, at the least, Admiral Khalihl has
been taken prisoner," Cabrenejos answered, his head still
down and his eyes on his hands in his lap. "That is the
most likely explanation for her lack of contact. She has
always been diligent in her reports."

"And what of Yscaaidt and his fleet?" Serjevko asked,
realizing as he spoke he too did not want to address the
issue at hand, that even he was deflecting and avoiding his
fear Khalihl was… he could not even bring himself to
think it.

"We received word just a few minutes ago a portion
of the Black Sun fleet had arrived at the prison planet as
Yscaaidt's soldiers were finishing up collecting everything
from the surface," Thans answered, looking over some
information on her pad. "We have been receiving
automated updates since then. Yscaaidt has engaged with
the enemy and is holding them off while his officers
complete a download of the compound's mainframe."

"Is that necessary?" Hujad asked. "Can't they just
destroy the computers and take the skip tech hardware?
We can't afford to lose ships in a pointless battle."

"The reports indicate Yscaaidt's first officer, Lensut, found data on the mainframes relevant to Ondrueut's transition from biological to digital consciousness," Asura answered, speaking for only the second time in the meeting. "Yscaaidt determined this information to be of strategic importance to the Inner Cluster, so they have been trying to retrieve as much as they can while they hold off the Black Sun forces."

"I agree with his decision," Serjevko said, "as difficult as it is. Whatever is in those mainframes may help us to better understand how something like Ondrueut could have happened. It may tell us how much of our history, as humans, over the last few hundred years was manipulated by his designs. It may give us what we need to protect ourselves from something similar happening again in the future."

"Are you sure that is the reason you want that information, Serjevko?" Isdet said, speaking for the first time in the meeting. Serjevko turned to face Isdet, drawn by the tone of the latter's voice. What was it he heard there? An accusation? Isdet faced him, his eyes as hard as stone.

"What do you mean by that?" Serjevko asked, bringing an icy calm to his own voice now.

"That kind of technology," Isdet waved a hand dramatically, rolling his eyes at the other Elder, "has... frightening implications for those in power. Imagine the ability to live forever. To transcend the mortal coil humanity has so long been trapped in. Are you sure there is nothing else you want from that ability?"

"What are you accusing me of?" Serjevko kept his eyes on Isdet. The others fell into tense silence. "Why don't you come out and say it?"

"Isdet," Cabrenejos said in a plaintive tone. "Surely, you can't be serious."

"Why not?" Isdet said, a certain amount of shrill beginning to permeate his voice now. "Is it hard to imagine someone accustomed to power, like the venerated Serjevko here, may want to find a way to hold onto his position? How long have you been in the Council, Serjevko? How long have you had a deciding vote in the destiny of the Cluster? 30 years? 50?"

"Isdet," Hujad said. "This is ridiculous. Serjevko does not need to prove his loyalty to you."

"And why shouldn't he?" Isdet's voice began to rise. "Why should he not? Why should not all of you? From what I have seen, the Cluster has lost its way since the Cluster Wars. Look at us! We welcome the enemy directly into our midst. Refugees," he nearly spat the word out. "These are the people who killed my family. Who killed so many here in the Cluster. And now we have sent our best to seek an alliance with the Black Sun, with the evil that has risen from the ashes of our victory over the Coalition."

"What are you saying?" Asura asked. All eyes were now on Isdet.

"I am saying the Council, indeed the Cluster, has lost its way," Isdet's eyes shone with energy now. "I am saying we have strayed from the path. I am saying we have lost the guidance Allah gave us so long ago."

"I have heard this kind of talk before," Serjevko said, allowing an edge of disgust to seep into his voice. "You sound like the proponents of the Original Way. You sound like a fundamentalist."

"So what?" Isdet screamed, his voice echoing through the chamber. "I have seen how we live in the Inner Cluster now. I have seen the sin permeating our culture. We have forgotten the truths of our ancestors. We have lost the way Allah intended for us. It is no wonder we stand on the brink of destruction from all sides now. It is no wonder Allah has sent the Watchers to destroy us."

No one spoke for a long moment, the only sound in the chamber Isdet's heavy breathing after his tirade. The others looked at one another in shock. Isdet had always been something of a dissenting opinion in the group, more prone to true belief than the rest of them, for whom the tenets of the Isla'hai equated to more of a cultural norm than a true religion. A sense of dread began to permeate Serjevko's being, and he wondered how they could have missed one of the Elder Council, one of their own, becoming radicalized like this. Becoming a part of the Original Way, as it sounded like Isdet had. He knew then he would have to tread lightly here, that Isdet was a dangerous man in a powerful position. Serjevko, like the rest of them, had heard the way those of the Original Way spoke of the Council. He knew their grievances, and he knew their purported solution. He shared quick glances with the others and could see their minds were following similar veins of thought as his was. They would have to be careful now.

"Isdet," Serjevko said, trying to project calmness with his voice. "How long have you been with the Original Way? How long have you followed their ideas?"

"I have always felt as such," Isdet said, turning his wild gaze onto Serjevko. "But I was alone – at least I thought I was – until they came. Until they gave words to my fears. Now I know the truth, and I see the way to that truth. The Original Way has given me my path."

With those words, Isdet reached into his pocket and pulled something out, some sort of small device. Serjevko instinctively reached under the arm rest of his chair for the button that would call security but stopped. The way Isdet held the small object gave its purpose away. *Too late,* he thought. As Isdet held the detonator high, Serjevko turned to the other Council members, a sudden sense of serenity washing over him. Their eyes showed the same recognition as his, the same sudden understanding.

"It has been a pleasure," he said, his eyes on the other men and women with whom he had so long served, "to be a member of this Council with you. May Allah forgive – "

The blast engulfed the chambers, cutting Serjevko off in a fury of light and noise.

<u>50</u>

*We all come into this world the same way. It is
how we leave that matters.*

-*Anonymous*

Come on, Yscaaidt thought as he listened to the reports
coming in over the alarms and the yelling of his bridge
officers. *Hurry it up Lensut. We can't hold them off much longer.*

He barked a command to his helm designating an
attack pattern and tried to take in all the information
coming in through his command panel. Men and women
sprinted back and forth throughout the bridge in the
flickering lights of systems' alarms and warnings, some
trying to contain the shorts threatening to send some
consoles into flames while others replaced fallen officers.
Everything seemed to be slowly descending into chaos, a
thin edge of control barely holding. The battle had been
going on for just a few minutes now, but the fighting was
vicious and the losses on both sides were mounting
already. The Black Sun fought without a sense of self-
preservation, ships careening into the Cluster formations
in suicidal attempts to break them up. And his own people,
the soldiers of the Inner Cluster, fought like men and
women on the edge of extinction, like their very existence
depended on it. *And it damn well might,* Yscaaidt thought
grimly as his ship was rocked by a near miss. *If the Black
Sun gains the technology to skip...*

326

He did not allow himself to finish that thought. Failure in his mission was not an option. If he failed, then the Inner Cluster would likely go down with him. That could not be allowed to happen.

"Reeigndrikt," he yelled over the noise permeating through the bridge. "Our ships with the tech from the planet. Are they gone yet?"

"Other than Lensut and her contingent still down there, yes sir," Reeigndrikt replied over the rising din.

"Order all damaged ships to get out of here," Yscaaidt said. "We cannot allow the Black Sun to capture even one of our skip-capable vessels."

"Yes sir," Reeigndrikt responded, immediately putting his head down over his tactical station and sending out the necessary orders. "A few ships are reporting their drives are damaged, sir. They can't skip out of here."

"Send out a general order: damaged ships that cannot skip away are to enact Order Ten," Yscaaidt felt a sense of hopelessness threatening to take over, but he pushed it back. He had never been forced to command Order Ten, the so-called "death order," but he had no choice. It would be up to the captains of each damaged ship how they wanted to proceed, within the specifications of the order. Either they abandoned and destroyed their ship, risking an open field of battle with a ruthless enemy in escape pods, or they fought to the bitter end, self-destructing when all hope was lost. He suspected most would take the latter, as the Black Sun was not known for following the rules of engagement. He turned to his comms officer. "Open a channel to Lensut."

"Open, sir," the officer responded.

"Lensut," Yscaaidt said, allowing the urgency he felt

to come out in his voice. "We can't hold on much longer up here. How much more time do you need?"

"We've hit a snag," Lensut said. Yscaaidt heard something in her voice he had only heard a few times before, a deadly determination. "We broke through one encryption sequence only to find another layered underneath. I suspect there will be layer after layer. There has to be some key log to them all, but I don't know if we can find it."

"Sir!" Reeigndrikt yelled. "A few Black Sun ships have broken through and are heading down to the planet. They will be at the complex in less than a minute."

"Copy," Yscaaidt responded, his mind racing through all the possible courses of action. "Lensut. You need to get out of there. Black Sun ships will be at your position in 45 seconds. Evacuate the compound and get back into orbit."

"We can't let them have the mainframe," Lensut said, the icy edge still there in her voice. "If they manage to get through the encryption, they will have everything they need to make their own drives, plus who knows what else is on here."

"That's an order, Lensut," Yscaaidt, even though he knew she was right, knew failure in this mission – allowing the Black Sun to get the information they came for – was not an option.

"You know as well as I do you can't give that order," Lensut's voice was quieter now, strong with a sort of resignation. "You'll have to target the compound, destroy it and the mainframes."

"Agreed," Yscaaidt said, having already thought of that option. "We will once you clear the blast zone. Now move!"

"It's too late for that," Lensut said. "Sensors show they've already landed outside. There are too many. We won't be able to break through them."

"No," Yscaaidt recoiled instinctively from the option even as a part of his mind already accepted it. "I won't. I can't. We will fight through to you. I won't let them."

"Jaier," Lensut's voice was soft now, gentle and soothing. "They are breaking in. You need to do it now."

Yscaaidt's mind raced, but he could not, for the life of him, think of another way. Reports were streaming in from the other ships in the battle; the Black Sun was taking control of the space surrounding the planet quickly. In a few more minutes, the battle would be over, and the Black Sun would control the planet and whatever information was left in the compound. The mission would be a failure. If the Black Sun gained the ability to skip, the Inner Cluster would lose its most important advantage: time. Still, Yscaaidt hesitated, his heart reaching out to Lensut on the planet and breaking.

"Sir," Reeigndrikt interrupted his thoughts. "More than half our ships have either been destroyed or have been forced to skip back to the Cluster. Our own shields are about to fail. We need to leave now if we are to avoid capture."

"Jaier," Lensut on the comm again. "Do it."

"Target the compound," Yscaaidt said, anguish and pain running through his mind and body but his voice strong with the years of command behind it. "Fire when ready. Give me a view of the compound." The viewscreen cycled to an orbital shot of the planet and then zoomed in until the compound was visible. Yscaaidt could not tear his eyes away as he heard, as if in a dream, Reeigndrikt confirm the orders and fire. "Lensut."

"I know, Jaier," Lensut said, her voice calm. "I love you too. In this life and the n – "

The transmission was cut off just as, on the viewscreen, the compound exploded in a flash of light. Yscaaidt stared for a brief moment before the gravity of the moment came rushing down upon him with crushing force.

"Order a general retreat," he said to Reeigndrickt before putting his face into his hands. "We're done here."

51

We view violence as undesirable, a final option, but, sometimes, you have to speak the language of the predator.

-Admiral Khalihl, in Lecture, Inner Cluster Military Academy

The explosion echoed down the narrow passageway Khalihl and the others were crawling through just as a blast of heat came rushing up behind them. Screams of pain and indistinct yelling came next. Wuou, just ahead of her and following the engineer Manhas, paused to listen for a moment.

"That will buy us a few minutes," Wuou said. "They will be wary of more traps."

"I hope you're right," Khalihl said. "We're going to need all the time we can get."

Behind her was Meiind followed by Cartage and the rest of the Black Sun defectors. The crawlspace, an engineering access strip, was narrow and hot with the heat of the ship's interior. Khalihl was not prone to claustrophobia, but, given the circumstances, she felt hemmed in on all sides, felt as if the walls were pressing against her. She swallowed and forced the thoughts back, forced herself to focus only on the task at hand: getting to the docking bay as quickly as possible. No doubt there would be a contingent of guards already there – the Black Sun had to assume they would be attempting to escape with their own ship – but she hoped their desire for a working skip drive would keep them from disabling the ship she and Meiind had come in. *A thin thread of hope,* she thought grimly, *but better than nothing.*

"How far is it?" she asked, casting her voice ahead.

"It will take us a few more minutes," Manhas replied.

"Be prepared to fight the moment we exit the strip," Wuou said. "They will be waiting."

Khalihl nodded though, in single file as they were, there was no one to see her acknowledgement. Still, the physical action seemed to cement the intention in her mind. She would be ready to do whatever it took to get clear of the Black Sun, if only long enough to get a message back to the Inner Cluster. Her mind was occupied with that one thought: the Council needed to know what she and Meiind had learned about the Black Sun. They were not dealing with a normal political force, one that could be reasoned and negotiated with, that could be understood and expected to act logically according to the normal rules of power. Rather, the Black Sun was something of a religious force bent on destruction and chaos as a moral endeavor. They were zealots, fanatics, the kind of people you could not hope to deter from their mission. Any attempts at diplomacy would be doomed to failure. And then there was what Meiind had experienced in his sudden trance during their meeting with the General. Whatever the Presence was, whatever this force which had intervened in human affairs through Meiind more than once, Khalihl could not help but think it would play some sort of role yet, that perhaps it could be of some kind of help in the coming conflict with the Watchers. If the reaction the Senders gave to Meiind's outreach was any indicator, they were going to need all the help they could get.

Stay focused on the task at hand, Khalihl told herself as she continued to crawl behind Wuou and Manhas, taking this and that turn until she was completely turned around. *First, you need to survive this. Then you can start thinking about the Watchers.*

Soon, Wuou and Manhas came to a stop in front of her just before a closed door. Khalihl could hear them speak quietly for a moment before Wuou turned and looked over his shoulder at her.

"We are here," Wuou said, sitting back against the bulkhead and checking his weapon. "This panel opens to the docking bay where your ship is being held. It will let us out in a back corner. With some luck, we will be able to exit the strip unnoticed."

"We will need another ship," Khalihl said. "Mine will not be able to carry all of you."

"There will be other ships in here," Manhas replied.

"One more should do to hold us all," Wuou added. "But I do not know how we will escape in a Black Sun ship."

"Leave that to me," Khalihl said. "I know a trick."

Wuou simply nodded his head, accepting Khalihl's claim without a second thought. He looked down the access strip, past Khalihl and Meiind to the other Black Sun soldiers.

"We will exit the strip silently and take stock of the situation," he said, casting his voice so the others down the line could hear it. "You are to follow orders from either Khalihl or me. Understood?"

There were murmurs of agreement and nods from the men behind them.

"Good," Wuou said. "Check your weapons. Be prepared to fight. Be prepared for Glory."

He caught Khalihl's eye as he turned back towards the panel before them, gave her a look and a bit of a shrug. For a moment, Khalihl wondered if he could be trusted, if this was all some sort of elaborate ploy, perhaps to infiltrate the Inner Cluster. She cleared her mind of the thought. She felt it was unlikely; Wuou had already killed his own in defending her and Meiind, had risked his life. And she could not begrudge him his adherence to the language of the Black Sun, considering how long he had been under their purview. Regardless, that threat could be assessed later, if they managed to escape alive. Until then, she needed him, and escaping was the priority.

Manhas, who had been tinkering with a control panel next to the door, turned back towards them.

"I've accessed the internal sensors," he said grimly. "There are dozens of soldiers guarding the ship and the entrance to the docking bay. We will be able to exit unnoticed, I think, but they have surrounded your ship."

"Just get me inside her," Khalihl said. "If we can do that, then we should be able to escape."

Wuou nodded and turned, tapping Manhas on the shoulder. Manhas turned back towards the panel and slowly, silently, pushed it outwards. Light came flooding into the strip, and for a moment Khalihl was blind. The sound of soldiers – voices calling out and footfalls echoing in a large chamber – came in through the entrance. Then

Manhas was gone, and Wuou soon after, exiting the access strip into the bright light of the bay. Khalihl followed close, leaving behind the narrow passageway and entering a huge room filled with the noise of many men. They exited directly behind some cargo boxes, but before she ducked behind them Khalihl caught a glimpse of her ship at the other end of the bay, surrounded, as Manhas had said, by Black Sun soldiers in their black and red uniforms. Soon, they were all out of the strip and huddled behind the boxes. Wuou, without speaking, made a series of hand movements the other defectors seemed to understand. They took position on either side of the boxes, preparing, it seemed to Khalihl, to fan out around the ships between them and her ship. Wuou turned to her, shuffling closer and leaning his head next to hers.

"We will rush them," he whispered, "and try to get into the ships as quickly as possible. We cannot survive an all-out battle – there are too many. But if we can get into the ships, then we can blast through the docking bay doors and make a run for it."

Khalihl simply nodded and looked over her shoulder at Meiind, who had positioned himself right behind her. He was not a soldier, had never been in battle before, but Khalihl was impressed with how he had held up so far. He now held a rifle – a little awkwardly, perhaps, without the ease of a seasoned soldier – and appeared to be ready.

"Whatever happens," she whispered to him, "stay close to me."

Wuou opened the bag he had been carrying and pulled out a number of small, round devices, passing them around. Khalihl took one and looked it over.

"Graviton grenades," Wuou said quietly, turning the device in his hands over and showing her a small slider on one side. "Snap the button upwards, and you'll have five seconds before it explodes, sending out a condensed gravitational wave. Use it to clear a path."

Khalihl nodded, the weight of the grenade comforting in her hand. *Maybe we have a chance,* she thought. Wuou, looking back at the other soldiers now positioned at the corners of the cargo boxes, made a series of quiet but sharp clicking noises with his mouth, some sort of battle language, Khalihl assumed. Silently, the entire group, moving as one, surged around the boxes and sprinted forward, towards the soldiers guarding Khalihl's ship at the front of the bay. They spread out, heading around the other ships and various objects stored in the chamber, keeping low and quiet until the last possible moment. Khalihl and Meiind followed Wuou and Manhas, staying close behind them, working their way forward. When they were only a few yards from the enemy soldiers, still unnoticed, Wuou stopped behind a few boxes. Leaning out around the corner, Wuou made a sharp noise with his mouth and lobbed his grenade into the space between them and the soldiers. Khalihl could see grenades from the others falling into the same space and threw hers as well. The clinking of the devices on the floor finally caught the attention of the soldiers standing there around her ship, who looked up just in time for the grenades to explode. There was the sound of rushing wind as the gravitational waves expanded out from the cluster of grenades, sending anything nearby flying outward from the focal point. Khalihl watched, even as she and the others rushed forward into the cleared space, firing their weapons into the now scrambling soldiers, as the guards closest to the grenades were lifted into the air and flung across the bay, some into the walls and some into their fellow soldiers, by the force of the waves. In the few moments of confusion after the explosions, Khalihl's group managed to take out a number of the Black Sun soldiers, but they quickly

recovered and began firing back. Soon, an all-out fire fight
was under way, bursts of charged energy crackling through
the bay, burning holes into cargo boxes and into the walls,
charring the bodies of soldiers who fell with screams of
pain. The docking bay flashed with electric blue light,
casting a crazy array of shifting shadows in every direction.
Khalihl found herself behind a small vessel with Meiind
and Wuou, each of them alternatively leaning out to fire
and ducking back for cover. The air was beginning to smell
of ozone, and static electricity – residual charges from the
blasts of energy flying back and forth – made the hair on
Khalihl's arms stand straight up. She could see the small
currents snapping back and forth between her and her
rifle, between her and Meiind where they crouched
huddled together. The sound of the rifles and of the
screaming men filled the docking bay.

"How long until their reinforcements arrive?" Khalihl
asked Wuou as they both ducked behind the vessel from a
volley of energy blasts.

"They will be here soon," Wuou said, leaning around
again to return fire and then crouching back. "30 seconds,
one minute tops. And they will come with overwhelming
force."

"Then we need to get to my ship now," Khalihl said.
"Cover me."

Her ship was only a few meters in front of them,
though the space was crossed with continuous rifle fire
spitting back and forth, charged particles of deadly energy.
She gauged the distance and tried to time the random
blasts of flashing light. She looked at Wuou, who nodded
at her and swung himself out into the open, strafing
sideways to the right from their cover towards another
group of their soldiers, sending gleaming lines of light
down towards their enemy and drawing their fire towards

himself. Khalihl, surging out just behind him, sprinted left towards the back of her ship, diving over the last bit of uncovered ground as the air behind her lit up with deadly current. Rolling into position with her back against the hull, she immediately swung around left, rifle up, laying three charges into the chest of a man who came around from the other side of the ship. She stepped over the screaming soldier, past the smell of burning flesh, and opened the panel to the entry port. She had the door open and was in the ship in less than a second. Wasting no time, she rushed into the cockpit which faced the enemy soldiers, from which she could see more now pouring into the bay, and began the startup sequence. It took two seconds for the ship to come alive; blasts of energy began to strike the hull as the soldiers turned their fire onto her ship. Khalihl started the weapons systems and, without aiming, laid a heavy blast into the area before her, the area where the enemy soldiers were now gathering their strength. The explosion of light was blinding, rocking her ship and sending bodies flying through the air and molten debris through the docking bay. There was a moment of silence, the eye of the storm, in the empty air left by the blast, and then Meiind and Wuou were in the ship behind her, other defectors entering the ship as well. Khalihl cycled the viewscreen, saw the others were taking the ship nearest hers. She cycled back to the screen showing the enemy combatants, saw they were beginning to recover and regroup.

"We will need to blast the bay doors," Wuou said behind her.

"No need," Khalihl answered. "Get on the comm and tell the others to fire into the bay entrance. We need just a few more seconds."

Wuou nodded and did as he was told. Khalihl, watching as the other ship fired and blew a massive hole into the area around the bay entrance, input a series of commands, her hands a flurry of movement over the controls. There was a jolt as her ship sent magnetic docking clamps flying through the space between her ship and the other, and then a heavy vibration and the screeching sound of metal on metal as she used the clamps to drag their ships across the bay floor, bringing them closer together.

"What are you doing?" Wuou asked.

Khalihl didn't answer, keeping her attention on the readings from her sensors. Energy blasts began to hit her ship again, rocking them in the cockpit.

"The hull can't take much more," Meiind, who had positioned himself in the tactical console, said.

"We only need a second longer," Khalihl hissed through her teeth, not looking away from the readings showing the distance between their ships.

As soon as they were close enough together, she activated the skip drive, input the navigational coordinates, and hit the sequence. There was the sound of tearing metal, something like a leviathan roaring around them, as the skip field, large enough to encompass both their vessels and some of the docking bay around them, tore through the fabric of spacetime and into anything not wholly encompassed in the field. In the view screen, the docking bay seemed to stretch outwards, and then it seemed to snap back. There was a moment of nothing, of complete emptiness, and then they were in open space, debris from the docking bay, parts of the massive Black Sun vessel torn asunder when caught up in the skip field and that they had taken with them, floating nearby. Khalihl pushed the air out of her lungs, heard Meiind and Wuou give the same relieved sigh, as they all sat back in their chairs.

"Welcome," Khalihl said, "to the Inner Cluster."

<u>52</u>

And behold!

The light of a thousand suns!

The fire that burns away the chaff of our dreams,

that takes with it all we hoped to be

and leaves only what we refused to see.

-Excerpt from "The Heart of Hate" by Perzen Ouobre

The hull of the first generation ship, the one closest to completion, tore open in a flameless breath, the exterior shearing apart as decompression jettisoned everything in that section of the ship into the void of space. The force of the explosion split the ring-shaped ship until it formed more of an open U, and then the hull began to buckle and collapse on the sides not blown open. Those sides went first, whole sections of the cylindrical ship separating from the rest until, finally, the last bit of curved hull broke apart, leaving the ship in four major parts and a cloud of debris. The ship's sublight drive went next, blasting the now disconnected pieces of the ship in all directions in a flash of light which could be seen for lightyears around. The large parts of the ship spun outward and broke apart, catching what was left of the orbital shipyard scaffolding surrounding it. More explosions blustered out as these building platforms collided with the now torn apart ship, sending still more debris outward in all directions. This growing cloud of metal, along with the ejected innards of the ship itself – bits of metal alloy and the bodies of the crews inside when the bomb had gone off – spread out from the focal points of the explosions. The ships that transported workers to and from each platform, the drones which brought materials up from the planet below, dozens of them, were shredded to pieces by the wave of debris and then caught up in the wave itself. This field of destruction, caught in the gravitational pull of the planet beneath it, reached the two other generation ships being built on either side of the first, bits of debris of various sizes now hurtling through space, a shotgun blast of metal, plastic, and flesh. The debris field tore through the other two ships, both incomplete rings heavily surrounded by builder ships and support structures, causing still more explosions as their engines lit up in flashes of white light. The annihilation of the shipyard was quick and complete: three massive generation ships – the Inner Cluster's and humanity's hope for evacuation before the invasion of the Watchers – destroyed, along with the entire facility that had allowed them to be built. The debris began to fall towards the planet, lighting the atmosphere in a wall of flame and light with the friction from their reentry. The people on the few ships which had survived the entire thing, as well as those on the planet itself, watched in awe as the destruction was finalized in a baptism of fire from the sky.

When all was said and done, there was nothing left but ash and destruction. It had all taken but a few minutes.

53

For so long — for thousands of years — conviction and faith were upheld in literature and politics as essential and worthy characteristics. The blunt and revealing lens of history, however, shows us how many times those traits have led to a breakdown of everything that has made the grand project of civilization possible. Truly, there has been no other threat greater to humanity than its own penchant for true belief.

-*Excerpt from* Spectrum Swing: an Analysis of Fundamentalism *by Kerrae Higdens*

The room was, at first, silent except for the sounds emanating from the medical equipment surrounding the bed in the center of it. Khalihl stood still, trying not to breathe, though she doubted she could manage even that. Her mind felt as if it had been opened and drained out of all its energy. Her body felt as though it would not respond to her commands. The room around her felt as though it was closing in, as though it was spiraling down atop her. She sensed the demon of despair threatening to wash over and through her, threatening to take over. *Keep calm,* she forced herself to think. And, not for the first time since returning from her failed meeting with the leader of the Black Sun, since she returned to an Inner Cluster in the throes of catastrophe, she wished Raasch was still alive, wished he was here to guide them. *What would you do? What would your plan be?*

She glanced up at the others in the room with her. Yscaaidt too stood silently, stoic with his back straight and his hands clasped behind him. Khalihl had read his report on what had happened at the prison planet, had read about what he had been forced to do. Her heart leapt out to him, but she kept silent. His mission had been a success – they had managed to get what was left of the skip technology which had been stored on the planet and destroy everything else that could have helped the Black Sun engineer their own skip banks and drives – but it had come at great personal cost for the man now standing before her. But she could not indulge her commiserating feelings, could not reach out and comfort him, not yet. They both needed to be strong, needed to keep face. There would be time to mourn, but now there was too much to be done.

On the bed before her, surrounded by medical equipment and with various wires and tubes coming to and from his body, was the only Elder to have survived the attack on the Council. Another stab of pain and sorrow seared through Khalihl. The Council gone! For her entire life, the Elder Council had guided the people of the Inner Cluster, had guided her, with their wisdom and their understanding of the many forces which drove humanity. And now, for the first time since the founding of the Cluster, they were without their main source of political cohesion. Khalihl had read the reports, had seen the images of unrest and chaos in the streets of New Mecca. Since she had returned, the police and military had managed to impose order, but no one knew how long it would last. The people needed leadership, especially in this time of existential threat, and the threat of the Original Way needed to be addressed.

Khalihl felt her face curl into a scowl at the thought

of the people who had perpetuated this crisis, who had destroyed the generation ships and killed all of the Council save one. She felt a kind of rage rising up within her she had never felt before. These people, the men and women who followed the Original Way – as well as the Christian fundamentalists who had helped them orchestrate their attacks, as the subsequent investigation had revealed – were true believers in the worst way. They had regressed to an ancient way of thinking, and in this way, they were no better than the Black Sun. They believed enough to kill for it, and Khalihl simply could not fathom the idea. She had killed, it was true, but always for the defense of herself or of her society, never in order to force some idea she had on others. That went against everything she had been taught. And the thing that appalled her the most, that was the most difficult for her to understand, was that the same culture which had produced her had also produced the Original Way, the men and women who had murdered thousands. This she simply could not reconcile. How was it that two such different realities could come from the same foundation? She knew this question would be on her mind for some time, would require some thought, but she pushed it aside for the time being. *There are other things to worry about right now,* she thought.

Serjevko, in his bed and with his wires and tubes and medical equipment all hooked up to him in various places, stirred and opened his eyes. Both Yscaaidt and Khalihl came to attention, straightening up. The doctors had said Serjevko would have brief periods of consciousness while he recovered – if he recovered – and there were some important things to be discussed while the opportunity was there. Serjevko looked up at Khalihl and offered a pained smile.

"I have left you quite a mess, my daughter," he said, quietly, the smile on his face belying the pain in his voice.

"This was not your fault," Khalihl said, reaching a handout to her old mentor, grasping his in hers.

"I bear some responsibility," the old man said, looking away but gripping Khalihl's hand hard. "We should have been more careful. We should have seen how prone to extremism Isdet was, should have been paying more attention. We were too tolerant of him and his."

"Tolerance is one of your strengths," Khalihl said, "not a weakness. Had you acted otherwise, you would not have been yourself."

"Perhaps that is the problem," Serjevko turned to Yscaaidt. "What is the current situation?"

"There is unrest in New Mecca," Yscaaidt responded. "Protests and counter-protests have broken out all over the planet. Members of the Original Way have publicly claimed the attacks, and some of the population supports them and their actions. They are growing. Most of the rest of the Cluster is operating as normal, just waiting to see what will happen. There has been a coup on Sahaj. The Christian fundamentalists who helped the Original Way in their attacks have taken power there, expelling the Sihken population and renaming the planet Trinity. They claim their independence from the Cluster."

"Let them have it," Serjevko said with a look of disgust and a wave of his hand. "Put up an embargo between the planet and the rest of the Cluster. Make sure the people there have what they need to survive but keep them from interacting with the general population of the Inner Cluster, especially the Original Way. They have already done enough." He turned back to Khalihl. "You must take control of the government. Declare martial law."

"Sir?" The shock was plain on Khalihl's face. Martial

law had never been declared in the history of the Inner
Cluster.

"I know it is not a desirable course of action,"
Serjevko said, "but we cannot allow the Inner Cluster to
fall into turmoil. Order will be necessary if we are to be
even remotely prepared for the Watchers and the Black
Sun."

Khalihl did not answer right away. The idea of taking
control of the Inner Cluster by force sent a spike of
emotion she did not quite recognize, something she had
never felt before, through her. She suddenly felt a great
weight descend upon her, the hopes of an entire people,
the judgement of an entire history. All she could manage
was a nod.

"My daughter," Serjevko said in a comforting voice,
seeing the turmoil on her face. "I know this is a fearful
course, that this will be a trying and difficult time. But it is
necessary. And I cannot think of anyone I would rather
trust with this responsibility than you. Your hesitation
itself is proof of your worthiness."

Khalihl glanced up at Yscaaidt, who was looking at
her intensely. He nodded.

"I agree with the Elder," Yscaaidt said. "You are the
right person for this. You will guide us well."

Again, Khalihl could not answer immediately. She
knew they were right, that order was necessary and
extraordinary circumstances called for extraordinary
measures to be taken. Still, she could not wrap her mind
around the idea she would be the one to take control of
the Inner Cluster. The idea felt distant, alien, impossible.
And yet, there she was. The last living Elder and the
military officer directly beneath her in rank telling her it

was to be done. *There must be another way,* she thought, though she could not see one.

"This is the only way," Serjevko said softly, as if reading her mind.

"Sir," Khalihl said, suddenly snapping from her melancholy as she realized, like it or not, indecision and inaction were worse alternatives. She turned to Yscaaidt. "Make the necessary preparations. I will make the announcement to the public tomorrow."

"May Allah guide you," Serjevko said, his voice waning as he appeared to slip back into unconsciousness, his job done for the time being.

For the first time in her life, that invocation offered no comfort to Khalihl.

54

For some, we lose a part of our humanity when we are unable to cooperate. For others, the same loss happens when we give up our individuality in order to work together. Many arguments have been made for either, many attempts to find a compromise acceptable to all, but, it seems, in the end, the gut reaction is all that matters. Some will always seek to find the common ground that allows disparate peoples to come together. And others will always seek to tear that fabric at the seams.

-*Excerpt from* Vice or Virtue: a Study of Human Cooperation *by Nigel Dentree*

The sight was difficult to fathom. No matter how long Meiind stared, his mind simply could not take in what he was looking at. It wasn't only the view itself, a perspective no human evolved to be able to understand and process, but it was the implications of the sight as well. *Now we have no choice,* he thought grimly. *We stay and fight. That is our only chance.*

The debris which had not burned up in the atmosphere of the small planet now formed a small ring of glittering metal around the planet's equator. Gravity had pulled the remnants of the destroyed generation ships, of the orbital stations and the support vessels that had been destroyed with them, into a tight line running from one horizon to the other in Meiind's view screen image of the planet. The metal in the ring reflected the nearby sun and, if he did not think about it too hard Meiind found the sight rather beautiful, as if the small planet was wearing a diamond necklace. He could not help but wonder how many bodies were in there as well. Many men and women had died in the explosions. The planet itself, a shade of color that seemed to change, in his eyes, from grey to blue and back, was utterly still and lifeless looking. The usual, constant stream of cargo ships coming and going from the surface had been stopped; there was nothing left for them to work on, nothing left for them to even work with. Even the lights which usually illuminated the dark side of the planet, the indicators of civilization's spread, had all gone dark. The planet had been, after the attack, evacuated, the people who lived there moved to one of the other shipyards in the Inner Cluster. Looking down at the planet, Meiind could not help but feel a sense of wonder. He had been to countless planets, dozens easily, and only once before had he seen one so dark and lightless. Every planet he had ever been to always blazed with the artificial lights of cities, of human activity. He saw the planet beneath him now, empty, void of life, with a kind of double vision. Twice now he had seen death on this scale, and the specter of Bodhi, dead like a blind eye, seemed to him now a portent of a possible future. Would this be what the planets of human space would look like after the Watchers arrived? Would the lights of humanity fade into the indistinguishable darkness of the void of space, lost for all time like a light simply shut off?

Meiind shook the thought from his mind, though the sense of despair accompanying it lingered. He could not help but think of the time they had lost when these ships had been destroyed, and he was ashamed the time lost bothered him even more than the lives destroyed. It had

taken them nearly a year to get as far with the generation
ships as they had. And at such cost! The timeline suddenly
struck Meiind. Eleven years since he had killed Ondrueut
and shut down the skip network, effectively causing the
collapse of the Coalition. A year since he had learned of
the Watchers, since the destruction of Bodhi and, with it,
of the life he had dedicated himself to. And now, as he
stood there looking at what was left of the ships which had
been meant to offer some sort of salvation to humanity –
the chance to, at the very least, survive – it became utterly
clear to him the remaining ten years before the Watchers
arrived would be the most difficult yet. His mind balked at
the thought.

The briefings he had been given to read by Khalihl,
who was now on New Mecca no doubt grappling with the
mess left over by the Christian and Islamic terrorists who
had destroyed the generation ships and killed all but one of
the Elder Council, had not given a favorable view of the
remaining timeline. Analysis showed they did not have the
resources to attempt to rebuild the generation ships they
had lost. Evacuation – escape – was no longer an option.
Thankfully, they still had their fleet, which was still
expanding with new, more powerful ships. The
fundamentalists had spared those; the building would
continue, though no one knew if it would be enough for
when the Watchers and the Black Sun arrived.

This drove Meiind's thoughts towards the terrorists
who had been responsible for the destruction of the
generation ships and for the deaths of the Inner Cluster's
leaders. With these thoughts, his sense of despair
increased, seizing him in its grip, and he was ashamed for
his species. With an existential threat imminent, the likes
of which humanity had never before faced, they, as always,
fell to petty differences and violence amongst themselves.
The predictability of it would have been laughable had the
stakes not been so serious, so terrifying. Here they were, in

the 25th century, freed from the bounds of their home planet and system, and still they carried with them the hate and destruction of their past. Still they fell to the old ways, the old beliefs, which had already, time and time again, proven to be destructive forces. How many times had humanity moved forward, made progress, only to be dragged back into disorder by the irrational beliefs of small but determined groups acting towards their own ends? What was it about these people, these inflexible fundamentalists, that made them so pernicious in the history of human progress?

Conviction, Meiind thought. *True belief.* The thought rang with truth in his mind. It was only the utter faith these people had that allowed them to act the way they did. He could not help but wonder at the two suicide bombers who had perpetuated the attacks on the shipyard he was now looking at and on the Elder Council. They had gone through with their actions knowing, without a doubt, they were going to die, overriding the most powerful of evolutionary forces. What was it that allowed them to send themselves to their own deaths? What was it that allowed them to take so many others with them in the fury and flame of their convictions? True belief. A belief in their own righteousness. A belief in the afterlife. A belief in the judgement of a distant God allowing for the murder of countless innocents. Nothing else could account for it. It did not matter whether they were Christian or Muslim; the content of the belief system was not relevant. It was the belief itself, faith in an untrue and unprovable system, that led, invariably it seemed, to conflict.

But, Meiind thought, *how many other beliefs we carry with us operate under similar principals?* He could not help but see the same kind of thinking throughout history, applied to non-religious beliefs. Faith in economic systems. Belief in progress. Hero worship and group solidarity in politics. In many ways, true belief seemed to be a natural state for humans, and even good ideas had led people to kill, to conquer, and to destroy. It was unfair to not acknowledge the fact. Had he himself not killed to escape the Black Sun? Admittedly, he and Khalihl had gone to the General with non-violent intentions, but, in the end, violence had been necessary. And had it? Was the morality of self-defense just another form of true belief? Did not all violence just perpetuate more of the same? What about his conviction that violence was always undesirable? Did that not as well have the tenor of righteousness and true belief?

Meiind shook his head to clear his thoughts, which were beginning to spiral. The experiences he had just gone through with the Black Sun and the state of the Inner Cluster on his return had affected him greatly, he realized. They had shaken the foundations of his being. He had always been optimistic about the goodness of people, had always believed humans were, deep down, social creatures and this meant cooperation was more natural to humans than competition. He still wanted to believe that, but now he felt unsure, felt shaky in this conviction. *There is this word again,* he thought. *It works its way into everything.* It seemed , no matter where he looked, true belief and conviction rested at the bottom of all his thoughts. And he could not help the thought that, perhaps, Eazkaii had been right. Perhaps chaos was the natural state of all things in the universe, including humanity. Human history, even the history Meiind was now a part of, seemed to pan that idea out.

Meiind turned from the view he had been staring at for so long now, from the ring of metal and flesh orbiting the planet, the debris from the destroyed generation ships which should have been humanity's best chance of survival, that seemed to so well encompass his thoughts and feelings in that moment. He could look at it no longer. Indeed, he had been so lost in thought he saw nothing anyways. And he realized then it was not his thoughts he was lost in. *No,* he thought. *I am lost in my own self. I no longer know where I stand or belong.* The thought passed through Meiind as a wave of despair. His entire life had been dedicated to the solving of human problems through discussion and understanding, and he had seen it work countless times, had helped many enemies see just enough of each other's perspectives to compromise. But now that seemed to him to have been folly. Now he felt a sense of futility in that. None of that had stopped the Coalition from attacking the Inner Cluster, had it? None of that could stop the Black Sun, could it? None of that would keep the Watchers at bay, would it? And, despite the best efforts of women and men like him, was not human history the story of one conflict after the other? This conclusion seemed inescapable: humanity was doomed to die by the cancer of its own inability to work together. It wouldn't be the Watchers who ultimately undid them; the Watchers would just be annihilating the leftover pieces of a species destroyed by distrust and hate of itself.

But, Meiind thought as he began to walk back to his quarters on the ship with which he had come to survey the damage, *that is not the entire story. Humanity is not the entire universe.* There was, he knew, the Presence which had, over the years, intervened in his life – in humanity's very history. And there was the fact he was, whether at the moment he liked it or not, a human himself. What was he to do? Allow despair to paralyze him? Allow his shaken faith in his own species to cause him to give up, to lie down and die without an attempt to save himself and to save his people? Even if it was a people he no longer felt like he understood, a people he no longer felt a part of… then it struck him. Then he saw a path out of his predicament, a light at the end of the deep, dark metaphysical and ethical hole in which he had found himself. In human history, conflict had always been tribal in nature. This tribe against that tribe, this city state against that city state, this empire against that empire, this nation against that nation, this planet against that planet, this region of space against that region of space. Even ideological conflicts could be looked at through the tribes of belief: this thought system against that thought system. And the evolution of conflict could be turned upside down to be seen as the evolution of human social structures; these structures, throughout history, expanded to include more and more people from more and more disparate backgrounds which, generations later, would see themselves as a single people from a single background. Perhaps he just needed to expand his view beyond humanity, needed to look outside to really see in.

At his room now, Meiind sat on the cushion he had set against a blank wall in an open portion of the space. He had received the cushion as a gift from Roshi Moyo – a stab of grief ran through Meiind as he thought of his lost friend and mentor – though he had not used it much since his return from the Black Sun. Meditation, a part of his life for such a long time now, had become difficult in the wake of what had happened to him and to the Inner Cluster. But now he sat with a new sense of direction. He knew where he had to look to find what it was he had always sought, all through his life: understanding and peace. He had to expand his view, had to seek his way outside the confines of what, from a large enough distance, seemed to be an arbitrary distinction of species, of space and time. He had to seek the Presence.

<u>55</u>

*When the dust settled and the board was set,
when all the players were ready for the final
confrontation, nothing was certain. The Coalition
was gone, having dissolved with the shutdown of
the skip network and leaving much of humanity
unorganized and unable to cooperate. The Elder
Council was destroyed by forces from within the
Inner Cluster, shattering the sense of unity that
had always pervaded their culture. The Watchers
and the Black Sun were closing in. And
humanity's most promising means of survival
were destroyed. It was a dark time indeed.*

> *-Excerpt from* The End of Times: a
> Brief History of the End of Humanity
> *by Ibn Dars-Elat*

Her first act as head of the Inner Cluster government
had been to preserve the state of the room she now stood
in, stopping the cleanup and declaring it a historical
monument. The people needed to remember. They needed
to see where their whims could take them if they were not
careful and vigilant against the demons of their natures. If
they were not skeptical even about their own feelings. If
they believed anything implicitly.

This was the tenor of Khalihl's thoughts as she
walked over the debris and around the blasted chairs,

charred and knocked over. Wood, brick, and stone littered the floor. The walls had been blackened in the explosion, the burn marks rising high towards the domed ceiling of the chamber. Half-burned papers lay thrown about. Bits of clothing and what appeared to be smears of blood could be found if one looked hard enough. In the air, the smell of sulfur. A scene of complete disarray, it matched her interior state. Khalihl did not know why she had come here, why she had come to see the place where the Inner Cluster she knew had been destroyed.

Already, and it had only been a few days now since the deaths of the Elder Council, since they had been killed here in this very room, Khalihl had done things she never thought she would see in the Inner Cluster, given orders that, in other circumstances and from another source, would have given her pause. Yscaaidt had given the "desperate times" argument, and Khalihl knew he was not wrong. These were indeed desperate times, as desperate as any she could remember or had learned about in the history of the Inner Cluster. Their enemies were closing in from the outside – by some infernal trick of fate, the Black Sun and the Watchers would arrive, ten years from now, at about the same time. They now knew they had enemies on the inside – no doubt the raids she had ordered, the ones she felt most guilty about, had not captured all of the members of the Original Way nor all the members of the fundamentalist Christians who had helped them in the attacks. They would be back, she felt sure, making preparations for the coming conflict difficult. As if it wasn't going to be difficult enough already. As if she didn't already have enough to worry about. These last few days, Khalihl had felt sick with worry, her head heavy with responsibility and her gut constantly tied in knots with anxiety. But she had tried to show a strong front, tried to project a confidence and assuredness she did not feel. This was a part of her duties now. Her people would rely on her strength, even if, ultimately, it was faked. And she had been faking it, pretending to the best of her ability to be confident when, in truth, she felt anything but. What she felt, instead, was fear: fear for her people, fear of failure, fear of annihilation. Fear she was not up to the task at hand.

A small scrap of paper caught her eye, and she knelt low to take it up gently between two fingers. Burned and blackened, like much of the room, she could just make out a few hand-written words, laid down in a beautiful hand Khalihl immediately recognized as belonging to Cabrenejos, one of the longest serving Elders on the Council, longer there even than Serjevko. She read the words, and they struck her as if she had been slapped, as if Cabrenejos had reached out from beyond the grave and grabbed her by the heart, grabbed her by her very essence, and shook her hard. She stood quickly, dropping the small scrap and watching it flutter back to the debris-littered floor where it settled face up so she could still read the words. She looked around her, looked at the ruined room, the place where she had, for so many years, sought wisdom and advice, had taken orders, had felt the reassurance of the Council's collective experience bolster her in whatever mission they assigned. For so long, this had been the place where the path of the Inner Cluster had been determined, a place where the line between practicality and idealism had been carefully walked, where the governing ethos of the Inner Cluster had been forged. It was here her people had attempted to put into practice the ideas of those first Musla who had come from so far away on the *Eden* so long ago. It was here her ancestors had created the society she had grown up to love and cherish, the way of life she had dedicated her life to protecting. It was here they had, with faith as their vision and history as their guide, created the Inner Cluster and everything it stood for. And, it was here faith had come full circle to conviction, had burned away all other prudence and had nearly destroyed everything they had worked so hard to achieve.

Khalihl suddenly felt it all threatening to come crashing down in the aftermath of what had happened. She felt her own faith slipping and with it the bedrock she had always stood on. The people who had done this, who had murdered so many and possibly doomed so many more, had they not done it on faith? Had they not operated by the same logic, belief in an idea, she also used to bolster herself in times of need? Khalihl could not help but wonder what this meant, what the implications were. She had always considered the faith she had been raised in, the ideals of the Isla'hai, to be a guiding force for good, a way to make the world better. But now, as she stood in the wreckage of a faith gone too far, of a conviction acted out in violence, her belief was faltering and with it her sense of being. She glanced down at the scrap of paper, at the hand-written words, the thoughts of a dead man, again. They read:

"Do what is necessary and let the rest fall into place as it will."

Khalihl took a deep breath, turned, and walked out of the room. There was much to be done.

EPILOGUE

History is the story of humanity as it has survived and been passed to us. How many unknowns have been lost to time? How many actors left unseen? For the historian, this is one of the paradoxes of our study: there are always shadows and darkness obscuring the truth in the distance.

-Excerpt from God's Hand: the Unseen in History *by Eldish Juret*

The Presence was not always there.

Before the Presence came to be, the space it occupied was empty, void of life and thought. An untouched… dimension? Parallel universe? Even now, it does not exactly understand its own existence.

In the beginning, it could only search itself, sift through its own thoughts. Strange things happened. There seemed to be the thoughts of others in its own mind – if a mind is what it could be called – and those thoughts grew more numerous daily, as if they were being added to from some unseen source. And it could sense others, different from itself but alive and there, just out of reach, as if on the other side of a glass pane. It focused its expanding energies on the others, and soon it could listen in, could watch, could pay attention. It was through this it learned more about itself through contrast with the others. The life it sensed, the lives it watched, seemed to exist in a different form. Their minds were similar, if smaller, but they were encased in temporary bodies, carried by physical forms which separated them from others of their kind and that eventually ceased to function. And when this happened, when the body died, the mind went with it.

Time did not exist for the Presence, but it watched generation after generation live and die. It watched and listened, but it could never communicate, could never find a hold in that world. Soon, it discovered more living beings, more lives and minds separated from itself by their corporal forms, and the Presence realized the physical world, a world it could observe but not enter, was teeming with others of like mind if of different form. And so it explored, and it listened and watched, and it learned. But the Presence always kept a piece of itself with the place it had originated, watching the ones it had first seen.

One day, something changed. The Presence felt it as a ripple in its space, and then he was there, roaming its space, getting lost in the world the Presence had lived in for it knew not how long. He was lost, and the Presence helped him find what he was looking for and then left him alone, left him to return to the physical world. The Presence had watched enough of these beings, had learned enough about humans, to decide prudence was the best course. These humans, the first beings he had seen and the ones, it thought, most like-minded to itself of all the life it had encountered and observed, did not react well to the unknown. They were chaotic and violent, even against their own kind. The Presence decided only to watch from a distance, especially this one who could traverse its space, who could enter its domain and communicate with it directly as no other life form had ever been able to.

Something changed. Again, a ripple in its space, but

this time the Presence did not find a physical being roaming its world. Instead, it found something more like itself, a mind of some sort, separate from physical matter as itself was. A mind, and a mind only, but somehow different from the Presence. Narrow. Confused. It, what the Presence had begun to think of as the Other, reacted negatively at the Presence's attempts to communicate, and the Other went into hiding, disappeared in the infinite space they occupied. For some reason, the Presence could not follow the Other the way it could follow physical beings; it could not read the Other's thoughts, could not see its path through space.

But the Presence did find clues as to the Other's whereabouts and actions, found the wake of destruction it left behind everywhere it went. The Other appeared to have some power the Presence did not. Not soon after first discovering the Other, after the Other first disappeared into the void of their existence, the Presence found the first casualties. An entire civilization of physical beings, creatures the Presence had come across and observed before – an enlightened culture of art and science – had been wiped of their thoughts. Their bodies still lived, but they had lost whatever it was that made them sentient, and their civilization had fallen into chaos as the mindless bodies, running on instinct alone, reverted to ancient, animal ways. An entire culture, a history and a people, forced back to pre-thought existence. It was devastating.

The Presence found more civilizations which had suffered the same fate. Billions of sentient beings wiped of their minds and left as if they had never had thought. Whole civilizations crumbled. It took the Presence some time to figure out what had happened, where this Other had come from, tracing its existence back to the first physical being it had made contact with, that human who had managed to enter its space. The Presence did not know how, but that being was somehow involved. And whatever it had done, it could do again. So the Presence watched, prepared to intervene if need be.

The need soon arose.

It was then the Presence understood. This human was special. It lived with a part of its mind in the space the Presence lived in, and it could interact with that part at will. What was more, it could kill with this ability, destroying a living being's mind and body. But this process was unnatural, and the Other had been born of the human's acts, had come from the human's use of this ability. Every time the human killed this way, the Other was added to, became stronger. The Presence did not know how many times the human had done this – enough times now to give the Other agency, it seemed – but it stopped him from doing it again, stopped the Other from gaining still more power with which to destroy the minds of the living.

For the time being, a crisis had been, if not averted, then at least stalled.

But the Other still roamed, still left mindless life in its wake. The Presence needed to find a way to stop it.

Keep Reading for a Preview of

The Cluster Saga

Book Three:

The Infinite Void

PROLOGUE

And I stood upon the sand of the universe, and saw a beast rise up out of the void, having seven heads and ten horns, and upon his horns ten crowns, and upon his heads the name of blasphemy. And the beast which I saw was like unto a leopard, and his feet were as the feet of a bear, and his mouth as the mouth of a lion: and the dragon gave him his power, and his seat, and great authority.

-*The* Holy Bible, New Interstellar Version, Revelations 13:1-2

"How old is she?" Michellne Joyne asked as her hands swiftly tapped over the control panel.

"Almost ten years old," Sadir Alhen answered, the thought bringing a small smile to his face as he looked over the most recent sensor report. "She already wants to be an artist."

"Such a wonderful age," Joyne replied, a tint of sadness entering her voice. "The whole universe, open and clear, ahead. So many possibilities…"

"That's why we are here," said Henrich Merkle, who had, up until this point, just listened to his comrades as they talked about their families. "To save that future for children like your daughter, Sadir, like your sons,

Michellne."

Silence descended, like a heavy blanket, on the room where they all sat, each at their own terminal watching closely over the equipment, monitoring the readouts. The conversation had been light, a purposeful attempt to avoid the reality of why they were there. But with Merkle's words, the gravity of their position reasserted themselves and, in the silence that followed, they each faced that truth in their own way, from their own hearts. In the open space between them was projected a star map of the surrounding area. The stars and planets gleamed with ethereal beauty, another reminder of the universe they lived in, of the job they had volunteered for. Joyne broke the silence.

"Why are you here, Henrich?" she asked softly, glancing over her shoulder at the stoic man sitting in the dark on the back of the station's control room. "Do you have family back home?"

"I am here for the same reasons as the two of you," Merkle said after a moment of thoughtful silence. "But no, I do not have any family left."

The word "left" hung in the air with a drip of past trauma and pain, heavy in the recycled air.

"What happened to them?" asked Alhen gently, turning in his seat to look at his usually taciturn fellow soldier. They had been here, in this remote station, monitoring the long-range sensors in the area, for weeks now, and Merkle had never offered any hint of willingness to open up, to talk about himself. While Alhen and Joyne had slowly gotten to know each other, filling the dull work with stories and memories, Merkle had simply listened, never joining in. Until now.

"My wife was an engineer," Merkle said, his voice flat

and empty of emotion. "She was working on the generation ships when the terrorists destroyed them."

"I am so sorry," Joyne replied after a moment. "You have no one else?"

"No," Merkle replied. For a moment, silence, and the others thought he had reached the end of his unusual loquaciousness. But then he said, "I am here to continue her work. She believed in the Cluster, believed in civil society, in the cooperation of people as their own ends. I was always skeptical, always afraid of the loss of individuality her beliefs implied. But, when she died, I was compelled to join and to do my part. And so here I am, with you both."

Again, the station was quiet except for the general background noise of the equipment running constantly. Each of them became lost in their own thoughts for several moments, reflecting on the last few years, on the pain and loss they had experienced personally and on a social level. But they each felt comfort, however slight, in the presence of the others, felt the foundational connection that can only be traced through shared experiences, shared goals. They were there because they believed, because they loved, because they hoped. In that moment of silence, nothing else seemed to matter, and the empty space surrounding them for lightyears was buoyed by their quiet resilience.

"Everything look alright with the canons?" Merkle asked after a few moments of silence, dispelling the heavy air with more immediate concerns.

"No changes," Joyne replied, her hands and eyes darting over the control consoles. The canons – was the reason they three of them were there. To monitor and control the massive spread of canons laid throughout the asteroid field where they were currently positioned, a few light years away from the Inner Cluster. A first line of defense against the… she did not even like to say the words in her thoughts. She looked up from the console and out of the port window in front of her. From their small, hidden station, she could see up into the field of massive, hanging rocks, a wall of movement. And beyond that, the deepness of the void broken by the light of stars farther away than the mind could imagine. She looked at her console again. "Everything is operating within specified parameters."

"And nothing new on sensors," Alhen said. But before the echo of his voice had died in the small chamber, the console before him lit up with color and gave out a small sound. "Hold that," his hands flew over the panel, making adjustments and reading the sensor logs. "There is something out there. Something big. Here."

As Alhen spoke, his hands still working the console before him, the star map projected in the center of their small space rushed inward, zooming in past their asteroid belt and into the space beyond. And then they could all see it. Alhen stopped and turned to face the projection in awed silence with Joyne and Merkle. No one spoke.

Before them, hanging in the air of their small station, was the image they had been waiting for and dreading simultaneously, the image they knew they would soon see but never truly believed would come. The three of them did not speak, only stared. They had been here, in this station, the first defense for the Inner Cluster, for weeks now, and each of them had been internally preparing themselves for this moment. But, now that the moment had come, not one of them could breathe, could even think. Before them was the image of the end, and now each felt within the true meaning of fear.

"Send a message to the Zaeim," Merkle said quietly, his voice heavy in the dense air. "Tell her the Watchers are here."

Made in the USA
Monee, IL
02 August 2020

37435954R00215